THE WAR HEIST

THE WAR HEIST

RALPH DENNIS

The author would like to thank the Crown, the Keeper of the Records, and the Public Record Office for permission to search the documents related to British War Cabinet and Admiralty matters in June 1940 He owes a debt as well to the staff of the War Museum in London.

This is a substantially revised edition of a novel that was previously published under the title *MacTaggart's War*.

ISBN: 1-7320656-9-1
ISBN-13: 978-1-7320656-9-7

Published by
Brash Books, LLC
12120 State Line #253,
Leawood, Kansas 66209
www.brash-books.com

In memory of Jessie Rehder (1908—67) a writer, a teacher at the University of North Carolina, and a valued friend

PART ONE

CHAPTER ONE

During the workday week of June 10 through the fourteenth 1940, in the cities of London and Manchester, in Liverpool and in Edinburgh, selected teams of bank officials and clerks worked late hours in the vaults. The overtime activity began when the daily banking hours were over and the other staff had left for the day.

In wooden crates the size of melon boxes, constructed to specifications furnished by the Bank of England, the bank staff packed the contents of certain vault compartments. The staff worked in two-man teams—a supervisor and a packer. The supervisor read a file number from a list provided by the Bank of England. The packer located the tied and taped packet; he read the file number to the supervisor, and, after the proper check was made on the list, the package was fitted into the packing crate. As each case was filled it was numbered, and the crate number was noted beside the packet file numbers.

The filled and covered cases were not heavy. They contained only paper. Each package—and they varied in size and weight—contained the investment wealth of one British family. At the beginning of the war, by emergency decree of the British government, private citizens were required by law to turn in their stocks and bonds to certain local appointed banks. Since then the dividends from these stocks and bonds had been collected by Britain and used to finance the war against Germany.

By the end of the week, by the fifteenth, the crates had been shipped by truck and rail to collection centers. There, under heavy security, they awaited shipping orders.

Altogether there were 488 cases.

The contents of these cases, when the final totals were computed at the Bank of England in London, were valued at something in excess of $400 million.

That same week, in London, two shifts labored in the caged vaults of the Bank of England. At a work area near the loading ramps, high stacks of special shipping cases ringed the space, leaving room only for an entrance and an exit.

Trestle tables constructed from thick raw lumber ran like a plumb line down the center of the room.

From time to time a rubber-wheeled cart was pushed down the aisle beside the tables. It was stacked with what looked like slabs of yellow tub butter. Each slab was a gold ingot weighing 27 pounds. At the established world price of thirty-two dollars an ounce, each ingot was worth almost fourteen thousand dollars.

Each shipping case was divided into four compartments. Loaded—the four ingots in place—each case held 108 pounds of gold. The value of each shipping box filled with bullion was something over fifty-five thousand dollars.

In all, during the week, the two shifts packed and sealed 2,229 cases of gold, a total of 8,916 ingots. The value of the whole consignment was in excess of $123 million.

As each case was closed and the straps attached and tightened, a man moved the length of the table with a stencil card and an ink brush. Across each case, before it was loaded on a cart, the man stenciled SALT FISH.

It was, for some reason, a big joke around the bullion yard.

The spring flowers were in bloom in Montreal's Dominion Square. In front of the Sun Life Assurance Company Building, the wide bands and sprays of yellows and reds danced off the gray, bleak stone.

The statue of the mounted horseman peering through binoculars at the South African landscape saw, instead, the girls in their spring dresses and the coatless men lounging in the sun on park benches.

It was the afternoon of Tuesday, June 11, 1940.

From his office high above the square the president of Sun Life watched the Bank of Canada official hesitate on the sidewalk before he crossed Rue Cathedral. A driver waited there beside the bank car.

The president backed away from the window. Two men were seated on the other side of his desk. Both men had attended the meeting with the Bank of Canada officer. One man, MacAndrew, was in charge of Sun Life real estate, and the other, Poole, was the company architect.

"He doesn't want much, does he?" The president's tone was amused. He gave Poole a questioning look, his eyebrows raised.

"It's possible," Poole said. "It's incredible but still possible."

"It has to be the third basement," MacAndrew said.

The third basement was far below the street level, cut from the rock that formed this part of the island of Montreal. The specifications the man from the Bank of Canada had outlined were within those available there: eight thousand square feet of work space and a vault that would measure fifty feet by sixty feet. The security for the work area and the vault had to be of the best design, to the standard of the Bank of England or the Bank of Canada buildings on Wellington Street in Ottawa.

"We'd better anticipate the problems," the president said. "It is one matter to agree to an official government request and it is another to be able to carry it out."

Poole, the architect, lifted his head from a pad where he'd been doodling. "Steel. Structural steel. Even with the proper priority there is just no way that we'll find the quantity of steel we need. At least, not from the usual sources."

"Even if we find the steel," MacAndrew added, "where in heaven's name do we come up with a vault door?"

Poole nodded. He made a large check that slashed across one of his doodles. "For the steel, we could use railway-track rails. That is, if there is a track left in Canada that hasn't already been salvaged."

The president edged his high-backed chair toward the desk and drew his telephone toward him. "Canadian National would know if there's an abandoned spur line out there somewhere."

MacAndrew stood. He circled his chair. "While you're on the phone…"

"Yes."

"Bank of Canada would know of a vault door under construction, one that's due to be delivered in the next two weeks."

The president lifted the phone receiver from its hook. "A bank somewhere will have to do without until the war is over."

Within twenty-four hours the workshops and the storeroom were cleared from the third basement of the Sun Life Assurance Building.

CHAPTER TWO

It was going to rain down on him. Torrents and hail as big as goose eggs and as heavy as bricks.

Seated behind his desk at Company D headquarters, Major Tom Renssler wasn't thinking about the rolling dark thunderclouds that he watched through the screened window. He had observed that swirl and tumble, the innocent menace, for the last twenty minutes. The storm on its way, the oppressive stillness in the air around him—those had given him the metaphor that fitted what was about to happen to his professional life.

"Let it come down." That was in *Macbeth* somewhere. So much for that kind of useless knowledge he'd picked up in the humanities classes at the Point.

And it would come down, this storm on the dusty parade ground at Fort Sam Belwin in the sandy coastland of North Carolina, in thick sheets, as if poured from a tin bucket. Perhaps they would have hail, too, the size of acorns. It would be a brief storm. The winds that brought it would carry it away, leaving behind only the soaked half inch of topsoil and the strong scent of dust that had been whipped up by the wind and the hard pounding of the rain.

Tomorrow or the next day—Thursday or Friday—it would be his turn. His time to stand bareheaded in the open. The reason for it was right in front of him, centered on the desk blotter. A gray cloth-covered book with COMPANY D RECREATIONAL FUND printed on its spine.

The final figure in the ledger, when he'd deducted the expense of *2 pairs boxing gloves, 4 checker sets, tips for pool cues, box chalk for same,* showed an unspent balance of $532.27.

Tom Renssler, without looking in the locked metal box in the file cabinet, knew that the actual amount left in the recreation fund was $32.27.

The other five hundred dollars, through a bad three-day run of cards at BOQ, was re-creating a certain Captain George Marsh. Marsh of all people. Marsh who didn't need the money, who had a steady income from a trust. After the third night, the final hand played, Marsh had folded the bills and stuffed them in the breast pocket of his shirt. He'd said, "After this bit of luck, I might consider trading in last year's Ford for the new model."

Tom laughed. It was all he could do. He had to pretend to be the good loser, the gentleman loser.

Already, minutes before, he had refused Marsh's offer of "eating money," the loan the winning gambler usually offered the big losers. He'd shrugged it off, as if to say there was still more where that five hundred came from. The fact of the matter was that twenty dollars wouldn't do much to solve the shortage in the funds. If he was going to be cashiered, it might as well be for five hundred rather than four hundred and eighty. Five hundred had a full round sound to it. Four hundred and eighty had the mark of a careful man, someone who'd stolen fifty dollars this time and thirty another. No, Tom Renssler was anything but a careful man.

The storm was almost directly above the camp now. The first rain hissed down. Dust swirled in the wind, and the window screens vibrated as if from an electrical charge.

Tom reached over the back of the chair and opened the file-cabinet drawer. He tossed the ledger on top of the cashbox. A nudge, and the drawer slid closed. That was that. That was the way the new Regimental Finance Officer would find them when, tomorrow or the next day, he came by to do his audit.

The quarterly audit wasn't due for another two or three weeks. The first of July. And that was normally more than enough time to cover the shortage. There was his pay, some borrowing he could do, and, if he had to, there was always an uncle or an aunt on the wealthy side of the Renssler family. If there was time.

Circumstances had trapped him this time. Old Major Sam Carter, a drinking friend, hadn't told anybody that he had requested a transfer to Oklahoma so he could be close to his mother who was ill. Perhaps he hadn't wanted to say anything about it because it might be turned down. The transfer had come through a week ago. That in itself hadn't sent out the danger signals. The audit still wasn't due until the first of July.

The bad news had come the first of the week through the Regimental grapevine. A new Regimental Finance Officer had been transferred in from Fort Jackson. A Major Griggs. He'd told his clerk, an enlisted man, that he intended to do an audit of all the company funds as a part of assuming the new post. His clerk told another enlisted man, and that one told another, and in two and a half days the information made its way across the camp. Earlier that afternoon, when Tom returned from lunch, Sergeant Jefferson stopped him on the parade ground and passed the rotten grape to him.

He drifted toward the window. Dampness blew in on him. It was raining harder now, curtains of heavy drops that sent the officers and enlisted men scurrying for cover. The parade ground was empty in no time at all. He placed his elbows on the window sill and leaned forward, closing his eyes, and let the cold mist wash across his face.

Tom Renssler was a tall man. Six-two in his bare feet. The uniform he wore had been tailored in London. His boots were made from the best English leather, from a shop on the Strand that specialized in military footwear. He knew to the penny what the uniform and the boots had cost. In his mail that morning, forwarded from the American Embassy in London, had been the third desperate dun from the tailor and the fourth from the boot makers.

His hair was black. His face was lean and tanned. The hawkish nose was the mark of the Renssler blood. It was all that he had inherited from the family. From ship's captains dealing in slaves, the Rensslers had gone on to own the ships, and, after the Civil War, they had left the ships and moved into banking. But somewhere in those last seventy years there had been a rupture, a tearing apart. One branch of the family retained the wealth, the position, and the prestige. The other, the branch that produced Tom Renssler, had been left only with the name, the hawk nose, and a knowledge of and taste for the kind of life it couldn't afford anymore.

Like the second and third sons of British nobility years ago, he'd been sent to the Army to make his living and his fortune. He'd done well at West Point. He'd applied himself, all his drive and his intelligence, and he'd graduated fourth in the class of 1930.

In ten years, in a peacetime Army where promotion and advancement came slowly, if at all, he was a major when other men with equal time in the service and equal skills remained in the grade of captain.

The post of military attaché in London had been the plum. He had used all the influence he could muster to obtain it. Since it had not cost them money, the wealthy side of the Renssler family had pushed him forward, collecting on some political IOUs. The story he'd heard later was that the Renssler influence had reached all the way to the back door of the White House.

Two years in the London post, if he'd handled it well, should have led to his promotion to lieutenant colonel. And with the war surely coming, colonel should have been the natural next step. With some luck, by the time the war ended, he might have been a general.

The gambling, the drinking, the mounting debts, and the halfhearted affair with Lady Denham had spoiled that pretty dream of the future.

His last fitness report, filled out at the Embassy in London, had followed him to Fort Sam Belwin. It was a collection of truths and half-truths. The result was that he'd been rated unsatisfactory. With that rating came the automatic Class-B status. At the next fitness report, if he wasn't classed as satisfactory or above that, he would be given one year's pay and discharged.

Not that it mattered anymore. The new Regimental Finance Officer, Major Griggs, would solve that for him. As soon as he checked the ledger against the cash on hand, Tom Renssler would be up on charges. You could forget the fitness report. One unit of paperwork less for the Army.

The center of the storm passed. A light rain trailed it as it moved inland. There had been no hail after all. Tom opened his eyes and ran a hand across his damp face.

Work to do. He had made up his mind that he would continue to work until Major Griggs arrived at Company D. He returned to his desk and stacked the accumulation of paperwork on the center of the blotter. For the next two hours he lost himself in the twists and mazes of it, and he was still working when Sergeant Jefferson, at 1630 hours, opened the door and pointed at his watch. Tom waved him away. After Jefferson left, he spent another ten minutes reading a report from the Surgeon General of the Army. The report, in almost sacred terms, worried about the spread of drunkenness in the enlisted ranks.

And what about the officers? Of course, he didn't write that in the margin. He initialed it in the proper space on the cover sheet and sailed it into the OUT basket.

Enough. He put on his cavalry hat and tucked his swagger stick under his arm. And then, as he was about to leave for the day, the impulse hit him. He opened the file cabinet and took out the ledger and the cashbox. He unlocked the box and dumped the bills and the change on the desk top. Without counting it he stuffed it into his pocket. He locked the cashbox and placed it in the file drawer. Another impulse. He opened the ledger to the last sheet where the balance was given. He wrote, in a thick slash of a pen, *IOU $532.27* and signed his name.

He dropped the ledger on top of the cashbox and locked the file drawer.

He left the headquarters building whistling. There, dammit. That was real style. Let the cashbox be empty, let the ledger confirm it. Let them hang him for $532.27. They could only do it once, and while he was waiting he might as well have a few drinks at the Officers' Club.

It was a hazy London morning. Duncan MacTaggart awoke with the sun balanced on the window ledge like a soft fried egg. Old man, he thought, you have done one more time what you usually do.

Not that he thought of himself as old. He was forty-six on his last birthday. That wasn't the end of the world. He had most of his teeth and all his hair, and there wasn't but a touch of gray in it; that was in the sideburns. The beer stomach was just beginning to lap over his belt. Not that there was much of it yet. He could still suck it in when he needed to. And on a man his size, six-four and about seventeen stone, it was hardly noticeable.

Had he been sleeping again? The sun had edged its way up until it looked more like a Christmas orange, the thin bottom curve shaded by the window ledge.

It was getting warm. The sun struck him directly in the eyes. The glare was there even with his lids squeezed closed. It was so warm he could smell his own bed sweat. No, it wasn't that. It was more than his smell. He tried to concentrate. It would come to him when his mind started working. If it ever did. All those pints of beer, the Guinness too, and the nightcap of gin doubles. He had a foul mouth. Taste of a dog's tail. A massive belch rumbled its way from the pit of his stomach and reached the back of his throat. He saw no reason to be polite and cheat himself of the pleasure. It thundered out. There now. Much better. That was half of the morning cure.

"You awake, dear?"

He recognized the other scent in his bed. Her perfume mixed with his sweat.

"I said, are you awake, dear?"

Peggy Sloan from down the hall.

"Not yet," he said. The second belch passed his breastbone. He choked this one and released it slowly. A hiss and a gurgle. He opened his eyes. Yes, he was in his own room at the boardinghouse. Paint flaked on the window frame, and there was the pint bottle of probably soured milk on the outside ledge. That confirmed it.

He dug an arm under him, raised up, and flipped over on his back. The ceiling blurred. He gave himself time for his eyes to adjust. Past his feet he saw Peggy Sloan seated in the stuffed chair next to the table radio. She was wearing only her pink knickers.

Her breasts were like Peckham pears. So that was what they were like. Blue veins in her skin, the thickness of pencil lead. She wore her red hair long. It brushed her shoulders. Slim legs with a slight bow to them. Her legs were crossed, and he could see the red nail polish on her toenails.

The face wasn't bad. Blue eyes in a child's oval face with the chin just beginning to sag.

"You might well ask me what I'm doing here," she said.

"I didn't ask."

"You promised me tea."

MacTaggart rubbed grit from the corners of his eyes. "When was that?"

"Last night."

"When?"

"When you happened to pass my room," she said.

He couldn't remember. It was true, however, that he had to pass her room to reach his. Hers was near the stairs, his at the far end of the second-floor hallway. In warm weather she had a habit of leaving her door open, she said to get a draft from her window. He thought he knew better. She'd had her eye on him for a year or better, from the time he'd moved into the boardinghouse. And, because she wasn't careful about the way she dressed when the door was open, he had to admit he had a way of looking to his left when he reached the hallway. Now and then she heard him and came to the doorway to ask for a match or a cigarette or to ask if he'd like a cup of tea. She'd be wearing a red silk robe he could see through.

He would furnish the match or the cigarette. He refused the offer of the tea. She lived too close. It could make problems. He'd never been in her room and this was the first time she'd been in his.

"Been waiting long?"

"For my tea? An hour."

"The water's in the kettle and the tea's in ..."

"I couldn't find a match for the gas ring," she said.

He kicked the twisted sheet from his legs and rolled to the side of the bed. He was naked, and when he stood he looked in Peggy's direction and saw her eyelids flutter. A flutter and another flutter and her eyes were wide open. He wobbled past her to the low shelf next to the door. The gas ring was there and right below it, as he'd thought, a box of kitchen matches. He broke two matches getting one struck. When the fire burned under the kettle, he measured tea into the pot. One cup for you and one cup for me and one for me after you've left.

His robe, threadbare and greasy, was on the hook on the door. He pulled it down and shoved his arms into the sleeves. He belted it. There now. A man felt better when there was something between himself and his nakedness. Unless he was passionate. And he wasn't. All he felt were aches and the bloat.

"Tea coming up, love," he said to the back of her head.

Peggy turned in the stuffed chair. Her head just cleared the high back of it. "I like the way you say that, Duncan."

"What?"

"Love."

MacTaggart stared at her.

"It means you remember last night." She hesitated. "You do remember last night, don't you?"

"Certainly," he mumbled. "Most of it."

"It's not my place to remind you, Duncan."

"It's foggy about the edges," he admitted.

"You said … it was just like it is in the films."

"Between us?"

She nodded.

"It's coming back to me," he said. It was bloody likely he had said that. Love at first sight. Like in the films. It was what he told a woman even when he hadn't been drinking. With some drinks in him it was as good as automatic.

"And later, much later …"

"We're engaged?"

Her eyes fluttered. A yes was in there somewhere. But, dammit, she wasn't supposed to believe it. That was baby talk to make a woman warm and loving.

"I wasn't sure you meant it, Duncan."

"I stand by my words," he said. "And we'll make it official as soon as I'm back from an important business trip."

Until that moment he wasn't sure he was going. It was between him and three others, which one would have to accept the rotten job. The other three were married. He thought he could make the argument that the single man ought to take the dangerous work. That it was only right and proper.

"You didn't tell me your business, Duncan."

"Banking."

"How long do you think it will be before …?"

"A month. It could be two months. It's so hush-hush I can't even talk about it. Not even to you. But you've my word of honor that as soon as it's completed …"

She stood and whirled to face him. Her arms were open.

MacTaggart knew it was going to happen. It was always like that after a night of hard drinking. Hangovers seemed to make it worse.

Peggy knew. Her eyes were on his face, but she knew. "After all, we are engaged," she said in a soft voice.

By the time he unbelted his robe and threw it aside, her pink knickers were in a pile at her ankles.

CHAPTER THREE

The Fort Belwin Officers' Club had been a gymnasium until the old Club burned to the foundations in the fall of 1936. The peacetime Army didn't have the money to rebuild it. The newer gym, the one the officers had used, was opened to all ranks. Exact scheduling assured that enlisted men and officers would not perspire in the weight room at the same time.

The old enlisted-men's gym was converted into the new Officers' Club. The basketball backboards were removed and the bleacher seats dismantled. A bar was placed against the wall between the twin entrances at the south end.

The floor was glass-slick where the basketball court had been. In the center of the dance floor the center jump circle remained. Crossed sabers and a springing-puma design filled the circle. The Pumas were the enlisted-men's basketball team.

An enlisted man working as bartender took the call from the Main Gate. He had his look to be certain that Major Renssler was still at his table. Then he returned to the phone and said, "He's here. I'll tell him." Captain Marsh was at the bar insisting upon a refill right away. By the time the bartender had mixed his drink and taken Captain Marsh's money, he'd forgotten one important part of the message. He couldn't, for the life of him, remember the name of the man who was waiting for the major at the Main Gate.

Major Renssler took it well. He didn't seem to care one way or the other. Of course, the enlisted man had heard the skinny on the major. The guys in D Company said the major might be regular Army but he wasn't dogshit the way some of the officers were.

One reason it didn't matter to Tom Renssler was that he had a good bourbon glow going. He'd spent $4.00 from the $32.27, and with the best bourbon going at 25¢ a shot, it was as much a forest fire as a glow. He had, however, had some help from the couple sitting at the table with him. He'd bought each of them two drinks. Captain Johnny Whitman was in his Company, and the woman with him was his wife, Lila.

"Ring the gate and say I'll be right there," he told the enlisted man.

The bartender said, "Yes, sir," and almost saluted before he walked away.

"A man, Tom?" Johnny grinned at him.

"That's what the kid said."

"Not the Simpson sisters?"

The Simpsons weren't sisters. They were cousins. They lived in a farmhouse on the outskirts of Fort Belwin. The land around the house was fallow, unplowed. The information was that the Simpson women charged some people and didn't charge others. Tom never paid, and one drunken night he'd escorted both of them to a dance at the Club. One colonel had been so angry that he'd stalked out, dragging his wife with him. His wife hadn't wanted to leave. She'd wanted to see how scarlet women conducted themselves in a real social situation.

"Not the Simpson sisters?" Lila Whitman put a hand on her husband's arm and pretended to be shocked. "You wouldn't, Tom. Not after the last time."

"You're not listening, honey," Johnny said. "It's a man." He gave Tom a sly wink. "Might be that Tom's going to change his luck."

Tom braced himself. He didn't react. The mention of *luck*, it could be casual, unintended, a fortunate hit. But, knowing Johnny's ways, it could be a dig at the card games last week at BOQ. Johnny hadn't been at the games the three nights when

Captain Marsh cleaned him. It wasn't to say that Johnny hadn't heard about it from one of the other players.

"My luck's fine," he said. "How's yours?"

Johnny nodded and winked.

Johnny Whitman was the golden boy gone some three or four years toward seed. At the same time that Tom was at West Point, Johnny had been a big man on campus and an All-Southern Conference halfback at Duke. In his senior year he made one All-America team, third string, and several Honorable Mentions. Even now he tried to keep himself in shape. He worked out with weights and ran mornings on the beach. At his last duty station, Fort Benning, he coached the base team and played a part of each game—at least a quarter—at his old position.

He gave the impression that he was taller than he was. On the base infirmary scales, in bare feet, he was exactly five-ten and one-quarter. What made him seem larger, especially when he was seated, were the wide, square shoulders with the twin humps of corded muscle that merged into his neck.

Everybody assumed that the weight training had produced Captain Whitman's thick upper torso. Johnny did nothing to discourage that belief. The truth was that most of the development had taken place in the coal mines in Walker's Creek, Kentucky. He'd gone into the mines for the first time when he was fourteen. He was big for his age. The shift foreman, a friend of his father, winked at the labor laws. Johnny worked a full night shift for the next four years. He'd come out of the mine at eight in the morning and blink into the daylight, and he'd wash the coal dust away and dress in his good clothes. He'd eat fatback and bread on the walk to school.

On top of school and the shift in the mine he played basketball and football. When he found time for sleep it was two or three hours at a time. Those nights when they didn't have a late practice or a game he got six hours of unbroken rest before he put on his work clothes and headed for the mines.

He knew there were better things ahead for him. They couldn't be worse than those four years. He believed this with the fervor of a primitive Baptist preacher talking about heaven and hell.

In his senior year, when the football scholarships were offered to him, he turned his back on the colleges and universities close to Walker's Creek. He rejected the University of Kentucky and West Virginia. He wavered between the University of Virginia and Duke. He couldn't decide. Finally he flipped a coin and Duke won.

The summer after he finished high school, he worked in the mines. He saved his money, all he could. That September he wore his best sport shirt and jeans on the bus trip to Durham, North Carolina. He checked his suitcase at the bus station and walked around town until he found a clothing store that had Duke emblems in the window. He bought two jackets and four pairs of trousers and a new pair of shoes.

Before he returned to the bus station for his suitcase he found his way to the YMCA. He sat in the steam room for a couple of hours until he was certain he'd sweated all the coal dust out of his pores.

He never went back to Walker's Creek again.

Tom squeaked his chair away from the table. He picked up his glass and measured the level of the bourbon. Too much to leave.

"Tom's in no hurry to get to the gate," Johnny said. "Maybe it's not even a white man."

"Could be."

Lila gave a little gasp and said, "Johnny, that's not nice." The shocked gasp was one of Lila's major accomplishments. She had perfected it during the time, as she liked to say, she'd been on Broadway. It was an all-purpose reaction. It could register the punch line of an obscene joke. It could show her shock at the hand that moved under the table and settled between her thighs. That was back in New York.

At Fort Sam Belwin nobody touched Lila under the table. Nobody touched her at all. They were afraid of Johnny Whitman. But she found ways to hand out her small pleasures. From the young second lieutenants to the colonels, all of them danced with her. These were the slow dances when the colored lights in the rafters were dimmed. Never to Johnny's face, always to his back, Lila knew how to do the pelvic ruffle. Around the Fort they called her Miss Dry Hump of 1940.

If Johnny Whitman noticed he didn't make a scene about it. Both of them knew, without having talked about it, that the marriage was almost over. He had courted her when he was on leave in New York and she'd been in the chorus line of the Broadway musical *Here Come the Girls*. The show only lasted three weeks. By that time Johnny had decided that Lila had more talent off the stage than on it. And she'd decided that any man who dressed as he did and threw money around, any man with his polish and manners, just had to be rich.

Of course, she was wrong. Johnny had only his captain's pay. Loans and some gambling winnings paid for the clothes and furnished the cash he spent on her. The polish and the manners were free. During the three years in the frat house at Duke he'd learned from his brothers how to dress and how to talk and what to drink—all the social graces that the rich learned at home.

Lila gave up her career and married him before she found out the truth.

Johnny accepted her complaints for three or four months. After a while she thought she had him cowed. She didn't. The bed was still good and he hadn't tired of her. Then she made the same complaint and he blacked both her eyes.

She screamed and cried, and he had to shout to be heard. "What career did you give up? Screwing fat Jewish producers?"

That was true to a degree. At least there was enough truth in it to make her stop and think. But not for long. She gave her practiced shocked gasp and cried on.

Her stage name had been Lila Browne. "With an *e*," she always said. Her real name had been Lillian Wychiek. As a child she had been skinny and all knees and elbows. At fourteen she stopped growing upward and started filling out.

It didn't take her long to discover that her body was a commodity. She could get anything she wanted by knowing when to withhold it and when to give it freely. At seventeen she was runner-up in the Belvoir, Michigan, beauty contest. Everybody, the M.C. and the young men from the Chamber of Commerce who ran the pageant, said she was a sure thing to win the next year. Each of them in his own way offered to help her prepare, to work with her to improve her speech and her poise and her talent. After she was Miss Belvoir she was a sure thing for Miss Michigan and on her way to becoming Miss America.

She believed them, but she didn't want to wait that long. In August, when she was about to start her final year of school, she decided she'd had enough education. Over a two-week period she borrowed from the young men who'd offered to help her. In return, she gave each of them an evening of her time. She had a train ticket to New York and a nest egg put aside. None of the men asked for her IOU. All they needed was her word that she would repay them when she could.

She reached New York and started going to the tryouts. She couldn't sing and could only master a few of the basic chorus-line dance steps. It didn't seem to matter at first. New York wasn't that different from Belvoir. Men would always do what they could for a girl with high breasts and a behind that didn't have a wrinkle on it.

Voice lessons and dance classes didn't help. She moved from chorus line to chorus line. And then she met Johnny Whitman. He was in town staying with an old frat brother who had a seat on the Exchange. He moved in the money world as if he belonged there.

So it was, one night on a balcony overlooking Riverside Drive, that she decided it might be nice to be married to a wealthy man. And Johnny Whitman seemed to be that man.

Tom threw back the shot of bourbon and felt the raw jolt of it. He tapped the glass on the table. He adjusted his cavalry hat at just the proper angle. "Back in a few minutes, no matter what color he is."

He passed the bar where George Marsh was buying a round for three junior officers from Company A. Marsh tipped a mock salute at him. Tom waved and smiled. The bastard. Spending *his* money on those shavetails.

His gray 1938 coupe, a Chevy, was parked on the street. He drove the four blocks to the Main Gate. He parked on the side of the road inside the military reservation. The sentry came out of the gate box and saluted and said, "He's over there, sir."

Tom followed the wave of the soldier's hand and saw him. A tall man with a ramrod back and a gray tweed suit that wasn't right for the weather had his back to Tom. He was paying a cab-driver for the ride and the wait.

He turned as the cab pulled away. Tom had a look at the ruddy face and the close-clipped mustache. The long horse face twisted into a grin. "Tom, how the bloody hell are you?"

A skip step, a long stride, and Major Robert Withers stuck out his hand. Tom took the hand, and, up close, he could smell the Scotch on Robert's breath.

"What a bloody awful posting," Robert said before he lurched away to find his travel bag.

Tom watched him stagger, and he thought, wryly, what the hell is the Crown Prince of Sloane Square, London, doing in East Jesus, North Carolina?

At Security Division, the Bank of England, Colonel Haggard's secretary, Polly, opened the door to the airless closet that was MacTaggart's office. Her plain face relaxed. "Thank God, Mac."

"Am I late?"

He knew he was. He'd rung in from the call box down the hall and said he'd be in by twelve or half-twelve. It was far beyond that time. Perhaps half-one.

The closet-office still retained the pegs they'd hung the dust mops on, a row of them all down one wall. The single narrow window was sooted over and it couldn't be opened. His scar-topped desk wasn't much wider than two children's school desks wedged together. One day, he promised himself often, he was going to trace that desk through the requisition paperwork and discover where they'd found it. He had a hunch it had been especially constructed for some twelve-year-old student whose thyroid had gone wild.

"He's been asking for you for hours," Polly said.

"Who?" MacTaggart tugged his hunter's-case watch from the small pocket below his belt. He ignored Polly while he flipped the cover and checked the watch face. It was 1:43. He closed the cover, keeping the catch open until the top was in place. He released the catch and heard the click. It was the only useful information his father had ever given him: how to close a hunter's case without wearing out the catch.

"You know *who*." Polly stepped through the doorway, pulled the door behind her, and leaned back against it. "I told him I thought I'd seen you in the hallway at half-twelve, going somewhere in a hurry."

"I think you did," MacTaggart said. "Tell the colonel you've found me and I'll be there as soon as I finish what I'm on."

"He said now, Duncan."

"Five minutes from now."

"Promise?" She didn't sound sure. But she opened the door and backed out.

MacTaggart nodded solemnly.

As soon as she was out of sight down the hall he went back to what he had been doing all the way across London, all the way from Shepherd's Bush on the underground. He was making a survey. He was trying to find out if he had any broken bones or torn muscles.

Poking and prodding at himself with his fingers. There. That was new. A soreness in his stomach muscles. Pelvic muscles. It was probably last night's exercises, the ones he had trouble remembering at all.

That Peggy-girl. She had the energy of a Morris dancer and the lungs of a Highland piper. She'd rattled the headboard of the bed against the wall until he thought the whole house shook, and she'd screamed until he was afraid somebody would come to see if Jack the Ripper was cutting up Marie Kelly all over again. Thank God everybody was off at work or minding their own business.

"Mr. MacTaggart."

It was the tone of displeased command. Though MacTaggart hadn't been in the Army since 1918, he reacted as if he were still on active duty. He rammed the chair against the wall with a shove and stood at attention. The sudden, abrupt movement set his stomach muscles screaming at him. He grabbed at the pain and doubled over.

Colonel Haggard said, "It would appear that you have some difficulty—" He broke off and stared at MacTaggart. "Are you ill, Mac?"

"I pulled something."

The bully-soldier evaporated from the colonel. He didn't handle command well. The peacetime Army in India must have been a casual affair. Nothing but sticking pigs with lances from horseback and drinking gin and tonic water.

Colonel Haggard's skin was the color of old leather. All the moisture must have cooked away. The wide, bushy mustache was red with streaks of gray.

MacTaggart, one hand clutching his stomach, backed away a few paces until his legs touched the chair. He eased himself into the seat. "I'll be fine in a moment."

"You certain, Mac?"

"I was storing some of my kit. One box must have been heavier than I thought." He gritted his teeth and let his breath hiss out.

"Storing...?"

"If I'm going to Canada..."

The colonel pulled the door closed. He did a step-step and he was against the desk front. He looked over his shoulder. "That is still secret, Mac. And I hadn't realized the decision had been made which one..."

"You can drop that pretense, Colonel. You know as well as I do that you've already decided." He ticked them off, each with a short nod of his head. "Troop's married. So's Billings. So's Matthews. I'm the one without the excess baggage." He sighed. "I'm not one to complain when a dirty job comes my way. Not even when I've no taste for seeing Canada. Still, I know how command decisions are made. And even when I think I've got the worst of it I'm not one to refuse a lawful order."

"I have to say that you're taking this well, Mac."

"It's my military background, Colonel. The same as yours." MacTaggart didn't mention that his highest rank had been lance-corporal. And the colonel, if he remembered MacTaggart's file, was too polite to remind him.

"The fact is... it's not for certain yet. We should know in two days, by Friday. The preparations are being made. The boys in the bullion yard... well, they've been busy. Now it's up to the big boys to give the final *go*."

MacTaggart forgot the pain from his pelvic muscles. A sour nausea floated in the pit of his stomach. "I'd understood, Colonel..."

"I think it's a *go*," Colonel Haggard said. "I don't think the War Cabinet would let it go this far and then pull it up short. It's not likely."

MacTaggart wanted to believe him. Either it was Canada or some awkward scenes at the boardinghouse. The Peggy-girl was nice enough, nicer than he thought she'd be, but he didn't think she'd turn him loose without a war.

The colonel backed to the door. MacTaggart, sucking in his stomach, eased from the chair and followed him.

"You'll be the first to know, Mac." The colonel winked. "I wouldn't unpack my kit if I were you."

"I won't."

"And you've been a real soldier about this. I can't slip anything past you. I can see that now."

"That's right, sir."

Colonel Haggard marched stiff-backed down the hall toward his office. All the talk of the military had infected him. He'd probably be that way the rest of the week without a letup.

MacTaggart circled his desk and slumped into his chair. He didn't accomplish a single thing the rest of the day.

Peggy waited for him in her doorway. She wore a white dress with lace around the neck and the sleeves. MacTaggart said, "Hello, girl," and her arm locked on his elbow and he was drawn into her room.

"Mackie, where have you been?"

"Working late."

She released him and did a model's twirl for him. "Like it?"

"Is it new?"

"The shoes are. I bought them on the way back from the factory." Peggy worked in a shop that made uniforms. Like him, she'd been late for work today. The shop foreman had given her a stern lecture on the importance of the war effort.

Then the dress wasn't new. MacTaggart wondered how long she'd had it packed away, waiting for the proper time. Like a summer wedding.

"Like it, Mackie?"

"Beautiful," he said.

"I'm glad." She leaned against him and reached past him to give the door a push. It closed with a smack.

He looked over her shoulder and saw that she had a proper setting at her table, a cloth to cover it and plates and even glasses. One plate held a little mound of cold meat pies and there was a bowl of salad and a Stilton the size of the palm of his hand. In the center of the table, next to the four-inch remainder of a candle, there was a whole bottle of plonk. A burgundy, he thought, from the shape of the bottle.

"Are you hungry, Mackie?"

He nodded. She stepped away and gave him a playful shove toward the table. "See how I think about you?"

CHAPTER FOUR

ajor Robert Anthony Withers gave his tweed jacket a good shake and draped it over a chair back. He was dressed in silk underwear, and now the whole room smelled of some kind of herbal soap he'd brought with him.

While Major Withers showered in the bathroom down the hall Tom had signed him into a guest room at BOQ as a *fellow officer, British Army.* There was a space in the book for his current unit, but Tom hadn't known what it was. When Tom had known him in London, during some long gaming and drinking sessions, Robert had been waiting for assignment, having recently left the Horseguards.

The bottle Withers had dragged from his travel bag was half empty. He tipped a long stream into his glass and carried the bottle to Tom. He touched Tom's glass, a courtesy pour, before he backed away. "Still don't fancy the peat, huh?"

"You finish dressing and I'll introduce you to some excellent bourbon."

"It's a well-meant offer, I know." Robert tipped his head toward the ceiling and took a long swallow. "When in Rome, you know. And I might have to cultivate the taste. I understand there is a shortage of Scotch here."

"Your war," Tom said.

"It'll be yours soon enough, chap."

Tom had a sip of the Scotch. "You didn't say what you're doing here in the States."

"Didn't I?" Withers pinched his lips between a thumb and forefinger and mumbled, "I'm not about to say, either."

"Something secret?"

Withers dropped his hand from his mouth. "Mum's the word."

"You can do better than that," Tom said.

"You force me to change the subject," Withers said. "Bill Templar said to remind you that you still owe him two hundred quid."

"Lucky him."

"He said he would be happy to accept American dollars."

"No doubt he would."

Withers placed his glass on the dresser top and reached both hands into his large bag. He brought out a slightly wrinkled Class-A summer uniform. "You think this will dazzle the ladies at your Club?"

"It might. These ladies don't get to the circus very often."

"That's a joke, I assume?" Withers stepped into the trousers and pulled them on. "A moment ago you had the sound of a man who's overdrawn at the bank."

"What bank?"

"Really, old boy, you ought to leave the cards alone. You really don't have the head for it."

"You're telling me that now?"

"There wasn't any reason to tell you in London. It would have ruined a good thing." He sat on the edge of the bed and drew his shoes toward him. "It happens I was furnished some American dollars for expenses."

"The Club will be glad about that."

Withers straightened the toe on one sock. "Any little birds at this Club of yours?"

"Women?" Tom shook his head. "They're all married. We'll have to stop in town for that."

"I trust you know a couple. I've had the most miserable voyage across on one of your destroyers."

"Which one?"

Withers shook his head.

"You dock at Norfolk, Virginia?"

"It's a fair guess, Tom."

"And you're headed for Washington after this side trip south?"

"You are persistent." Withers stood and put his back to Tom. "Let's talk about the birds."

On the way past the Duty Office where the enlisted man kept the phone watch, Tom touched Major Withers on the shoulder and turned him toward the counter.

"You'd better sign in, Robert." Tom leaned on the counter top. "Let me have the guest book, please."

"Yes, sir." The corporal opened the ledger and placed it on the counter.

Tom turned the book toward him. "This is Major Withers." He stared at the single entry on the page. "I wasn't sure about your present unit," he said.

"Of course you know it, old boy." Withers took the pen the corporal offered him and scribbled the final part of the entry in the ledger. "Same as it was the last time I saw you in London."

Tom glanced at the ledger before he closed it and pushed it across the counter toward the corporal. *Horseguards,* Withers had written in the space on the far right of the line.

"Back with your old outfit?"

"I never left it," Withers said.

Johnny Whitman had his back to the dance floor and Tom looked past his left shoulder. Lila and Withers were in the center of the mob of dancers. From the last look Tom had had of the major's face, he knew that Lila was giving him the base welcome, that slightly upward movement of her hips that was probably the next best thing to being in bed with her.

"My Blue Heaven" ended. Withers stood on the edge of the dance floor, talking to Lila, before he stepped away from her and offered her his arm. He returned her to the table.

After they were seated, Johnny Whitman had his slow, long look at Major Withers. "You haven't said much about the way your war's going."

"What war?" Withers sniffed his bourbon and water before he gave it a tentative taste. He swallowed and gave a mock shudder. "It's not a war. It's a disaster."

"The French..." Johnny began.

"The French, as they've done in all the wars since the Franco-Prussian one, are about to roll over and play dead dog."

"How long?" Johnny stared down at his empty glass, but he made no effort to refill it.

"This month. Next month. At the least, a fortnight."

Lila leaned forward. "That's two weeks."

"Good girl," Withers said.

Johnny ignored his wife. "And then?"

"Within a month of the French surrender I expect the German Army on the beaches of England."

"And that's the end of it." Johnny looked at Tom.

"Perhaps," Major Withers said.

"You don't seem to be convinced by your own facts," Johnny said.

"The sun never sets on the British Empire," Major Withers said. "At least we were taught that in school."

"You're being cryptic," Tom said.

Lila's lips moved, forming the word. "What does...?"

"That's your interpretation, old man," Withers said to Tom.

"Drinks?" Johnny held up his empty glass.

Major Withers pushed back his chair. "I believe it's my round." He dug a wad of American money from the inside pocket of his uniform jacket. "I need another lesson in what dollars are worth."

"I'll go with you." Tom picked up Lila's glass and Withers got Johnny's.

They headed for the bar, dodging dancers on the way. Withers grinned back at Tom and stuck out his elbows. He knifed his way to the bar. Tom followed him. They lined the glasses on the bar and waited for one of the bartenders to notice them.

Withers tilted his head toward the table where the Whitmans sat. "You ever try that one?"

"What?"

"Lila."

"No. Not a brother officer's wife."

"Ho," Withers said. "That one's asking for a pronging."

"Not from me," Tom said.

"A bit of a tease, I suspect."

Tom leaned forward and called out his order to a passing bartender. When he backed away he said, "Let's just say that nobody wants Johnny Whitman mad at them."

"He's quite much, isn't he?"

"A bit of a roughneck."

"And an officer and a gentleman?" Withers asked.

"By act of Congress."

The drinks came. It had been a simple order. Four bourbon and waters. Tom picked up two of the glasses and waited while Major Withers paid with a ten. He stared at his change, bewildered, before he stuffed it in his pocket. He scooped the other two drinks from the bar. They moved away from the crowd. Withers stopped. "You know, I was prepared to leave tomorrow afternoon. I might remain another day."

"How long were you at sea, Robert?"

"Eight days," Withers said, "and a bloody awful day on the train getting here."

"I think I know the cure for your disease."

"Disease?"

"I think you're lonely," Tom said.

"Will I die of it?" Withers grinned at him.

"Not if I make a phone call to town."

"Good man."

They returned to the table. Tom excused himself and found a telephone in the lobby of the Club.

The Simpson farmhouse was set far back from the highway. A bumpy road ran between fenced-in pastureland, and the headlights of the coupe lit up a slab-sided horse asleep standing beneath a huge old oak.

Buck, the chained dog in the front yard, started barking when the car was still a hundred yards away. By the time Tom braked the coupe next to the screened porch, the answering barks came from all the points of the compass.

Withers sat with a full bottle of Scotch clamped between his knees. "My secret reserve," he'd said when they'd stopped by BOQ before driving into town. Now he stared at the dark farmhouse. "This is it? It doesn't look like much."

A light flared on in the living room beyond the porch.

"Don't let the wrappings on the package fool you."

"I think you'd better know that I've been warned about snipe hunts."

Emma Simpson, barefoot and wearing a cotton bathrobe, stepped onto the porch and peered out at the car. "That you, Tom? You coming in or are you going to stay out there with the bullfrogs all night?"

Withers laughed and grabbed the neck of his bottle. "If that's a snipe I don't believe that I'll mind."

Tom followed him up the steps and onto the porch.

Withers, about to pass Emma, stopped and leaned over her. He wrapped his arm around her shoulders and pulled her close to him. "I was told to award this to some deserving young lady in America." He kissed her, and his free hand, the one that wasn't holding the Scotch bottle, slipped under her robe.

At the doorway, dressed in a nightgown, her cousin, Betsy, opened her arms to Tom. "It's about time you dropped by," she said.

MacTaggart rolled to the edge of the bed and reached for his shoes. It was within seconds of the air-raid sirens going off across London.

His shoes weren't there, not where he usually placed them. Damn. He dropped to his knees and reached both hands under the bed. He was like that when Peggy stepped over him and groped her way to the window. She'd left the blackout curtains open to let some fresh air in. Now she drew them closed and found her flashlight. The beam swept across the bed and stopped on him.

"Are we going to the underground or the basement shelter?"

"Neither bloody place," he said, "until I've found my good shoes."

His clothes were draped over the back of a chair. His shoes were there on the rug in front of the same chair. He dressed quickly.

On the way to the basement, leading the way with her flashlight, he worked the watch from his pocket. He flipped the case open. It was 1:34.

It was sticky and airless in the basement bomb shelter. There was the smell of dust from beyond the concrete walls and dry rot from the timbers above.

Peggy brought a blanket and a pillow with her. MacTaggart spread the blanket in a space along one wall. He sat with his back against the wall and placed the pillow on his thigh. Peggy stretched out and got comfortable, and he put a hand on her shoulder.

She said, low-voiced, "I'm glad you're with me, Mackie. It's bad here when you're alone."

"Get some sleep, girl."

It was too dark to count them. MacTaggart estimated that there were fifteen or twenty people in the shelter. At least one baby. It cried and got teat. The *suck-suck* sound was obvious. Another older child cried and was shushed.

During the first hour everybody settled down to wait. There was a loud snore from one corner. And an old man calmed his wife: "You'll see. It will be like last time. They've turned away, so there's nothing to worry about."

And then it was still until the lovemaking began a few feet from where MacTaggart sat. It was secretive. It was hushed. Only the ragged breathing gave it away. Near the end, when it went out of control, toward orgasm, there was the squeaking and the *whack-whack-whack* of hard pounding on the floor.

Peggy heard it. Her hand moved up his leg and stopped high on his stomach. He caught her hand and held it for a time, pressing it, and then he moved it away.

MacTaggart thought of other places.

Canada was big and cold, wasn't it? There were ice and snow everywhere and trees as wide as houses that reached all the way to heaven and back.

Nobody there spent their nights in basements.

And there you weren't forced to overhear some frightened couple's desperate lovemaking.

The all clear sounded a few minutes after four. The German planes had turned toward Portsmouth.

CHAPTER FIVE

Tom Renssler opened his eyes. In the darkness, at first, he wasn't sure where he was. Then he heard Betsy's deep-sleep breathing. It was somewhere between a snort and a gurgle. And now she smelled like she'd been dipped headfirst into a vat of Scotch. He eased his way across the bed. His feet touched the floor, and he reached behind him with both hands to steady the mattress so that the movement of his weight, when he walked away, wouldn't awaken her.

One, two, three. He couldn't move. He reached *four* and leaned forward. The bed creaked. He staggered a few steps before he got his balance.

Dear Lord, he didn't want to awaken Betsy Simpson. What they said about grass widows was true. That woman had worn the skin off him, and the last time, before they went to sleep, he'd felt she was drying up his bone marrow.

He didn't remember all of the night. There'd been the bourbon at the Club and then Robert's hoarded Scotch after they arrived at the farm, and when that was gone they'd had a quart of the pop-skull—the white whiskey—that Emma furnished from the cupboard under the kitchen sink. All that mixed and stirred together explained the way his head felt. It was like a paper sack filled with muddy water.

He crossed the bedroom and reached the door. He eased it open a couple of feet and stepped through sideways. He was on the narrow second-floor landing. He reached behind him and pulled the bedroom door toward him until he heard the latch catch.

The living room was below him. There was an old sofa with the stuffing beginning to show at the arms. And, he smiled to himself, the rocking chair with Robert Withers's uniform draped over the back of it. That was a Britisher for you. The trousers carefully folded to retain the crease. The uniform jacket arranged so the edges wouldn't touch the floor. Give Major Robert Withers ten minutes for a shave and a wash and he could pass parade for the King.

Tom wobbled his way to the bottom of the stairs. That was the difference between Robert and him. He couldn't remember where he'd left his uniform. He looked back at the landing. Perhaps the uniform was in Betsy's room. But not likely. He remembered, just then, something that had happened in the kitchen. How many hours ago had that been? They were drinking the white whiskey and Robert said something about it being bloody warm. He'd marched off into the living room, and when he'd returned, he was stripped down to his silk underwear.

After that there wasn't any doubt about the way the evening would go. In no time at all, Emma Simpson was waving Robert's silk undershorts over her head, and Betsy, leaning close to Tom and running a hand over his groin, asked him if he was feeling overheated too.

"That you, Tom?"

Tom hitched up his shorts and walked into the kitchen. Robert sat at the kitchen table with his chin anchored in his hands. He was wearing Emma's robe. His eyes, when he looked up at Tom, were bloodshot.

"I felt the need for another drink."

"You look in the cupboard?" Tom waved a hand in the direction of the sink.

"I wasn't certain which was the whiskey. All of it smells like cleaning fluid."

"I'll have a look." Tom squatted next to the cupboard. He found a two-quart Mason jar and unscrewed the top. One sniff and his nose was clear. He carried the jar to the table. "Try this on for size."

Robert drank from the jar. A swallow and a gasp and he put the Mason jar on the table with a thump. "Are you reasonably certain this is safe for humans?"

"Emma and Betsy drink it all the time."

"From preference?" Robert pushed the jar across the table toward Tom. He wiped the back of his hand across his mouth. "And these are what you call red-neck ladies?"

"When we call them anything at all."

"I want the exact designation." Withers grinned. "War stories for the mess, you know?"

"When will that be?"

"Pardon?"

"When will be you heading back to England?"

"I don't know. Perhaps never."

Tom picked up the jar in both hands and had a sip. "What does that mean?"

"I have a set of emergency orders."

"I don't..."

"If the worst happens, I'm to head for Canada."

"Why Canada?" Tom asked. He slid the Mason jar toward Withers.

"Why not Canada?" He lifted the white whiskey and looked across the lip of the jar toward Tom. "My friend, do you really know how desperate matters are in England? The real truth, not the swill for the public trough."

"I know what I read in the papers."

"Lies," Robert said. "Of course, the Prime Minister and Chamberlain and Eden don't confide in me. That is a pity. But at the same time I have a certain amount of intelligence. I am not your ordinary run-of-the-mill fool. I have had a vision that the War Cabinet is prepared to make a run for Canada."

"Why?"

"To continue the war from there, old chap. As soon as England is invaded..."

"I don't believe it."

"Americans are so naïve," Withers said. "It is one of your better qualities."

"But Churchill said they would fight on the... "

"That's talk for the war morale. Let me tell you something, Tom. I am here in your United States of America to prepare for the arrival of a vast amount of British wealth which will be stored in this country."

"Purely a safeguard," Tom said.

"We're speaking of billions and billions of dollars."

"To buy weapons and war materials?"

"Over the next few months the complete liquid assets of the Empire will be shipped to North America."

"That's hard to believe."

"I said you were naïve. Let me prove it to you. On the morning of July first or second—one or the other—the first shipment will arrive at Halifax, Nova Scotia. It will be aboard a ship of the line, H.M.S. *Emerald*. Altogether, the cruiser will transport a cargo worth more than half a billion in dollars."

"Why?"

"Consider the possibility that the war may have to be fought from Canada. If England falls."

"It'll never come to that," Tom said.

"That first consignment consists of four hundred million in stocks and bonds and a hundred and twenty-five million in gold."

"That much?"

"Those are rough figures," Withers said. "Since I'm translating the pounds into dollars."

"It sounds fantastic."

"And that shipment is only the beginning. If *Emerald* reaches Halifax without problems, a second, larger shipment will leave the same port, Greenock, within a matter of days."

"What's your part in this, Robert?"

"I am not, as you guessed, in Horseguards anymore. I've wormed my way into Army Intelligence."

"I thought you were here scavenging for arms."

"Not this trip." Robert pushed back his chair. He got to his feet and almost fell. He caught the side of the table to steady himself. "Did someone invite me to a party?"

"I think that was the general idea."

"Then I should say my good-morning to one of the ladies." He staggered around the table and headed for the staircase that led upstairs. Tom followed him.

"Emma's room is down here," he said.

Robert climbed the steps. He reached the landing outside Betsy's bedroom. He turned very slowly. "I know that, old boy. The trouble is that Emma is a very tired lady."

Tom stared up at him.

"Do you mind?" Withers waved an arm at Betsy's door. "Am I not a guest?"

"You are."

Withers adjusted the cotton robe and marched toward the bedroom door. "Knock on the door when you're ready to leave."

The door slammed behind him. Tom returned to the kitchen and made a pot of coffee. From the other wenching times with Robert he was fairly sure that Emma was a tired woman. Robert's bedroom endurance was a legend in certain parts of Chelsea.

The June 13 morning meeting of the War Cabinet began at 11:30.

The Chief of the Imperial General Staff, Sir John Dill, took the floor first. His briefing concerned the situation on the western front.

Winston Churchill looked glum. The Prime Minister's talks with Reynaud on French soil had brought out the actor in him.

He'd shown a confidence that wasn't with him now. The raid scare the night before had disturbed his sleep, and he had still been recovering from his dangerous exploit when bad weather grounded his fighter escort and his plane had to return to England alone.

Little had changed since the Vice-Chief's summary the day before. West of Rouen the reports were vague and spotty. What was known was that two battalions of the Fifty-first Division had crossed the Seine to the south. A brigade of the Armored Division faced the Germans there. Perhaps the two battalions of the Fifty-first could be used to solidify that front. The Fifty-first, however, was short of ammunition, fuel, and food.

The overall projection wasn't hopeful. There were signs of a buildup for a strong German offensive to the east of Reims. The French Army, by retreating on the Marne, had opened a door for a German advance that could lead straight to Paris.

The Prime Minister tossed the stub of his Corona-Corona over his shoulder. It landed in the red fire bucket of sand that was always behind the Chair. "What preparations has Paris made for its defense?"

Sir John Dill considered his answer. Then he admitted, with a shrug as bleak as his words, that he had received no intelligence about plans for a Paris defense.

Churchill nodded. The briefing went on.

Discussion ended on the final minute of the morning's scheduled business. The Prime Minister, by prior arrangement, dismissed the members of the Secretariat. When the door closed behind them, he looked the length of the table. "I believe it is imperative that we make a final decision on Operation Salt Fish."

Churchill drew a prepared file toward him and opened the top cover. As he spoke he leafed through a thin sheaf of Admiralty memos. "His Majesty's Ship, *Emerald,* is on the high seas bound for Iceland. It should complete its duties there on the afternoon of the sixteenth of June, three days from now. Barring any unfortunate and unexpected happening, *Emerald* will dock at Greenock on the eighteenth of June." The Prime Minister pushed the Admiralty messages to one side.

"The Bank of England informs me that the shipment has been readied. Collection centers in Liverpool, Manchester, Edinburgh, and here in London hold the packaged investment wealth. The bullion has been crated and, at my orders, has been marked as salt fish." He smiled and lifted his hand in a cupped mock toast. "Confusion to our enemies."

The Bank of England notations joined the Admiralty papers. "In Canada, a special depository is being constructed in Montreal, and the Bank of Canada has cleared and reserved special vaults in their Ottawa central building. Even at this moment, as I speak, a special train is being assembled by the Canadian National Railway. The security preparations will be staggering."

The Prime Minister drew the memos together as if collecting playing cards. He tapped them on the table edge and placed them in the folder. He closed the cover with a hand slap. "Some men might view our intention as a desperate gamble. I prefer to think of it as a realistic alternative." He stared down the table. He saw a nod, an agreement, here and there. "The forecast from France is bleak, to say the least. My recent firsthand assessment did nothing to reassure me. In two weeks we may be facing the German Army across the Channel. In three weeks we may be facing them on our shores." He paused and cleared his throat. "It is time for a decision on Operation Salt Fish."

Churchill counted the solemn nods. "No one opposing?" He waited a long moment. "Then God help us all."

The morning meeting of the War Cabinet was over.

The new Finance Officer, Major Griggs, did not appear that day; Thursday, either. One more day. Another day, and he would have the weekend ahead of him.

That morning in the shower at BOQ, Tom Renssler remembered the wild and improbable story that Robert Withers had told him at the Simpson farm. In the alcohol fog he wasn't entirely certain he hadn't dreamed it. If he had, was the whole night a dream as well? The antics of Betsy and Emma? The constant lustiness of Robert Withers?

No, too much of it was real. But the story itself was absurd. England would not take that kind of risk. He thought of England as an aging, cautious player that did not have an all-or-nothing gamble left in her.

The lie, he decided as he dried himself, was Major Robert Withers's creation to cover some important mission that had brought him to the States. A man with a life like a tall tale could probably invent them with the best liars in the world.

Withers slept until noon in the guest room at BOQ. After lunch at the Officers' Mess, Tom drove him into town to catch the 2:15 train north. With four hours of sleep Withers looked as fresh and unblemished as a choirboy.

For all that, he appeared withdrawn and thoughtful. Tom noticed this, and after he'd walked to the edge of the platform and stared down the tracks to the south, he returned to Robert and said, "It can't be that bad. I have a month's proof the Simpson ladies didn't infect us."

"If they did I'll never forgive you, Tom." Robert shook his head. "It's not that, old boy. Last night, did I say anything I shouldn't have?"

"You insulted me a few times, but I considered..."

"No, blast it, did I talk about secret matters?"

It seemed the proper reaction to assure Withers that he hadn't talked out of line. The train arrived. A relieved and relaxed Major Robert Withers, formerly of the Horseguards, boarded one of the day coaches.

As the train pulled away from the station, Withers comforted himself with the thought that if he had revealed too much to his American friend he could thank his lucky stars that Tom Renssler had been drunk and didn't remember.

Officers' Row smelled of garbage cans and diapers and neglect. One of the married officers who'd graduated from the University of Virginia called the long streets of wood-frame houses the Slave Quarters.

The houses were painted a flat, dull white once each summer. A detail of enlisted men mowed the lawns every week or two. A narrow border of earth was left bare on both sides of the front steps, for gardening if the tenants wanted flowers. Only the older military wives worked in their yards. For the younger wives, uncertain about the length of their stay at Fort Belwin and depressed by their living quarters, it hardly seemed worth the trouble. Lila Whitman didn't garden. She didn't do much cleaning or dusting, either.

Johnny came home and looked through the house before he pushed the back door open and found his wife sunning herself on the back steps. It was 4:45, and the sun slanted directly on her. She was wearing her one-piece swimsuit, the white one that was almost transparent. Head back, eyes closed, and legs wide apart, she faced the back doors of the officer housing on Pershing Street.

He stood on the step above her for a time. At an angle, to his left, he thought he saw a curtain move at a rear window. It was at the Clifford house, the bathroom window. That old goat, Colonel Clifford, was doing his afternoon sightseeing.

"You're better than a strip show," he said. "Or a blue movie."

Lila's lips hardly moved. "Him across the way? It makes his life bearable."

He stepped around her and planted his feet in the grass and turned. "It's too bad he's not filling in my fitness report. I think he'd want to keep your floor show in town."

"What's for supper, honey?"

"Nothing. Chilled nothing for appetizers, stewed nothing for the main course, and frozen nothing for dessert."

"That's witty." He sucked in a long breath through his teeth. "There's got to be something. I invited Tom by for supper at seven."

"We were going out tonight." *Out* meant to the Club or to one of the roadhouses outside of town for a steak sandwich and a few drinks.

"Maybe tomorrow," he said. "We'll go to that seafood place up the coast."

Promises. She choked back a rush of harsh words. It wouldn't do to have another quarrel outside. As it was, the neighbors knew more about their personal business than they had any right to. That she had been a New York show girl, that they fought about money all the time, and that Johnny was waiting out his Class-B status.

"You sent out the invitation," she said. "You cook the supper." She smiled sweetly, and her tone of voice had sugarcoating on it. She pranced up the steps and into the house. In the kitchen, next to the dining table, she hesitated to see if he was following her. He wasn't. She stomped down the hall to the bedroom. The image of the kitchen remained in her mind's eye. The table still littered with the breakfast dishes, the sink stoppered and piled high with plates and pots and pans. Damn him anyway.

She sat on the edge of the bed and kicked off her shoes. She heard the back door slam. He'd followed her inside after all. She stood and put her back to the open bedroom door. She eased the straps from her shoulders and peeled the bathing suit down to her waist. She knew he was behind her, in the open doorway. She pretended she didn't know. The swimsuit fell to her ankles. She pulled one foot free and kicked the suit across the room.

Even before the suit landed she turned to the dresser and picked up her hairbrush. She stroked her hair, counting, and by the time she'd reached fifty she could hear the crackle of static.

At seventy-five she lowered the brush. She turned to the doorway. She knew how she looked. As she whirled she prepared the surprised laugh she'd give when she discovered him staring at her.

The doorway was empty. A few seconds later, as if to answer the unspoken question, she heard the rattle of dishes in the kitchen. He was cleaning up.

CHAPTER SIX

All day Thursday there'd been no word from Colonel Haggard. That evening, because MacTaggart told himself that he couldn't spend twelve hours a day in bed with Peggy, he took her to Piccadilly Circus for a night on the town. He liked cowboy films, and Gene Autry and Jane Withers were in *Shooting High* at one of the theaters. The queue, when they got there, was blocks long. It looked like every soldier and sailor in London liked cowboy films as well. "Another night," he told her, and he walked beside her through the crush and press until he found a place where he could buy them supper.

On the underground headed back to Shepherd's Bush, a pair of drunk sailors across the aisle had their stare at Peggy; one of them said something to the other in a whisper. The sailors had their eyes on MacTaggart to see how he'd react. MacTaggart looked straight at them and blew his nose.

Words wouldn't light the gas or cook the stew.

Above ground, on the walk to the rooming house, Peggy took his arm like a lady and matched him stride for stride. Her face close to him, she said, "You miss not being in uniform, Mackie?"

"Not me, girl." He broke stride. "I've had my war. I don't know what a man has to do to deserve more than a single war in a lifetime."

"Oh, don't lie to me."

"I'm not lying."

"I saw how you looked at the uniforms," she said.

"I was figuring how many board feet of timber it would take to bury them."

She wasn't sure whether to believe him or not. "How many, Mackie?"

"I stopped counting at a million," he said.

And then he saw her stricken face. He'd been joking, still angry with the sailors in the underground, and he realized that it hadn't been a joke after all.

"What's wrong, Peggy?"

"I've got brothers. One in the Navy and one in the Army."

He held her in a dark doorway until she was calm again. He cursed himself for being a hundred kinds of fool.

And then on Friday the colonel showed up at his closet-office.

The colonel said, "I hope you've got your sea legs."

"It's not my legs worry me," MacTaggart said. "It's my stomach. I get a sick stomach just looking at photographs of ships."

"The decision's been made. It's on."

"How long?"

"You'll have ten days to put your affairs in order."

"No," MacTaggart said. "How long will I be at sea?"

"Eight days."

MacTaggart closed his eyes and thought of eight days of twenty-four hours, with each hour having sixty minutes in it, and all of them packed and crammed with seasickness. It wasn't a pretty thought.

The truth, he knew, when he'd allow himself to face it, was that he was becoming fond of that Peggy-girl. Once you got used to that driving passion of hers to get married, that fear she had of being an old maid, there wasn't much better company anywhere. Out of bed as well as in it.

Fool man that he was, he'd talked himself into eight full days of agony when, now, he wasn't sure he wanted to leave London at all.

What Johnny Whitman served for supper was half a brown-sugar-baked ham. After he finished cleaning the kitchen, he had a look in the pantry. Nothing there worth serving anybody. He made a phone call and drove across the base and parked behind the BOQ mess hall. Anything was possible if you knew the right people. Johnny knew the right people and the dishonest ones as well. A certain mess sergeant named Bachman owed him a favor that he had been collecting for the last year or so. One night when Johnny had the duty he happened upon Bachman on his rounds. It had been after midnight, and Bachman had been loading twenty steaks into his car. Johnny hadn't reported it. If he had, it would have put Bachman in front of a military court. It would have meant at least the loss of one stripe and perhaps some time in the post stockade. Bachman still had his stripes and Johnny had a friend in the mess kitchen.

There was, however, half a ham less for the Saturday night supper at BOQ. Bachman had a full day to figure some way to cut down on the portions.

It was a warm night.

After supper at the table in the kitchen, Johnny broke the seal on the fifth of bourbon that was Tom's contribution to the evening. Earlier in the day, when he'd asked him to supper, he'd said Tom could bring a girl if he wanted to. "One of the Simpson sisters, if you like." Instead, Tom had offered the bottle and said that this was his date.

"I knew you had taste," Johnny had said.

He mixed drinks while Tom carried three chairs into the backyard and placed them on a patch of lawn beyond the steps.

It was cooler in the yard. A damp wind blew from the east, from the direction of the coast.

Tom, even after the heavy meal, felt as uncomfortable as he had all week. Major Griggs hadn't reached D Company that day, Friday, either with his audit. Tom had a grace period of at least forty-eight hours. Perhaps longer. He knew if he could find the time, a few hours for some intense thought, he could come up with a way of replacing the five hundred-plus dollars. A loan if he could. But not from Johnny Whitman. Johnny didn't have two one-dollar bills to rub together.

He'd never been fooled by Johnny's surface game. It was pose and nothing else. Maybe Tom had never had the wealth, either, but he'd been allowed his slow and careful look at it. And he'd lived, until he entered West Point, on the crumbs from that side of the table.

A cool breeze blew across the dark yard. Above them, the wind skimmed the clouds away and revealed the evening sprinkle of stars. Star light, star bright, first star I see tonight... I need $532.27.

Might as well offer a prayer while he was at it. For all the good it would do.

It was a bad night for the Whitmans. Tom could see that. There was a stiffness between them, a lack of ease. It was, he was sure, another quarrel about money. Tom felt like groaning. It was one of those evenings when money was on everybody's mind.

The after-dinner talk was strained. Lila was bored and angry, and she didn't bother to hide it. Johnny was grim and edgy. He was drinking like he wanted to see the bottom of the bourbon bottle.

It was going to be a long hour, Tom figured. For minimum politeness, he would have to stay at least that long before he could say his good-night and leave. In desperation he searched around for something to talk about, a way to interest one or both of the Whitmans. Otherwise, it was going to be a long, long night.

"I poured Withers on the train north yesterday."

"The Englishman? I thought he was nice." Lila smiled.

Johnny laughed. "You take him on a tour of the countryside, Tom?"

"Some of it."

"Old Mill Road?" Old Mill Road was where the Simpson farm was located.

"Only because he insisted," Tom said.

Lila was puzzled. "What's on Old Mill Road?"

"One of the historic battlefields," Tom said.

"Oh."

Johnny laughed. He collected the glasses and carried them into the kitchen. He mixed drinks and returned. As he handed Tom his drink he said, "What was Withers doing down here anyway?"

"Checking on me."

"No. What's he doing in the States?"

"Something hush-hush I think."

Tom knew he shouldn't talk about it. But what the hell? What harm would it do? After another drink, pressed by both Lila and Tom, he told them what Withers had revealed to him in the Simpson kitchen.

At the end of it, Johnny Whitman put back his head and roared in a voice that could be heard the length of the Row, "I don't goddammit believe it. I just don't."

When Tom opened the bathroom door he saw Johnny waiting in the hall. He released the light cord and left the overhead bulb burning. "It's yours."

Johnny blocked the hallway with his spread arms. "You know, I've been thinking about it. I think we could do it."

The bourbon bottle was empty, stuffed upside down in the trash can. Tom had drunk his fair share of it. He closed his eyes and shook his head. The fuzz wouldn't go away. "Do what?"

"We could rob that train."

"You and me and Jesse James?"

"Huh?" Johnny blinked at him.

"On second thought, you and Jesse do it." Tom pushed Johnny's arm aside and stepped around him. He reached the kitchen before he realized that Johnny had followed him. The dining table was cleared. The dishes soaked in the sink.

"Say it's a tactical exercise, Tom."

"It's one they don't teach at the War College."

"Look here." Johnny reached across the kitchen table and picked up the salt and pepper shakers. "Watch this."

"Forget it." Tom looked toward the screen door. The hour was up. He could say his good-night to Lila and leave.

Johnny held the salt shaker toward him. "This is Halifax, Nova Scotia." He placed the shaker on the table surface. "Right here."

"I've got to leave, Johnny."

"You've got a minute." He waved the pepper shaker at Tom and then placed it about two feet from the salt. "This is Montreal."

"Look, we've been drinking. It's late. Tomorrow..."

"Hear me out." Johnny cupped one hand around the salt shaker and one around the pepper. "Halifax and Montreal. What's between them?"

"I don't know." He also told himself that he didn't care.

Johnny poured a tablespoon of salt into one hand. He spread a thick trickle that led from one shaker to the other. "Tracks. The tracks of the Canadian National Railway."

"Okay, Johnny." He decided that he couldn't get away by putting the idea down as nonsense. He'd hear Johnny out and leave and hope that he didn't remember much of it when he was sober. "Tell me about it."

"Now you're talking."

"But we're discussing a tactical problem. That and nothing else."

"That ain't the problem. This is the solution." Johnny pulled back a chair and sat down. He looked across the table at Tom. "There are three parts to it, the way I see it. Part one. It's got to be shipped from London or wherever. Trucks or trains, that doesn't matter because there's no way we could get to England to do anything about it. So we strike out part one. Part two. It's loaded on a ship or on ships. Armed and escorted, you can bet on that. I can't see any way you're going to rob a British ship at sea. So we forget part two. That leaves part three." Johnny touched the salt-shaker cap. "The stuff's unloaded at Halifax. It's put on a train for Montreal and points west. That is where it's vulnerable. It's locked in." He traced a route through the thread of salt. "The tracks. The train's got to stay on the tracks. It's not like an army on the march. Cut off, ambushed, it moves to the north or to the south or back to the east. You can't do that with a train. It runs from Halifax to Montreal. Period."

They heard Lila's footsteps on the back stairs. She entered and stood in the doorway. "I thought you'd left, Tom."

"I'm trying to."

Johnny said, "I'm not done yet."

"Some other time."

Lila edged past Tom. She looked down at the table top. "What's this?"

"The Canadian National Railway tracks," Johnny Whitman said.

"It looks like a mess to me." Lila reached for a damp cloth on the sink counter.

CHAPTER SEVEN

Tom avoided Johnny Whitman all day Saturday. There were two messages in his box at BOQ when he returned from lunch. He didn't call the Whitman quarters as the notes asked that he do. He picked up his bathing suit and a towel and drove to Officers' Beach. Two hours later, when he entered his room, he found a note under his door. He wadded the message and tossed it in the trash without reading it.

He spent Saturday night at the Simpson farm. He didn't drive back to the base until late Sunday afternoon. He had a sense, a feeling, that Johnny Whitman wasn't going to give up that absurd idea until he'd sweated all that alcohol out of him. That might take another day.

He hadn't wanted to return to the base at all. Betsy Simpson was cooking fried chicken for supper, and Emma, who did most of the baking, was shelling pecans for a pie. What forced him back to the base was the appointment he'd made earlier in the week for a few games of handball. He'd tried to reach Lieutenant Mellows by phone and couldn't. No one had seen him at BOQ since the night before.

Mellows wasn't at the gym when he arrived. There was always the chance that he'd been trying to reach Tom to cancel the games. That would be in the pattern of his luck. The crappy luck he'd had the last week or so. Tom dressed in his sweat clothes and went to the court he'd reserved. He batted the ball around for a few minutes and was thinking of giving up on Mellows, when he heard the dry cough from the spectators' catwalk high above the court.

Johnny leaned on the railing and grinned at him. "Hello, good buddy. How are you?"

"Stood up. You want a quick game?"

"Not today. Today my mind's on other matters."

"Too bad." Tom slapped the ball against the corner and caught it backhanded when it fired back at him. "I've got time for one game before I'm due back in town."

"Not today."

Tom left the court. He flipped the light switch outside. He undressed in the locker room and took a quick shower. When he returned to the locker room he found Johnny Whitman there. He was seated on a bench near Tom's locker, legs crossed, head back, smoking a cigarette. "Most people would be curious why I'm leaving messages under rocks and ..."

"That was booze talking Friday night."

"You and me, we could plan it." Johnny tapped the side of his head. "That's where it works or fails, in the planning."

"As a party game it might beat playing bridge. And that's all it was, a party game. Some way to pass the time while the host and hostess aren't speaking to each other and it's still not time to say good night and leave." Tom dressed quickly. He looped the tie under his collar. "If you believe you can pull this off, all it means is that too many footballs bounced off your head." He tossed his sweat clothes in the wire basket. "Anyway, I've got other plans."

Johnny trailed him from the locker room to the equipment compartment. He watched as Tom pushed the basket through the window to the attendant. "Going to Kansas, huh?"

"What does that mean?" Tom stepped around him and stood in front of the mirror. He began tying his tie.

Johnny leaned toward him and grinned into the mirror. "You know. What's the town there where they've got the stockade where officers do their prison time?"

"I wasn't thinking about Leavenworth."

"It might not be your choice, Tom."

Tom adjusted his tie. An itching began high up, between his shoulder blades. "What does all this mean to me? You're talking nonsense."

Johnny backed away. His eyes flicked toward the attendant behind the equipment cage. "Not in here."

Tom waved a hand at the attendant and pushed through the door that led to the parking lot. A blast of hot air hit him as soon as he reached the stairs. The full sweat broke out over the length of his body. He raised a hand and wiped his forehead.

"You can give me a lift," Johnny said from behind him.

"Where's your car?"

"Lila dropped me. She was going to the beach."

"All right." Tom led the way to the Chevy coupe. He got behind the wheel. Johnny entered from the passenger side, but he didn't close the door. "I guess you didn't hear what happened last night."

"What?"

"They'll want to talk to you."

"Who?"

"The Provost Marshal," Johnny said. "Somebody broke into Company D last night."

"Is that right?"

"They pried off all the locks and broke into all the cabinets."

"Who?"

"Nobody knows. Probably some dogface needed booze money." Johnny put out a hand and touched the dashboard. He drew his hand away. "Hot as a griddle." He turned and stared at Tom. "They broke into your office, too. I understand they emptied the Company Recreation Fund."

"My cabinet?"

"You're slow today, Tom. They took everything that was there."

"It should have been more than five hundred dollars."

"Should have been," Johnny said softly.

"You put a funny emphasis on *should.*"

"Maybe it deserves one." Johnny closed the door on his side of the coupe. "That dumb dogface did a night's work for very little pay."

"That's a funny remark."

"Of course," Johnny said, "nobody knows this but the thief and me."

"It doesn't bother you that you seem to know what the thief knows?" Tom put the Chevy in reverse and backed out of the parking spot. He turned into the road and headed for Married Officers' Row.

"You'd be surprised all I know. For example, I hear you had rotten cards last week."

"They were so-so."

"They were dog slime, and you know it. You might say I've done a study of your gambling habits. All on the quiet, you know."

"Of course."

"The run of cards you had last week. Somebody might get the idea the thief was doing you a favor."

Tom turned onto Custer Road. Johnny's house was halfway down the street on the left.

"But we know better," Tom said.

"Know what?"

"We know it's blackmail."

"How can you blackmail an innocent man?" Johnny stretched and yawned. "I understand that dogface even stole your account book."

"I guess that's why the Provost Marshal'll want to talk to me. He'll want to know the balance in the fund." Tom swung the coupe across the road and braked in front of Johnny's quarters.

"Maybe. On the other hand, if the Provost knew about your gambling, he might have some other questions for you. The way I heard it, you lost somewhere between four and five hundred dollars to George Marsh." Johnny pushed the door open and stepped into the road. "Come in for a few minutes."

Tom leaned on the steering wheel. "What were you doing last night, Johnny?"

"Me? Nothing. Lila was feeling sick, so we stayed home and listened to the radio."

"All evening?"

"The whole evening." Johnny rounded the front of the Chevy and opened the door on the driver's side. "And we did a lot of talking. You know what? Lila thinks the trip to Canada is a great idea."

"That makes all the difference in the world," Tom said.

"Don't it?" Johnny waved a hand at his house. "Come on in."

Tom followed him up the walk to the front porch.

Lila had made a pitcher of tea before she left for the beach. Johnny got a handful of ice from the refrigerator and dropped it into two glasses. While he poured the tea, Tom stood at the screen door and looked into the backyard.

It had happened there. Damn himself for a loose tongue.

"Have some tea," Johnny said. "It'll cool you off."

"I'm not hot."

"You're boiling." Johnny held the glass toward him.

Tom moved from the doorway. He took the glass. "Say the rest of it."

"I don't like the word *blackmail*."

Tom sipped the tea. "It's a rotten word."

"But say somebody tried to do you a favor. Say it was a way of making you owe them. Instead of that, while they were doing the favor, that person got his hands on something really damaging."

Tom knew. It was the operatic gesture, the *IOU $532.27* scrawled in the ledger to balance the books for Major Griggs when he came by. And he'd signed it, in inch-high letters.

"If that evidence, if we call it that, got mailed to the Provost, all hell'd break loose. Somebody'd hang by the balls."

"If it got mailed," Tom said.

"That's right. What's bad about blackmail is that it means you're forcing somebody to do some action they don't want to. It means you're pulling at them and they're digging in their heels the whole way. It's a waste of time and energy dealing with them."

"The solution's simple. The one who's reluctant, you let him sit out the game."

"It's not that easy."

"Why not?" Tom said.

"The way I figure it, at a minimum, we need at least two chiefs and six indians. One chief can't handle all the details."

"Find another chief. Promote somebody."

Johnny shook his head. "That's another problem with blackmail. The one who doesn't want to go along with it, say you let him out. What's to keep him from coming by afterward and doing his own version of blackmail?"

"His word," Tom said. "His complete lack of interest."

"In a hundred million dollars?" Johnny stared at him, his look steady and unblinking. "No, the other chief is in it, like it or not. Of course, it would be better if he liked it."

Tom placed his glass of tea on the table. "Can I use your bathroom?"

"Like it was your own."

Tom ran water in the sink until it changed from lukewarm to cold. Then he filled the basin and ducked his face in it several times. He dried himself on a towel that smelled of Lila's perfume.

He could fake it. That was the only choice he had. The whole idea had an ice chip's chance in hell of getting under way in the first place. Johnny said he needed two chiefs and six indians. Against that number, there was the Canadian National Railway and the Canadian Army and the Mounties and British security and God knows who else.

He could go along with it until Johnny got deep enough into it so he'd see how impossible it was. It might take a matter of days, no more than a week. Humor the child until he discovers that the puzzle he's putting together is too difficult for him. It was that or he'd have to explain the accounts to the Provost. That could, as Johnny had warned him, mean prison time at the stockade in Leavenworth, Kansas. It wasn't a pleasant prospect. No, he'd humor the child for a few days.

When he returned to the kitchen, Johnny was seated at the table. There was a sheet of paper and a pen in front of him.

"I guess I'm in," Tom said. "But I can't lie about it. One heel's still dragging."

"At least it's progress."

Johnny capped the pen and shoved the paper across the table. When it was closer, Tom lifted it and saw that there were six names listed on it.

Randy Gipson
Clark Gipson
Harry Churchman
Vic Franks
Richard Betts
Gunny Townsend

"You know them?" Johnny took the list from Tom and placed it on the table in front of him.

Tom nodded. "And every one of them is trouble." He leaned across the table and drew a line with a fingernail under Clark Gipson. "Except him. He doesn't fit in with that bunch. Why do we need him?"

"We don't. But we need Randy, and without Clark we don't get Randy."

"Two for the price of one?"

"A fire sale." Johnny tapped the list with a finger. "First thing in the morning we see what the Army's got on them. Home addresses, Army addresses."

"Harry Churchman's out. He's been ex-Army for months. Vic Franks took his discharge. So did Betts. Gunny Townsend retired with his full time in. I don't know about the Gipsons. Hell, they're all grown boys and they won't be home with their mothers."

"I didn't say it would be easy."

"I'm glad you didn't say that."

"That's why I've given us three days to locate them." Johnny Whitman folded the list and stuffed it in his shirt pocket. "And not one day longer."

Talking is the easy part. It's no trouble making a list of names.

It was small comfort, no matter how much Tom tried to convince himself.

The son of a bitch really thought he could do it.

But in a few days, in a week...

CHAPTER EIGHT

Money changed hands. Captain Whitman and the clerk in the records office knew what twenty dollars was worth. The hunt for the six men began in the files early Monday morning, as soon as the office was open for business.

Gunny Townsend was easy. It was simply a matter of finding out where they mailed his retirement check each month. One call, and the clerk had that address for Johnny.

The Gipson brothers weren't much harder. Randy Gipson, as he'd been most of his Army time, was in trouble, and he was serving his sentence in the Fort Bragg stockade. Clark had taken his discharge about a month before. There wasn't any address for him, but he wouldn't be far away from his brother. He'd be somewhere in Fayetteville. The Gipsons were like the evil and the good halves of a character in a Russian novel. Find one, and the other would step out of a doorway down the street.

The enlistment papers for Vic Franks showed that his mother had signed for him so he could join up at seventeen. The chance was that she might know where her son was. It was, however, a long shot. Maybe they weren't in touch.

That was the morning's work. Two definites and two possibles. A good start when you considered that he'd allowed himself three days.

At noon, on his lunchtime, Johnny drove into town and sent two telegrams from the Western Union office. One to Gunny Townsend and the other in care of Mrs. Franks in Detroit. Both telegrams were the same.

I HAVE A BIG PROJECT. UNLIMITED
FUNDS. CONTACT ME NOW.

Ten words exactly. Right on the head for the minimum length.

The enlisted men's mess was through serving for the day when Johnny got back from town. He walked around the building to the loading platform. Lunch might be over, but the cleaning up was still going on. Johnny found the mess sergeant's desk and asked for Alvin Hart. The sergeant checked a clipboard and directed him to the pot sink.

Hart, a sad-faced private with bad skin, was there, up to his elbows in soapy water. Mountains of dirty pots and baking pans surrounded him.

Yellow meat-grease scum floated around his elbows. His fatigues were soaked down the front, and he stood in a pool of the same water.

Private Hart saw Captain Whitman and didn't know whether to salute or stand at attention.

Johnny solved it for him by saying, "Stand easy."

"Yes, sir."

"You about done here?"

"I ain't hardly started," Hart said.

"Somebody told me you buddied about some with Richard Betts." The somebody was Sergeant Jefferson.

"That's right, sir."

"You hear from him?"

"I had a letter a week ago," Hart said.

"It have a return address?"

Private Hart nodded. "The letter's at the barracks."

Johnny looked around. The mess sergeant stood at a distance, watching them. Johnny waved a hand at him and the sergeant trotted over, quick step.

"Yes, sir, Captain?"

6 4

"I need Private Hart for a special detail. Somebody else will have to take over the pot sink until the breakfast shift in the morning."

It didn't matter one way or the other to the sergeant. The peacetime Army didn't have any shortage of warm bodies. The only one it mattered to was Private Hart. He'd miss the lunch and the supper cleanup. That was two less sessions in the grease barrel.

Within ten minutes Johnny had an address for Richard Betts. He copied it from the pencil smear on the envelope. Private Hart had a free afternoon and he considered it a fair swap.

Ex–Master Sergeant Harry Churchman was a hard man to find. He hadn't left a lot of footprints behind when he took his discharge and left the Army. Added to that, he had always been something of a loner, a man without anybody you could call a close friend.

Half a dozen phone calls and twice that many questions, and Johnny didn't know one new fact about Harry. He'd walked off the base with the discharge in his hand and dropped right off the edge of the world. That's the way it seemed.

And then, around suppertime, Johnny drove off the base to the Green Lantern Tavern.

The road outside the military reservation, as it was at Bragg and Jackson, was elbow to elbow with junk-car dealers and road-houses and trailer camps. And during his time in the Army, Johnny Whitman didn't recall one of these payday strips that didn't have one tavern called the Green Lantern.

A former top sergeant named Billy Corkran owned the one in Fort Belwin. He had the big belly of a man who'd spent half his life in mess hall and might have slept there between meals. His head was as bald as a peeled onion.

Johnny found him in a room in back of the Green Lantern. It was a makeshift office. His desk and chair were planted in the middle of stacks and stacks of beer crates and soft-drink boxes.

"Harry? That bastard."

"I thought you used to drink with him, Billy."

"I drink with anybody."

"You know where he is now?"

"I heard something," Billy said. "I forget what it is I heard."

"You're not much help, Billy."

"You maybe noticed I didn't stand up and salute when you walked in here. It might be because I ain't in that man's Army anymore."

Bastard. But Johnny kept it easy and even. "Where'd you hear this about Harry? The part you don't remember anymore?"

"I think it was from a girl works night at Emma's." Billy gave Johnny an amused look. "You wouldn't know Emma's, would you?"

"Only from the VD reports that go across my desk."

"The girl goes by the name of Angela."

"That's a classy name," Johnny said.

"Ain't it though?" Billy shifted his weight and made a reach into a beer crate. He pulled out a warm beer and pried the cap away on the side of the desk. A swallow and he said, "Oh, hell, this is a waste of my time. It's not like I gave a crap one way or the other. Look, I'll save you a trip over there. Lord only knows why. This girl from Emma's comes in one night and she gets in my private bottle back here, and it turns out she'd been giving it to Harry on her free time. She got it in her head, the dumb cow, that Harry was going to send for her as soon as he got settled up north. She heard from him this once. She got to worrying, and she got this guy she knows in New York to look him up." Billy tipped the bottle and the warm beer slid down. "This guy—I think he was a pimp—tracked Harry from a flophouse on Second Avenue to a fancy penthouse on Riverside Drive. It turns out that Harry is now working for Mr. Arkman. That scares the pimp or whatever and he backs off."

"Harry works for who?"

"Arkman. He's a mob money man."

"He got a first name, Billy?"

Billy laughed. "He don't need a first name."

That night, with a fake leave excuse—an uncle who'd had a heart attack in New York—Johnny Whitman drove to Raleigh, where he caught the night train.

He left the Gipson brothers to Tom Renssler.

It was hell to be old. To be useless. To be tossed on the junk heap and treated like some piece of machinery that wasn't worth using or repairing. To be at a time of your life when all the food you liked didn't agree with you and even if you lived with the heartburn your bowels didn't want to move for you.

Gunny Townsend had a roll call of all the bad there was about being fifty-one years old—and hell to know you weren't one quarter of the man you'd been twenty or even ten years ago.

Thirty years in this man's Army, and faster than you could remember how to say "Kiss my ass" in French, you were retired and it was *that* man's Army you were talking about. You were on the outside, drawing the check every month, and it was supposed to be the time of your life. That was what they told you, but it was a far piece from being the truth.

The time of your life was being a green recruit and getting your butt rubbed raw on a saddle chasing Pancho Villa all over the American side of the border and even down into Mexico. And, Lord, those Mexican women felt like their bodies had trapped the sun's heat.

And it was France during the Great War. It was when being an American meant something, and having that second stripe was about like being a sergeant was now. It was coming out of the trenches after two or three months with the dirt and the rain and the rats, and you soaked the mud off—it peeled off in layers— and you got dressed in your Class-A uniform. You got yourself a bottle of that popskull they called Cognac or Calvados, and you drank it down like you couldn't taste how bad it was. That was so you could forget how those French women smelled and how hairy they were. And, hot damn, the amazement that first time when you found out those French women did better with their mouths than with the other part the good Lord intended it for.

After the war was over, there was post life. People still respected the uniform. He'd made his third stripe over there, and he was all piss and vinegar and full of himself until he laid eyes on the top sergeant's pretty daughter, Amy Loughlin. After that first look at her, there just wasn't any woman in the world could shine with her. He just had to marry her. It was that or settle for a life where the beer was always flat, the whiskey sour, and the food all had the taste of sawdust and old newspaper mixed together and fried.

He married her, and it had been a good life, most of what he wanted, though Amy said she didn't care what those French women did, all it did was just prove how nasty they were.

Two children were born of that marriage. Bobby was older by a year. The girl, Cathy, was only a few months old when Amy died. It was cancer, and Amy was like a dried stick when he buried her. He didn't marry again. There wasn't any woman who could match Amy. No use looking. He raised the two children with the help of a sister who was a widow.

Bobby saw all he wanted to of the Army while he was growing up on all those posts. As soon as he was out of high school he took the first job offered him. It was driving a milk truck. What you could say for him was that he did have ambition. He worked his way up until he managed the whole fleet of milk trucks.

Cathy wasn't Army either. At seventeen she married a short-timer who was waiting out his discharge for his first hitch. The husband, Jeff, wasn't worth much, and it wasn't any great surprise to Gunny when he walked right out of the Army and took a job working in a mill.

When the children were gone, Gunny lost interest in them. He told himself that that was the end of them. He saw Bobby about once a year or every two years. Cathy was different. She acted like she cared about him. She remembered Father's Day and his birthday, and she named her first boy after him. Junius. And when she heard he was retiring, she wrote him and said that she could not bear to think of him living alone in some rooming house somewhere. And, now, she was not going to take no for an answer. She fixed a room for him, one that she had been renting out before, and told him she would rather do without the rent money and have real family living with her.

Not that she did without. Gunny cashed his check each month and put half of it aside for himself and gave the other half to Cathy.

That was how Gunny Townsend came to be living at 103 Blanding Street in Sumter, South Carolina. Fifty-one years old and going on fifty-two. In a house that had a bathtub but didn't have hot water unless you heated it on the stove. The house was on the next-to-last white street before black town began. With a daughter who was getting fat from eating too much and a son-in-law who worked at Williams Furniture Factory.

Every Saturday Gunny's routine was the same. That Saturday the middle of June wasn't any different. After breakfast he poured himself another cup of the Eight O'Clock coffee that Cathy made. He went out and sat on the front porch, mostly hidden by the tins and lard cans of flowers that Cathy potted and placed on the porch railings. He sipped his coffee and read the *State,* the newspaper from Columbia. He read it from cover to cover except for the advertisements.

At 11:00, exactly, he returned to his room and undressed. He put on clean underwear and clean socks and his best clean shirt. He left the house and walked up Liberty Street to the YMCA. For a quarter he got a towel and a small bar of soap. If it wasn't crowded, he stood under the hot shower for ten or fifteen minutes.

Then, dressed, feeling clean for the first time in a whole week, he walked over to Main Street. It would be just 12:00 noon by the City Hall clock. When he reached Main Street he took a right and headed for South Main. That was where the taverns were.

Sumter was the county seat, and Saturday was the big shopping day for the farmers. The streets got packed with them from dawn to dark. Their mules and wagons filled the rutted back lots. And all the niggers came in, too.

By noon the streets smelled of hot dogs cooking in grease and hamburgers with the raw, sliced onion that came with them. The children lined up at the Rex Theater for the early showing of some cowboy movie. The popcorn machine in the entrance-way of the Rex flooded the summer streets with its special brown scent. You could smell the popcorn and the butter all the way down South Main.

Saturday, June 15, wasn't any different. Just the routine. At least it started that way. He sat at the counter of Bob's Jewel Café and had his first ice-cold Pabst a few minutes after noon. With his second beer he had one of Bob's hamburgers with a thick slice of onion. The hamburger, he said, was to soak up the beer, and the onion was to keep all the pretty girls from bothering him during his drinking hours.

He was on the fourth Pabst when he felt the tickle in the back of his throat. He fought back the urge to cough. He didn't panic. He put down his beer and mashed out his cigarette and walked out the back door. A narrow catwalk there led to the bathroom. He went inside and locked the door and waited. He leaned over the grimy, splattered toilet with the busted seat, and this time, when it came, he didn't fight it back. He coughed and it broke out of his chest. The hamburger came up and part of the last beer and a ropelike clot of something. Blood. For the first time in months he was coughing up blood again.

He remained in the toilet for ten or fifteen minutes. He wanted to be sure he'd coughed all of it up. Somebody tried the door and found it locked. He banged a time or two and grumbled as he walked away. Then Gunny was pretty sure it was over. He wiped his mouth with toilet paper and used a wad of it to clean the blood from the rim of the bowl. He flushed the toilet a couple of times and went out to the catwalk.

A young man with greasy black hair that smelled of hair tonic was waiting there. He pitched a cigarette over the railing and stared at Gunny hard. "I thought you died in there."

"Almost," Gunny said. "Almost."

He had a swallow of the beer and left for home. His face, in the bedroom mirror—the pasty, yellow sheen of his skin—scared him, and he could feel the fever that came with the new outbreak.

The doctors had said it was cured. They'd said there was only a ten-percent chance the TB would come back.

"And if it does come back?"

There had been a lot of fumbling talk but no exact answer he could take home with him.

That night he told Cathy he didn't feel good. She brought him a bowl of homemade vegetable soup. He sat up in bed and ate a few spoons of it. After she left, he waited a few minutes and then carried the bowl of soup to the bathroom and flushed away what was left.

The chills and fever were on him bad. Twice during the night he had to make a run for the bathroom. He hoped nobody heard him coughing.

After the second time he carried the washbasin back to his bedroom. He placed it next to the bed. The next morning, Sunday, the basin was about one-quarter full of curdled blood and tissue. He got the basin emptied and washed before anybody else was up. All morning he stayed in bed. He coughed and nothing came up. His lungs felt sore, constricted, so that he counted each breath he took.

He didn't want Cathy to worry. He had Sunday supper with them. He picked at the fried chicken and the baked sweet potatoes. He had trouble swallowing—his throat didn't want to work—but he forced enough down to satisfy Cathy.

He was in bed the next afternoon. In his fever, like a dream, he was trying to figure out how long he had left. Days and weeks and months. Cathy heard the knock at the front door. She brought the telegram to Gunny. She sat on the edge of his bed and watched him while he read it.

The telegram was from Captain Whitman, the one who was a lieutenant when Gunny served under him. He read the message through a few times. Maybe it was the fever. It didn't make much sense to him.

"Is it bad news, Daddy?" The concern and worry was on her face. Telegrams did that to some people.

"Not a bit." He folded the telegram and stuffed it in his pajama-top pocket. "Some old Army buddies are having a reunion."

Junius, the boy named after him, was around the house. It was summer vacation from school. Gunny wrote out the message he wanted sent:

FINE WITH ME. WHEN AND WHERE?

Junius took the message to the Western Union office downtown. Gunny paid him a quarter to do it.

The return telegram came the next morning. It was from Major Tom Renssler. He'd been a captain the last time Gunny'd seen him.

COME FORT BELWIN SOON AS YOU CAN.

After lunch Gunny packed a bag. He told Cathy he would be back in a few days. He caught the bus to Columbia where he transferred, after a two-hour wait, to the bus headed north.

Richard Betts knew it was time to be moving on. He knew it gut deep, all the way down to his toenails. There wasn't anything wrong with the job. Hell, as work went, it was fine. You got all the suntan you'd get at some beach and all the ticks and bugs you'd get while big-game hunting in Africa.

What was wrong about the job was all the way personal.

And it was just too damned bad. The pay was good, and it looked like the job might last through the summer. It was 1,900 acres of land that was thick-assed with stumps from the last two or three times the timber crews worked their wide path across it. The last pass by, they took every tree as big as three inches in diameter.

It was good land, land that didn't know what a plow was yet. It would know soon. But now, all you could see in all directions were the stumps sticking up two or three feet in the air. Except where Richard and his crew had been: there, there wasn't anything but pocks where the stumps used to be. That was the job. Richard and his crew—two powder monkeys—trying to keep half a day ahead of the mule crew: the twenty mules, the ten blacks, and the white boss.

In a good day, taking it slow and careful with the sticks and the caps, working from first light to last light, Richard and his crew could clear maybe two acres of land.

Right behind them, dogging them, the mule crew followed. The drag chains attached, two mules to the stump, one black leading the mules, and the white boss, Ben Chambers, yelling the whole day. The stumps were hauled away, stacked, and left for the night fire crew. All night long at the company tents, you could smell the green-wood smoke and see the bonfire glow.

It was a good operation. Timing and planning went into it. When the land was cleared, it was going to grow cotton until hell froze over and there was a market for ice cubes. It was going to grow more cotton than any other plantation in the whole state of Alabama.

Wouldn't you know it? You had to know it. The only problem was a woman. Both the powder monkeys worked their tails lean.

They were good learners and they knew the dangers of working with the sticks. The burr in Richard's hide was that one of his crew, Bill Truesdale, had a wife. He hadn't wanted to leave her at home, and he talked the company into hiring her to cook for the whites, for him, for his helpers, and the boss white.

Now, Lord, Bill's wife, Ethel, wasn't no Jean Harlow. Far away from that. During Richard's hitch in the Army he wouldn't have pissed on most women as plain as she was. But the backwoods wasn't Fort Belwin or Fort Jackson, Columbia, South Carolina. These backwoods were the ass-end of anywhere. A week of waking up with that fence pole in the cot with him, and Ethel started looking more and more like a movie star all the time. And, hell, up against Bill Truesdale, he supposed he'd always looked handsome to her. He hadn't done much. All he did was give her his hundred-watt smile and talk nice about how good she could cook. She didn't say much back, but he could see her begin to act girlish around the kitchen tent. It wasn't no accident that she pranced by his tent that night about midnight when he was sitting out there smoking the last one of what had been a whole pack two hours before. And it wasn't no accident that the camp stool he was sitting on just happened to have a blanket on it that he was using as a cushion.

He walked a distance from the camp with her. It had been grease-slide easy. All he had to do was say that he sure had fallen in love with her and it sure was his bad luck that she had to be married.

It didn't take much more saying before the blanket was spread and they were down on it making more noise than two hogs in a dry cane field. And he had been like a boar hog having all he wanted of her, and her acting like love had just come to her at the age of thirty.

Damn, but she was dumb. Now she was looking at him with those doe eyes in the kitchen tent, and, late at night, she kept going on about how much she loved him and how they were going to have to tell Bill soon. Bill was, she said, getting suspicious anyway.

And damned if he wasn't. That last weekend he came back from all of Saturday and most of Sunday in Dothan, and the first sight he saw in the kitchen tent was Ethel with a fat, puffed lip. One look at him and her mouth jerked open, soundless, like a live fish on dry land. All the time Bill sat there looking at Betts with eyes like a cluster of birdshot.

That was at Monday breakfast. Even then, already, Bill must have worked it out in his head. Could be he'd been planning it the whole weekend. Bill wasn't all that bright. What it took somebody else an hour to figure out it would take Bill ten or twelve.

After breakfast, they walked over to the blasting ground. Bill didn't say anything about Ethel. Except for his sullen way, it could have been any other morning.

The blacks had gotten drunk that weekend. They were sweating stink stronger than hot muleshit. The boss was yelling himself right into a sore throat.

The blasting crew was going one-two-three, just the way it was supposed to be.

Bill and the other powder monkey, Tod, cleared the space under the stumps for the charges. Richard would look at the stump and the roots, and he'd estimate what he needed, one stick or two. Sometimes three or four. The charge bundles were made up, taped together. All Richard had to do was attach the blasting cap and the fuse. Twenty seconds on each fuse.

When the space was dug under the stump, Richard would pass Bill or Tod the charge and they'd insert it and move away. Richard lit all the fuses himself. He'd put the match to it and yell, "Fire in the hole," and even an acre away the blacks would stop and stick their fingers in their ears and bend over.

It was clockwork until right before noon quitting time. Richard decided they'd do two more stumps and that would take care of it until after chowdown. Both stumps were big ones, green wood that hadn't dried yet. Richard got two of the three-sticks out of his bag, and by the time he'd worked the blasting caps and the fuses, Bill and Tod had the holes dug under the stumps. They were waiting for him. He passed the first three-stick to Bill and saw him insert it and lay out the fuse. Richard walked past him and handed the other charge to Tod.

Tod was on his knees. He slammed the three-stick home and stretched out the fuse tail. Richard waved him away and struck a kitchen match. He touched the fuse and the count started in his head. It had reached five by the time he reached the other stump. Bill stood there, blocking his path. Richard started to step around him. Bill took a step to the side and bumped against him. Richard said, "Watch out," and raked a kitchen match down his leg.

The count on the lit fuse behind him had reached ten.

Richard cupped the match flame in his hand. He put out his free hand and pushed at Bill.

Bill caught his arm. "I got to talk to you about Ethel."

"Nothing to say." Richard's eye was on the match.

It flickered in his cupped hand. Bill swung an open hand and hit Richard's cupped one. The match flew away and went out.

Richard said, "Now look here, Bill…" He could smell smoke close by. Not the other charge behind him. The count was now fifteen on that one. It was shaving it close. "Bill, dammit…"

He looked down and saw a curl of smoke drift past Bill's leg. He understood it then. Bill had already lit the other fuse. He was doing his own count in his head. He was going to delay Richard until, when he did reach the fuse, it would go off in his face. It was supposed to be about the same time Richard realized there wasn't any fuse to light.

Richard said, "You dumbass." He turned and leapfrogged two stumps. He was flying through the air, turning, falling on his side, when he looked back and saw the surprised look on Bill's face. That was a split second before both the charges went off at the same time. Tod was yelling, "Fire in the hole" over and over again.

At the last second Bill tried to move. The dumbass had the count wrong in his head. A piece of green root the length and circumference of a man's arm blew up Bill's ass and came out his throat, taking his chin with it.

The white boss, Chambers, and two blacks took the body back to camp, wrapped in a tarp, over a mule's back.

Richard and Tod stayed in the field and worked until full dark.

When they arrived at camp they found that Chambers had driven Ethel, with the body of her husband, into town. They fixed a poor supper for themselves, and Richard was in his tent later that night when Chambers returned. He stopped in the tent opening and gave Betts a sour look before he tossed some mail on the foot of the cot.

The first envelope he opened held a note from Ethel. It was in chicken-scratch, grade-school handwriting.

Dear Richard,

I know you did it for me and I love you still. What you did has not changed my mind at all. I will be in Dothan at the bus station this coming Saturday at 12 noon.

Love, Ethel

The other piece of mail was a telegram that had been sent to the company headquarters in town.

One reading and Richard packed his barracks bag and placed it by the tent flap. He trimmed the kerosene lamp and stretched out on the cot. He closed his eyes and rested. He didn't sleep.

At 3:00 A.M. he stole Chambers' flatbed truck and drove it all the way across the state line into Georgia. He abandoned it in a dirt lot in Atlanta and took the train north from there.

CHAPTER NINE

The Chevrolet coupe was parked outside the Fort Bragg Main Gate. It had been backed into the diagonal parking slot so that the two men inside could look through the windshield and watch the entrance to the military reservation. It was 8:00 A.M., exactly.

The two gate guards paid them no attention. They weren't on the post, and therefore not the soldiers' concern unless they crossed the thick white line that ran across the road at the front edge of the sentry box.

It was so quiet that Tom Renssler heard the hard boot heels even before the three men rounded the corner about a full city block away. They turned past a huge white-frame building and marched straight down the middle of the road.

Tom leaned forward and braced his elbows on the wheel. Next to him Clark Gipson put both hands on the dashboard. He edged forward until he was almost pressed against the glass. The anguish on his face told Tom all he needed to know.

He asked it anyway. "That him?"

"It's him." Clark put out his right hand and fumbled for the car door handle. "It sure is him."

Tom clamped a hand on Clark's left shoulder. "Not yet. It won't do any good."

"But it's my..."

"Not until he's across the boundary line," Tom said.

Clark Gipson tilted away from the windshield. His back settled against the seat. It was an outward thing, a loosening of muscles. The inside of him, Tom knew, was in knots and tangled coils. That was how he'd been when Tom found him in the flophouse hotel in Fayetteville the night before. He'd been sitting in the dark, smoking cigarette after cigarette while cockroaches the size of half-dollars climbed the walls of the room. Tom had bought him supper and a few beers while they talked. And he'd waited for the tension in Clark to pass, but it hadn't.

Clark had been mustered out, an honorable discharge, four weeks before. The past two weeks, waiting for Randy, he'd washed dishes in a downtown restaurant kitchen. He was pale and sallow, in a town where everybody was beginning to acquire their farm or parade-ground tans.

He looked thirty. Tom knew from Clark's records that he was twenty-five. He had dark hair. There was Welsh or Scots blood in some part of his family a hundred or so years back. He was lean and narrow-shouldered and slightly bowed in the legs. His eyes were a milky blue. Now they were masked behind narrow slits as he stared at the three men marching toward the Main Gate.

Two of the three men, the ones on either side, were over six feet tall. Big and oakwood hard. They'd been selected for the job on the basis of size and toughness. These two men wore leggins and boots and peaked caps. Each one carried a .45 automatic in a leather holster with the flap closed over it. And they carried long polished billy clubs.

The man in the middle was dwarfed by them. He wasn't more than five-four or five-five. He wore wrinkled tan trousers and a white-tie shirt with the sleeves ripped off at the shoulder seams. He carried a rolled-up, untied bundle under his left arm.

The little man, Randy Gipson, marched slightly out of step. The huge soldier on his left, a sergeant, called the cadence. "Hup ... Hup ... Left, right, left."

Clark's voice was a whisper. "They've skinned him."

It was true. Now that the men were closer Tom could see that Randy Gipson had had his head shaved to the skin in the last day or so. His hair was as dark as his brother's, and the hair stubble made his scalp look like it had been dyed blue.

The two gate guards circled the sentry box until they were on the right side. The three men marched toward them. When Randy Gipson was level with the gate box the sergeant bawled out, "Prisoner … halt."

The other stockade guard, a corporal, circled the prisoner until he was behind him. He grabbed the bundle from under Randy Gipson's left arm. He threw the bundle like a football. It hit the road some twenty feet outside the military reservation. The bundle bounced a couple of times and fell open.

One of the gate guards laughed. "You gonna do it, Dewey?"

"Don't I always?" the big sergeant asked.

The corporal remained where he was. He unfastened the flap that covered the .45. His hand wrapped around the butt of it. The big sergeant saw this and nodded. He walked in a half-circle until he stood directly behind Randy Gipson.

"The U.S. Army has something to say to you," the sergeant yelled.

It was reflex. Randy started to turn his head.

"You're at attention," the corporal shouted at him.

Randy Gipson sucked in a breath and went rigid. He was like that when the big sergeant took two steps forward and kicked him squarely in the butt. Randy hadn't expected it. The force of the kick threw him headfirst across the white boundary line. He landed on his hands and knees and slid for a short distance.

"And don't you ever come back," the sergeant bawled.

In the Chevrolet, Clark Gipson grabbed the door handle. This time Tom didn't stop him. Clark got out of the car and closed the door carefully behind him. He walked slowly toward the sprawled figure in the roadway.

The gate guards watched him. They didn't say anything. The stockade guards turned their backs as Clark leaned over his brother, caught him under the arms and pulled him to his feet.

Randy struck his brother's hands away. He walked stiffly toward the Chevrolet where Tom waited. He kept his hands away from his sides. Blood dripped from cuts and scrapes on his hands and elbows.

Behind him, Clark squatted over the open bundle. He began collecting the underwear, the spare trousers, and the socks. When he reached the car door Randy whirled and looked at him. "Leave it where it is," he said.

Harry Churchman backed out of the kitchen carrying two cups of coffee. He placed his cup, black and no sugar, on the low table beside his chair. The chair's high back was against the main entrance into the penthouse apartment. Anybody who wanted to enter the apartment, if they got past the doorman downstairs, had to come in over Harry Churchman.

He carried the second cup, cream only, to one of the six men grouped around the poker table. It was a new table, covered with heavy green felt, and it had an adjustable hanging lamp over it that threw its circle of light only as far as the outer rim of the table.

Like a trained waiter, which he wasn't, he approached Mr. Arkman from the right. He placed the cup and saucer on the table without spilling a drop. Mr. Arkman glanced up briefly, a flicker of his eyes that took in Harry's steady hand. Then he looked down at his cards. Backing away, Harry saw that Mr. Arkman had kings and tens. The trash card in the five-card draw was a six of diamonds.

Harry was careful. His face didn't change. He had worked long enough for Mr. Arkman to know the rules. No pleasure when his boss had a good hand working and no disappointment when he had a poor hand. It was better that way. At a poker game, the other players watched a lot more than the way the cards ran.

Harry settled into his chair at the door. He had to reach across and adjust the shoulder holster under his cord jacket. Bothersome fucking thing. But it was part of working for Mr. Arkman. His boss was a gambler and a speculator and the moneyman for a good number of shady deals. They were the high-risk deals nobody else wanted to touch. And when Mr. Arkman put his money in a deal, he skimmed a straight and even forty percent off the top before expenses. He didn't make friends with that kind of cut. He'd also made a lot of enemies with his touch for the fast-buck deals he handled himself.

That was why he needed Harry Churchman. And that was why his driver, as well, was armed. A man with the class of enemies Mr. Arkman had didn't take chances and last long.

Harry had been on the job six months. The man who'd had the job before him had let the pressure squeeze the guts out of him. He got shaky and he started drinking too much. When he couldn't tie his shoelaces he was fired, and Harry got the chair by the door.

Until eight months before, Harry Churchman had been regular Army all the way. He was going to be a twenty-year man or maybe even stay for the full thirty. That was the way he planned it.

Harry came out of a little town in the Texas Panhandle. As a boy growing up there, he got tired of the heat in the summer and the cold winds in the winter, and he knew he was going to leave. He watched his father and mother working themselves to death without any hope of being any better off when they died than they'd been when they were born. He couldn't change it for them, so he decided that he wouldn't stay and watch it happen.

At sixteen he joined the Army. The recruiter, a corporal with ten years in, didn't believe he was eighteen. It didn't impress him when Harry said he'd been born on the farm with a midwife rather than a doctor and that the birth certificate never was filed. The recruiter said, "We all got our crosses to bear, boy," and gave him a paper that he was supposed to have his daddy sign that swore he was eighteen. Harry knew his daddy wouldn't do it. He was free labor for them until he came of age. So he walked around town until he found a man who signed his daddy's name for him. He was gone, on a train headed for basic training, before his daddy and mama even knew he was missing.

He was Army for sixteen years. After twelve years in he thought he had it made. He was a lifer and twenty years wasn't that far off.

He made master sergeant in his fifteenth year. It was supposed to lock him in tight. It hadn't. He knew damned well what he was. He was the best small-arms man in the whole round-assed Army. The Army knew it too. They hadn't wanted him to leave. They tried to talk him out of it. He said, "If I am so necessary to this man's Army, why am I getting field-hand pay?"

The major who'd been trying to talk him into re-upping couldn't answer him. He wasn't all that pleased with his own pay scale.

So, at the age of thirty-two and going on thirty-three, Harry took off his uniform and went looking for somebody who'd pay him what he thought he was worth. It took most of two months to find the kind of job he wanted. He turned down some offers. And then the luck was with him, when Mr. Arkman's bodyguard got so shaky he couldn't even tie his shoelaces.

The pay was eight hundred dollars a month. Danger pay. Room and board went with it. One night off a week when Mr. Arkman was staying in and the driver could guard the body.

It was the fat life, that's what it was.

The high cotton.

It happened so fast there wasn't anything Harry could do about it. He was half dozing. It was about an hour after he'd taken Mr. Arkman that last cup of coffee.

He knew four of the men in the game. They were regulars who played every week if Mr. Arkman sent them word the game was on. The other two men in the game this time were from out of town. One was from Texas and the other from New Mexico. Both slight little men, quiet-spoken. Nothing to worry about from them, Harry'd told himself. And anyway, as part of his job, he'd patted them down from their necks to their ankles.

The first thing he heard was when the Texan, a slim dark man about forty who looked like he might be tarred with some Mex in him, said, "... shaved edges on them cards, and I damned well know it."

His voice was soft and southern, and there didn't seem a touch of anger in it. It was almost matter of fact.

The other stranger, the one from New Mexico, said, "Let's have a look at the deck."

It was still low and easy. They could have been talking about the weather.

But Harry heard the words and he shook his head to clear it. He gripped the arms of the chair and leaned forward. He was just getting to his feet when Mr. Arkman shoved back his chair and stood. The move was too abrupt. His head was turned, looking for help from Harry Churchman, when the slim Texas man reached across the table and swung his arm. There was a steel flash in his hand. He'd pulled a blade from his boot top, and when Mr. Arkman made his sudden move he'd reacted in panic. The knife had the edge of a straight razor. It cut Mr. Arkman's throat deep and wide and all the way to the neck bone.

Harry got to the table two steps late. The Texas man was leaning across the table, about to take his second cut, when Harry hit him behind the head and floored him. Harry kicked the chair aside and hit the man two more times. One blow flattened the Texas man's nose, the other broke his jaw. Harry located the knife and kicked it across the room.

He had to take care of the trouble before he could look out for his boss. One of the regulars had caught Mr. Arkman before he fell and lowered him face down on the poker table. The pooling blood, buckets of it, soaked into the felt and smeared the cards and the chips.

Harry circled the table and reached under Mr. Arkman. He got his hand bloody to the elbow trying to find a pulse, a heartbeat. There wasn't one. Mr. Arkman was dead and running out of blood and turning into cold meat.

Harry Churchman was out of work again.

Early the next morning a garbage scow, twenty miles out of New York harbor, dropped two extra bags over the side. In one was the 120 pounds of what had once been Mr. Arkman.

The other bag, almost a twin in size and weight, held what was left of the little Texas man. Two of the regulars had beaten him to death in the bathroom with blackjacks, for spoiling what had been a good weekly poker game.

The New Mexico man had insisted he was deaf and dumb and would remain that way for the rest of his life. In fact, he promised he was leaving town on the next train. When he got back to New Mexico he was going to tell everybody he had been to San Francisco.

The disappearance of Mr. Arkman worried some people and made others happy. It was about an even split.

The New York Police Department didn't seem to care one way or the other. Perhaps it was only a formality, but they put out the word on the streets that they wanted to talk to Mr. Arkman's bodyguard and his driver.

Harry Churchman was down to his last hundred and thinking about taking any kind of work, when Captain Whitman found him. He was sleeping at a one-dollar-a-night flophouse on Second Avenue.

They didn't like him at the Transcountry Hauling and Transport Company, and Vic Franks knew it. They called him "Soldier Boy" to his face. That started because, waiting for his first payday and short of cash, he'd worked in his Army uniform with the corporal stripes cut away. It was like the old lifer in Company D said: "They love you and buy you drinks and pat you on the back when there's a war going on. Ain't nothing too good for you then. Peacetime, they think there's something wrong with you for being in."

Vic took the crap. He thought, if he took it well, it would stop in time. He needed the job and work was hard to find. It was a measure of how much he needed work that he took a job on the loading dock. What he wanted, what he felt he was qualified for, was work in maintenance or driving the big rigs. Oh, the hiring boss had made promises. He was up for the first opening in the garage or the first driving seat that didn't have a butt in it. He didn't believe him. That talk was the carrot for the horse, and he wasn't any dumb horse.

Vic worked the loading dock from 11:00 P.M. to 8:00 A.M., five days a week. It was gut-busting and backbending work. He'd load the trucks and then watch the drivers come in in the morning. It burned him. The drivers would be hungover, and they'd tear up the gearboxes because their hands and their heads weren't together.

In the beginning, maybe he did believe the carrot. During his 4:00 A.M. break, when the others on the loading crew flaked out and rested, he'd trot over to the garage. What he saw there—the shoddy mech work, the "lick and a promise" engine overhauls—disgusted him. If you loved engines, any and all kinds of engines, you didn't treat them that way. No more than you beat your children or abused a woman if you loved her.

Could be he should have kept his mouth shut. It was what you learned in the Army. But wasn't he out of the Army now? What was all that talk about freedom of speech? Well, it didn't seem to apply at the Transcountry Hauling and Transport Company in Newark, New Jersey.

So he made some enemies. On all sides. The dock and the garage. He heard them talking just loud enough so he would hear them. "Soldier boy don't like the way we do things here" and "Might be he ought to sew them punk stripes back on and go back to Mama."

He could put up with the talk. That wasn't any red off his candy. But the dirty tricks came next. One morning he found that somebody'd poured a can of motor oil in his good shoes. That was in his locker where he kept a change of clothes. There wasn't a thing he could do about it. That was eight dollars' worth of good shoe leather gone to hell.

Another time he opened his locker and caught the strong smell of urine. Somebody'd pissed in the bottom of the locker. The piss pooled there. He had to take it. He didn't complain. He got a wad of rags and cleaned it out. Even motor oil was better than that.

Bad enough. That was bad enough. Then it really got serious. It was during the shift on the night before the mid-month payday. They'd have fixed him good if he hadn't left the dock while the other two loaders were taking the 4:00 A.M. break. What he needed was the spare pack of Camels he kept in his locker. He got the smokes from the top shelf and was backing away, closing the locker door, when he saw the pile of cleaning rags on the bottom shelf. He pulled the rags away and found two whole quarts of Old Grand Dad.

He didn't have to spend time worrying about the meaning of shipping goods in his locker. He knew. He carried the two bottles to an empty locker down the line a ways and left them there.

At 8:00 A.M. the day foreman passed out the pay envelopes on the dock. The foreman, Vic thought, wasn't part of it. He had always been fair.

The foreman said, "Word came back about a shipment went out yesterday, one loaded during the graveyard shift. There was some shorts. I guess I've got to do a shakedown."

Vic's locker was the last of the three the foreman searched. While the foreman poked around in his belongings Vic didn't watch him. His eyes were on the other two loaders. When the foreman lifted the pile of rags and backed away he said, "Nothing here either." Vic saw the look that passed between the other two loaders. The question was there: What went wrong?

Vic knew it was over as far as the job went. Once they went that far they wouldn't stop until they got him some way or another. He'd been lucky this time. He might not be the next.

After breakfast that morning, on the way to the room where he stayed, he made two stops. At a hardware store he bought a funnel. Next he bought two ten-pound sacks of sugar at the grocery store around the corner from his rooming house.

He arrived at work that night about half an hour early. The evening shift was done, caught up with their loading, and they were sprawled around the dock drinking coffee and thinking about harder stuff. Vic didn't have to make the suggestion. One of the early-night crew did it for him.

"Since you're here early, Soldier Boy, I guess we'll go on home." They didn't wait for him to agree. They left for the nearest bar.

He watched them go, and then he went to the clump of hedge that ran down one side of the loading area. He'd left the bag with the sugar and the funnel there on his way to the dock.

There were three trucks backed up to the dock for loading during the graveyard shift. Before eleven, before the other two loaders showed up, he inserted the funnel in the gas tank of each of the trucks. He poured between six and seven pounds of sugar into each tank.

He worked the full shift. He was standing on the dock the next morning when the trucks left on their runs.

At the rooming house he paid up what he owed. He packed his few belongings. He rode a bus for a day and a half to reach Detroit. All the trip, seeing it in his mind, he knew what the sugar was doing to the engines. The sugar burning with the gas, syrup at first and then as hard as rock.

The way he felt about engines it was almost enough to make him cry.

He had been at his mother's house, looking for work, for almost a month when the telegram came from Captain Whitman.

CHAPTER TEN

MacTaggart didn't return to the boardinghouse from his office. Not right away. He found a pub and had a few pints. He thought about Peggy and how his life and hers were growing together, no matter that he had approached her at first like a ram in rut. It was different now.

When he got to that point, when he felt he'd digested the lumps and the curds, he finished the pint he was on and returned to the boardinghouse and to her bed.

Short of breath, afterward, he left the bed and poured two drinks from a half bottle of her Irish. He brought the glasses to the bed and sat on the side and placed her tumbler on her flat, bare stomach. The blackout curtains were closed. A single candle burned in a dish on the nightstand.

"When I first met you all I wanted was your tall, handsome body," she said, picking up the tumbler.

"That's always the way it's been," he said.

"But now I've decided you're more than just a tall, handsome man." She sat up and smiled at him before she took a swallow of the Irish.

"Now you've made me happy," he said. "It's a painful life, Peggy, if you don't learn what to keep and what to throw away."

"I think I know now," she said.

He let her sleep with her head on his shoulder. He didn't disturb her even after his arm went numb. He was awake when the first threads of light pushed through the blackout curtains.

❦   ❦   ❦

Johnny Whitman returned from New York on Thursday the twentieth. The two, almost three days, that Johnny had been away from Fort Belwin had been busy days for Tom Renssler. Besides his Army duties, now there was Lila on the phone at all hours with jobs for him to do. Gunny Townsend was at the bus station and needed someone to pick him up and take him to a rooming house. Richard Betts had called from the train station in Raleigh. Would Tom talk to him when he called back? Betts insisted upon knowing more details about the project before he was willing to catch the next train to Fort Belwin. And when Vic Franks sent a telegram from Detroit, Tom had to drive into town and cable him to remain there until he received further instructions.

On top of everything else, he had to babysit the Gipson brothers. Randy, after his time in the stockade at Fort Bragg, was a short fuse looking for a match. His brother, Clark, couldn't handle him alone.

The message from Johnny was waiting for him when he returned to BOQ after a couple of hours soothing Randy Gipson's impatience. Tom was angry and frustrated and had the beginning of a stomach burn when he drove across the reservation to the Row. It took about ten minutes to fill Johnny in on what had been happening while he was away. Johnny made notes on where the Gipsons, Gunny Townsend, and Richard Betts were staying. He'd drop by later to see them. It was time to start them north. And, on the way into town, he would stop by Western Union and wire Vic Franks. If Franks left Detroit first thing in the morning he could be in New York some time Sunday.

"How do we get together up there? It's a big city."

Johnny had planned that. He'd stayed at the Hotel Earle and he'd thought ahead enough to make a reservation for Lila and himself for Sunday. The Gipsons, Townsend, and Franks could reach him there, and he'd set up the meetings.

"That settles it for everybody but the two of us."

"You take three weeks of leave," Johnny said.

"It won't be easy," Tom said. "Both of us on leave at the same time. It leaves the Company short."

"Not both of us. You take the leave. I've put in my resignation, effective immediately. I'll take some accumulated leave while the discharge is being processed."

"They'll have to replace you."

"In this cowshit Army? The way they feel about me?" Johnny walked to the screen door, pushed it open wide, and flicked a cigarette into the backyard. "I told them I was leaving for business reasons. I said I need a quick discharge so I can take a job with a stock company in New York. The way I put it I've got to be in New York on Monday. I don't think they'll bother to check it out, but it's a real offer."

"I doubt..."

"Look, the way I see it, Colonel Harper probably worked late today. I'd guess he hand-walked my papers through just to be sure I didn't have time to change my mind."

"He loves you," Tom said.

"And I love him back."

There was a loud thump from a room in the front of the house. "Lila's packing," Johnny said.

Tom nodded. He got his campaign hat from the hallway table. Johnny followed him to the front door.

"I'll put in for leave first thing in the morning."

"You don't have to, Tom."

"Huh?" Tom turned to face him.

"I sent the request in for you this afternoon. It seems you need time off to arrange your marriage plans with some wealthy girl or other."

"A girl in New York?"

"That's right."

"I signed those papers?"

"With a flourish," Johnny said.

"I've signed the papers," Colonel Harper said. "I was given to understand there was a legitimate reason for haste."

Tom Renssler stared at him. He didn't know what the Colonel was talking about.

"Captain Whitman told me in strict confidence."

Tom lowered his head and stared at his desk.

"My boy, there's no reason to be embarrassed. Many marriages begin with … these circumstances."

Then Tom understood. Johnny Whitman had gilded the facts around the bogus wedding in a way that assured that there would be no problem with the leave.

"The girl is from a good family?"

"The best," Tom said. "Amelia and I have known each other for years, since we were children."

It was Friday afternoon. Colonel Harper had dropped by after lunch. The whole time, Tom had the feeling the colonel was staring at the new file cabinet in the office.

"When is the wedding, Major?"

"We may elope," Tom said. "We think it might be easier that way on her family."

"It might."

The colonel left.

Tom's supposed engagement was the talk of Company D. Everywhere he went someone congratulated him. From the looks he got, he also had the feeling that everyone had heard that it was going to be a shotgun wedding.

❧   ❧   ❧

"You should have heard him," Johnny Whitman said.

"Who?"

"Colonel Harper, that's who. I'd said something about how I was sorry this business opportunity was going to leave him short of officers."

The late train from Raleigh that Friday night was crowded. There was only one sleeping berth available. Lila had taken it and had gone to bed about an hour after the train pulled out of the station. Now it was midnight; the dark Virginia land rolled past, and Tom Renssler and Johnny Whitman sat in one of the day coaches and passed a bottle back and forth.

"When was that?"

"When I picked up my leave papers," Johnny said. "Harper gave me this look, toenails to eyebrows, and said, 'This Army can function quite well without you, Captain John Whitman.'"

"Too bad you couldn't tell him you had some girl knocked up."

"You found out about that?"

"He'd have been sympathetic," Tom said.

"That was in confidence," Johnny said. "That man broke his word."

"What the hell? It worked, didn't it?"

CHAPTER ELEVEN

MacTaggart felt that he was nailed to the wall. It happened so fast.

As soon as he reached his office Colonel Haggard sent for him. It was under way—the whole mission—and the colonel hadn't known about it until the night before. Of course, he'd been expecting it, but he'd assumed there would be more warning. He'd tried to call MacTaggart, but the phone in the hallway at the boardinghouse wouldn't ring. He'd sent a messenger across London to inform MacTaggart, but there had been no one in the room.

"Dammit, Mac, don't you ever sleep?"

MacTaggart was thinking the same thought. It had been a sleepless or almost sleepless night with Peggy on his shoulder most of it, and he didn't feel very fresh. He'd hoped he'd have a chance to get a couple of hours of rest at his desk. Usually that was possible.

"It leaves Euston Station," the colonel said. "They're assembling the train now. The boxes from the collection center here should arrive there about three this afternoon." The rest of the paper shipment, from Liverpool, Manchester, and Edinburgh, would be time-staggered and shipped directly from those cities to Greenock. "You'd better get over there now, Mac."

"My kit?"

"I'll send Billings around with a car to relieve you at six or half-six. You'll have an hour."

It would have to be enough.

❧   ❧   ❧

The train was assembled in a barnlike shed in the freight section of Euston Station. It consisted of an out-of-date passenger coach and eleven boxcars. A squad of Scots Guards, hastily assigned, paced the length of the loading platform and stood watch at the entranceway to the truck ramp that led down from the street.

A working party of twenty young men from the Horseguards training school arrived at two in the afternoon and waited for the first truck to appear. It was a long wait. The first truck didn't arrive until almost four.

It took an hour and fifteen minutes to unload the four trucks and reload the boxes into one of the boxcars. The boxes weren't heavy. They held the stocks and bonds that had been packed in the London banks almost a week before. MacTaggart counted each box as it came off the truck and counted it again as it went into the boxcar. When the boxcar was locked and sealed it held 203 cases of paper wealth.

There was a break of forty-five minutes and then the trucks began to arrive from the bullion yards of the Bank of England.

MacTaggart had the unloading and reloading under way when Billings arrived with the car and relieved him. He turned the job over to his relief. By 6:20 he was at the boardinghouse in Shepherd's Bush. He left the driver waiting outside and took the steps up to his floor in twos and threes.

There'd been no way to reach Peggy. Now she came to her door when he knocked and the fear and anxiety left her face and she made a leap at him. "You said you'd be here at five and ..."

He shushed her. "That trip I said I had to take. It's here." He held her for a moment longer and then he turned her and led the way to his room. While she watched, he packed his battered leather handbag. Underwear, socks, a couple of spare shirts, and the zipper bag with the .45 Colt automatic and the three spare clips. His shaving kit went on top.

He put that bag aside and dumped the rest of his belongings into the cardboard-sided suitcase. "You'll have to keep this for me."

He carried both bags to her room. There wasn't much time. He stored his suitcase in the back of her closet. He sat at her dining table and did some figuring in his head. He owed the landlord for a week. He counted out the money and placed his key with it. She would handle that detail for him.

He stood and looked around. "I've got to go. I can't say where I'll be. I'll be gone about three weeks. At the most a month. I'll write you when I can."

"I wish we had more time, Mackie."

"I do too, girl."

He held her for a time. When he backed away she was trying to smile. It was a wounded smile. "Where you're going, will it be cold and wet?"

"It might be." It was on the tip of his tongue to tell her; as much as he wanted to, he couldn't give her any clues that might suggest his destination.

He'd misunderstood her. He watched as she crossed to the table. She returned with two bottles of her Irish, a gift from her mother. "It will help you think of me, Mackie."

He packed the bottles in his bag and wrapped his spare shirts around them for extra protection.

He kissed her good-bye in the doorway. He didn't let her follow him to the street.

At Euston Station the original working party of twenty men had been reinforced with the arrival of another twenty men from a casuals depot, a unit where soldiers waiting reassignment to other units stayed until their orders came through.

Billings remained while MacTaggart ate a beef and cheese sandwich at the canteen that had been brought in to feed the working party and the soldiers.

While MacTaggart was gone, they'd loaded two of the box-cars with bullion cases. Now, with Billings gone, it all fell to MacTaggart. As soon as one truck pulled away from the platform and up the ramp to the street, another pulled in.

The next four hours, clipboard in his hand, he checked each bullion crate off the truck and checked it into the boxcars. The first nine of the remaining cars were loaded with 225 crates of gold bars. The final one held 204.

Just before midnight, while the engine was backed into place and joined, MacTaggart made his final check of the ten boxcars. When he was satisfied with the count, the cars were locked and sealed.

He signed the Bank of England's manifest. It was his full responsibility from that point on.

A squad of armed soldiers marched down the ramp and, under the command of a captain, filed into the passenger coach at the rear of the formed-up train.

MacTaggart followed them in. He placed his leather bag and his black raincoat, what he called his travel mac, on an empty seat and looked in the private compartment at the front of the coach. Five men were crowded in there. All of them were neat and well dressed, wearing ties and suits. They had the mark of clerks and bankers on them.

MacTaggart knew the man in charge, Craig. He got introduced to the others, to Phelps, Crewshaw, Forrest, and Kent.

Each of the men carried a single suitcase. With the exception of Craig, they looked stunned and bewildered. MacTaggart understood that. Only Craig knew the details of the mission. The others had been recruited at the last possible moment, on purpose, so there'd be little risk of the information leaking out.

MacTaggart left the bankers to their compartment. He didn't feel he belonged with clerks and bankers.

He took his seat among the soldiers.

The blackout shades were pulled down and fastened before the train left Euston Station.

Ten minutes out of London MacTaggart was asleep and snoring.

Behind them, in London, the secret train had not remained secret. By morning rumors about the train swept through the city. The story given the most credence was that the train carried the Queen and the two Princesses, Elizabeth and Margaret, and the Crown jewels on the first leg of a trip that would take them to the safety of Canada.

The morning of June 22 it was cool and clear in Greenock. The temperature was in the mid- to high fifties most of the day. In the distance, above the Greenock harbor, the dark green of the summer land edged down toward the paler green of the sea.

On the cruiser H.M.S. *Emerald* the bosun piped the hands to cleaning chores at 0800 hours. The *Emerald* was "laid down" in 1918. It had been designed for World War I but was not completed until 1926. With the coming of the war in 1939, the cruiser toiled those early difficult months in the important but less-glamorous backwaters of the North Atlantic merchant convoys.

She was an E-class cruiser. Her silhouette stamped and marked her. There were two funnels just behind the bridge. Then there was a space, an interval, where the third funnel should have been but wasn't. The third funnel was where the fourth one usually was. Outlined against the sky, the profile was that of a grin with one tooth missing.

At 0940 a working party from the starboard watch was sent ashore to await the arrival of the train that carried the assigned cargo. The train from London arrived at 1000 hours, and the engine shunted the boxcars to the harbor siding.

Under the supervision of a tall man in a dirty black raincoat the seal on the first boxcar was broken and the door unlocked. The working party from the *Emerald* worked for almost an hour unloading that boxcar and stacking the crates on wooden cargo skids. At 1120 hours the bosun's pipe was for the remainder of the starboard watch to assemble to handle cargo. Winches lifted the cargo skids to the deck of the *Emerald*.

H.M.S. *Emerald* was not a cargo ship. It was a ship of the line. As a warship it was not constructed to carry large quantities of anything other than provisions and munitions. Storage for 2,717 boxes and crates created a problem that was solved only by using the weapons and ammunition magazines as cargo holds.

There was a break for lunch. During the afternoon, as unloading continued, three other boxcars arrived at the harbor and were shunted onto the siding. One car was from Liverpool, one from Manchester, and the other from Edinburgh.

At dark the working party was dismissed and a guard posted on the remaining boxcars. The first day they'd unloaded eight of the fourteen boxcars.

The tall man in the dark raincoat slept that night in the passenger coach. During the night, at one- and two-hour intervals, he could be seen prowling the length of the train.

At 0730 the next morning the bosun piped the same watch, the starboard, to stations to handle cargo. The starboard watch worked through the morning until it was relieved by the port watch at 1300 hours. The watch going off duty was granted shore leave until 0700 hours the next morning.

The port watch had it easy. Another hour and the last of the cargo had been received and stored away. The working party was secured. The tall man in the dark raincoat came aboard and stored his bag in the compartment assigned to him and to three of the bank officials.

Accompanied by the cargo officer, he made the rounds of the storage holds. He did not seem pleased that the cargo shared space with powder and shells.

Nobody on H.M.S. *Emerald*—the working parties—knew what the cargo was. There was some joking below decks about the markings on the crates. SALT FISH.

"Why the hell do they need salt fish in Canada?"

"I suppose they shipped it here by mistake and want it back now."

The men with tired backs and sore muscles had some doubts that salt fish could ever be that heavy. "It's like bloody lead weights," one rating said.

Speculation continued. It would not be confirmed what the shipment was until the *Emerald* was a day at sea.

MacTaggart slept that night aboard the ship. He slept through breakfast. He would have slept through dinner as well if one of the bank officials hadn't come into the compartment to get a package of pipe tobacco. Awake finally, he still felt tired and dizzy. The strain of the last three days and the fitful sleep the first two nights had him jumpy and nervous.

He had dinner in the ratings mess. He spent the afternoon walking around the ship. It was larger than he'd first thought it was. It was like a small town, a world of its own.

At dusk, before he went ashore, he asked that a guard be posted on the magazines until the ship left the harbor.

By dark, still wearing the stained raincoat and needing a shave, he made the first of his pub stops. He worked the waterfront area, the public houses near the port. One pint here, one pint there, talking little, mainly listening. He seemed turned back on himself, deep in other thoughts and other places.

He wasn't. He heard every word said around him.

At half-past nine, satisfied that there was no street talk about the shipment, he returned to the harbor and the *Emerald*. He sloshed with the beer he'd been drinking. He wobbled on his rounds of the cruiser while he checked to make certain that the watch was still posted on the cargo.

He found his way to his bunk. He stretched out and either slept or passed out within minutes.

He didn't notice the weighing of the anchor at 2254 hours. Forty minutes later H.M.S. *Emerald* passed the boom and headed for the open sea.

PART TWO

CHAPTER TWELVE

Harry Churchman picked the meeting place. It was his town, wasn't it? Didn't he know the back streets and the side alleys? You worked for Mr. Arkman and you got to know the seamy side of the city. Penthouses and the East Side, townhouses and Park Avenue—those were for the big ones, the guys behind the money masks.

The ones on the way up, the bright guys with the new hustles—they came from grubby places and wore all they owned on their backs. A good tailor was better than a good address with them. The new hustler wore some tailor's best on his back and about fifty dollars on his feet, and he walked out of some slum apartment and turned a corner and waved down a cab. By the time he left that cab somewhere in midtown nobody could tell where he lived.

But Harry knew. He had to hunt them down. He delivered the operational money for the risky deals, and sometimes he had to collect Mr. Arkman's share. The hard-way collections.

Harry selected an abandoned garage on Tenth Avenue. That part of Tenth was residential, working-class houses and rented rooms in shotgun flats. The garage tenants hadn't made rent and expenses for more than a year. Now the corrugated-tin sides had scrawled obscenities on them, child high, and the windows had been smashed even before they'd been boarded up.

Harry arrived in a cab about half an hour early. He had the cab drop him a block away. After the cab turned a corner he walked back to the garage and tripped the heavy padlock on the office door with a key about the size of a paring knife.

The office was empty. No furniture at all. Just the paper trash on the floor and the dust balls that had collected. It was warm inside from the June heat. A door that hung on one hinge led to the work space with the grease pits and the divided stalls where the mechanics had worked.

There was a skylight above this main work area. It was dirty, but it let in enough light so that Harry could find the electric switch box just beyond the wrecked door. He threw a couple of switches. Banks of lights flared on. He cut those and tried another. He experimented until he found one bank of overhead lights that had some burnt-out bulbs mixed in. He wanted only the minimum light. Too much light, like too much noise, would advertise the meeting.

A long wooden table was directly under the skylight. Its top was scarred and scratched and, here and there, showed the black puckers and pocks of cigarette burns. There were six mismatched chairs around the table. Harry leaned across the table and ran a finger down the center of it. Dust rolled ahead of the finger in waves. He blew the dust from his finger and looked around. He found the bathroom. There was a cloth-towel roller on one wall. He ripped the towel from the box. It came away easily. Rotten. He tore away a long section of the towel and carried it to the table. He wiped the top and the chair seats. A hit-or-miss job. It didn't matter to him. He wasn't any goddam house maid. Screw it. He picked himself a sturdy chair that would hold his weight. He eased into the chair and checked his watch. Still twenty minutes to wait.

The garage, until a few months before, had been a numbers collection center. For electricity they'd tapped into another line down the street. Getting water was almost that easy. You slipped a few bills to an off-duty man from Water and Sewage.

At one time all the runners—the collectors—brought the day's take to this table. It came from all across the city. It came in leather bags and brown-paper sacks. Once it got to the table, it received a count that would have pleased any big-city banker. On peak days all six chairs were filled. Underlings did the count, and the boss circled the table the whole time. The boss verified each count and kept his eyes open for sticky fingers.

Mr. Arkman had some points in the numbers business. It was one of his dozen or so continuing enterprises. At least once a month, without warning, Mr. Arkman dropped by the collection center to do his own check. Harry went along as his gun.

Back around the first of the year, the collection center had started drawing attention. They'd had to buy a policeman and then his buddy. It was all those arrivals and departures at a deserted building. In April the collection center moved to another location. Maybe in a year they'd rotate back to the garage. That was why they hadn't done anything about the electricity or the water.

When Harry began to look for a place to hold the meeting, he remembered the unused collection center. It had been easy enough to find one of the runners and talk him into the loan of a key.

Captain Whitman walked in two or three minutes early. He wore a new gray lightweight suit. His tie shirt was wrinkled, and the collar was rimmed with a dark sweat line. "Hot out there," he said. He tossed a long tube wrapped in brown paper onto the table. The tube rolled toward Harry.

Harry put out a hand and checked it. "Maps?"

"The latest I could find." Johnny walked away from the table and looked into the bathroom. "I'm the first one here?"

"You're the whole fucking gang."

"Lucky me." Johnny pulled a chair from the table and sat down. He was across from Harry. He grinned. "You and me, Harry, we could probably pull this off alone."

"It's a dogshit idea. The two of us have about as much chance as eight of us do. That is, not much chance at all."

"You were eager before," Johnny said.

"That was before."

"And you're backing away now?"

"I say that?" Harry tipped his chair and balanced it on the back legs. He stared up at the skylight. It was almost full dark outside. "Let's say I quit drinking tit milk a long time ago. And there ain't anybody can force-feed it to me. It just happens it might be better if I spent some time in Canada. This fairy-tale job works out, I can use the money. It don't, and I still won't be in New York City."

"Who's looking for you?"

"Who said anybody was looking for me?" Harry snorted. "You jump to funny conclusions, Captain."

"Strike the conclusion, then. You ready to leave?"

"I could leave yesterday." Harry lowered his head. His eyes were closed. His face was a death mask. Then he opened his eyes slowly, degree by degree, as if getting used to the light. "This bunch of crazy dogfaces you put together. You must like failure."

"It was the best I could do on short notice." Johnny hesitated a beat. "You know them?"

"The way I know you." Harry made a fist with his right hand and uncurled one finger. "Gunny Townsend. Learned most of what I know from him. A good man one time, the best there was. He's sick, old, and tired now."

"There might be one campaign left in him."

Harry poked out another finger. "Richard Betts. Might be he knows his job. Word was that he did. The way I think, though, anybody plays with matches and fuses didn't start with a full fifty-two in the deck."

"An occupational hazard?"

A third finger. "Vic Franks. I don't know him except to wave at."

"He talks to cars and trucks," Johnny said, "and they talk back to him."

"And that's not crazy?" Harry held out the full hand, the little finger and the thumb showing now. "That leaves the Gipson boys. Clark ought to be preaching hellfire and damnation in some backwoods church in Alabama or Georgia. Randy, his brother, is only a slightly higher form of life than a cockroach."

"They know railroads."

Harry dropped the hand, palm down, on the table top. "That's the lot. It's a rotten stew."

"You missed one," Johnny said. "Harry Churchman."

"Him? He's the biggest nut in the whole batch. You know why? Because he knows better. He's got good sense. He don't do dumb things. And, with all that true, he's about to go waltzing away to Canada after a trainload of gold that might exist and then again might not."

"The gold's real."

"You say."

"More people than me say it," Johnny said. "For one, there's a British major named Withers. I've known him a time. He let it slip, and the next day, when he realized what he'd done, he almost crapped in his uniform."

"And he heard about it on the streets?"

"At British Intelligence."

"It might make a difference." Harry scratched the side of his nose. "You believe him?"

"One hundred percent. Major Renssler believes him too. That ought to mean ..."

"That reminds me," Harry said. "He's the other one we didn't talk about. The boy scout from West Point."

"He's smart like you. He knows the gold is coming in, but he's against the whole idea."

"I might marry him," Harry said.

The street door opened. Both men turned and looked in that direction. Vic Franks and Gunny Townsend had met down the street while they were searching for the address. They walked past the sagging door. Vic Franks nodded at the captain and took a seat. Gunny circled the table and put out a hand to Harry.

"It's good to see you."

"How are your lungs, Gunny?" Harry gave the hand a squeeze.

"Sound as a dollar."

Harry laughed. "I didn't know the dollar was in trouble."

"It's not."

"I hope that's true, Gunny."

"It's fact." But he dropped his eyes and turned and looked for a chair.

The others drifted in during the next ten minutes. There was talk about old times in the Army and in Company D. It was a lot like a reunion.

Tom Renssler was the last to arrive. Johnny nodded at him in passing as he went to the office doorway and locked it with an inside slide bolt. When he returned all the chairs were taken. He stood at one end of the table. Tom sat on the edge and crossed his legs at the knee.

Johnny looked at Tom. "You want me to start?"

"It's all yours," Tom said.

"Might as well, then." Johnny took a deep breath and looked around the table. "There's something you might not know. There's a difference in time zones between the States and England. It's a matter of five or six hours."

Randy Gipson turned to his brother. "This a school?"

"It's seven in the evening here now. It's midnight in England. About now, give or take a few minutes, a cruiser named the *Emerald* is going to leave a port on the west coast of Scotland. It's carrying a lot of paper, stocks and bonds and that kind of crap. Stuff I wouldn't wipe my ass with."

Johnny stopped. He dug a pack of cigarettes from his shirt pocket. He took his time getting one lit. When he looked the length of the table he saw the confusion, the disappointment that was registering on the faces. He took a couple of puffs on the Camel. "And, besides that worthless paper, the *Emerald* is carrying something on the other side of a hundred million in gold bars."

He had their attention.

When MacTaggart came to he didn't know where he was or how much time had passed. He was damp-wet and was stretched out in a narrow bed. The strong smell of medicines and disinfectants told him he was in sick bay. There was, he realized, a new lump on the back of his head that felt about the size of a tennis ball.

The light blinded him. He could see the blur of shapes above him, crowding around him. Then he got his eyes to focus. A naval officer wearing a yellow rain slicker moved closer to the bed and leaned over him. Water dripped on MacTaggart from his rain hat.

"Who the hell are you, sir?"

"MacTaggart."

"What the bloody hell is a MacTaggart?"

MacTaggart didn't answer. He closed his eyes. His bladder was empty and peaceful. The pain from the back of his head didn't outweigh that.

It was, he decided, a fine time to complete his night's sleep.

CHAPTER THIRTEEN

It took a few minutes for the meeting in the Tenth Avenue garage to settle down again.

In the talk and excitement that followed Johnny's announcement of the estimated value of the gold, Gunny Townsend went into the bathroom and closed the door behind him. There was a muffled sound of coughing. When he returned a few minutes later he wasn't coughing but he was pale and his hands shook when he lit a cigarette.

Harry Churchman watched him. He saw the tremor in Gunny's hands and thought, no matter how I feel about the old man, I don't want my ass to depend on him backing me. The shooting starts and his lungs get to itching, I might get some rounds in my back by mistake.

Randy Gipson, still with the bluish shaved head from his time in the stockade, had spent the last two days trying to drink all the whiskey in New York. He hadn't had a drink for almost an hour. He felt sick and logy, and he sweated an oily, rank perspiration. It was enough to clear one end of the garage. It was the smell of cheap whiskey, and it was even worse because he hadn't had a shower since they'd reached New York. Clark hovered over his brother, soothing him and promising him another drink as soon as the meeting was over. It was the only way he could get Randy to concentrate on their part of the problem.

Richard Betts looked bored. He stared down at his hands. He smiled to himself every now and then—that was at the thought of

Ethel, two days ago, waiting at the Dothan, Alabama, bus station for him. Lord, dumb as she was, she might still be there.

Beside him, Vic Franks had his eyes closed. In his mind he had X rays, cutaways, of engines. Big truck engines choked and died as the sugar in the gas turned to black stone.

Tom Renssler had a headache. He'd been short of money when he'd arrived in New York. He'd thought of a West Point friend, one who'd stayed in the Army for five years after graduation and then resigned. In the years since then, Mark Swift had published one book of poetry and one novel. It turned out he lived in the Village on a trashy street a few blocks away from Washington Square. The Village was where all the writers lived that year. The apartment, when Tom finally found it, was a cold-water loft above a garage. Everything smelled of gas fumes and oil. The headache either came from the fumes or the raw, sour wine Mark drank all day.

What concerned Johnny Whitman was problem number one. Everything depended on a solution. With an answer, they could move on to the other questions: what kinds of weapons they'd need, the transportation, the type and amount of explosives.

It was a puzzle he'd put to Randy Gipson.

There is a train. It is made up of several freight cars. We don't know how many, yet. Some of the cars will carry paper we don't want. Others will carry the gold bars we do want. While this train travels between Halifax and Montreal, how do we cut out the boxcars that hold the gold bars?

Randy licked his lips. He was sweating. "You don't," he mumbled.

Tom put a hand over his mouth and yawned. He'd spent a few hours trying to come up with a way that would spoil the plot. He knew now that he had wasted his time. The confusion and the stupidity, the building chaos, would do it for him. The meeting was already at the point where it might break up at any moment.

He counted heads as he looked around the table. Harry Churchman was on the fence. He was a nudge, a push, away from going to Canada by himself. Richard Betts, almost burned black by the sun, looked coiled, trapped, about to lunge for the door to the street. Vic Franks didn't appear to be listening. His mind was somewhere else. Gunny Townsend was in, but he was so ill that he might fall over any minute.

The Gipsons, bless them, they were the real roadblocks.

Johnny leaned across the table. "What did you say?"

Clark stared at him with an open mouth and then looked at his brother. "He said..."

"I said... you don't."

"Goddam." Johnny hit the table with a balled fist. "You're supposed to know trains. That's why you're here. And all you can do is sit there on your ass and say we don't?"

"If I'm your expert," Randy said, "then why the shit don't you listen to me?" He reached a claw hand into his brother's shirt and came out with a crumpled pack of cigarettes. He dug about for a cigarette and then tore the top from the package and pulled out the last one. He turned to Clark. Clark struck a match and touched it to the cigarette. "What I say is that you don't and you can't."

Harry Churchman grunted. It was like a yes to a question that he'd asked himself. "I don't know about the rest of you. Maybe you got more patience than I've got. Me, I'm tired of listening to this moron."

"Wait a minute." Johnny waved a hand at Harry. He moved down the table toward the Gipsons. "Go on, Randy. Tell me what you mean."

"I mean you don't know shit about trains or about the air-brake systems. Once that train is moving there just ain't no way you're going to make a break in that system. You ain't going to be able to cut out this car or that one."

Johnny looked at Clark. Clark nodded.

"That's the truth of it, Captain."

"Explosives," Richard Betts said. "We blow up the whole fucking train. Then we walk around and pick up those gold bars right off the ground."

Johnny put his back to the Gipsons. He seemed to be considering the Betts proposal seriously.

Randy blew smoke at his brother. "You remember that time in Montgomery?"

"The hotbox?" Clark said.

"That was it." He winked at Clark and faced down the table. His grin, his look, was almost sober now.

"One time in Montgomery, this foreman had it in for Clark and me. He said we was soldiering on this job. The way he told it, we'd made this whole shipment of gravel late for consignment. He fired us right on the spot and he went over to the office to get our pay. That right, Clark?"

"That's right."

"It was four gondolas, open bed. While the foreman was over at the office I crawled down under those cars and I emptied the hotboxes."

"What's a hotbox?" Johnny was puzzled by the story, but it interested him. He wasn't sure there was a real point to the tale. On the other hand, there might be, or there might be some way that he could use what he learned.

"It's this box next to the axles. It's full of cotton waste that's soaked with oil. It keeps the axles oiled so they don't overheat and seize up."

"What good would emptying the hotboxes do?"

Randy laughed. It was almost a giggle. "Well, we can't say we followed that train to find out. We took our pay and left the train yard. That was after we cussed back and forth some with the foreman."

"Our guess," Clark said, "is that, about fifty or sixty miles out of Montgomery, somebody noticed smoke and sparks and maybe even fire coming from under those four cars. That was from the axles heating up and turning red and getting so hot."

"What happens then?" The puzzled look on Johnny Whitman's face was changing. It wasn't a smile yet, but there was the frame, the outline, for it.

"They ain't got a lot of choice. Either they stop right there on the track for a few hours, and might be they get another train rammed up the ass of this one, or they take it slow and easy until they get to the closest siding. More than likely they'd go for the siding. They'd cut out those four cars and shunt them off on the siding. Next they got to send out a crew to work on those axles and those hotboxes."

"You see?" Clark said. "Instead of that rock gravel being two or three hours late, turns out it was maybe a day and a half late. All because that foreman got on Randy and me."

"All right," Harry Churchman said, "I've listened to this dummy's story and ..."

Johnny shook his head. "No, you haven't been listening at all, Harry. What Randy's saying is that the air-brake system makes it impossible for us to cut the boxcars we want out of the train." The grin swept across his face. "But nothing says we can't give them a nudge so they'll cut those cars out for us."

"That's it," Randy said. "They do it for us."

The meeting was on schedule once more. The agenda Johnny had prepared in his mind was tailored to ease them past the hard questions. Those would be command decisions. His decisions, made after a consultation from time to time. The U.S. Army wasn't a democracy, and this outfit wasn't going to be one either.

Gunny Townsend was talking about weapons. Thompsons if they could get them. Shotguns, rifles, grenades. Gunny wheezed when he talked. There was a flutter to his breathing. The way he saw it, if there was going to be any fighting, it would be brush-fire, short and in close quarters. The Thompsons and the shotguns were best for that. Nothing better. The Thompsons for rounds per minute and rapid fire. One Thompson was the equal of five men using the old Springfields. And the shotguns were to blow down anything the Thompsons couldn't find. And they might consider getting some tear gas and masks if they could find them. You never could tell what might come up.

Johnny nodded. Yes, yes.

"Of course," Gunny said, "those Thompsons are hard to find right now." He looked at Harry Churchman for confirmation. Harry looked away. "Feds make it hard for you to own them. And, from what I hear, most of what the U.S. could spare and about all they had in Canada was shipped to England. So, if we found them, we might have to pay a price for them."

"How much?" Johnny tore a piece of brown paper from the map wrapping. He uncapped a fountain pen.

"It's according to the shape they're in. Used or still in the packing grease. Used would be cheaper. But that's like buying a used car. New would be best. Now we could figure a fair price and add about twenty percent above that." Gunny paused and took a deep breath. "But there's no reason to worry about the cost unless we can find them."

"You know anybody?"

"I've got a name in Montreal," Gunny said.

Harry hadn't joined in on the talk about weapons. His knowledge was as extensive as Gunny's. Now he scraped back his chair. "I the only one that this talk about how much a Thompson costs bothers? Anybody else?"

"What do you mean?" Richard Betts asked.

"All this crap about money. Anybody see a dollar of it yet?"

"I've been paying my meal ticket and my room," Betts said.

"That's what I mean." Harry nodded at Randy Gipson.

"Clark and me, we're down to a twenty and some dimes."

"You," Harry said to Vic Franks.

"I was hoping somebody here had a twenty that needed a home."

"I've got a couple of hundred I can spread around," Johnny said. "Anybody short can see me after the meeting's over."

"That won't do it," Harry said. "Where's the big money coming from? I'm not talking about meal money. If you can't give me an answer I'm going to waltz my ass out of here."

"You've been listening, Harry. You tell me what we need."

"You really want to know, Captain?"

"I want to know."

"Forty or fifty thousand. That's at the top. Might be we could shave some edges and bring it in for thirty thousand."

"You heard it from the master criminal," Johnny said. "That's what we need."

"Put it on the table, Captain."

"We'll have it, Harry."

"When? Now is what bothers me."

"It's waiting for us on the way to Canada," Johnny said.

"Where?"

"It's in a nice little family bank in Upstate New York." Johnny Whitman waved a hand in the direction of Tom Renssler. "The major there used to work summers in it. Told me about it one time. Funny thing about that little bank. It's in a town named Renssler. And that town's just one big spit from the Canadian border."

"They lend it to us?" Harry asked.

"Oh, no, they wouldn't do that." Johnny hesitated a few seconds. "We take it from them."

"That easy?"

"That easy," Johnny said.

Harry shook his head. "That's one mistake on top of what might be the really big one."

"If we can't rob a crackerjack box of a bank and get across the border we might as well forget about that train and that hundred million-plus that it's carrying. Call it a shakedown for the outfit, an exercise."

Harry thought about it for a minute. Why the hell not? It was some cash. Even if nothing came from the train job the cash would be living money while he got himself settled in Canada.

"I guess I'm in," Harry said.

Randy Gipson laughed. It looked like more and more fun all the time.

"The offer of a few dollars tonight still holds," Johnny said. "And after we do the bank everybody turns in expenses to this point. Travel, hotel, and meals." He grinned at them. "But no padding, you hear?"

Tom Renssler closed his eyes and let his breath hiss out. The rank S.O.B. thought of everything.

CHAPTER FOURTEEN

The three bank officials were gone when MacTaggart sat up and looked around the compartment. The two bunks across from him were made, the blankets folded and the suitcases stored away carefully. He didn't have to check the bunk above him. That one would be the same. These boys had been well brought up.

His own bag, an affront to neatness, was open on the deck next to his bunk. Underwear and socks spilled over the sides, half in and half out. The neck of one bottle of Irish stuck up like a swollen thumb.

He pulled the bag toward him and selected a clean set of underwear. His shaving kit stared at him. He pushed it toward the bottom of the bag and covered it with socks. Being at sea was roughing it, wasn't it?

He undressed and changed his underwear. He put on the same trousers and the same shirt and covered it all with the clammy weight of his raincoat. The way his life was going, the raincoat might stay wet the whole eight days.

He went on deck. It was gray and gusty. The ocean swells had calmed some. The wind beat at him, still strong, from the west.

His walk carried him the starboard length of the cruiser. Near the stem of the *Emerald* he leaned on a railing and watched the drama in front of him. Straight ahead, not more than a hundred yards away, a destroyer plowed the rough sea. In its wake, H.M.S. *Emerald* executed a zigzag pattern.

While he stood there, appreciating the expert ship handling, a young officer came out of a doorway behind him. MacTaggart looked over his shoulder. The officer stopped and gave him a puzzled stare. Then the officer nodded to himself and walked toward MacTaggart. It was an easy gait he had, one that appeared to predict even the slightest roll of the deck beneath him.

"Mr. MacTaggart, I presume?"

"Which ship is that?" He nodded his head toward the destroyer that kept its course straight into the wind.

"*Cossack.*" the young officer said.

"That's the whole escort?"

"Another one back there somewhere," the officer said. "It can't keep up."

"That's reassuring."

"Then you haven't heard the other news?" There was amusement on the young man's face, as if he were half of a comedy team and he'd been awarded the punch line.

"What news is that?"

"I assumed you'd been told."

MacTaggart shook his head. Cheeky bastard.

"Captain Flynn had a wireless from Admiralty in London. Admiralty believes there are at least three U-boats out there waiting for us." The young officer waved a hand in a rough 180° sweep. "Have a good day, Mr. MacTaggart."

The young man gave him a satiric salute and walked away with the same effortless stride.

MacTaggart watched him go. He stared down at the wind-stirred and whipped sea for a long time. Great Limping Jesus. How in the name of Him was he supposed to protect the shipment from three or more U-boats? It wasn't in any of the instructions he'd received from the Bank of England.

He felt foolish. If anyone saw him now they'd think he was standing watch.

He left the rail and wobbled his way along the port side of the cruiser. He did his check at each of the magazines. The hatches were closed. The guards, now that they were at sea, were gone.

Well, that was all he could do.

His stomach growled and rumbled at him. Breakfast was past and it was time for dinner. He followed his nose. It didn't matter which mess he found, officer or enlisted. In his circumstances, neither fish nor fowl, either would do.

If there were submarines out there, if he were going to drown in a freezing ocean, it might as well be with a queasy and full stomach.

The dinner MacTaggart forced on himself, some thin soup and a chunk of greasy beef, didn't stay down long. It hardly settled in before it was gone. By then he was in good company. Even the salts, the ratings with years at sea, were turning a shade of green and passing up food in favor of steaming mugs of tea.

The wind was gale force once more.

H.M.S. *Emerald* bobbed like a cork in the wind and the ocean swell.

He had little to do. Every hour or two he checked the hatches on the magazines. Other than that, he stretched out on his bunk. His eyes closed, he thought of jugs of beer and hot meat pies, hissing steam, that were served on tables that weren't moving from side to side or up and down.

He began writing a letter to Peggy in his mind. It helped pass the time.

> *Dear Peggy-girl:*
> *I have discovered a new cure for sickness at sea. When I return to you in London we will become rich selling it*

from door to door. Every hour, on the hour, or at those
times when you feel the flutters, you wet your tongue with
a taste of good Irish.

Vic Franks found the unlocked door on the passenger side of the
1940 Ford sedan. It was on a dark street that was bordered on
both sides by huge apartment houses. He hot-wired the ignition
while Harry Churchman stood in the shadows of a doorway and
watched for police cars.

Harry had him drive around for an hour. "Take that street,"
he'd say, or "Take a right." They were on the edge of Brooklyn
when Harry said, "Here."

Vic pulled to the curb. They were in front of a sporting-goods
store.

Harry checked his watch. "I've got one-thirty-five."

"The same," Vic said.

"That alley there. I want you to pass it every five minutes
until you see me. Pace yourself."

"All right, Harry."

"And if you hear an alarm go off, you get here flat out."

Vic nodded. Harry got out. Vic watched him stroll past the
store front. S. H. ARNOLD AND SONS was painted on the glass of
the windows. Harry stopped at the mouth of the alley. He looked
both directions and ducked in there. Vic put the Ford in gear and
pulled away from the curb. There was a light in the alley. By the
time Vic passed it, there was a *ping* and it went dark.

Vic made seven circuits. Each time, passing the store, he
slowed down and looked into the alley. Once, on another street,
quartering away, he passed a police car parked in front of an all-
night diner. He took another route the next circuit. It wouldn't
do for the police to notice the Ford or the regular routine he
was on.

On his eighth loop, a cigarette butt flipped out of the alley and hit the Ford's windshield. It threw a shower of sparks. Vic braked. Harry Churchman sprinted out of the alley, bent over, his arms loaded. Vic reached over the seat back and pushed the door on the curb side open. Harry dumped a clanking, wrapped bundle on the floorboards of the back seat.

"Watch both ways," Harry said. He whirled and ran for the alley again. He made three more trips. He carried boxes and bags and long boxed shapes that had to be rifles or shotguns. By the final load Vic could feel the weight pushing down on the rear springs.

Harry slammed the back door and got in next to Vic. "Take it slow and easy," he said. He was breathing hard.

"Where?"

"The garage on Tenth."

It was a long drive. Vic waited until Harry got his breath evened out before he asked, "What'd you get?"

"Everything." Harry sucked on a cigarette and stared at the dark passing streets. "I got everything but Daisy air rifles and heavy artillery."

Talking about money—how you could spend it, a catalog of what you could buy and own—turned on some secret tap in Lila Whitman. Johnny knew women, and it hadn't taken him long to pinpoint that aspect of her during his brief and expensive court-ship. A lavish dinner in *the* theater restaurant of the month, the charade of knowledged talk with the wine steward, the crepes flamed next to the table, and the offhand way he settled the check, as if he were buying a newspaper or a package of cigarettes—all these brought the warm sexual oils flowing to the surface in Lila. As did the feel of fur, the sparkle of gems.

And because she didn't know a precious stone from a chunk of quartz, green glass unglued her the way an emerald should have.

It was a joke he stored in his mind. What he'd do to her one night before he was done with her. He'd be ass deep in Lila and he'd chant the list to her.

"Emeralds, black opals, and pearls."

Wham, wham, wham.

"Ermine, mink, and sable."

Grunt, grunt, grunt.

"Cords, Rolls-Royces, and Bentleys."

Hump, hump, hump.

And right at the end, when she was on the edge, and he was about two lunges away, he would lean over and whisper in her ear, "Hundred-dollar bills."

Then, as he was pulling out, he'd say, "Nickels, dimes, and quarters."

Lord, it would chill her. It might even make her frigid the rest of her life.

If she understood what he'd done to her. There was always the chance that she wouldn't.

After the planning meeting was over at the garage on Tenth he'd returned to the hotel where Lila was waiting. He showered and changed into a dark suit. He took her for a late supper to Emilio's, the restaurant in the theater district that had been the *in* place when he'd done his whirlwind courtship. Now he didn't know any of the waiters or the maître d', and Lila didn't see one friend from her days in the theater. In fact, the few customers in the restaurant seemed to be tourists from somewhere in the South or the Midwest.

They returned to the hotel a little before midnight. On the way through the lobby, Johnny asked room service to send up a bottle of chilled champagne.

So far it was going well. Why not splurge?

They drank the champagne in bed.

"A hundred million," he said, "and if we split that eight ways …"

"No," Lila said, "you're being too generous." She reached over him and lifted the champagne bottle from the ice bucket. The icy water dripped across his bare chest as she passed it over him and had a swallow from the mouth of it. "At least one-fourth of it is ours. You're planning it, honey. It's your idea."

"Maybe." He let himself sound disinterested.

They'd had no talk of the split at the meeting. Perhaps they'd all assumed that it would be a straight eight-way division. Anyway, that could come later. If they got the gold, if they got it across the border, if they found a buyer for it. And also, after they'd counted heads to see how many survivors were left from the original eight.

"You know it, too," she said. "Brains have to count for something."

It was almost dark in the hotel room. A dim light near the door to the hall, shielded by the foyer wall, lit only the bottom part of the bed.

"When it's done, I'll put in my bill," he said.

"Think of all the places in the world we can go."

He did. Already half of the world was closed off by the war. In the Far East that door was slamming as well. It was only a matter of time. It didn't leave much. But he didn't tell Lila that. There was no reason to spoil her fun.

She took the last swallow from the champagne bottle. When she leaned across him to drop the bottle back in the bucket he lowered his hand and placed it on her thigh. Her leg jerked as if he'd touched a match to it. He moved his hand upward and her legs opened.

Yes, all that money talk. It worked with her. It felt like warm oil flowed up his hand to his wrist.

Nickels, dimes, and quarters.

✣ ✣ ✣

It didn't take long for MacTaggart to become a familiar figure on the ship. The crew stopped smiling at his soggy raincoat and his heavy street shoes that squeaked with water.

He really made his reputation the first time he showed up for the day's rum ration. That was at 1100 hours, the second day at sea. The routine called for a representative from each division to bring a container. He got a measure of rum from the demijohn for each man on the rolls. At the end of the count a measure of water for each tot of rum was mixed in. The mixture was the precaution the Navy took so the ratings couldn't hoard their ration for a couple of weeks and then go on a drunk aboard ship.

The officers got their rum neat. The Navy trusted them.

MacTaggart figured that if he could be trusted with about £125 million of the assets of the British Empire, he could be allowed his rum neat.

The rating with the demijohn didn't agree.

MacTaggart argued, he cursed, and he held up the whole line until the word came back from the Executive Officer. "Mr. MacTaggart can have his ration in any manner he likes it."

He drank it on the spot. One long swallow, and the raw burn clawed at his throat as he walked away.

At supper that night he watched the old sailors. They stayed with the hot tea, and he did the same. The sea was rough and the *Emerald* pitched and rolled in it.

Around dark, after a final check of the magazines, he returned to his compartment. He stripped down to his underwear and got into his bunk. A nip from the bottle of Irish and he could sleep, no matter what the gale-force winds did to the ship.

He awoke to stillness. The heavy darkness, the oppressive air told him where he was. He dressed and made his way to the head.

Two ratings were there before him. They were either going off watch or about to go on. They were having a smoke, rolling their own. One rating, an older man with a pocked face and a Yorkshire accent, nodded at MacTaggart and passed him the makings. MacTaggart fumbled for a time and produced a poor twist of a cigarette.

"How's it out tonight?"

The rating with the pocked face took the sack of makings and stuffed them in his waistband. "It's not getting any better."

"Any more talk about U-boats?"

"In this weather?" The younger man shook his head.

The older rating lit MacTaggart's cigarette. He blew out that match and struck another to light his smoke and the other man's. No three on a match, even if the bad weather did protect them from submarines. "The big news is that we're to go it alone from here in to Halifax."

"How's that?"

"Captain Flynn and the captain of the escort decided it. The destroyers couldn't keep up in this gale. It's holding us back." He looked at the younger rating. "What are we doing now, Fred?"

"Twenty knots."

The older man nodded at MacTaggart, the nod meaning that what he'd said was confirmed. "We've been held to fourteen or fifteen so we wouldn't outrun the escort."

"When does it happen?" MacTaggart puffed carefully on his cigarette. It was beginning to fall apart on him.

"It already has."

"The escort turned back at twenty-three-fifty hours," the young rating said.

MacTaggart tugged out his hunter's-case watch. He opened it. It was 12:14.

The older rating leaned over and looked at the watch. "Twenty-four minutes back," he said.

He wasn't sure the bank official was talking to him. Not at first. MacTaggart was bent over, fussing with a knot in his wet shoelaces. It was early the next morning and he was thinking about breakfast even though he knew he'd settle for tea again.

"We're in it by ourselves now," the bank official said.

MacTaggart lifted his head. He looked around the compartment. He was the only one left in the room with the bank official.

"Pardon?"

"Did you hear?"

"I didn't hear anything," MacTaggart said.

"France surrendered. The wireless operator got the message last night. The surrender took effect at one-thirty-five the morning of the twenty-fifth."

About two days ago. "Bloody awful" was all he could say. He freed the knot in his laces and got them tied. He struggled into his raincoat. A nod at the bank official, and he left for his round of the magazines. Breakfast could wait that long.

Yes, he thought. Yes. Now he understood it. Churchill and the War Cabinet had expected it. They'd known it was going to happen.

A gamble. A roll of the dice.

There'd been three players. One had dropped out. Now it was between the final two.

And here he was, Duncan MacTaggart, right in the middle of the first desperate roll in the new game.

The storm they'd encountered when they'd rounded the northern coast of Ireland remained with them, ahead of them, as H.M.S. *Emerald* headed west.

MacTaggart moved about the ship now with more assurance. He had, he thought, his sea legs. He found he didn't bounce from passageway wall to passageway wall below decks, and topside, he could almost walk a chalk line on the deck. If there had been a chalk line there.

He was on his way to getting his sea stomach as well. He'd had to take the risk. He tired of the constant rumble of his stomach. For a man who loved his food, there was nothing exciting about cups of hot tea or the chocolate bars he bought during the hours the ship's canteen was open.

So he crept up on his stomach. He allowed himself a child's portion the first time, and when that stayed with him, he increased it slightly the next meal. Still, he knew it would take time. He went to sleep with his stomach growling at him and awoke to the same sound. It made him wonder how many feet of intestine were still empty after the early fasting.

Even though the wind and the high seas pounded at the *Emerald* the routine business continued. It appeared, every time he found a comfortable spot and settled in for a rest, there was a call for emergency stations or the abandon-ship drill.

The ship was making good time. He heard that from all the seamen around him—the ones he talked to on deck and the ones he shared mess with. MacTaggart could notice the difference himself, now that the escort had turned back toward the Clyde. They were averaging about twenty knots an hour.

It didn't matter that the *Emerald* carried precious cargo. It had its wartime purposes as well and didn't neglect them. On the second day out of Greenock, the twenty-sixth, a little after nine in the evening, H.M.S. *Emerald* had left its course to identify a ship that was sighted on the horizon. It had turned out to be a Latvian freighter, *Everalda*. The ships exchanged greetings, and the cruiser wished the freighter well before it turned back to its established course.

It bothered MacTaggart. There was, however, nothing he could do about it. If the ship had to play traffic warden, that was the Navy's business. He had his doubts that Captain Flynn, up there on the ship's bridge, would want his landsman's opinion.

On the morning of the third day the wind weakened some. It was from the south. All that morning MacTaggart felt himself adapting to the softer rhythms of the sea. But by noon the wind was stronger, this time out of the southwest. There was another shift later in the day. The sea was rough again by evening and the wind was gale force from the northwest.

By nine that evening the ship's speed was cut to eighteen knots.

About this same time MacTaggart was seated on his bunk. He was hunched over, thinking of pints of beer and slices of roast beef as thick as the plates that held them. He heard the compartment door open. He didn't look up. He assumed it was one of the bank officials. It wasn't as if he had much to say to them.

The door closed. He heard a cough and, after a few seconds, another cough.

A young naval officer stood with his back to the doorway. He was so young he didn't look like he shaved yet. "Mr. MacTaggart?"

"Why?"

"You're the gentleman in charge of the cargo?"

"I am."

"I've got something to show you, sir."

At least he was well brought up and polite. MacTaggart looked at the face of his hunter's-case. "Now?"

"Now, if you don't mind, sir."

"And if I do?"

"It's important, sir," the young man said.

He put on his damp shoes and his raincoat. He followed the young man to the passageway. "What is it?"

"I'd rather show you, sir."

They reached the ladder at the end of the passageway. MacTaggart grabbed the rails and started up. The young officer called to him, "This way, sir." MacTaggart backed down the ladder and followed the thin shape down a dim walkway and down another ladder. At the base of the ladder there was another passage. In the distance, low and muffled, he could hear engine sounds.

He was lost. That was the truth of it. He'd learned his way to the deck and to every other location he found from the deck and downward. Now it looked like the young man was taking him on a snipe hunt.

The officer stopped in front of a closed hatch, a doorway. He raised a flashlight and touched the switch.

"Where are we?" MacTaggart said.

"You've been here."

"Pardon?"

"This is the forward magazine."

"Which one is that?" MacTaggart said.

"The one where the two thousand crates of heavy cargo are stored."

That one. The gold bullion. He closed his eyes and made the walk in his mind. Very well, he had the forward magazine placed. "What is it you want…?"

"This." The young officer opened the doorway and stepped inside. MacTaggart followed him. The flashlight beam swept over the stacked cases. The stacks reached as far as MacTaggart could see. Piled on top of the crates were the shells, the projectiles, that usually filled the magazine.

The officer walked to the edge of the front stack of cases and squatted. MacTaggart did the same. "See this?" The young officer reached into a jacket pocket and brought out a steel bearing about the size of a child's marble. He placed the bearing on the metal plate flooring and watched it roll away until it touched a bullion case. He scooped up the bearing, and, reaching to his right a couple of feet, he did the same again. MacTaggart picked up the bearing and looked at it.

"I don't know what you're saying."

"The weight of the cargo..." the officer sputtered.

"Yes?"

"It's bending the bloody angle irons under the magazine."

"Let me have your flashlight." He didn't wait for an answer. He grabbed the flashlight and carried out his own check. He took his time with it. He wanted to be certain that he understood. It wasn't easy to spot. They were probably hairline bends. Not that obvious yet.

MacTaggart stood and stretched his legs. He switched off the flashlight and returned it. "What's your name?"

"Sub-Lieutenant Carr, sir."

MacTaggart stepped out of the magazine. The officer followed and closed the doorway behind him.

"Well, what do you think we ought to do?"

"We've got to shift the cargo, sir."

"The floor likely to collapse in the next four days?"

"I doubt it, Mr. MacTaggart, but..."

"The cargo stays where it is."

"It's damaging the structure of the..."

"You report this to Captain Flynn yet?"

"No, sir."

"Then you tell him." MacTaggart started down the passageway. He stopped and turned. "And then you let me know what he thinks we ought to do... first thing in the morning."

In the end, lost again, he allowed Carr to lead him until he recognized *his* ladder at the end of the walkway. He waved at Carr and took a left and headed for his compartment. When he reached the doorway he looked over his shoulder. Young Carr was still there, staring at him in bewilderment. MacTaggart grinned at him and the young officer swung around and trotted up the ladder and out of sight.

My God, he thought. If it was that young sub-lieutenant's decision to make he'd dump £30 million worth of bullion over the side of the ship to save a few angle irons.

It was like those bloody American films where the airplane is flying on one engine and they throw everything out of the cargo hatch to lighten the load.

He closed the compartment door. He sat on the edge of his bunk and unzipped his bag. He tugged the half-empty bottle of Irish from the mass of clothing. He allowed himself a long swallow. The truth was he needed it.

He didn't see young Carr the next morning. He heard nothing more about shifting the cargo. He did notice, however, that there were regular inspections of the plate flooring in both magazines.

That was after he began to make his own daily checks as well.

CHAPTER FIFTEEN

Around the turn of the century Renssler, New York, wanted to style itself the "Newport of the North." The Renssler family was there first; it was the town's society, and they built their summer home on the south end of Lake Buckner. It was an Italian villa constructed from white marble and native stone. It had wide terraces and walks, a formal garden, and about four acres of sloping blue-green lawn that ran down to the lake.

The Renssler villa was an example of what the family expected the other summer places along the lake to be. When it was completed, the Rensslers sat back and waited confidently for equally wealthy and prominent families to move north and join them.

Only one other summer mansion was built. It was erected on the north side of the lake, facing the Renssler villa. The owner was a rich Irish-American politician from New York City. He'd made most of his money in sewer construction. He was the new money, and the older Irish-American families, the ones that had been in the country fifty or sixty years longer than he had, didn't receive him or his family socially.

Edward Brophy selected the Renssler site because he hoped that some of the Renssler-family polish and prestige would reflect upon him. It didn't. The Rensslers were very careful that it didn't. The Rensslers wanted nothing to do with anyone with a name like Brophy.

For five years the Brophy clan spent their summers at the lake. They had a summer home they called the "Castle," a somewhat scaled down model of Ballyseede Castle in Ireland, complete with the turrets and the crenellated walls. It was built from stucco rather than marble or stone.

The lake was Mrs. Brophy's pride. Each summer she stocked the lake with swans. The swans always left the first week. It was a mark of Mrs. Brophy's new-world optimism that she always believed that the swans would return. Her daydreams were that she would go down to the lake one morning and find a hundred swans there paddling about, the forty she'd bought and placed there and the natural offspring and increase.

After the fifth summer the Brophys returned to New York. During the winter one of the Brophy girls, a girl with rare beauty and grace, became engaged to one of the sons of a real-lace Irish family in Boston. The Brophys now had a minor toehold at last.

The Brophys didn't return to Renssler the following summer. The Castle was offered for sale. There were no takers. It was boarded up and forgotten.

The Rensslers always believed that the garish Brophy Castle had kept other fashionable builders from moving to the lake. Who would want to live near that? Renssler, New York, did not become the social summer resort they'd hoped for. The dream was lost. The town and the Renssler family went back to lesser expectations.

During the early years of Prohibition, one of the black-sheep relations of the Brophy clan used the Castle as a halfway house for liquor smuggling across the border from Canada.

It was extremely profitable. It spawned a whole new wealthy branch of the Brophys. After only three years, when that part of the border was closed down to whiskey traffic, Joseph Brophy took his earnings and moved to Hollywood. By the time Prohibition ended he was a producer. His Westerns, produced in seven days, stocked the Saturday-morning theaters across the country.

The Castle was deserted again. Tom Renssler, as a young man, used the Castle grounds as a lover's lane. All the high-school crowd did.

❖ ❖ ❖

During the early morning hours of Thursday, June 27, Tom
Renssler guided the caravan of two stolen automobiles along the
lake road to Brophy Castle. On the north side, the road ended at
a massive wrought-iron gate. It was locked. Harry Churchman
stepped out of the second car and broke the padlock with a
wrench from the car's tool chest.

They drove down the narrow, tree-lined road to the Castle
and parked in the drive that circled the huge tiered fountain that
faced the front entrance.

It was still an hour before full light. They'd been driving
most of the night. They'd made a late start because Vic Franks
was selective about the cars he stole. He'd discarded one of the
first two because he didn't like the way the engine sounded. That
had meant another run to find a car that satisfied him.

Tom got out of the lead car and toed the mixture of sand and
broken shell that formed the driveway. Johnny Whitman left the
back seat of the same car and joined him. Tom pointed down at
the drive. The headlights lighted the area. There were two contraceptives there, side by side.

"Nothing changes," Tom said.

Johnny grinned and turned away. Randy Gipson walked over
and had his look and kicked the contraceptives away. "I could use
some poon myself."

They settled in for the wait.

At first light Tom saw on the lake, in the distance, a pair of
white swans gliding by. Poor Mrs. Brophy.

At eight Harry Churchman and Gunny Townsend opened
the trunks of the two cars and passed out the hardware. Shotguns
and handguns and the ammunition.

At 8:50 they loaded into the cars according to the assignment
Johnny Whitman made. At 8:55 they began the slow, timed drive
into Renssler.

✤ ✤ ✤

The old square at the center of the town was a reminder of what the town had been once. At the north end of the square was the old red-brick courthouse. It had been built right after the Revolution.

"That's the bad news," Johnny Whitman said at the briefing in New York. They were at the garage on Tenth waiting for Vic to steal the cars. "The police station's in the courthouse. Right in front. It's too close." He nodded at Tom. "How many cops?"

"Three, the last time I was there. It might be four now. I don't think it could be more. The town hasn't grown much the last ten or fifteen years."

"How many police cars?"

"Only one, as far as I know."

"They make rounds?"

"Only at night," Tom said.

To the east and west of the square, on those sides, there were shops and stores. All of the shop fronts, under city-council law, preserved the village quality of a hundred years before or fabricated it.

The First Bank of Renssler occupied most of the south side of the square. It had been built out of the same red brick used in the courthouse. In the beginning the bank building housed a carriage-manufacturing company. That business went into a financial decline even before mass-produced cars drove horses and carriages off the streets and roads.

The village green in the center of the square covered almost a city block. It was landscaped, and there were wooden benches along the paths. One tree, the Captain Buckner oak, towered above the scrubs and orderly beds of flowers.

A Civil War monument took up the center of the Green. The solider, weary but valiant, leaned on his rifle and faced the courthouse steps.

At 9:01 the two cars entered the square from the north, on the street that ran next to the courthouse. The street that ran around the Green was still paved with brick. At each corner of the square there was an access street.

The lead car was a 1939 Ford. It was driven by Vic Franks. Johnny Whitman was in the passenger seat next to him. In the back seat, wedged shoulder to shoulder, sat Harry Churchman, Randy Gipson, and Richard Betts.

The 1940 Packard followed them. It was driven by Clark Gipson. Clark hadn't wanted to be separated from his brother. He'd argued against that part of Whitman's plan. Finally, urged by Harry, Randy took his brother aside and convinced him that, driving the backup car, he could bodyguard Randy better.

Tom was in the passenger seat beside Clark. Gunny Townsend had the whole back seat to himself. He needed the space. There were a shotgun, a Winchester lever-action .30-30, and two long-barreled target pistols on the seat next to him.

The drive through town brought back a powerful rush of memories to Tom Renssler. They'd passed the grammar school on the way to the square, and the empty yards and buildings made him think of Sylvia Campbell, the blonde girl he'd loved in the fourth grade. And, approaching from the north access street, they'd passed the all-night café that had been owned by the old Greek man whose name he couldn't remember now. He thought of hamburgers and milkshakes and the everything-on-it pizza the old Greek made, and late nights there after football games.

The lead car passed the Green and made a left that brought it directly in front of the bank. Vic Franks eased it to the curb. He braked so that the car doors faced the bank door. There was a No Parking sign painted on the sidewalk and a length of the curb was painted a dark red. Vic got out of the Ford and hurried around to the hood. He lifted it, set the brace, and leaned over the engine.

The Packard pulled in behind the Ford. The bumpers almost touched. No one left the Packard. In the back seat Gunny Townsend shifted his way across the seat until he was against the window on the left side. It faced the front of the courthouse. He cranked the window all the way down.

As soon as the hood was raised on the Ford, the doors on the curb side opened. Johnny Whitman stepped out first. He carried a handgun, a .44 with a six-inch barrel. Harry Churchman was right behind him, first out of the back seat, swinging an automatic shotgun up and against his hip. Richard Betts was on his heels, a double-barreled shotgun at the ready. Randy Gipson brought up the rear. He carried the twin of the .44 that Johnny had. Just before he ran into the bank Randy swung around and waved at his brother.

Johnny reached the center of the bank. He raised the .44. "Nobody moves," he shouted.

There were three teller cages. Only two were operating. A gray-faced old man was in one, a plump blonde girl in the other.

At the rear of the bank, behind a low wooden railing, were the bank officers' desks. Past those was an open walk-in vault. Only one desk was occupied. As soon as Johnny yelled his order, a portly, balding man pushed back his chair and made a lunge for the vault door.

Johnny pointed the handgun at him. "You. One more step and you're dead."

The man jerked to a stop. His hands went over his head and he turned slowly to face Johnny.

Richard Betts trotted past Johnny and pointed his shotgun at the banker. Harry Churchman stood facing the teller cages. He nodded at Johnny.

Johnny shoved the gun in his waistband. He pulled a pillow-case from his hip pocket. He pushed through the gate in the low railing and headed for the vault. Randy Gipson followed him, shaking out another pillowcase. After Randy passed through the gate he swung right and moved toward the teller cages.

There was only one customer in the bank. A thin, hump-backed little woman with gray hair. She appeared to be deaf. She stood with her back to the robbery, at a desk against the wall. She was writing a check and balancing her bankbook, oblivious of what was going on behind her.

Randy emptied the till at the old man's cage first. He took it slowly. Bills only, no change. He reached the blonde girl's cage about the same time Johnny Whitman trotted out of the vault. A half-filled pillowcase was in one hand, the gun in his other.

Johnny took a couple of steps toward the teller cages. He was about to shout at Randy to let it go. It was then that the blonde girl screamed.

"What the hell...?"

Randy Gipson laughed as he backed out of the girl's cage. "Just getting a feel," he said.

"Outside."

The blonde girl screamed again.

While everybody in the bank, except the deaf little lady, turned toward the blonde girl, the portly man reached out and touched the alarm button on the side of his desk. The alarm rang loud and harsh across the Green.

Harry Churchman spun slightly on the balls of his feet. The shotgun was at his shoulder when he completed his turn. He pulled the trigger and the portly man's left arm and shoulder blew away. The man fell out of sight behind the desk.

"Goddam," Johnny said. He vaulted the low railing. Randy was behind him. Richard Betts was next. Harry Churchman was the last one out of the bank, covering them, backing until he reached the doorway.

The little lady finished writing her check. She turned from the wall desk just in time to see Harry Churchman and the shotgun go out of sight.

At the lead car, the Ford, Vic Franks heard the scream and backed away from the engine. He slammed the hood down. Then he heard the second scream and the alarm. The shotgun boomed, and he ran the length of the car and got behind the wheel. The engine was still running. He put it in gear.

Above the engine sound he heard Clark Gipson yell something from the Packard behind him. He looked to his left and saw two men in blue, policemen, run down the front steps of the courthouse. Both men carried handguns.

The doors to the Ford opened. Johnny lunged into the seat next to him. The others jammed into the back seat. When the doors on the curb side were pulled shut, Johnny said, "Go, Vic."

The Winchester opened up behind them. Vic looked past the village green and saw one of the policemen fall, knocked down. The other policeman froze for a couple of seconds and then he turned and ran up the steps toward the courthouse entrance.

In the Packard, the single round Gunny fired from the Winchester deafened Tom. Gunny levered another round into the rifle's chamber. He was settling the butt against his shoulder and sighting in on the thick back of the second policeman on the steps when Tom shouted, "That's enough, Gunny."

Gunny was either deaf also or he ignored Tom. He was getting ready to squeeze the trigger when Tom reached over the seat back and grabbed the barrel of the Winchester and pulled it aside. "Dammit, Gunny, that's enough."

The lead car pulled away from the curb. It made a sharp right turn to the access street and headed away from the Green.

Clark Gipson put the Packard in gear and followed. Just before the Packard made the turn Tom looked back and saw that the policeman who'd been shot was on his knees. Both hands were pressed against his left side.

CHAPTER SIXTEEN

It was a back road that Tom Renssler discovered the summer he was seventeen. He was just out of high school, waiting for the fall when he'd start at West Point. He'd thought of it as a conditioning hike, a preparation for the hardships of the Army. He'd walked along the lake road and cut across the Brophy land and circled the Castle. There was a crumbling stable behind it, and past that, a stand of pines.

The road was there, concealed by a high mound of dead brush and tree limbs. He'd bypassed the barrier, and there was the road. It pointed directly north. That day he'd walked about ten miles of the road. Another day, about a week later, he'd borrowed a car and driven the whole length of it.

He never knew if the road had been cut through the trees for the run from Canada. There was always the chance that it had been a wagon road at one time, before cars came in and brought with them a demand for straight and level stretches of highway. Later, hearing the stories about the black-sheep member of the Brophy family, he knew that it was the bootlegger road.

It wasn't on any of the road maps of the day.

In the years since that summer the road had been accidentally seeded with grass and pine seedlings. There were ruts and slashes across it where rain and groundwater had eaten it away.

It took the Packard and the Ford almost two hours of slow and careful driving to cover the twenty-five miles. Every mile or so there was a bad spot in the road, and they'd have to detour into the woods and then back onto it. It was almost noon when they reached the end of the road. There was a white stone marker in the open field. The stone, plain, without any lettering, marked the dividing line between the States and Canada.

They bumped their way across the open field, passing the stone, and they were in Canada.

Past the field, a couple of hundred yards into Canada, they reached a dirt road. It might have been designed for carts and wagons. It was hardly wide enough for two cars.

Johnny waved the cars to the side of the road. He got out and Tom Renssler joined him as he spread the map on the hood.

Montreal was to the northwest.

"No way we're going directly there," Johnny said. "Not in these cars."

"East then," Tom said.

"It's the only choice," Johnny agreed.

Johnny waved Vic Franks to the right.

After an hour the road took a bend to the northeast and they were driving parallel to a raised track bed. Johnny relaxed. If there was a track then there had to be a train station and a train.

Around two in the afternoon they could see a town in the distance. A dingy white church steeple stood out alone, and then a few more miles, and they could see the rows of weathered wood-frame houses.

They drove through the center of town. All the shops and houses appeared to cluster around the train station. BUTLER, the sign in front of the depot said in big block letters.

Johnny noted the name and then pointed Vic down a side street that took them away from the center of town. There was no way of knowing if police in the small Canadian towns got bulletins about bank robberies below the border in the States. It didn't make sense to risk it. There was always the chance that someone in the town of Renssler had written down the license-plate numbers.

✤ ✤ ✤

They parked beside a combination gas station and grocery store. While the others were inside the store buying cheese and crackers, sardines, and soft drinks, Johnny and Tom sat in the Packard and spread the map between them. It was there. Butler. The town was on the main line between Montreal and Halifax. Johnny estimated the distances. It was about 150 miles west to Montreal and about 700 east to Halifax.

While the rest of the group had their lunch, Tom and Johnny walked the half mile back to the center of town. It was dark and cool in the train station. The clerk behind the ticket window interrupted a late lunch and came to the window brushing crumbs from his mustache.

Johnny was first in line. He asked about the train to Montreal. If it was on time, the clerk said, it would arrive at 5:28. Johnny said that was fine and bought two coach tickets. He paid for them and left the station without looking at Tom.

Tom leaned on the counter and asked about the next train to Halifax. It would be through about midnight, the clerk said, but it didn't usually stop unless he wired down the track and told them there were passengers. Tom said he understood. He didn't buy a ticket. He said he'd have to think about it.

Johnny waited outside the station for him. He passed Tom one of the tickets for Montreal.

"Halifax?"

"Midnight," Tom said.

Johnny shook his head. "I don't like it. Leaving the Gipsons here in town for six or seven hours. That's a risk."

They walked down the street toward the gas station–grocery store. "Harry can handle them if anybody can," Tom said.

"That Randy. I still don't believe what happened in the bank."

"Crazy."

"If I didn't need the two of them I'd break both Randy's arms and legs," Johnny said.

"I'd help."

"They can still mess it up."

"Not if Harry puts a dog collar on them."

They'd have to hope for that. It was too late to be looking around for replacements.

The train to Montreal was ten minutes late.

Before Johnny and Tom left for the station Tom saw that the cars were abandoned some distance away and the license plates removed and buried. While that was going on Johnny opened the suitcase where he'd stored the still-uncounted money from the Renssler bank. He gave each man two hundred dollars for past expenses. This was his way around the listing of expenses that he'd proposed at the planning meeting in New York. The money for the Gipson brothers, however, was given into Harry Churchman's care.

Besides the expense money, he gave Gunny and Betts and Franks cash for the train fare. They'd take the same 5:28 train to Montreal.

Harry and the Gipsons would be heading in the other direction. Johnny estimated train fare to Halifax and expense money for a few days. While he counted that money into Harry's palm he suggested that Harry ration the two hundred dollars he owed each of the brothers. It would be a way of keeping them in line.

Randy didn't like the arrangement. He bitched until Harry told him to shut up. Either that or he'd break his mouth for him. "I already owe you for that crap in the bank," he said. The threat quieted Randy, even if it didn't satisfy him.

At 5:38 Johnny and Tom boarded the train heading west. Gunny and Betts and Vic Franks bought their tickets at the last moment and took seats in a different day coach.

Head back, trying to catch some sleep, Johnny worried about the three men he'd left behind in Butler. A lot depended on them. One whole half of the plan he'd put together. They screwed up in Halifax, and you could forget the whole deal.

It was up to Harry. He trusted Harry. He had to.

Tom sat in the window seat and watched the passing countryside. An hour out of Butler they passed through a heavy rainstorm. Rain covered the window in sheets. With nothing to watch, he closed his eyes and tried to empty his mind.

It was a backwoods café and bar. It was directly across the street from the train station. Outside, you could smell the grease from a block away. Inside, that scent was overpowered by the odor from new oilcloth that covered the tables.

The customers were all working people, men from the trainyard and from the sawmills outside of town. It was hot in the café, and the ceiling fan didn't do much more than stir the heat and the smell.

The few women at the tables were heavy and thick-legged. The waitress was on the other side of fifty. Everybody seemed to know everybody. There was talk and joking—some of it in French—from table to table.

It was still early when Harry took the Gipsons to the café for supper. He ordered three bowls of the beef stew and bread and coffee.

Harry ate without any real interest in the food. For him, eating was putting gas in the car or stoking the furnace. Anyway, didn't it all turn to shit in the end? Whether it was fancy French food, the kind Mr. Arkman had liked, or chicken potpie.

He kept his eyes on the Gipsons. Clark wasn't a problem. He was docile enough. Most of the time he acted like sweet little Jesus. Randy was another matter. The dumb shithead. Harry didn't have any regrets about the banker, about having to point the power at him. He asked for it. Still, it wouldn't have been necessary if Randy hadn't needed a feel of the blonde's bottom. Goddam, and right in the middle of the job.

Dumb. Double dumb.

It was an indication of the weakness of the outfit that Randy was as close to a train expert as they'd been able to find. He hadn't been important in the bank job, and he'd just about done that in. How the hell would he be when the outcome really depended on him? It wasn't a happy thought.

While Harry ate his stew he made himself a promise. When the job was over, whether it came off or not, Randy was expendable. Expendable was one of Mr. Arkman's favorite words. As soon as it was over, Randy lost his value. He'd be left somewhere, buried or unburied. Let the dogs eat him.

It was such a pleasant thought for Harry that he relaxed. He didn't notice that Randy had developed a strong interest in what was going on in the other half of the café building. The part that was the bar. A doorway connected the café to the bar. Most of the diners, after they'd finished eating, passed through that doorway and out of sight.

Randy finished his beef stew and mopped his bowl with a chunk of French bread. He gulped his coffee and wiped his mouth with the back of his hand. "I sure could use a beer," he said. "How about you, Clark?"

Harry lifted his head. He put his hard eye on Clark. He realized that it was a play script. Clark knew, without being told, what his answer was supposed to be.

"It's been a long day all right," Clark said. "We've come a far piece. A cold beer might cut the dust."

Harry looked at his watch. A little after seven. It was a long time before the midnight train to Halifax. Too long to ride herd on them. Hard to expect them to sit on their hands in the train depot for five hours and be good.

Too bad about the movie. He'd considered that earlier. The only movie house in town, the Gem, was showing some film called *21 Days Together*. It starred somebody named Vivien Leigh and Laurence Olivier. Love mush, it looked like from the posters outside. It wasn't the kind of movie that interested Harry, and he knew it wouldn't hold the Gipsons for an hour. Damn the Gem anyway for not having a war movie or a cowboy picture. Anything but a sappy love story.

"It's dusty all right," Randy said. It was part of his act not to look at Harry. He even managed a feeble cough.

"Might be," Harry said, "if I get your promise."

"You've got it," Randy said.

"Don't you want to know what you're promising?"

"Oh, sure." The bland, idiot's face.

"No trouble. That's the promise. We have our beers and we don't mess with anybody."

"You've got my word," Randy said.

And you damned well better keep it, Harry thought as he paid the supper check for the three of them.

The promise lasted two beers and almost into the third.

The waitress working the tables and booths didn't appear to belong in the bar or the town. She wasn't huge and cowlike. She was a baby step past being a child. She was thin and awkward with the first buds of breasts beginning to push out at her gingham blouse. Her legs were like plaster slats. Her straw-colored hair was loose and reached her waist. Her face was that of an innocent who sees everything but doesn't understand one tenth of what she sees.

Harry had his back to the wall, relaxing, feeling good. There wasn't a woman in the bar worth making trouble over. If that was what Randy had in mind, then he had drawn one big goose egg.

Randy and Clark were on the aisle side of the table.

It was going too well. Harry should have expected it.

The young girl came from the bar with three bottles of Moosehead on a tin tray. As she reached the table, she stepped forward, between Randy and Clark, and reached across the table to place a bottle next to Harry's empty glass. It happened then.

Randy leaned down, as if to tie his shoelaces. He was bent over. It was then he reached a hand up the girl's skirt and rubbed it across the girl's almost hairless crotch.

The girl's eyes widened. Her mouth sucked at air and then she screamed. The tin tray flipped out of her hand. One bottle of beer hit the floor. The other turned over and spilled across the table and into Clark's lap.

The scream brought every head in the bar up and around. The bald man behind the bar counter reached down and brought up about half a pick handle. Three men at the bar, closest to the girl, pushed away and headed for the table. One of them, the one in the center, was a bruiser with a bent nose. He reached out gently and put an arm around the stunned girl. He led her to the side, away from the table. When he returned he looked at Randy. He brought up his huge hands. The skin on the palms and the knuckles were like dried leather. He closed the hands into fists and hissed something. It sounded like "pervert."

Harry stood. Randy was still seated. He was grinning, the dumb shit.

"Randy?"

Randy turned to face Harry. "Yeah?"

It was close, too close. It wasn't a choice anymore. Not that Harry would have chosen otherwise. There was the matter of the broken promise.

Harry hit him. It was a short punch, but it had all Harry's weight behind it. The fist hit Randy in the corner of the mouth and the cheekbone. The chair Randy sat in tipped over. Randy rolled across the floor and landed at the feet of the man with the huge hands. He wasn't out but he was stunned.

The bruiser opened his hands and looked at Harry. There was a puzzled, questioning look on his slow face.

"My cousin," Harry said, "would apologize if he was still awake."

The big man smiled.

Harry circled the table. He did it slowly so the big man wouldn't misunderstand. When he passed Randy he drew back his foot and kicked Randy in the ribs a couple of times. "Wouldn't you, cousin? Speak up."

The bruiser's smile got even wider.

Harry nodded across the table at Clark. "Take him to the depot. Clean him up and keep him there."

Clark didn't move.

"Do what I say." Harry reached across the table. He swung his open hand and cuffed Clark across the mouth. "Do it now."

Harry walked away. He put a hand on the big man's shoulder and eased him toward the bar. The bartender still remained at the counter with the pick handle in one hand.

The girl sobbed on the shoulder of a fat woman. It was a muffled crying, and Harry was glad about that.

Everybody stared at Clark and Randy. Randy was sitting up now, wiping at blood that trickled from his torn mouth. Clark hunched over him, trying to get him to his feet.

The big man nodded. The blood seemed to satisfy him.

"I don't want you to think all men from the States are that kind of scum," Harry said over his first drink.

The big man heard him. He didn't agree or disagree. But he did drink the beer Harry bought him.

Harry bought two rounds for the bar. He told a funny story. The big man, in return, told a funny story that Harry didn't understand. It was more than a hour before Harry could get away from the bar.

But he'd calmed it down. Nobody followed him from the bar. He stood outside the train station for a few minutes and watched the street to be sure of that.

He'd smoothed the waters. There wasn't going to be a lynching in Butler tonight.

It was 8:30, full dark, when the train arrived at Bonaventure Station in Montreal.

The five of them walked down Peel Street in a light mist of rain. They carried their suitcases. Either it was the war or the late hour. There hadn't been a cab at the station.

Vic Franks and Richard Betts took turns struggling with the extra bag Gunny had packed before they abandoned the cars back in Butler. The extra bag weighed over a hundred pounds, it seemed. In it were the handguns, two stripped-down pump shotguns, and several boxes of ammunition.

Ahead of them, Johnny and Tom took turns with the extra bag that held the money. It didn't weigh very much at all.

At the Mcnt Royal, Johnny and Tom went in to check on rooms. The others waited outside, getting their breath. On the way through the lobby, Tom bought a Montreal *Daily Star*.

The headline was: RUMANIA ACCEPTS SOVIET DEMANDS.

Tom left the inquiry to Johnny. He settled into a chair and watched as Johnny joined the end of a line and worked his slow way toward the desk clerk.

The *Star's* right-hand column had a smaller headline.

NAZI BOATS MUSTERED IN NORWAY. SMALL
CRAFT MAY BE USED IN U.K. ATTACK.

London, 26 June. Germany today was reported concentrating a fleet of small ships in Nazi-occupied ports facing Great Britain—arousing speculation as to whether the hour was near for Adolf Hitler's expected attempt to invade the British Isles.

Tom folded the paper and looked around the lobby. It was crowded for that hour of night. And he noticed, for the first time, that everybody under forty seemed to be in uniform. It shouldn't have surprised him. He'd been in London when the war started. But, here, only hours from the American border, a country was at war. Not that you'd know it on the American side. Johnny reached the desk. Tom watched him arguing with the clerk and he knew he wasn't having much success. Johnny was red-faced and angry when he walked over to join Tom.

"Full up. The man says there is a war going on over here."

Tom stood. "Other hotels?"

They walked toward the entrance.

Johnny shook his head. "He says our best bet is one of the tourist homes."

Outside the hotel they flagged down a passing taxi. The driver took them on a tour of Montreal while they tried three tourist homes. At the fourth one, on Rue Ontario, they found rooms.

Johnny locked the door to the room he and Tom had been assigned. It was a small room, two cots almost side by side, a closet next to the door, and a washbasin in one corner.

Johnny unbuckled the straps on the imitation-leather suitcase. He dumped the contents on the cot. It was a jumble of money. Some of it, what he'd taken from the bank vault, was counted and banded. The rest of it, what came from the teller windows, was a mixture of denominations.

It took the better part of half an hour to sort the bills and do a count. The final total, apart from the cash he'd already handed out as expense money, was $52,826.

It was, Johnny said, more than enough for the expenses.

After they returned from supper that evening, Johnny portioned out about half of the cash to Gunny Townsend, to Betts, and to Vic Franks.

It was time to collect the hardware.

The last time Clark Gipson saw his mother alive she was in the Buncombe County Hospital. She was in a ward, in there with ten other women, the beds all crowded together. It was the poor ward. He knew that, and she knew it too. It shamed her.

The tumor that had been growing in her stomach for a year, the growth she had concealed while she prayed to God that it would go away, finally was too large to hide anymore, and the pain of it sapped her strength. She had to give in and ask Clark to drive her to the hospital.

Randy wasn't at home then. He'd been away forty-five of the sixty days he'd received from Judge Bennett. It was road-gang time for breaking into the soft-drink machine in front of Stovall's Gas Station.

During those last minutes with his mother, all she could talk about was her worry about Randy. He'd been the last born, her favorite, Clark knew, and he sorely disappointed her hopes for him.

"You are going to have to look out for him," she said.

"I will." There was a damp cloth on the table next to the bed. Clark used it to wipe the pain sweat from her face.

"I would pray to God to change him," his mother said. "I would. I swear I would. If I still believed in him."

For a time Clark wasn't sure which *him* she didn't believe in. God or Randy.

Later that day, in the waiting room, while they operated on her, he asked God not to let her suffer, and God had taken him at his word and He took her right there on the operating table. And that confirmed God in Clark's mind.

If it had not been for his promise to his mother he would have left railroading and would have answered the Call. God's Call to the Chosen. Not that God had called him yet. That was because God knew that he was his brother's keeper and could not answer the Call. God would not ask the impossible, would not ask him to break his deathbed promise to his mother.

Still, he knew he was of the Chosen. When he was free of his promise, then he would receive the Call. With God's Call he would not need to go to college like those fancy preachers did. It did not matter that he had never delivered a sermon. When he stood before a congregation God would touch his tongue, and the proper words would come out.

After he buried his mother and Randy was off the road gang, they went back to railroading. It was the life they knew. They'd have gone on forever if there had not been that trouble over the girl that Saturday night in Atlanta. That trouble put them in the Army and as far away from Atlanta as the Army would send them.

The girl had been fourteen, it turned out. Her age had worried Clark, but Randy said she had had a lot of experience. She had, he said, as much as begged him to do it to her, and she'd been rubbing it and spitting on the head of it, about to put it in, when her daddy's car pulled up in the driveway. She was scared of her daddy; her daddy had told her what he was going to do the next time he caught her with a man. That was why she started hollering rape and all that.

That might be the truth. But the girl was underage. No way Clark could talk himself around that fact. So he convinced Randy to join the Army, and they took the train across the state border into South Carolina using their railroad passes, and they enlisted at Columbia. They did their basic training at Fort Jackson, and Clark watched his brother and thought it was working the way he'd hoped it would. The discipline and the hard work was good for Randy.

But as soon as they left Fort Jackson and reached their unit it started up all over again. It was like the Devil had taken Randy for a friend.

He did his best to protect his brother. He tried to be understanding the way He would be. It was a moment of weakness near the end of their enlistment when Clark got angry. It was over Randy taking ten dollars of Clark's money, right out of his locker, and spending it on whores. Right then and there he asked God to chastise Randy. He wanted God to break his spirit.

God answered him by putting Randy in the stockade for being AWOL and by giving him a dishonorable discharge.

It was not God's fault that the stockade and the way they treated prisoners like animals had only driven the meanness and the Devil deeper into Randy, the way a fisherman sets the hook deep in the guts of a fish.

At the Fort Bragg Main Gate, watching them march Randy there, he knew. Clark knew that he would never be free of his promise to his mother until he was dead or Randy was dead.

There is no other way. He is my Cross and he is my Job's sores. And my brother.

Randy had his shoulder pressed against the train-coach window, his face printed on the glass. His breathing was somewhere between a blocked nasal snort and a wheeze.

Clark had the aisle seat next to him.

Harry Churchman was in the seat directly in front of Clark. Oh, that was a smooth man for you. He was slick as warm pork fat. He'd explained all of it away. It was either that he hit Randy and slap Clark as well or they'd have been booted and stomped to death by those bastards.

Clark pretended to believe him. He'd acted like he wasn't mad about the slap Harry gave him. What Clark really believed was that, if they'd wanted to, they could have stood shoulder to shoulder, the way friends do, and they could have taken on that whole bar and come out all right.

"The girl was thirteen," Harry said.

Clark nodded. The rage in him, unspoken, had answered: Then if she is that young what is she doing in that shitty tavern? And then he'd asked God to forgive him his bad language. Please, Lord, I won't again.

"She's the daughter of the bartender," Harry said, as if he read minds. "The men in that bar all think of her as a little girl."

Old enough to bleed, old enough to butcher. No, that was what Randy said. He never allowed himself to say nasty things. Not before now. That is the rage, the anger, talking in me.

"You see the boots they were wearing?"

Clark shook his head.

"Hobnails. You ever see what hobnails do to a man?"

Clark shuddered. He didn't have to see. He knew. But it would not have happened if Harry had stood shoulder to shoulder with them.

"I did. Once in Washington State. It wasn't pretty. The man's face looked like chopped meat. You couldn't tell where his eyes had been, or his nose."

Clark shuddered again.

"It was better the way I handled it," Harry said. "Randy got part of what he deserved and he got off without being stomped. Let's drop it at that and call it even."

"All right, Harry." I am lying, Lord.

"But the next time he gets out of line I am going to come down on him like the wrath of God."

That is a mistake, Clark thought. If that is not taking the Lord's name in jest, then I do not know what is.

"After this is over you two can do anything you want to. I don't give a moral shit one way or the other. You two can have all the ten-year-old girls you want."

Clark agreed. Not that he wanted any ten-year-old girls, and Randy didn't either. But he would try to control Randy the best way he could.

There is, he told himself with tight lips, a reckoning to come. It is a day that belongs to the Lord God and me.

Harry didn't sleep much that night. He wanted to be sure where he was. Now and then he'd have a chat with the conductor to get his bearings. At first light the train was still around four hundred miles from Halifax.

When first call for the dining car came, he awoke the Gipsons and they ate early.

At some point about two hundred fifty miles from Halifax, Harry tapped Randy on the shoulder. Randy moved into a window seat on the left side of the coach. Clark kept his window seat on the right. Both men had pads and pencils.

They were careful. Harry kept a watch. It was wartime, and they didn't want to be taken for spies.

Randy and Clark charted the last two hundred or so miles of track. Stations and sidings and the terrain, too.

When they reached the gray flint banks outside Halifax, Harry nodded at the Gipsons, and they closed the pads and passed them to Harry.

It was done, he hoped.

CHAPTER SEVENTEEN

"No room at the stable," Harry said. It was what he'd expected.

Harry returned to the Halifax train station under the Nova Scotian Hotel. The Gipsons had waited there while he tried the hotel. The clerk at the Scotian had looked at him like he was speaking some foreign language. As if questions about vacancies hadn't been asked since the war began.

They tried several other hotels. The last one was the Carleton. Nothing available there either, not even when Harry offered a bribe.

When they left the Carleton, their baggage stored there for a fee, they walked down the sloping road toward the waterfront.

You could tell them right away. The uniforms weren't the ordinary ones, not Navy and Army, the ones that packed and massed on the streets.

Theirs were the uniforms of yellow sweat and grease and dirt and oil. There weren't any standard colors or designs to these uniforms. They were tan cotton or blue denim and even bib overalls.

Harry and the Gipsons found the day train-yard crew in a Chinese café called Toy's. It was on a narrow, sloping street a few blocks up from Water Street.

It was funny as hell. Harry almost broke into a laugh. There were about a dozen of the roughest, hardest-looking men Harry had ever seen, and they were sitting at tables in Toy's and drinking tea from those delicate eggshell cups.

Harry had his look. He dropped an eyelid at Randy and Clark while he ignored a Chinese waiter who wanted to seat them in the far dining room. Harry took a table right next to one where four of the trainmen were.

The waiter got a pained look on his face and looked toward the heavens. What could he do? He seemed to be asking that. Then he trotted away and returned with menus.

Harry tossed the menus back at him without looking at them. "We want what they're drinking," he said.

"Tea?"

"If that's what it is," Harry said.

The waiter returned a few minutes later. He placed the eggshell cups on the table and poured the pale-brown liquid into them from a ceramic pot. He backed away, smiling.

Harry had a swallow. It was tea, goddam scalding tea.

Randy turned in his chair and stared at one of the trainmen. A squat man with thick shoulders and a broad, flat face. The man saw the question on Randy's face and leaned toward him.

"What you drinking?" Randy asked.

The broad face broke into a grin. Teeth missing top front. He passed the cup he had to Randy. Randy sniffed at it.

"What is it?"

"Rum," the trainman said. "Newfoundland Screech."

Randy passed the cup back to him. "How do we...?" He tipped his head toward his own cup.

"From the States?"

"Yeah," Randy said, "and me and my brother used to railroad if it makes a difference."

"It might." The man had a sip from his cup. There was a hesitation while the man read them. He took most of the time trying to figure Harry. He didn't look right. "We got to be careful," he said. "We don't want to get Toy in trouble, and we don't want to dry up the well, either."

"No danger from us," Randy said. "We're tourists."

"Shorty." The man waved a huge arm at the Chinese waiter. "Over here." The waiter trotted over and made a little bow. "The special tea for my friends from the States."

The waiter hesitated only a moment. Then he nodded and swept the cups with the real tea from Harry's table. When he returned he brought fresh cups and a different teapot. He poured each cup full to the brim.

Harry had a sip. Yes, that was the real, raw stuff.

"On my check," the broad-faced man said.

"Yes, Mr. Cody."

After that drink Harry bought a round for the other table. It turned out that Cody was the crew foreman. A sip into the second drink, and the Gipsons and the other crew members were talking railroading. More drinks. The rounds kept coming. Harry passed Randy some bills under the table when it was his turn to buy a round.

It was getting dark, dusky, when the train-yard crew began drifting into the street. It was time, Cody said, to make room for the real customers, the ones who came to Toy's for the food.

On the street Harry mentioned to Cody that they were having trouble finding a place to stay.

"I can find you a bed for a night or two," Cody said. "It's not the luxury I understand you Yanks expect."

"I'm not shy," Harry said. "You ought to see some of the places I've camped out in my time."

"It's a boardinghouse. Most of the train crew sleep there."

"No matter," Harry said. "It's got to be better than sleeping on the street."

"A bit," Cody said.

They circled by the Carleton Hotel to collect their baggage. Then they walked the seven or eight blocks to the boardinghouse.

It was dark by then and the streets swarmed with soldiers and sailors.

Cody led them through some dark streets where lines seemed to be forming up outside dark, curtained houses. "This what I think it is?" Harry said.

"It's a booming profession," Cody said. "It's the only product you can sell all day and night and still sell all over again the next day."

At an open window on the second floor of one of the houses, a girl naked to the waist leaned on the window ledge and gulped fresh air.

Gunny Townsend was lost. He had been turned this way and then that, and all the Montreal streets had started to look the same.

For the best part of two hours, after meeting them on a street corner, he'd been driven around the outskirts of Montreal, wedged between two swarthy men who smelled of garlic and perfume. The two men were silent most of the time. When they did speak to each other it was in French, and that was as bad as Greek as far as Gunny was concerned. All he remembered from his time in France in World War I was how to say hello and how to ask for a piece of ass. Neither of the men, when they did speak, said hello to Gunny or asked if he wanted a girl.

Finally the driver pulled to the side of a street and puffed his garlic breath at Gunny. "Do you know where we are?"

"Not a bit," Gunny said. "This is nowhere close to my briar patch."

The driver looked around Gunny toward the other man. He said something in French. It had a rise at the end like there was a question in there somewhere.

The other man who smelled of old sweat and some kind of perfume as well as the garlic said, "It is his way of saying that he is lost."

"That's right." And it was the Lord's truth. The streets all blurred and ran together. It had been a long day. After all the phone calls, the call to this number and the call to that one, each time using the phrase *scrap pipe,* he'd reached the right man. The man had sent these two to pick him up on a street corner down the way from the boardinghouse on Rue Ontario. It had been full dark then and now it was dark as night in a bat cave.

"He'll be at the Club now," the driver said to Gunny.

"I'm in no hurry," Gunny said. "It is not every day that I get a free tour of nighttime Montreal."

The driver stared at Gunny. The other man said, "He is making a joke."

"It is not much of a joke," the driver said in that prissy French way that bothered Gunny.

The driver was wiry and about as hairy as a pig-bristle brush. He looked something like a monkey that has almost grown to a man's height and has just learned to walk on his hind legs. He wore a starched white shirt with the sleeves rolled high, almost to the shoulders.

The other man was tall and bony. His head was bald-slick and he wore a crushed gray-felt hat. The hat was sweat-stained above the black band that ran around it. The man's nose had been broken a time or two and the tip of it curled off to the right side of his cheek.

The driver pulled into the street once more. He did a few more circles. Maybe he didn't believe Gunny when he said he was lost. Another ten minutes, and he pulled off the wide main street into a narrow one. There was very little light on the street. There were shops on both sides and the windows had been blanked by shades that had been drawn down. The street was rough, paved with cobblestones.

Halfway down on the left a neon light fluttered. It was above a doorway that was outlined by a string of blue lights.

The driver was looking for a parking space. He pulled past the neon sign and the lighted doorway and bumped the car up over the curb. He braked it on the narrow sidewalk. The man in the felt hat got out and held the door for Gunny.

They crossed the street and Gunny noticed that they still kept him flanked, one on each side. Closer, almost at the doorway, he could read the fluttering neon sign. PAPA JEAN'S. Just before they stepped through the doorway, the driver pushed past Gunny and went in first. The other man motioned him to follow and walked in after him. Straight ahead, after they'd entered, Gunny saw the maître d' behind a high podium-like reservation desk; beyond him, the glare of white tablecloths and the diners. It looked busy, almost all the tables occupied. Gunny could smell butter and fish and spices.

The driver took a sharp left as soon as he was past the doorway. There was a staircase there, going down. One flight down, and there was a light above a closed door.

The sign on the door was in English as well as French.

MEN'S CLUB ONLY

NO WOMEN ALLOWED

MEMBERS ONLY

The driver stopped in the circle of light and flipped through a heavy key ring. He selected a brass key. The door opened with a single twist of the key, and the driver withdrew the key while he held the door open and motioned Gunny inside.

It was a dim, small barroom. There were a few tables along the edges of the walls, but they weren't being used. The customers were all at the square bar, on the three sides that were lined with barstools. The fourth side was the bar shelf with its display of bottles and glasses.

There was a man in a white jacket at the near corner of the bar. He turned his barstool, and his feet touched the floor when he saw Gunny. His face had "mean" and "go away" written on it. Then the driver stepped around Gunny and waved at him. But he remained standing until he was approached by the driver; then he turned his ear and let the driver whisper something to him.

The man in the white jacket nodded. He waved Gunny and the other two men down the bar. He backed away and lifted his butt and put it on the stool. Even as he turned, his head lifted and he stared up at the ceiling.

Gunny moved down the bar until the driver touched him on the arm. He sat in the seat the driver indicated. The driver took the stool on his left, the other man in the felt hat, on his right.

"What do you drink?" the driver asked.

He wanted Southern Comfort but he knew they wouldn't have it. "Brandy," he said.

The bartender arrived just in time to hear Gunny. He swung away and returned with a glass and a bottle. He poured a large one without using a measure.

"Usuals?"

The driver nodded. Gunny had a sip of the brandy. It was raw fire.

"I understand you wish to speak to me."

Gunny heard the voice on his left. It wasn't the voice of the driver. He looked around and found that another man had replaced the driver on the stool there. The driver was on his feet, just behind that man's back.

This man was in his late forties or early fifties. He looked like a movie actor. The one who always played the rich father. He had gray hair, and his face and his hands were tanned. He smelled of some kind of flower soap, lilac or verbena. His eyes, even in the dim bar light, looked like gray metal washers.

"If you're the man with the hardware..." Gunny stopped and corrected himself. "If you've got the scrap pipe."

"That is better," the man said.

Gunny edged his stool seat to the left so that he could lean toward the man. "Thompsons?"

"I have the new models."

"The 1928s?"

"That is correct."

"I need five," Gunny said.

"Drums as well?"

"A fifty-round drum with each and a spare and a couple of cases of ammunition."

"Five 1928s, two drums with each …"

"And two cases of ammo."

"That is possible." The man nodded at the bartender, and the bartender brought him a glass and a small crystal pitcher of water. The glass held a clear liquid that turned cloudy when the man added a few drops of water to it from the pitcher. "The 1928s are rare now. There is a shortage here in Canada."

"But you have them?"

"I have them," the man said. "I thought you should know how rare they are."

"But not priceless," Gunny said.

"There is a price for everything," the man said. He had a sip of his cloudy drink.

"I could also use a case, maybe two, of grenades." Gunny was close enough to smell the man's drink. It smelled like licorice.

"Are you starting a war?"

"There's already one," Gunny said. The man's face didn't change. Gunny shook his head. "My boss likes to hunt deer with the 1928s."

"And the grenades?"

"For fishing." Gunny smiled. "My boss is not a patient man. He doesn't have time for the fish to take the hook." Gunny pantomimed pulling the pin and tossing the grenade. "All the fish he wants for supper float to the top."

"He would seem to be eccentric, this boss of yours."

"You have the money?" the man asked.

"I have it."

"My price is five hundred American dollars for each of the 1928s. At that price, I throw in the drums and the spare ammunition. The case of grenades will be two hundred dollars."

"Too much," Gunny said. "Even in mint condition they're not worth more than a hundred dollars."

"I have told you how rare they are."

"Mint condition?"

"They have not been used," the man said.

"I can go as high as two hundred for each of them."

"You are wasting my time," the man said. "I might consider an offer of four-fifty for each of them."

"Two-fifty," Gunny said.

"I am sick of this. I do not like to haggle. The five 1928s are yours for a round sum of two thousand dollars. One hundred for the spare ammunition and one hundred more for the grenades. That is a grand total of two thousand and two hundred dollars."

"If that is the best you can do."

"It is my final offer," the man said.

"We deal then," Gunny said.

"When do you want them?"

"Tonight."

"It is possible," the man said, "but we have done much talking, and we have made a deal, and I have not seen your money."

"Half now, half on delivery?"

The man nodded.

Gunny had to stop and think. He had five thousand on him. Two thousand in hundreds buttoned away in his hip pocket. One thousand in fifties in his right-hand trouser pocket. Two thousand in mixed bills pinned in his inside jacket pocket.

He had to choose. He didn't want to show too much money. He sensed that the driver and the bald man would kill for twenty dollars. And he was caught between the sums in his pockets. Eleven hundred owed.

He reached into his hip pocket and brought out the two thousand in hundreds. He kept the wad of bills low but he smelled the strong garlic and knew that the driver was pressing closer, watching him. Nothing he could do about that. He didn't open the fold. He did a cut he thought was a bit more than halfway through the wad. He placed the heavy part of the cut on the bar and replaced the remainder in his pocket. He picked up the hundreds from the bar and counted out eleven of them. He still had two hundred left. He stuffed them in his front-right trouser pocket. "There." He pushed the wad of bills toward the man on his left.

The man took his time. He counted the hundreds, and then he inspected each bill, feeling the paper and staring at the engraving.

"It's not phony money," Gunny said. "If that's what you think."

"It was my thought."

"Check the serial numbers," Gunny said. "No two alike. If they all had the same numbers, they'd be phony."

The man checked the numbers. He nodded that he was satisfied. "Jean will deliver the pipe to you in two hours." He indicated the driver. "You pick the location for the delivery."

The driver, Jean, nodded.

Gunny pushed back his stool. He had the rest of the brandy. It jolted him and burned a place in the pit of his stomach.

"Drop me at Rue Ontario. I'll wait for you there."

The man with the gray hair nodded at the driver.

Gunny followed the driver and the bald man to the exit.

CHAPTER EIGHTEEN

The way Vic Franks heard it, Jules Harpur saw the war coming as early as 1937. That wasn't to say that it was a religious vision or anything like that. The rest of the world had seen the same signs. The difference was that Jules, even that early, decided that there had to be some way to take advantage of the war when it came.

Jules owned a junkyard, and part of his business was buying old cars and stripping them down before he sold them for scrap metal. That alone gave him a head start, because he realized that with the coming of the war there was going to be a shortage of cars, trucks, tires, and all parts.

The junkyard did well. Jules made expenses and a good profit. He didn't, he knew, have the cash to put his big idea into operation. It took him time to work up the nerve to go to his Uncle Robert, the relative that the whole family talked about in whispers. What they said was a mixture of respect and fear. From nothing, his Uncle Robert had skimped and saved and cut corners, and now, at sixty, he owned whole blocks of slum property and even land in the better parts of Montreal.

It was not a long conversation. The small man with the face of an ill child listened after the first question. "What is it you want of me, Jules?"

Jules had brought his notes with him. He knew almost to the penny. He needed the money to buy the twenty acres that joined the junkyard on the west side. The money to hire three or even four men to send on expeditions to the outlying, small-town sections of Canada with enough cash in hand to buy every used truck and car they saw. Payment on the spot—that was important. And storage. He would need to construct sheds and other buildings so that he could protect and hide what he collected.

"There will be no shortage," Uncle Robert said. "There will be steady flow from below the border."

Jules shook his head. "The United States will be in the war themselves."

"You are certain?"

"One reads the newspapers. That man, Roosevelt, will help the British. It is as if they are family."

The old man believed him. He stared at Jules for a long time. "I thought all the blood in the family had gone thin and weak as water."

Jules blushed. He did not know what to answer.

"There is a further matter," the old man said. "You must tell me why I should let you have the money. You have offered me your idea without strings, free of any charge. Is there a reason why I should not take your idea and go and do with it what I please? I have the money to finance it and you do not."

"There is no reason," Jules admitted. And he felt the sinking feeling in his stomach.

"There must be a reason you can give," Uncle Robert said, "or I will do just that."

"It is my business. I know it and you do not." He sucked in a breath and rushed on. "I will do all the work. I will handle every part of it. By the time the war is one year old or two years, we will be dividing large profits each month."

"How would we divide those profits?"

"Fifty-fifty," Jules said.

"Money itself is more than an idea or the sweat that makes it work."

"Sixty to you, Uncle, and forty to me."

The old man agreed. Within the month Jules had his seed money.

Now the war was a year old. Steel was short. Everything went into the war effort. Soon, if he understood the newspapers as he believed he did, the United States would be in the war. It would be hard for them to stay out of it.

The stockpile on the additional twenty acres grew. The profits were just around the corner. The old man, his uncle, was even more patient than he was. He knew that if there were profits to be made now, those profits would double in another year.

Other men, slower than Jules Harpur, had the same idea. They were too late. They found the surrounding countryside had been stripped almost bare by the Harpur advance men.

Vic Franks found him in his office near the front gate of the junkyard. It was a one-room shack, a wood-frame building that was covered, roof and sides, by tar paper. The floor creaked, and it was black with tracked-in oil and grease. Metal shavings and filings made a grain in the wood floor.

The desk Jules sat behind was a flush door laid over two fifty-gallon oil drums.

"I do not understand," Jules said. "Is there some reason why you should come to me? I am, as you can see, in the junk business. I do not sell trucks or cars."

"A man..."

"Is there a sign outside that says that I sell trucks or cars?"

"A man in a bar gave me your name," Vic said.

Jules Harpur lifted his hands over his head, the gesture of ultimate exasperation. His arms were thick and short. "And now people are talking about my business in bars? People talk freely..."

"It wasn't all that free," Vic said. "I had to pay him a hundred dollars."

"Did this man … this paid informer … give his name?"

"I didn't ask it. His name didn't have anything to do with my business."

"You are saying," Jules said, "that you are discreet?"

"I've got a mouth that shuts like a bear trap."

"I see." Jules fiddled with a tin can on the front of his desk that held a number of pencils. "And, what exactly is your business?"

"That's my business," Vic said.

Jules pushed himself up from his chair. He was wearing bib overalls with a blue shirt. The bib wasn't hooked. It hung down, flapping against the front of his legs like a butcher's apron.

"It will do no harm to look around and see what we can find."

"My thought exactly," Vic said.

The bib flapping against his knees bothered Jules after a few minutes of walking. He hooked it in place while he showed Vic through the old part of the junkyard.

"Do you see anything that interests you?"

Vic pointed toward the west, the new part of the yard. "Let's try that direction. I can smell a truck a mile away."

Jules unlocked a high fence gate. They walked through rows of crudely constructed storage sheds. The sheds had walls but no doors. From outside, Vic could see the racks of engine parts. He looked at Jules.

"Guard dogs at night," Jules said, answering the question before it was asked.

Past those sheds, and they were in a different area. The buildings looked like oversized carports. Each shed, without walls but with a tin roof, held five or six cars or trucks.

"I told you my nose was good," Vic said.

Jules led him through the larger sheds where the trucks were stored. They passed bay after bay where the trucks were parked.

All of the trucks were on blocks, tireless, and they were covered with waterproof tarp.

Vic had his look. Then he touched Jules on the arm and they walked back to the second shed, where he stopped in front of two three-and-a-half-ton Mack Company Bulldogs. Vic knew the Bulldogs had been built from 1915 to 1937 with almost no changes in the design.

He removed the tarps. "1935?"

"I understand they are 1935 or 1936."

Vic opened the hoods on both Bulldogs. The engines were clean. They'd probably been steamed and sprayed with oil. He ran his hands over the wiring, looking for rot. The wires appeared solid. He backed away and looked for a tool bay. He found a toolbox and selected a spark-plug wrench and pulled a couple of plugs on each truck.

Fouled points. He tossed the plugs away, skipping them like stones across the shed.

"They need plugs."

"I have them," Jules said.

"Tires?"

Jules waved a hand at a wired-in cage where there were stacks of tires.

"These two, they running when you brought them in?"

"Drove them right through the gate," Jules said.

"I'll change the plugs and tune the engines. You have somebody who can set the tires for me?"

"For a fee," Jules said.

"Of course."

They set the deal in the open shed. The price was high. Jules wanted ten thousand dollars for each Bulldog. He'd bought them, he remembered, from a construction company that had gone out of business. He'd paid five thousand dollars for the pair of them.

Vic argued him down to six thousand dollars each.

It was a good morning's profit for Jules and his uncle. The seven-thousand-dollar profit was an indication of things to come.

Jules left him with the trucks. Vic stripped down to his undershirt and went to work. By late afternoon he had the plugs changed and the engines humming to suit himself.

The tires were worn but still had plenty of tread.

By five in the afternoon the trucks were parked on the road outside the main junkyard gate.

Hess said, "The money is fine. Something else bothers me."

Richard Betts had done his cock-and-bull at the Melton Construction Company, asking about work, but mainly he'd been interested in locating the shack where they stored the explosives. It had been easy to locate. It was set apart, distanced from the other buildings and sheds. And then, when he'd been told there wasn't work, he had a few beers and a sandwich at the bar down the street where all the workers from Melton had lunch. A few casual questions and he had the name of the night watchman. That was easy enough, but he backed away. He didn't want anybody remembering him. It took a phone call to get Hess's address. He said he was the old man's nephew from Ottawa and he was passing through Montreal on the way to his new duty station with the Army. The war was big, and everybody tried to do all they could for the servicemen. He got the address.

Will Hess was about fifty-five. He had a bad hip from the other war, and he dragged the leg when he walked. If it wasn't for the fact that he was a veteran and there was a shortage of men, he probably wouldn't have kept the job any time at all.

At first, when Richard approached him at his boardinghouse, Hess had been surprised and even outraged. That would be dishonest, to take a man's pay and then stab him in the back. It was what some dirty German might do.

Richard Betts accepted the mouth from him. It always took a man time to talk himself out of thinking that he was honest. You let him blow it out, work his rage off, and then run down.

Then you say, "Look, I am going to find somebody and give him this five hundred dollars, and if it happens that you are independently wealthy, then I guess I'm just wasting your time and mine."

You show the money, you fan it in your fingers like a card hand. A couple of fifties, some twenties, and the rest in tens. It makes a big wad that way. And then you fold the money—after the greed starts getting to him—and you put it away.

And you watch him break down the middle from all the things he knows he can buy with five hundred dollars, and you wait for him to creep up on you and accept the deal.

His hand will find the right pocket.

"What do you need?"

Betts just looked at him. "That's for me to know," he said. "It ain't none of your mix at all."

"You ain't going to hurt anybody with it? I would not like to think…"

"I've got this logjam in my backyard," Richard said, "and I need enough sticks to blow it loose." Then he decided he ought to calm the old fart. "Of course, I ain't going to hurt nobody."

"And you said five hundred?" Hess had his eyes on the pocket where he'd stored the money.

"Half now, the rest tonight."

Hess held out his hand.

At about eleven o'clock he stole a car a few blocks from the tourist home on Rue Ontario. He drove across town to the Melton compound. Hess met him at the gate and let him drive in. He parked next to the explosives shack and used a short piece of pipe to pry the lock and the hinges from the door. Hess, nervous and shaking, held the flashlight while Betts selected the sticks, the caps, and the coils of wire that went with the black box.

He loaded what he wanted in the back of the car and then drove to the gate and got out. Next to the guard shack Betts counted into Hess's hand the two hundred and fifty he owed him.

That was when Hess said that the money was fine but something else worried him.

Betts understood. "You got some place where you can put the cash so it won't be on you?"

Hess carried the money into the shack. He'd just stepped out of the doorway when Betts hit him. Betts caught Hess as he started to go down. He rammed him against the side of the shack. The shack shook.

Hess said, "That's enough."

"No," Betts said, "that is not enough to fool anybody." He hit Hess in the nose and broke it. Then he worked Hess over. He pulled his punches some, but he wanted to be sure there were plenty of bruises on his chest and ribs.

Finally, he was getting some blood on himself from the broken nose Hess had, and he decided it was getting messy. Hess had earned the five hundred.

He let Hess fall face down in the dirt.

It wasn't just to protect the old man. They'd believe him, they'd see the beating, and there would be fewer questions. If they didn't push at the old man, then he could probably stay with his story. That way Betts would remain a ghost.

He left the gate open. He drove to the junkyard where the trucks were waiting. Gunny and Vic Franks were there. By now they should have received the shipment of arms.

Richard Betts thought right away that there was something wrong. The two Bulldogs were parked side by side on the driveway that led to the main gate of Harpur's junkyard. There wasn't anything wrong with that. It was where Gunny and Vic had said the hardware would be delivered. What was wrong was that there was a low wooden-sided truck parked behind the Bulldogs, blocking access to the road. And there was nobody showing, not even when Betts hit the horn a toot and slowed down.

Not right. The plan was that they'd load the explosives and head for Gilway, a railway stop about two hundred miles from Halifax. It was going to be a hell of a drive, all night and part of the next day.

So Gunny and Vic should have been waiting by the trucks. They weren't. Richard Betts changed his mind about turning into the drive. He eased the accelerator down and drove past. He followed the fence that surrounded the junkyard until he found a place where he could make his turn. Then he forked the car around and headed back the way he'd come. A hundred yards from the gate he cut the lights and the engine and coasted a few yards while he pulled to the side of the road. He got out and stood there for a time. He didn't have a weapon. He'd refused one when Gunny had offered him his choice from the suitcase. Shit. That was smart at the time, but it seemed dumb as hell now. He walked to the trunk of the car. He fumbled about in the clutter until he came up with a jack handle. Best he could do, he guessed. He carried it over his shoulder the eighty yards or so to the junkyard gate. He walked on the dirt and grass. Playing cowboys and Indians, he was going to be the Indian.

He ducked when he reached the truck with the plank-wood sides. He had a look in the cab. Nobody there. The smell of rank cigarettes and some kind of perfume. An awful stink. He moved to the bed of the truck. A canvas tarp was thrown there in a heap. Nothing under it. He bent low and ran for the Bulldog on the left. The truck bed was empty. He rounded the side to the cab. The Bulldog had a sliding door. He eased it open slowly. Nothing on the seat. He'd backed away when he saw the shape of the suitcase on the floorboards. He reached in and grabbed the handle. It was the right one, so heavy it almost pulled his arm off at the socket. Yes, that was Gunny's war bag. He lifted the suitcase from the truck and lowered it to the ground. He squatted over it and worked at the two leather straps. He opened it and did a braille reading of the contents. A pump gun would be better. He didn't want to take the time to assemble it. He settled for a .45 Army automatic. He put that aside and found a loaded clip. He ran a fingernail down it until he was sure it was a full load. He slapped the clip home, worked the slide, and knew a round was in the chamber.

Careful of his feet, wary of where he stepped, he reached the gate. The chain hung down, the busted lock on the ground. The gate was parted a couple of feet. He walked through sideways.

He started across the yard toward the office shack. After two or three steps the toe of his right shoe touched something huddled on the ground. He kept his balance and leaned down. He was afraid it might be either Vic or Gunny. It wasn't. It was some man he didn't know. Probably the night watchman at the junkyard. The man was out, his breathing shallow but steady. His hands were tied behind his back with a piece of rope.

Betts straightened up when he heard voices from inside the shack. A growl or a shout. He followed the angle of the building and ducked beneath a window. He avoided the light and peered over a window ledge. He saw Vic Franks. He was backed against a wall. Blood, from a number of cuts and tears, covered his face. While Betts watched, a tall bald man stepped forward and caught Vic by his shirt front.

"Tell him," another man off to the side, at the desk, said.

"Fuck you," Vic mumbled.

The bald man hit Vic. The building shook when Vic fell back against it. Stunned, blinking, he bounced off the wall and back toward the bald man.

Betts didn't see Gunny at first. Then he stretched to his full height and could see the whole room. Gunny was on the floor on all fours. He'd been beaten, too. He looked like he was trying to pull himself together, his head shaking like he was trying to clear it.

The man behind the desk was armed. He was waving around what appeared to be a lady's hideout pistol. It was pearl-handled and it looked like it was probably a .32 with a short barrel.

The bald man doing the rough work didn't have a gun showing. Betts decided he'd have to play it that way. One armed and one unarmed. He was backing away from the window when the man at the desk spoke. "My friend and I do not have all the patience in the world. Tell me why you need these weapons or ..."

Betts lost the rest of it. The building shook and Betts knew that Vic had taken another lick.

There had to be some way to let Gunny, if he wasn't too dazed, and Vic, if he wasn't out on his feet, know that he was outside. They had to be expecting him. The fact that there had been no one outside to watch for him meant that the two strangers in there didn't know he was coming. Otherwise they'd have planned to ambush him too. Gunny and Vic expected him. That was why they were willing to take the beating.

And then Betts had an idea. On the train, all the way to Montreal, he'd bored the hell out of them doing birdcalls. He'd done all the calls one of the blacks on the mule chain had taught him.

He stepped away from the window and did a bobwhite. He repeated it. Then a third time. He circled the building until he reached the rear of it. He did the caw of a crow. After a pause he repeated it a second and a third time.

He threw out another bobwhite and another crow call while he circled the side of the building and headed for the main door. It was silent inside the shack. He wasn't sure what that meant. He arrived at the door and leaned forward. He ran a hand around the outside of the door until he found that the hinges were placed inside. The door would open inward. He put his back to the wall to the right of the door and did a whippoorwill. He pursed his mouth to do the whippoorwill a second time and then heard the floor creaking. The steps came toward the doorway. He heard the man who'd done all the talking say, "…a wild-bird refuge?"

The door was jerked open, inward. The barrel of the pearl-handled pistol came through the doorway first. The man was following it when Betts chopped at the hand holding the gun. The gun shook loose. At the same time Betts rammed the point of the .45 into the man's gut. The air went out of him. He was beginning to slump when Betts caught a shoulder in him and pushed him back into the room.

Bad action in there. Vic was slumped against the wall. No help there. The bald man was reaching for his hip pocket. Whatever he had there wasn't to blow his nose with. Betts shoved the man in front of him to the side and brought up the .45. He took in Gunny, still down on his hands and knees. The man didn't pay any attention to Gunny. The hand came away from his hip. He held some ladies' pistol in it. Maybe a .22. He brought up the pistol and, at the same time, began to step around Gunny.

He should have watched Gunny. Before Betts could get the .45 sighted in, Gunny reached out a thick arm and hit the bald man about ankle high. It was like being hit by a rolling log. The strength of the arm and the man's moving forward floored him. The .22 skidded across the floor toward Betts.

Gunny wasn't that much out. He moved like a fat possum climbing a tree. He landed on the bald man and planted a knee in his kidney and clubbed him in the back of the neck.

It was blood-and-spit time after that. Betts stood aside and watched Gunny and Vic get theirs back. He let it go a time and then he stepped in and stopped it short of killing. The slicker who'd had the gun was missing a couple of teeth, and he probably had a bad jaw and some floating ribs. The other man, with the bald head, took his beating and kicking while he was still unconscious.

They shoved the wood-sided truck into a ditch, to get it out of the way. Betts drove the stolen car to the driveway. The explosives were loaded into Gunny's truck. The other Bulldog, the one he hadn't checked, was already loaded with the Thompsons, the spare ammo, and the grenades.

The two trucks trailed Betts a mile or so, until he found a place to ditch the stolen car. Then, because he could see that Gunny was shaky, Betts took over for him and got behind the wheel of his Bulldog.

"Scum was curious why we wanted these weapons." Gunny was bent forward, hugging his ribs. His breathing was rough.

"I guess we should have expected it."

"Birdcalls," Gunny wheezed. "That was good as string music."

"I didn't know you appreciated them."

"I do now. And one more thing."

"Yeah?"

"In Vic's truck. Those are cut-rate weapons. Scum got so anxious they didn't wait to collect the other half of the payment."

"Better and better," Betts said.

"They were overpriced anyway."

After a couple of hours of rest Gunny said he felt good enough to drive. Betts shifted to the other truck and relieved Vic.

They were on a tight schedule. As soon as Johnny and Tom heard that the arrangements were being made, they'd taken the train to Halifax to meet with Harry and the Gipsons. That had been early evening.

The Mack Bulldogs rolled east the whole night.

CHAPTER NINETEEN

Henri Lebeque did not think of himself as a criminal.

No matter how other people saw him, he thought of himself as a patriot. From the time he was a small boy he'd been involved in the Movement. There was to be a Free Quebec, and it would be separated from Canada, and it would be governed by the true French-speaking. It would be the real New France.

He had learned his politics at his grandfather's knee. His grandfather had come from France and had refused to learn English. If the old man had to speak English to ask for a glass of water or to order a meal, he would prefer to die of thirst or hunger. His grandfather was a great man.

Henri waited until his grandfather died before he let anyone in the family know that he understood and spoke English. The Quebec Movement needed money, and it needed arms, and the English seemed to have most of both.

Ten years before, at the age of thirty-four, after he had worked himself up to head clerk in the shipping department of the Canadian National Railway, a once-in-a-lifetime chance came to him. He was working in Ottawa then, and a shipment of fifty used Mausers and ten thousand rounds of ammunition had reached the depot. It was intended for a sporting-goods wholesaler. Henri misrouted the consignment, and it arrived at a newly rented storefront in Quebec. By the time the misrouting was discovered, the arms were in the Movement's cache, and Henri Lebeque had disappeared from Ottawa. There was a price for everything, and it was almost five years before Henri could come out of hiding. He'd aged during those years, his hair had gone gray, and he had been furnished a newly created identity. Henri Leveque was how he was known now. It was his own idea to set up in Montreal. With the Movement's contacts and with some starter money, he settled into the criminal world. He started with gambling and moved from there into any and all traffic that would bring in money. It amused him that the English-speaking Canadians, with their vices, pumped cash into the war chest of the Separatists.

Then came September 1, 1939. The bond the Movement felt with old France postponed their war of independence. Most of the young men in the Movement believed their first war had to be fought to keep their real homeland, France, free. They joined the Canadian Army in hundreds, and the older men, when they became used to it, decided that it was not all bad. Let the English teach the young men to fight, to fire weapons and kill. It would rebound on them later, when the time came.

And then France surrendered. That was two or three days ago. All the anger Henri felt against the English increased. It was at the boil. Churchill had betrayed France. He had not given the help and the support he had promised. He had withheld his Air Force. France had fallen because Churchill was too concerned with keeping England strong, with keeping Germans off British soil.

But the young men still enlisted. Now the cry was that they had to liberate the homeland. Their own part of Canada, Free Quebec, would have to wait until the war was over.

The model 1928 Thompsons had come into his hands through a fluke. A happy mistake. Henri had arranged the hijacking with the information that the truck carried passenger-car tires, new ones, worth all that the traffic would bear on the black market. He sent out his men, four of them, and they'd caught the truck on a narrow road and blocked it at both ends. The two men in the truck hadn't given them trouble. Henri's men were amazed to discover that the men were in Canadian Army uniforms, and even more surprised when they'd lifted the tarp from the truck and found the cases of Thompsons and the boxes of ammunition.

The cases held fifty 1928 Thompsons. It was like finding a gold seam. The leader of the squad of hijackers knew that the heat would be on. The soldiers had seen too much of them. He took the two soldiers into the woods, off the road, and executed them, thinking of it as war. He had made his nervous explanation to Henri, and Henri had agreed with his decision.

He hadn't been able to move the Thompsons. Henri considered burying them until the war ended. It was then that the old American began asking in the grapevine about scrap pipe.

If Henri could not move them, if he had no use for them until the war was over, why not sell five of the Thompsons to the American for a high price? The Movement would be able to use the money. Henri thought that way when he made the bargain with the old American.

Later, looking at the crisp, new hundred-dollar bills, he had second thoughts. The evening paper he read after he left the private club where the deal was made had a small article on one of the inside pages. A bank had been robbed across the border in the United States. In a town called Renssler. The robbers had taken what was estimated at fifty thousand dollars. A large part of that money, the article noted, was in new hundred-dollar bills.

The bank robbery and the hundred-dollar bills aroused his curiosity.

Some time later, when Jean and the bald man, Pierre Picard, arrived at his home to carry the Thompsons and the other goods from his cellar storeroom and load them in a borrowed truck, he had a talk with Jean. A deal was a deal, he told him. There was no doubt a deal had been made. Still some questions had come up. He needed to know why the old American wanted the Thompsons and the grenades. Jean would find a way to learn the truth. If it was only a matter of buying weapons to take over the border to the States, he could go on with the deal.

He might, however, try to raise the price if the old American would allow it.

If the facts were otherwise, if the American had some kind of adventure planned for Canada, Jean was to bring the old man to him. He himself would discover if there was some way in which the Movement could profit from it.

He heard them tell their tale. The old American had gone from being alone to having another man with him when they met him at the junkyard. And if that was not enough, there was another man as well, a man who waved a huge pistol about that was the size of a cannon.

More and more curious, Henri thought.

One man had grown to three. Could not those three have grown to six or even ten? How many had crossed the border? At least five, he thought, because they'd bought five of the 1928s. So what were five men going to do with five 1928s and a case of grenades?

Jean, his driver, sucked breath through a gap in his teeth. His jaw was swollen, but he did not think that it was broken. "Whatever they are, however many they are, I think the old man we dealt with is not a true indication of the quality of the others. The others are very, very tough."

Henri dismissed them. Both Jean and Pierre went to see a doctor.

At first he had been angry with them. How could they let the Americans handle them so easily? And how could they neglect to collect the second half of the payment? He calmed himself down. It was not all bad. If they were really tough, they would not have disclosed what they intended anyway. Tough men never did. They died first.

Perhaps if the Americans would not tell him what they planned, they would show him, instead.

By four in the morning the word had passed through the Movement's grapevine. There was a description of the two trucks and the three men. Locate them and report to Montreal.

He would handle it himself this time. When he knew where they were, that would be the proper time to discover what their real business was. He would mix and stir in it. After all, had they not made a binding deal? One half of the money when the bargain was struck and the final half upon delivery. The old American had broken his word.

If it turned out that their business—why they needed the arms—did not interest him, the eleven hundred dollars did. It was the Movement's money.

It was a cloudy, cool day in Halifax.

According to plan, the Gipsons had wormed their way into the center of the train-yard crew. When Cody and his crew left the boarding house for breakfast at six in the morning the Gipsons trailed along. The story they gave was that they wanted to see how railroading was done north of the border. Harry rationed them breakfast money, lunch money, and a few dollars for drinks at Toy's after the workday was over.

"Show them you know the business," Harry said.

"That ought to be easy," Randy said. "We damned well do."

Harry let that snot pass. It wasn't worth the trouble it took to level the smartass. Later. That would come later.

The crew left. Harry rolled back into bed for two or three more hours of sleep.

He spent the rest of the day wandering around Halifax. The old town was bursting at the seams. It was overcrowded with the influx of servicemen, whores, and workers. Housing couldn't be bought for double money. No booze for sale anywhere in the city except at the ration stores, and you had to have a card for that. That was all right with Harry. He could settle for the rum at Toy's. And the shortage might hold the Gipsons down for a few days. Might. Just might. He didn't really believe that anything but a bullet between his eyes would hold Randy in check.

At four in the afternoon, legs weary from all that walking, he was at a table in Toy's when Cody and his crew streamed in. The Gipsons were all buddy-buddy, and that much of it was fine. They'd had a good day playing trains, and they hadn't shown any crazy at all.

Harry waved his cup of Newfoundland Screech at Cody and he yelled at Shorty, the Chinese waiter, that the first round was on his ticket.

The talk that afternoon over the drinks was about the war. It wasn't going well. Invasion across the English Channel was expected any hour. The way the war was going, they might start cutting the exemptions for work that was considered essential. That happened, and the train crews might end up working at half strength. As it was, they were working a man or two short in each shift.

Harry made his joke. "You could hire these two good ole boys for about fifty cents an hour. It's about all they're worth."

Cody took it as a knock on the Gipsons. He didn't take the offer seriously. Not completely. But there was a hesitation before he said, "I lose a man or two and that's not such a bad idea."

And then the offer got lost in the noise of the next round being ordered.

Harry didn't push it. He settled back and let the suggestion sink in. He'd planted it, and that was all he wanted to do. It was there in case the need came up. And it would. He would see that it did.

Harry finished his bath in the community tub down the hall. He returned to the room he shared with the Gipsons. It was a bare living space about twelve feet by twelve. Two double-decker bunks, a card table, and a couple of chairs were the only furniture.

The Gipsons were gone. Harry didn't let it panic him. He dressed in clean underwear and walked the length of the hall. He asked his question and got the same answer everywhere. Nobody had seen the Gipsons since they'd all returned from Toy's.

Harry thought of one possibility. He returned to his room and took his trousers from the wall hook. He counted the wad of cash in the hip pocket. He knew what he'd started with in Butler and he made a quick estimate of what he'd spent in Halifax.

He was short about a hundred dollars.

The urge was in him so strong it dried his mouth. He wanted to find Randy and kick the living crap out of him. No matter what. Even if he busted some knuckles on his hard head.

But he knew he didn't have the time to go looking for them. The captain and the major were due on the early-evening train from Montreal. He and the Gipsons were supposed to meet them. It was a fucked-up situation anyway. There'd been no way to contact them in Montreal because they hadn't known where they'd be staying, and the captain and the major hadn't known how to reach him in Halifax. It was damned poor communications for people who'd been trained in the U.S. Army.

He finished dressing. Before he left the room he found the mapped tracks, the sketches Randy and Clark had put together the last two hundred miles or so on the way to Halifax. He'd been over the maps with them. It had been a surface look. It hadn't seemed important at the time. The Gipsons were supposed to do the reading for the captain and the major. And now the Gipsons, damn them, had decided to take a vacation.

Maybe he knew enough. Just maybe.

He was late. He found Captain Johnny seated on a high-backed bench in the waiting room. His head was back; his feet blocked the aisle between the benches. The bustle, the crush, in the train station was incredible. Uniforms and more uniforms, and here and there a woman or a woman with small children. Harry looked at the women and he knew, from his day's walk around Halifax, that the chance of housing was zero. Good luck, ladies.

He stopped in front of Johnny, who had his eyes closed. Harry was about to speak when he felt a touch on his shoulder and looked around. It was Major Renssler, freshly shaved, with his kit under his arm.

"By yourself, Harry?"

He nodded.

Johnny opened his eyes. He stood. "Let's walk and find some fresh air."

They pushed their way outside. There were a couple of battered taxis at the curb. They passed them by and walked a few blocks until they found a greasy-spoon café. It was almost empty. Johnny led the way to a table in the back of the café, apart from the few diners. There wasn't much choice in the dinner menu. They selected the broiled fish.

There'd been little talk on the street. Johnny had said that they would be taking the next train out. That was about two hours away. "I feel like a goddam rubber ball," Johnny had said.

Now, after the waiter left with the menus, Tom planted his elbows on the table. "Where are the Gipsons?"

"I wish I knew." Lying wouldn't do any good. "They slipped me an hour ago while I was in the tub."

"You were supposed to hold them down."

Harry looked at Johnny. "I can't take baths with them."

"What do you think?" Tom said.

"A hundred or so is missing from my pocket. I think they're visiting the pro ladies."

"You think they're coming back?"

Harry nodded. "Otherwise they'd have taken more than the hundred."

Johnny looked grim. "Slap them down when they come back."

"My pleasure." And it would be.

"They do the charting?"

"They did." Harry dug the folded pad sheets from his hip pocket and made room on the table so that he could spread them. "These are composites. It's what they put together from the charting Randy did on one side of the train and Clark on the other." He put a fingertip on HALIFAX and moved it left along the crossed twin lines that stood for the tracks. His finger stopped at a big X with the square block of a house drawn next to it. "This is Wingate Station. It's about a hundred or a hundred and five miles out from Halifax." His finger moved past the X and followed the track until a thin line curled away from the double lines. "This is a siding about forty miles or so farther out. That puts it about a hundred and forty or forty-five miles from Halifax. The way the Gipsons see it, even if the hotbox goes bad after the train passes the Wingate Station, they'll decide to back the train up and uncouple at Wingate rather than use this siding."

"Why?" Tom rubbed his eyes and yawned.

"The size of it," Harry said. "Randy says there's a crew there. And there'll be telephones and a telegraph, and there are a couple of sidings." Harry tapped the siding about a hundred and forty miles out. "This one is just a siding in the woods. Nothing else."

"How do they figure…?"

Tom broke off as the waiter arrived with their suppers. Broiled fish, watery potatoes, and green peas.

The waiter left. Harry had a bite of fish and then, guessing, he finished Tom's question in his mind and answered it. "Randy says they'll try to use whatever crew there is at Wingate to repair the hotboxes. That way they won't have to send a crew from Halifax. The Wingate crew does the work while a spare engine comes redballing out to pick up the cars when they're ready to move again."

"What happens if they decide to fix the hotboxes while the whole train waits?"

"Randy says that won't happen. It's an important shipment, and he's sure they're going to have a clear track for it. But they're not going to tie up the track for hours. Randy says they'll shunt off the cars with the bad hotboxes, and the rest of the train will leave. For one thing, they've probably got a schedule to meet. That and not tying up the track all day."

Johnny turned the chart toward him. He studied it while he ate. "We're going to look silly if we're waiting at Wingate and that train roars past ... and don't come back."

"That's the risk," Harry said. "But Randy says, and Clark backs him, that if we mess with those hotboxes, there's no way those freight cars are going to get far beyond Wingate Station."

"That worries me. Having to put much store in anything the Gipsons say."

"They're *your* experts," Harry said.

"Damn them," Johnny said.

Tom asked if he'd made contact with the train crew.

"Easy as pie. And they're short of crew now. The work's essential, draft exempt, but a couple got patriotic and went off and volunteered. They haven't been replaced yet. Also, by the time that ship reaches port here, that early crew is going to need two more good men. I've got it planned they'll be bone short."

They finished the meal in silence. Johnny settled the bill, and they walked back to the train station. There were still about fifty minutes before the train headed back toward Montreal.

Johnny and Tom wouldn't have to ride it the whole way. If there were no hitches, they'd meet Gunny and the other two at Gilway, about two hundred miles down the line from Halifax.

Harry left them outside the station and walked his way through the darkening streets to the boarding house. The angry burn was in him all the way. He wanted to kick some ass. Those rednecks had made him look bad with the captain and the major.

But he still needed the Gipsons, and they knew it, and they were playing it for all it was worth. That meant he couldn't kick and stomp. He'd just rough them up and add some bruises around the edges.

That decided, he kicked off his shoes and stretched out on his bunk. He needed the rest, and Lord knows when the Gipsons would run short of money. He hoped it would be soon.

CHAPTER TWENTY

As soon as Johnny Whitman settled into the coach seat at Halifax his head went back and his eyes closed. Within ten minutes he was asleep.

All the rail travel hadn't tired Tom Renssler that much. He felt it in his lower back, and he told himself that another six or eight hours on horsehair seats and he'd have saddle sores. He wasn't like Johnny, who had the athlete's looseness, an ability to drop off for an hour at any time and any place. His body seemed to tell his mind to shut up, and that was all there was to it.

It was a grace that Tom didn't possess.

Twenty minutes out of Halifax, the coach lights dimmed now, Johnny began to dream. The even breathing changed to a series of grunts and snorts.

Enough. More than enough.

Tom left his seat. He stood in the aisle for a time. He tried to remember the train as it was when they'd boarded it. And then, not sure he was going in the right direction, he went looking for the canteen car. If there was one. He wasn't sure there would be. What he wanted, more than a cup of coffee or a beer, was to get away from Johnny Whitman for an hour or so. With any luck, Johnny's dream would have ended by the time he returned to his seat.

He passed through several cars. The train was crowded. Uniformed men—Army and Navy—filled most of the seats. Here and there, spotted about the cars, were the usual card games that went on either by the dim overhead lights or by hand-held flashlight.

He didn't ask directions. It was almost a child's game. Even if he didn't find a club car or a canteen, the time spent away from Johnny's animal dreams was its own kind of reward.

I'm getting warm, he thought. That was when he entered a Pullman car. Two stewards, too busy to notice him, were converting the coach into a series of beds. He passed them and pushed through the rear door. He stopped in the connector section between cars. It was drafty there, and then he lurched for the door handle and caught it and entered the next car.

The smell stung his nose. It was the smell of a hospital. The strong disinfectant felt harsh in his lungs. He couldn't breathe for a moment. He lurched and caught his balance, and then he narrowed his eyes so that he could see.

It was like a Pullman car, but the bed litters were open. War wounded, he thought, and he turned and would have gone back the way he came. What stopped him was the panic-constricted voice of a young man off to his right.

"Sister? Is that you, Sister?"

"No," Tom said. "I'll find her."

"Please..." the man said.

Tom leaned in. The man was on one of the bottom litters. "What is it?"

"It's the one above me," the wounded man said.

Tom squatted, and, on level with the man, looked up. A dark stain covered the canvas of the litter. It was blood, and as Tom watched, he saw the blood dripping on the man who'd called out to him. The same dark stain covered the man from the neck to his knees.

Tom stood. "I'll find the nurse."

He backed away, hit the door, and then he was in the connector. The fresh air cleared his lungs, and he was leaning against the door, coughing and gagging, when the Sister, the nurse, passed him. While the door to the hospital car was closing Tom heard the same man calling out to the nurse.

He moved to the window and looked out at the passing land, the lights in the distance. A few more seconds, a few more deep breaths, and he could head back to his seat in the coach.

It happened that MacTaggart's rounds—his inspection of the magazine where the bullion was stored—matched that of Sub-Lieutenant Carr's on the morning of June 29. H.M.S. *Emerald* was two days out of Halifax.

MacTaggart had requisitioned a light for his inspections. That is, he found a poor, lost, orphan flashlight on a shelf in an empty compartment as he'd passed by. He'd stuffed it into his shirt before anyone realized that it was lost.

He spent twenty minutes checking out the floor plates around the stacked cargo. It wasn't that he was worried about the *Emerald*. Frisky girl that she was, if her knickers got a tear in them, there was always the dockyard at Halifax for repairs. What he had nightmares about, unlikely as it was, was that the angle irons might bend, the floor plates buckle, and several crates of the gold bullion might tumble into the area below the magazine. Down there, wherever that was, the cargo would be plunder for the souvenir hunters aboard the *Emerald*. It was not a happy thought to the man who'd signed for the shipment: each and every man on the ship having his own personal twenty-seven-pound bar of gold stored away in his seabag.

Carr joined him about the time he'd finished. MacTaggart stood aside while Carr tested the incline of the floor plates. Done, Carr switched off his light.

"She's bearing up," Carr said.

"No worse?"

"A fraction. I suspect it's acceptable under the circumstances."

They walked single file down the narrow passage. Carr led the way.

"The captain decided not to throw it overboard?"

Carr turned and laughed. "I'm afraid Captain Flynn didn't even see the humor of my suggestion. He had a double handful of my fur about it."

"Sorry, Mr. Carr."

"It wasn't your fault."

They reached the passageway that led to MacTaggart's compartment.

"A cup of tea, Mr. MacTaggart?"

"A pleasure."

At the Officers' Wardroom, Carr filled two mugs with tea from the urn and brought them to the table. He added milk to his. MacTaggart shook his head and took his straight.

"I suppose it's about done for you," Carr said.

"The consignment?" He had a sip of the tea and burned his tongue. "Hardly."

"I thought..."

"Two things could happen on the voyage. Both bad. The storm could break up the ship and we'd sink, or the Germans might find us and sink us. We've passed the storm, and I have it on good authority that we won't meet U-boats or raiders this far west."

Carr nodded. "Their hunting grounds are behind us. The closer we get to land, the more we come under the air-search umbrella. U-boats don't like air search."

MacTaggart blew the steam from his cup. "You ever been to Canada?"

"Only to Nova Scotia," Carr said.

"Not into the interior?"

"Not even beyond Halifax," Carr admitted.

"My responsibility for the shipment doesn't end when we reach port."

Carr sipped his tea.

"I understand," MacTaggart said, "that it is a vast, vast country inhabited by bands of marauding redskins."

Carr smiled at him. He waited to see what MacTaggart would add to that statement. He added nothing. He sipped his tea, his eyes closed, for all the world looking like a dozing cat.

Harry heard the door ease open.

He wasn't half puma and half alligator for nothing. He sat up and dropped his legs over the side of the bunk bed. He was fully dressed except for his shoes. His feet touched the board floor and he told those boards not to squeak. They didn't.

Harry was two paces from the doorway when a hand from the hallway caught the doorknob and jerked the door to a stop, open just wide enough for a man to step through sideways. A triangle of light ran across the floor of the room.

Harry knew the first man through the doorway. It was the runt, Randy.

Give your soul to Jesus. Planting his left foot firmly, Harry hit Randy in the stomach. He pulled the punch at the last moment, until it was only about three-quarters strength. There was enough left. The rank breath blew out of Randy. He staggered and grabbed his gut and doubled over and sucked for breath.

There wasn't any fight in him. Harry caught him by the shoulders and half walked, half dragged him across the room to his bunk. Harry lifted him, shook him, and tossed him into the bottom bunk. He was limp as a bag of rags. "Not a word out of you," Harry said. He backed away and found a match and struck it on his pants leg. He lit the kerosene lamp on the card table. He trimmed the wick so that the light was dim. He capped it with the glass chimney.

He had his look at Randy. Sweaty and about to puke. Harry put his back to him and went to the door. Clark stood there, blinking at him.

"Come in," Harry said. "This is where you live."

Clark wobbled past him. He smelled of rotgut and something else. "You do remember where you live, don't you?"

And then the smell fixed itself in Harry's mind. Jesus, pale Jesus, the kid has been sheep-dipped in perfume and cunt.

"You going to hit me, Harry?" Clark didn't put up his hands to defend himself.

"Not tonight. Your night's been busy enough." He backed away from Clark and sat on the edge of his bunk. He stripped off his socks and dropped them in his shoes. "How was she, Clark?"

"Who?"

"Miss Halifax of 1940. Who the hell do you think I mean?"

The kid started crying. His face twisted up and then he was blubbering. "I didn't want to."

"None of my business," Harry said. "Go to bed. You get four hours sleep before you go socializing with the morning crew again."

"I told Randy..."

"Go to bed."

Randy had his breath back. "Shut up, Clark."

Clark climbed into the top bunk above his brother. He didn't undress. Harry looked at the two of them. Dogshit that walked. Then he blew out the lamp and finished undressing in the dark.

He set his body clock. Up in four hours.

He listened to the breath gasping, the easing on the lower bunk. For a few minutes more he heard the sniffling from Clark. Then it turned into a mumbling that could have been a prayer.

What a crew.

Dogshit.

If he got through the next day or two...

And then he was asleep.

Gunny Townsend wasn't sure exactly when the major and the captain would arrive at the Gilway railway station. He and Vic

Franks, relieved from time to time by Richard Betts; drove all night. At dawn they stopped for breakfast. The Mack Bulldogs could get out and run, a lumbering, awkward, ground-eating trot. Vic kept his ears on the engines, listening to them talk, and what he heard pleased him. Lord, they are like coon dogs that have been locked up all summer and now it is fall, and they can smell the leaves burning, and they know they will run off the summer fat as soon as they smell that first coon.

Stopping only for fuel and a sandwich or a soft drink, they continued the eastward run. They reached Gilway in the early evening, near dark, and drove down the two blocks of main street and parked on a side street.

Betts and Franks remained with the trucks. Gunny walked around town. It wasn't more than five minutes in any direction. Gunny found a deserted barn on the edge of town, off to the north-west, and he asked around until he found the owner. The house he got sent to was diagonally across the street from the barn. A dour, ruddy-faced man named MacGregor gave Gunny his keen Scots look and said that he might rent Gunny the barn for the night for ten dollars American. He'd furnish a lamp, but they couldn't smoke or cook in the barn.

Gunny agreed. He returned with the trucks ten minutes later, and MacGregor was waiting in front of the locked doors. MacGregor kept them waiting while he unlocked the padlock and spread the high doors. He stood aside and watched the trucks pull inside and park. Then MacGregor held out the padlock key, and Gunny passed the ten-dollar bill to him.

MacGregor was curious about the trucks. He loafed outside the barn, examining the ten-dollar bill, until Gunny explained that they were over the border on a camping trip. The trucks carried equipment their bosses would need in the wilds. In fact, he checked his watch, the train bringing them ought to be arriving any time.

"A considerable amount of camping equipment it would seem to me," MacGregor said.

"Rich people can't do without their comforts," Gunny said. "Why, they've even got a portable bathtub in there."

Gunny was waiting on the platform when the captain and the major stepped off the train. Gunny had drawn the first watch, the short straw in the straw game.

Tom had taken a couple of steps toward the street when he stopped and came back. He turned Gunny so that the platform light struck him full in the face. The bruises were getting dark, going toward blue.

"Trouble, Gunny?'

"You wouldn't think so if you saw the other two. They got the rough end of it."

Gunny led them off the platform to the street. He told them the rest of it through a puffed mouth.

"You think that's the end of it?" Johnny asked.

"That's my guess. They didn't get the full price but they got more than the going rate for the hardware."

"How is the hardware?"

"Still in the packing grease. And first things first, I want to clean and test-fire them."

"Down the road," Johnny said.

"How far?"

"I'd say two or three hours to Wingate Station."

"All right," Gunny said, "but the sooner we get settled in, the better."

"A hotel in town?" Tom looked over his shoulder at the part of town they'd passed through.

"I saw something passed for one," Gunny said.

They entered the barn. Betts and Franks sat in the cab of one of the Bulldogs and passed a quart of beer back and forth between them. The lighted lamp hung from a nail on a rafter off to the side.

Johnny had his look around. "Somebody'll have to sleep with the trucks tonight."

"We can split watches," Betts said.

"The straw game?" Franks got out of the truck and stretched his legs.

Gunny shook his head. "You get some sleep. I'll do the night turn."

"How do you feel?" Tom asked.

"Never better." And it was true. Even with the beating, the aftereffects of that, he hadn't been coughing, and there hadn't been any blood spotting. "I've got a can of solvent. I thought I'd spend part of the night cleaning the Thompsons. I can nap on the road tomorrow."

It was settled. Vic stayed with Gunny to help him strip down the Thompsons. Richard Betts said he was hungry, and he led the way to the hotel.

Johnny and Tom kept him company at supper. Both ordered only coffee and pie and shared a carafe of the house wine that tasted of rust.

The waiter was a dark man in his forties. He might have passed for Italian if it hadn't been for his slight French accent. To the displeasure of the townspeople at the other tables, the waiter hovered over the Americans. The townspeople thought that he probably smelled a large tip.

His name was Gilles. Earlier in the day he'd received a request from the Movement that he watch for a party of Americans. These were Americans. He could tell that from their accents. But they seemed ordinary enough, and none of them showed the marks of the beating that was part of the description he'd received.

The three Americans finished and left, and Gilles was considering whether it would be proper to send the message. After all, these did not fit the descriptions, and it might cripple the search if he sent in the information and it was not useful.

He was in the kitchen getting an order when the other two men entered. One look at the bruises on their faces, and he knew these were the right ones. For the short duration of their meal he bustled around them. He tried to overhear what they said. These two did little but eat. They did not appear to believe that conversation was a part of dining.

Five strangers, five Americans, in one day in a town that hardly saw that many in a whole year? He assumed they were together, the three who had eaten before and these at his table now. It proved to be a correct guess. These two separated after they left the dining room. Gilles watched them from the doorway and saw one seat himself in the lobby. The other went out.

Gilles found reasons to pass the doorway every minute or two until he was rewarded. He saw the bruised man who'd remained in the lobby joined by the three that had eaten earlier. He watched them check in at the hotel desk.

The dining room did not close until ten. It took another half an hour to straighten it and set the tables for breakfast. When that was done, Gilles slipped through the back door and trotted to the train station.

The depot was closing for the night. There were no more local trains until the next morning. The telegrapher took down the message and counted the words and took payment. He told Gilles that the cable would not go out until the first thing in the morning.

Henri Leveque received the telegram while he was having breakfast.

FIVE MEN GILWAY. COULD BE MEN YOU ASK ABOUT.

He finished his breakfast—French-roast coffee, black, and fresh croissants that flaked to the fork, and country butter with the flower-mold imprint—and then he reread the message.

After a second cup of coffee he called Jean at his apartment. Jean said he was packed and ready. It would take half an hour to pick up Pierre at his residential hotel across town. He would arrive at Henri's home in forty-five minutes, unless the traffic delayed him.

In his upstairs bedroom, Henri packed for three days. He did not believe that his business with the Americans would take more than a day or two.

He carried the suitcase downstairs and left it beside the front door. He passed through the dining room and entered the kitchen. At the rear of the kitchen, near the pantry, there was a locked door. A flight of stairs led down into Leveque's wine cellar. It was not an impressive collection. It numbered a few more than two hundred bottles. All of the wines were French. No others were worth drinking. And now, except for wines already in stock in Canada or the United States, there would be no more until after the war.

That thought, not the first time it had come to him, stopped him at the bottom of the stairs. He reminded himself. When he returned from the trip he would send letters to several wine brokers in Canada and in the United States. He would ask about certain vintages. Certain years. It might be a long war. Another ten-dozen bottles might be a reasonable purchase.

There was a single light in the center of the cellar.

High wooden racks lined the stone walls on three sides. There were spaces, altogether, for five hundred bottles.

The rear wall, the one without a length of wine rack, appeared to be solid wood panels. It was a work area with a heavy trestle table. Henri pushed the table aside. The wall panels were held in place by metal frames at the top and bottom. He leaned over and tripped a catch at the bottom left of the metal frame. Standing, he pushed the panel about four feet to the right.

The opening led to a cave that had been cut from solid rock. A candle in a dish was on the floor just inside. Henri lit the candle and stepped into his arsenal.

For the most part, the racks and shelves in the cave held a motley collection of arms. Many of them had been stolen. Others had been bought in pawnshops in Canada and below the border in the States.

The newest acquisitions, the Thompson 1928s, were stacked at the far end of the cave, still crated except for the one open case. The five he'd sold the old American were from that box, as well as the two that he'd had cleaned and test-fired.

Those two 1928s were in standing rifle racks. He wrapped them in an old blanket and placed them on the worktable outside the cave. His second trip, he carried out two fifty-round drums for the Thompsons. His final time in the cave, he selected a handgun for himself, his favorite, a Colt .44 revolver with a six-inch barrel and the kick of a mule.

He pushed the panel back into place. He carried the .44 revolver upstairs and placed it on top of his suitcase. The 1928s and the drums were still on the worktable in the wine cellar. Jean and Pierre could bring those up when they arrived.

After he washed his hands and patted the patches of perspiration from his face, he returned to the dining table and poured himself a final coffee.

He was a man who liked puzzles. He liked putting this part next to that part and taking this piece from far over there and moving it about until it fitted. Everything made sense if you knew there was an overall design.

The first part. Here was an old man, an American, past his prime but still with an unusual toughness. He wanted five Thompsons and spare ammunition and a case of grenades. When you asked why he needed those arms he gave flippant answers.

The second part. There was the matter of the trucks. Jean said that when he'd arrived at the junkyard, there were two Mack Bulldogs, three or three-and-a-half tons, parked outside the fence. Henri's check with Harpur confirmed that the trucks had been bought from him that day for cash money. The man who bought them was an expert, a specialist with engines.

The third part. The radio, the day before, had noted in the news broadcast that a watchman at a construction company had been brutally beaten during a robbery. An undetermined amount of high explosives had been stolen. The newspaper that Henri read that night speculated that a German Fifth Column might be operating in Canada. Who else would need such large quantities of high explosives?

Who indeed? Another element fell into place after Henri called a lawyer he knew. Could he find out when the robbery at the Melton Construction Company took place? The lawyer could and did. The time was not exact but it was about the time that Jean and Pierre delivered the arms and did their questioning of the old man and the engine specialist. Could it be that the third man, the one who arrived at Harpur's junkyard with the pistol like a cannon, was the same man who had beaten the old watchman and stolen the explosives? Was that a coincidence?

He did not think so.

Five men, the telegram said. His three men had grown to five. What did five men want with Thompsons and grenades and high explosives?

It was a puzzle to end all puzzles.

And there were still missing pieces.

They drove straight through to Gilway in Leveque's 1940 Cadillac. They made good time, with the two men taking turns at the wheel while Henri dozed in the back seat.

It was Sunday; the church bells were pealing away. All morning they passed the churchgoers in their Sabbath best on the roads.

It was the supper shift for Gilles at the hotel dining room. He came to the lobby and spread his hands in helplessness. The four men who had stayed at the hotel had checked out after breakfast. The other man, the fifth one, had eaten later.

By the time Gilles was free of the dining room and could look for the men and the trucks, they had disappeared. He had, however, discovered that the Americans had stored their trucks in the MacGregor barn overnight.

The barn was clean as a dog's tooth.

Leveque, after Gilles got the key from old man MacGregor, searched the barn without finding anything. Then he went outside and walked around the perimeter edges until he caught the scent of something strange. He squatted and reached under a low bush. His hand came away greasy. He sniffed the smear of dirt and recognized it. He had spent much time around weapons, and he knew that he had found the place where someone had dumped the wash from a weapons cleaning.

Another part. If the weapons had been bought, as he had assumed earlier, for use below the border, why were they being cleaned in Canada?

Since there was no way to learn which direction the Americans had taken, Henri decided to stay the night at the hotel in Gilway. As soon as he was settled in he placed a call to Montreal. All telegrams and phone calls from the Movement network were to be sifted and the important information passed on to him.

He did not believe that it would be a long wait.

The Movement's network was as dense as a spider's web. The flies would bumble against the web without knowing that it was there.

By a phone call he had shifted the center of the web. Now, instead of Montreal, it was located in Gilway.

It was only a matter of time before he felt the distant touch on the web. An hour or a day.

By Sunday, June 30, the major part of the construction in the second basement of the Sun Life Building in Montreal had been completed.

One drawback in the early planning sessions had been the acute shortage of steel. Contacted by the president of Sun Life, the engineers at Canadian Railways had located an abandoned spur near Quebec. A crew recovered 870 rails from that track. The steel was shipped to Bonaventure Station in Montreal and trucked the few blocks to the Sun Life Building.

Space for the construction work was limited in the second basement. That created another problem. The architect's estimate was that a million pounds of concrete would be needed for the vault walls. There wasn't, however, room for the mixing equipment in the basement. An experiment was suggested. Two huge compressors were set up on the Mansfield Street level at the rear of the building. Concrete was mixed there, and the compressors blew the mixture through large hoses into the basement where it was formed around the steel structure.

The Bank of Canada found a vault door. It was being fabricated in Ottawa for a bank in Toronto. In the name of the war effort, the finished door was diverted and shipped to Montreal.

In usual times two elevators connected the main lobby of the Sun Life Building with the third basement. One elevator was altered so that it would not go below the second basement. The other elevator was converted into an express that did not stop except at the lobby and the third basement.

As soon as the vault was completed, a team of specialists from the Bank of Canada arrived and installed a delicate alarm-and-detection system.

By June 30, a unit of Canadian Mounted Police guarded the lobby desk, the express elevator, and the third basement, twenty-four hours a day.

PART THREE

CHAPTER TWENTY ONE

The church bells welcomed them to Wingate Station.

They heard the tolling for more than half an hour before the two Mack Bulldogs eased over the low rise and the town was spread below.

Vic Franks drove the lead truck. Johnny sat in the middle of the cab. He leaned away to make room so Vic could shift gears.

Johnny pointed at the shoulder on the other side of the road. "Let's have a look."

"Here?"

"Here."

Vic swung the steering wheel and crossed the midline. He cut in front of the Bulldog Richard Betts drove and Betts hit his horn. "Damn you, Vic." He whipped past the first Bulldog and parked in a cloud of dust.

From the rise Wingate Station looked like a child's model of a small town.

The ribbon of black double tracks ran toward them from the curve of the horizon. That direction was east, Halifax and the coast.

As the tracks approached the town there was a flow of gray buildings, weathered and with the dull glint of windows, like the downslope movement of lava. The tilt toward the tracks formed the neck of a pipe. The tracks funneled through the pipe for a distance before it reached the white-frame train station with its black-slate roof.

From where they stood, the train station was on the left side of the tracks. On the right, across those double tracks, there were several large buildings that were probably warehouses. Behind their high frames there were even rows of streets with a pattern of small houses. The countryside and the green farmland began there and spread south.

The main part of Wingate Station, what there was of it, was on the side of the rails where the train depot was. The taller buildings crowded there, some with three and four stories, along with the shops and stores and cafés and perhaps a hotel or two. The spires and towers of four churches reached upward.

Beyond the center of town there was another cluster of homes and a peppering of trees, and a thick road broke out of the crowded mass and rammed its way north. It was a clean line beyond the town. This same road blurred in Wingate Station, it wobbled its way, and then it appeared on the other side of the train station. It crossed the tracks, was hidden by the warehouses for a time, and then it was free and heading directly south.

The double ribbon of tracks passed the station and squeezed through an identical pipe mouth as it headed west. When it was clear of town, the track bed began a slow incline, and the tracks passed below and within fifty yards of where the five of them stood beside the two Bulldogs.

"Toyland," Tom said.

"What population?" Richard Betts wanted to know.

"Eight or nine thousand," Johnny said. "Maybe ten on the high side."

"It could be your hometown," Vic Franks said to Richard Betts.

"Maybe," Betts said, "if I hadn't burned it down before I left for the Army."

"Peaceful-looking," Gunny said. "It could be half the towns in South Carolina."

Vic Franks said, "It ain't Detroit."

Tom mashed a cigarette on the sole of his shoe and field-stripped it. The tobacco fell in a stream, and he wadded the paper before he tossed it away. "What's the brick building by the depot? The one next to the warehouses?"

It was red brick, two or three floors high. There was a glint from the roof. It appeared to be a mass of window glass.

"Beats me," Johnny said.

"Another warehouse?"

"We'll check it."

"As long as it's not an Army barracks," Gunny said.

They returned to the trucks and followed the bells into town. The last few miles they bogged down in the churchgoing procession of trucks, old cars, and even horse-drawn wagons.

They planned the day over lunch at the Wingate Inn Hotel. The dining room was almost empty. Church services had just started, and the first of those diners didn't arrive until Johnny paid the bill and they were seated in a corner of the lobby.

The way out was the first concern. Tom Renssler and Vic Franks were to take their Bulldog and find the U.S. border and a way to cross it. They didn't want to attempt a crossing at the border station. Two truckloads of gold, several tons of it, wasn't likely to pass even a casual customs check.

Tom settled into the passenger seat and closed the sliding door. He made a note of the last three digits on the mileage meter: 649.

"Find the border, Vic."

"That all you want?" Vic put the Bulldog in gear. "I ought to be able to smell it from here."

The road they took through town cut across the tracks east of the train station. It angled past the fronts and then the sides of the warehouse buildings. A siding curled away from the main tracks there. The siding ran parallel with the road for a short distance and then it ended, swallowed up by a closed metal doorway. They were high doors, and they were the entranceway into the red-brick building Tom had noticed on the leg-stretch look at town.

Vic slowed down. Closer, the top third of the walls and most of the roof seemed to be glass.

"What the hell is it?"

Tom shrugged. He would have to leave that to Johnny and the others. Their afternoon was to be a slow, careful walk around Wingate Station.

The first few miles out of town the road was clogged with the churchgoers on their way home. A few minutes of passing cars and trucks and the Bulldog was free, in the clear.

"What's your guess? The mileage to the border?" Vic said.

"Somewhere around a hundred and fifty," Vic said.

Two hours and forty minutes later and 126 miles by the meter, and the road began to squeeze, grow narrow. Another mile or two and they saw the first sign. It pointed to the west, CANADA–UNITED STATES BORDER STATION.

Vic slowed the truck. The road was empty, nothing in front and nothing behind them. "Which way, Major?"

"Let's take a look at the border station."

Another ten miles by the meter and they reached a second sign. This time it pointed away from the main road. They passed the turnoff at a crawl. Tom had his full look at the border station. Down the narrow road there was a kind of gateway with facing booths.

It didn't look busy. The security between the borders wasn't that tight, anyway. The border was almost an invisible line as far as coming and going went. Maybe two or three people on duty there, just enough to check for contraband and screen out aliens.

A couple of miles past the border station turnoff, Tom said, "Let's picnic here."

Vic eased the Bulldog to the side of the road.

They got out and walked it, crossing the field and stopping about where they estimated the border line was. It was fairly flat land. It had been turned by the plow but not planted. The even rows had been smoothed by wind and rain. Obviously somebody had planned to seed it and changed his mind.

A slow 360° turn while they searched for houses. Nothing close by.

"There," Tom said. In the distance, on the American side, about half a mile away, a row of poles and black wire strung between them. "You ever see telephone lines that weren't by the side of a road?"

Vic shook his head. "I'll check the maps."

They returned to the truck. "It'll be dark the next time we're here," Tom said. "Find some markers."

Vic looked around. "I can find it."

They drove back toward Wingate Station. Dark thunderclouds rolled toward them as they turned north. A rainstorm was headed across the border into the States.

Betts left to watch the truck.

Gunny and Johnny set out on a block-by-block, house-by-house study of the town. First a door-to-door on the side of the street where the hotel was located. Then they crossed. They were halfway down the block when Gunny touched Johnny on the shoulder and pointed upward at a metal sign attached to the side of a building. The sign was above a narrow alley. At the dead end there was a low set of stairs and a small building. It was the police station.

"I'll have a look." Gunny left Johnny to have a smoke. He mounted the steps and swaggered inside. He was inside two or three minutes. When he rejoined Johnny he said, "Two." They moved away from the alley. "That's a guess. One desk. I'd say one cop on duty days and one night man."

"Just a guess?"

"There's a coffeepot on a hot plate. Two cups on the rack over it."

"Weapons?" Johnny said.

"Side arms. A locked case with two Winchesters in it. No shotguns I could see."

They angled across the street and passed the hotel again. Down a short street, and the train depot was straight ahead.

"You think they patrol?"

"I doubt it," Gunny said. "No car. Maybe a shop-door shake at night."

"We'll need to check it," Johnny said.

Gunny nodded.

They rounded the station and stopped on the platform. "My turn," Johnny said. "Might be a telegram for me."

"You arrange it with Harry?"

"The name's Jim Whit." He left Gunny on the platform and entered the station. Off to one side there was a cage with side-by-side windows. A gray-faced man was behind the ticket window. Johnny leaned in. "You got a telegram for Jim Whit?"

"Down there." The man indicated the other window.

Johnny turned with him and followed him. The man picked up a stack of telegrams and flipped through them. "You say Whit?"

"Yeah."

"You got one." The agent passed it through the window.

Johnny thanked him and carried the telegram outside before he opened it.

SHOULD BE TOMORROW. I WIRE ARRIVAL TIME. HARRY

He passed the telegram to Gunny. Gunny read it while they walked along the track bed. They crossed the tracks where the highway did. Here there was a switch and the metal flag. A siding butted against the main tracks and curled south. The rails ran between the warehouses and the road for about two hundred yards.

Gunny folded the telegram and passed it to Johnny. "Time's getting cut short."

"With this crew it might be the best thing could happen." Johnny stuffed the telegram in his hip pocket.

The siding ended abruptly. The high metal doors were closed and locked.

Gunny looked at the red-brick building. "The major's got a good eye. Glass up there and on the roof, just like he figured."

"I wish it wasn't Sunday. I'd like to see if it's being used."

"Used how?"

"I think it's a roundhouse. Where they do repairs on the engines."

"I can't see it matters," Gunny said.

"It would if they shunted those broke-down boxcars in here to work on them. Or just for storage."

"It's like a fort," Gunny said. "Except for all that glass up there."

"It could be a problem." Johnny turned and walked back toward town. "Bring Betts by later. We might have to plan to blow a few holes in the side of it."

"Soon as the major and Vic get back."

They reached the main tracks and took a turn to the east. They followed the tracks for half a mile or so and then turned north. It took another hour to box-step their way around Wingate Station.

The sky darkened above them. A scattering of heavy rain made them run for cover when they were still a block or so from the hotel.

Constable Lafitte didn't put all the parts together until about nine that night. He was on his first rounds, the quick circuit of the main business district that took exactly thirty-three minutes, when the heavy truck swung out of a side street. The taillights flickered as the truck headed north on the main road.

Lafitte shook the door in front of Poole's Café and stepped out of the doorway. Just then, the second truck, the twin to the first, turned in the same direction and went out of sight.

It clicked then. The two parts of it. There was the old American who came in the police station about lunchtime. His face had faded bruises on it. At the time, Lafitte had thought the bruises might be part of a birthmark. Had not his cousin, William, had such marks from the day of his birth until he died the year before?

The old American had asked about fishing. His eyes, now that Lafitte thought back on it, seemed more interested in the furnishings of the room rather than the answer he'd given.

And now the trucks.

The click of two objects running together. Now, if there was a third...

Halfway through his round he passed the hotel. Usually he passed it. Tonight he went inside and talked to the clerk. The clerk had gone to high school with him. Yes, Graham said, he had rented double rooms to the Americans.

He finished the rounds. He sat in the station, behind the single desk, and stared at the phone for another hour. It tempted him. Still, he knew that he would have trouble explaining a long-distance call.

He was ready to leave when the night man, Parsons, arrived at 10:05. He rushed out while Parsons stood at the hot plate and bitched because he had not made a fresh pot of coffee as he did most nights.

Lafitte did not have a phone of his own. The widow Jervis, who rented him a room, did, but there was no privacy there because the phone was in her bedroom.

He stopped at his room long enough to pick up the Movement number in Montreal. Then he walked the two miles outside of town to the Berger farm.

The Berger dog wanted to take off one of his legs. Old man Berger had to get out of bed and chain the dog before Lafitte could cross the backyard to the kitchen.

"It is important," Lafitte said. "It is the business of the Movement."

"It had better be important," the old man said.

It took time for the operator to place the call to Montreal, and the charges had to be reversed. Otherwise, old man Berger would not allow the call.

The man at the other end of the line took his message. He wanted details before he seemed satisfied. Finally, he said that a Mr. Leveque would be in touch with him the next day.

It was after midnight before Lafitte got to bed. He was tired, and his boots were muddy, and he had a bad headache.

He fell asleep wondering what the hell it was all about.

CHAPTER TWENTY TWO

The train crew huddled over their eggshell cups of rum at five that afternoon when Harry entered Toy's.

Randy was telling some long and probably dirty story to Cody. He broke off long enough to nod at Harry, but he didn't seem to want to leave the table where he was. Clark was at the outer edge of the group. He got Harry's look and brought his cup of rum to the table Harry picked. He arrived about the same time the waiter brought Harry's first rum of the day.

Clark pulled his chair close and leaned across the table toward Harry. "It's tomorrow for sure."

"Cody say so?"

Clark nodded. "There's an early call in the morning. They're to be at the yard at four A.M. Word is they're putting together fifteen boxcars, three coaches, and a caboose."

Harry marked that in his mind. Coaches meant troops, guards. He looked across the table and saw Clark's mouth moving, as if he had more to say and didn't know how to put it. "Yeah?"

"It's funny about those coaches and the caboose. Most of the time they wouldn't be part of the morning orders. I mean, they wouldn't be on the work sheet. The work sheet would show the fifteen boxes. Later, after they were loaded and ready to move, the train would pass through the yard and pick up the coaches and the caboose."

"What does it mean?"

"You see the security around the piers?"

"Yeah."

"I think, once the train's assembled, they haul it behind those fences and it stays there until they're ready to redball it west. No stopping to pick up coaches, no stopping for a caboose, no stopping for anything."

"Two things," Harry said.

"What?"

"You and Randy ask around the crew. See if you can find out when the train leaves the piers. Cody might know."

"All right."

"And the two young guys you were drinking with yesterday."

"Phillips and Mass?"

"Those two," Harry said. "Talk to them about a couple of drinks later tonight."

"Ought to be easy."

"Do it," Harry said.

"It's good as done."

Harry reached deep in his pocket. "How are the two of you fixed for money?"

"Getting short."

Harry peeled away a couple of tens. He passed them across the table to Clark. "That'll hold you until I see you back at the boarding house." He tipped the cup of rum and pushed back his chair. "Got some business." He waved at the train crew and dropped a dollar on the table for the waiter.

Harry wandered around in the mazes and the stews.

It was still light. None of the brothels, the low-rent ones, were open yet. Not that he was interested in that kind of woman. If he wanted a woman, it would be the kind Mr. Arkman had at the apartment now and then. The sweet-cream ones, clean and young, and they acted like ladies.

No, he was interested in the blind pigs, the illegal bars. And not just any one of those. It had to be the right one. A rough place with some of the fur still on it.

Too early, dammit. It would have been easier around midnight. Timing was a factor. He couldn't wait that long. What he wanted he needed now. Half an hour ago.

The second blind pig he visited was the right scum world. The bottom. It cost him a dollar, paid to a bum in the street, to get directions to it. And once he found it, up two flights of stairs in a slum that smelled of overflowed toilets or no toilets at all, the man on the door didn't want to let him inside. Maybe he looked too neat and clean. Harry yelled that he was a tourist, a damn American tourist, until the bouncer gave up and waved him in.

A quick look around and he thought he'd found the right one. It was one large room with a makeshift bar off to one side. Rough planks over sawhorse frames, a shelf behind the bar that held glasses and a few bottles of clear liquid: gin, from the labels. There was a large wooden keg with a tap. Probably the rum.

Benches along the walls. No tables. The floor pocked with cigarette burns and littered with last night's trash.

Two British sailors slumped against one wall. Either it was an early start or a drunk that was still running from the day before.

"What's yours, gov?" The bartender was a man about fifty. He needed a shave, and there was a thumb missing from his right hand. He wore a dingy white shirt with the cuffs rolled up to his elbows.

"What's the choice?"

"Gin and rum."

"Rum," Harry said.

The bartender held a glass under the keg tap and drew a shot by some measure in his mind. He placed the drink on the plank bar and scooped up the dollar Harry put there. He didn't offer change.

Harry picked a hair from the rim of the glass and had a swallow. It was pure fire all the way down.

"American, huh?"

"That's right. I'm taking a summer vacation."

"Sight-seeing the war, huh?"

"Not exactly," Harry said.

"You'd be surprised how many of the tourists are," the bartender said.

"They'll have their own war soon enough."

"You see it that way?"

Harry nodded. He finished his shot and tapped it on the bar.

"Another?"

"One won't kill the germs," Harry said.

The twenty-dollar bill was in his front-left pocket, apart from the main wad of cash. The bartender placed the glass on the bar and looked at the twenty when Harry dropped it next to his glass.

The bartender picked up the bill and stared at it. "This the smallest you got?"

"Afraid it is."

"I can't change it yet."

"Who said I wanted change?" Harry lifted his glass. "Have a drink with me. What's your name?"

"Call me Bill." The bartender poured himself a shot of the gin. He nodded at Harry and put it back in one swallow.

"You make that yourself, Bill?"

"Don't everybody? What else is a tub for?" Bill looked at his empty glass and waited. The twenty was still in his hand.

"I've got a sick hunting dog, Bill."

"Is that right?"

"I think I'm going to have to put him away. Poor old Shep."

Bill shook his head, a mock sympathy without any real belief in the story.

"I think I'd like to knock him out first, you know."

"Tender feelings," Bill said.

"Why, Shep is almost part of the family," Harry said. "If I knocked him out, he wouldn't be looking at me when I do it."

"How're you planning to do it?"

"Cut his throat," Harry said.

Bill nodded as if that didn't seem at all remarkable.

"Or shoot him."

"And you want to knock him out first?"

"I think I have to," Harry said.

Bill stared at him for a long moment. Then, decided, he stuffed the twenty in his trouser pocket. "Watch the bar a second for me." He ducked under the bar and headed for a door at the rear of the room. The door was open for a brief moment, and Harry saw the bed and a couple of chairs.

Bill returned a couple of minutes later. His left hand was closed over something. Harry finished his drink while Bill ducked under the bar and walked down to face him.

Bill held out the closed fist, the knuckles up. Harry put out his open palm. Bill dropped a small bottle into his hand. "Another drink?"

Harry shook his head. He looked down into his hand. It was a small medicine bottle with an eyedropper cap. "What's the dose?"

"For a dog like Shep, I wouldn't know," Bill said. "For a man, it takes one eyedropperful."

"Half that much for Shep," Harry said.

Bill nodded. The hard eyes read Harry.

It was dark by the time Harry reached the boardinghouse.

It was drunk out. Rip-roaring and piss-in-the-streets drunk.

It was wet, too. Raining and miserable in the streets. All the dead scents seemed to be revived by the dampness. Not even the smell of the sea, the freshness of that, could reach those dark corners of the stews.

Phillips and Mass were from the Maritimes, and they drank like they'd got a taste for it from the tit. And they knew places that the Gipsons never would have found. Bars as small as an outhouse or as large as a barn.

Of the two, Clark felt closer to Andy Phillips. They were about the same age, and they'd both been born and brought up dirt-poor or worse. They'd talked some about religion, too. Andy went to church every Sunday when he didn't work, and when he had to work he went to evening services.

There was one more bond as well. Andy had a sister, Susan. He talked about her all the time. Susan was seventeen and she was plain, according to Andy, but when he brought out the photograph, Clark decided that she wasn't plain at all. She had pale skin, and her hair was long and black, and Clark thought she was about the most beautiful girl he'd ever seen.

It seemed to Clark, if the Lord got past what happened the other night, if the Lord had tested him and the Call was going to come, that he would need a wife. Nobody trusted a preacher if he was not married. One look at her picture and Clark began daydreaming. His own church, and him married to Susan, and with Andy, when it happened, his good friend and his brother-in-law.

And Andy said he thought that Susan would like Clark. "We're alike, Susan and me. She likes people I like."

Bob Mass was an odd one for Andy to pair up with. Bob was every bit as hard and tough as Randy was. That kind of person. And, to tell the truth, Andy didn't have the excuse that Clark did. Bob wasn't Andy's brother. He didn't have to carry that burden.

Maybe it was the young man who looked up to the older man. Something like that.

All evening Randy and Bob huddled over their drinks. They were talking big, and half of it was lies. Clark and Andy had their own conversation. The drinking pace was different, too. Randy was drinking two to Clark's one, and it was about the same way with Bob and Andy.

And then it was 12:20. Cody had told the crew it was a special shift and he didn't want anybody staying out after eleven. The deadline didn't seem to bother Bob. He said he could work one day without sleep. Andy was the one with the responsible streak. He kept mentioning how early 3:00 A.M. was when you hadn't even had an hour or two of sleep.

The fuss might have lasted another hour except for Randy. He smothered a huge yawn and said that Andy was one hundred percent right. It wasn't fair for him and Clark to keep working-men out late when they had a hard day coming up.

"But I want another drink," Bob said.

"That's easy," Randy said. "We'll get us a bottle to nip from on the way back."

Randy left the table and leaned across the bar to speak to one of the bartenders. The bartender pointed toward the door and said a few words. Randy nodded. On his way past the table he gave Bob a lazy wink. "Good as done."

Randy reached the door to the hallway before the panic hit Clark. All the drinking he'd done must have fogged his mind. That wasn't the way they'd planned it. Harry didn't trust Randy, and he'd entrusted the bottle of knockout drops to Clark. "I wouldn't trust you to piss on a fire," was what Harry had said to Randy.

Clark pushed back his chair. Bob and Andy stared at him. "I'd better make sure he's got enough money," Clark explained.

He caught Randy in the hallway. "I'll buy the bottle."

Randy gave him an insolent smile. "Where you going to buy it?"

Clark looked back toward the blind pig. He realized he didn't know where the bootleg shop was. "But I've got to doctor it the way Harry said." He reached in his pocket and pulled out the small bottle.

"I can do it," Randy said.

"Harry said..."

"I know what Harry said." Randy put out a hand and grabbed the knockout drops from Clark's open palm. "Screw what Harry said." He turned and started down the hall.

"I'll go with you."

"You better go back and keep them company. First thing you know they'll come looking for us."

Clark stopped and looked toward the bar. It was like Randy to be stubborn. Harry had made him mad, and he had got it into his head to doctor the rum come hell or high water. It was his way of getting back at Harry.

"Go on," Randy said.

Randy waited until Clark entered the bar. Then he went looking for the rum. The bartender's directions took him down the hall six doors to the left. An old woman there, in a room the size of a broom closet, sold him two pints of rum at five dollars a pint. He stuffed one bottle in his coat pocket and carried the other.

In the dim hallway, before he returned to the blind pig, he used a fingernail to tear away the top right-hand corner of the label. He uncapped it and took a swallow. That done, he placed the bottle on the floor and squatted over. it. He tried to doctor the rum the way he had heard Harry tell Clark it was supposed to be done. It was too much trouble to measure the drops and he was afraid somebody might come out of the bar and see him doing it. Finally he stood and held the rum bottle in one hand and the medicine bottle of knockout drops in the other. He poured in half the drops, and he should have stopped there. But he got to thinking. If half the knockout drops would do it in minutes, then the whole bottle would do it twice as fast. It made such good sense that he poured the rest of the drops from the medicine bottle in the rum. He capped it and gave it a shake to make sure it got spread around.

On the way out of the building Randy fell behind a few steps with Clark. He explained it. No drinking from the bottle with the torn corner. You could pretend but no swallowing. And, when he could, Randy would switch bottles. They could drink then.

"It's not going to hurt them?"

"Naw," Randy said. "I had a Mickey myself once in New Orleans. All it gave me was a rotten headache."

Hooting and hollering, that's how it was in the wet streets. The rain had cleared some. A light drizzle now, just enough to soak a man through.

Staggering and dancing. Now and then they'd step into a doorway and point the rum bottle toward the sky.

Two blocks and half the bottle of doctored rum, and Andy said he didn't feel good. Bob leaned against a wet building front and said the rum was getting to him too.

Randy took that chance to switch the bottles. He said, "It is all that exercise you had," and he lifted the bottle and let the rum pour down his throat. "Or it's that you two are half-assed."

"You say." Mass grabbed the bottle, and the drinking started up again. The third block, near an alley, Andy grabbed his stomach and fell down. Bob leaned over him and lost his balance and dropped to his knees. His head landed on Andy's chest.

Both were out cold.

Randy looked down the street and then behind him. Nobody coming in either direction. He grabbed Bob Mass under the arms. "You get Andy." They dragged them down the alley and left them propped against a wall under a flight of stairs.

Clark looked at Andy. "You're sure they're all right?"

"They're horses," Randy said. He uncapped the doped rum and poured it into a mud puddle. He tossed the bottle away.

At 3:00 A.M. Cody came down the hall and pushed the door open without knocking. He shook Randy until he was awake.

"You went off with Bob and Andy last night?"

Randy blinked at him. "Last night? Sure."

"Where'd you see them last?"

"Some bar or other," Randy said.

"When was that?"

"About midnight. We left, but they said they wanted one more drink."

"They didn't make it," Cody said.

Randy swung his legs over the side of the bunk. He reached up and gave Clark's shoulder a hard push. "Get up."

"Huh?"

Randy stepped into his trousers. He was buttoning his shirt when Cody said, "You going looking for them?"

"I wouldn't know where to look," Randy said. He sat on the bunk and pulled his shoes toward him. "You're short men. You need us, and we'll work the shift for you."

Cody hesitated. "I don't know how I can pay you."

"You've been friends," Randy said. "We'll take our pay in drinks at Toy's."

"You don't mind?"

"Naw. You want us?"

Cody nodded.

Randy gave Clark's mattress another shake. "Up, Clark."

Clark jumped down and began to dress, yawning the whole time. It had been a short night's sleep.

CHAPTER TWENTY THREE

Around 0500 hours on the morning of Monday, July 1, a gray shadow of land was sighted from H.M.S. *Emerald*. The Nova Scotia coastline was dead ahead.

Duncan MacTaggart, his soiled raincoat flapping around him like black wings, was on deck when the *Emerald* passed the protective boom and entered the harbor at 0649 hours.

By 0720 the cruiser was secured to Pier 23, the Halifax Ocean Terminal. Already in place, the assembled train waited on the tracks that ran the length of the pier. The engine that had backed the train into place at 6:00 A.M. was still attached. From the deck of the ship, while he watched the docking crew, MacTaggart counted the units of the train. Fifteen boxcars, three coaches, and a caboose.

Satisfied, he went below and collected his gear.

When the gangplank was in place, MacTaggart went ashore and stored his bag and his raincoat in the last day coach, the one nearest the caboose. Clipboard under his arm, he walked past the day coaches and stood in front of the first of the boxcars.

At 0745 a company of Royal Canadian Navy Cadets marched smartly into view. Within minutes the unloading began.

The lights burned late behind blackout curtains in the Prime Minister's bedroom at 10 Downing Street.

It was a harrowing time for Churchill, a night for long thoughts and a decision.

What occupied the Prime Minister this night and for the days since the surrender of France was the French fleet. It was the nightmare come true. Since the early days of June, the War Cabinet had sought assurances from the French admirals that the fleet would not be turned over to the Germans.

Now, most of the French ships were berthed in North Africa, at Oran and Mers-el-Kebir. A decision had to be made.

It was the P.M.'s determination, with the backing of the War Cabinet, that not one French ship of the line was to fall into German control.

Churchill plotted the options that he could offer the French admirals. The French pride, damaged by defeat and surrender, had suddenly hardened. All negotiations had come to nothing. The French delayed, marked time, and the outcome did not look promising.

It was an impasse. The French felt honor-bound to resist all British pressure. The British had to press for a solution before time ran out.

The courier from the Admiralty arrived at 10 Downing Street a few minutes after 2:00 A.M. The locked metal dispatch case was signed for and taken directly to the Prime Minister's bedroom.

Churchill sat up in his bed, a tattered robe wrapped around him. One of his huge cigars, unlit and with the end chewed, rested in a dish on the night table beside the bed. An untouched glass of brandy completed the late-night still life.

Churchill read the message. It was the first good news of the day.

In regard to your continuing concern: we respectfully submit that His Majesty's Ship *Emerald* entered Halifax, Nova Scotia, harbour at 0649 hours 1/7/40.

Before the Prime Minister returned to the problem of the French fleet he scribbled a note.

Prepare new Salt Fish shipment.
Alert Admiralty, Bank of England.

By lunch break, noon, MacTaggart figured that a third of the consignment had been unloaded. The paper shipment—the stocks and bonds—had been packed into the first three freight cars, the ones at the caboose and day-coach end of the train.

The Royal Canadian Navy Cadets had larked through those, tossing them from hand to hand, down the pier and up and into the boxcars.

The first of the gold crates changed that. The groans sounded and the officer in charge moved down the line saying, "Watch your toes, men." Even with the warning, a dropped case here and there, and young men limped away from the loading line.

When lunch call came one boxcar was only partly filled with the gold crates. One hundred cases by MacTaggart's clipboard count. He sat in that open boxcar doorway. A young cadet brought him a sandwich, an apple, and a mug of hot tea from their rations.

The sandwich was tinned beef with butter spread on one slice of the thick white bread.

Clark was almost useless when it came to doing much of anything that took guts. First of all, he'd been worrying all morning about that Andy Phillips kid. Had they given him too much of the knockout drops? Was Randy sure that Andy had been breathing when they left him in the alley? All that mewing like a goddam baby. When, to tell the truth, it didn't matter a rat's ass one way or the other.

He'd worked well putting the train together. No doubt about that. Clark had been railroading almost as long as Randy had. He knew enough not to lose his head on a low bridge, and one near miss uncoupling the air hose years back, and now he did it by the book.

But there was no way around it that he was chicken. He knew what had to be done and instead of doing it, he was standing around, hands in his pockets, and looking punk, while he sweated the rum from last night.

It wasn't to say that it was easy. Back in the train yard, when they'd been putting it together, it would have been easy. They could have emptied every fucking hotbox in the yard. No questions asked, and that was for damned sure. But that wasn't the way it had to be. Not according to Harry. Harry said they had to pick and choose. Otherwise, they'd have the whole damned train laid up at Wingate Station and the whole Canadian Army would be camped around it in layers.

No, it had to be done at the dock.

The plan was to wait until the boxcars were loaded. Then he'd know which ones held the gold and which held the paper shit. You mess up those boxes early, Harry said, and we might end up with fighting a war over paper not worth wiping our asses with.

All the morning, while the crates and boxes were being put over the side of the ship and humped into the boxes, he and Clark had wandered up and down the pier with oil cans. Cody and most of the rest of the crew had found a coffee urn in one of the watch shacks. They were off there, taking it easy and waiting until the boxes were loaded and sealed.

There was a lot you could learn if you used your eyes. Take the difference in the way the boxes of paper were handled. Tossing and throwing them like they had feathers in them. And then the gold: the grunting and sweating and the rigid backs—that told the story.

One time Randy followed one of the Navy cadets into the latrine.

"Getting wore down?" Randy asked from a place a few feet down the trough.

"I do believe I've broken something," the cadet said.

"Heavy?"

"Those boxes might weight ten stone."

"Huh?"

"A hundred and forty pounds." The cadet buttoned up. "It might be less. Perhaps a hundred and twenty pounds."

"It looks like tons," Randy said.

"Over two thousand cases." The cadet headed for the door. He took a ragged breath. "I don't know if I'll last the day."

Randy followed him back to the train. The cadet rubbed at the small of his back with both hands.

They'd tailed the train onto the pier. After the caboose, the next three cars were day coaches. Next to the passenger cars, the first three boxcars were loaded with the paper cargo. That meant that all the other boxcars, all twelve of them, would be transporting the gold bullion.

Randy put Clark to watching the loading of one car. From the beginning until they closed the door and locked it. "Two hundred cases exactly," Clark said.

He wasn't good at math. Two hundred times one hundred and twenty... that equals... no, forget that. Two hundred times one hundred, just to keep it simple. Now, say one ounce is worth thirty-two dollars. Sixteen times thirty-two dollars times twenty thousand and you've got...

He gave it up. Past him. But he damned well knew that it was a hell of a lot.

Randy figured the best time would be the lunch break. Everybody would be off eating. Nobody would be around except maybe some guards. None of them would think anything about a couple of men from the train crew going on with their work.

He gave them ten minutes. Time enough to leave the train and line up at the canteen where the food was being served. Time to sprawl around in the sun.

He nodded at Clark. They walked down the train. It was then he noticed that Clark was scared yellow.

"Lots of soldiers here," he said.

"And not one of them," Randy said, "knows a train from a cat's puckered ass." He put a hand on Clark's shoulder. "Hold it together, boy. Twenty, thirty minutes, and we've got it done."

"All right." But Clark didn't sound sure.

"Harry said three boxcars."

"That's a lot," Clark said.

"Not for the Gipson boys." He grinned at Clark. "Can you whistle 'Dixie'?"

"Sure."

"That's all you got to do. You got an oil can. You do some oiling. I go under and mess with the hotboxes. Somebody comes you whistle. You do that?"

"Sure," Clark said.

Make it easy for them, he thought. He counted the three coaches, then the three boxes that held the paper. Then he stopped next to the seventh car. A nod at Clark, and he skinned under. Close fit. Still hot under there, and it had a oil stink to it.

Ten minutes. It took that long, working as fast as he could. Cover off, pull the cotton wadding out. Spaces in the pier below the tracks. Shove the cotton waste through those openings. Out to sea. Close the cover.

Out in the fresh air. "That was pie easy," he said to Clark.

Clark tipped his head toward the main part of the train. "A man's watching over there."

"Screw him."

They reached the eighth car. Before Randy ducked under he stopped and had his look at the man Clark had noticed. Long legs hung over the side of the box. He was seated in an open doorway, the tenth car over.

"Pucker up," Randy said and then he ducked under the boxcar.

Then he was stretched out on the crossties. The cover didn't want to give. One slot ruined. He hammered at it and he felt it coming when he heard Clark whistle. It wasn't exactly "Dixie." It had gaps and holes, but it was close enough.

"What're you doing down there?"

The cover fell away.

The voice had a kind of burr to it. Not quite English. Something else.

Randy turned his head. The man squatted there, his head to the side so that he could see under the train. Gray hair, a long serious face.

"Inspecting," Randy said. He turned away from the man. All right, so he'd check this one. He spent a couple of minutes repositioning the cotton wadding. That ought to bore the hell out of him.

He turned and looked. The man was still there.

"What does it do?" the man asked.

"You know trains?"

"No."

"It takes too long to explain." Randy fitted the cover and fastened it in place.

He crawled out. The man backed away. He was a tall one. Over six feet and about as big as a tree. Randy nodded at Clark and headed for the ninth box. The man followed. He was munching on an apple.

The man remained with them. He watched while Randy checked the ninth car. There the whole time, so that Randy had to give it up. It wasn't possible. Damn that man anyway, whoever he was.

He snaked his way from under the box and stood dusting himself off. Twenty thousand pounds of gold. It would have to be enough. "Ready for lunch?" he said to Clark.

"That all you're inspecting?" The man finished the apple and tossed the core over the edge of the pier.

"Got to leave a few for the rest of the crew," Randy said.

He and Clark went off at a fast walk. The tall man followed them as far as the tenth car. When Randy looked over his shoulder the man was seated in the boxcar doorway once more.

Henri Leveque was up early that morning. The bed in the hotel room had been lumpy and he had not slept well. There was no one moving in the hallway. He bathed in the bathroom down the hall and dressed at his careful pace. On the way toward the stairwell he stopped long enough to awaken Jean and Pierre. Idiots. They could sleep anywhere.

He had the dining room to himself. The waiter, Gilles, hovered over him like he was royalty. The attention did little to improve the coarse food, the overcooked eggs, the side order of hashed brown potatoes that he had not ordered.

Still, Gilles had his uses. Over his second cup of coffee, Henri wrote out the Movement's number in Montreal. Gilles carried it to the desk clerk who put the call through. Five minutes later, about the time Jean and Pierre appeared at the table, the Gilway operator had placed the call.

Henri took the call at the only phone, the one at the desk. In Montreal the phone watch had not been busy. There had been two calls. One placed the Americans in a suburb of Ottawa. The other, from a Constable Lafitte, had located them in a town to the east of Gilway. The latter was more likely, and Henri made a note before he ended the conversation.

"I will call early in the afternoon and give you a number where I can be reached in Wingate Station. The Ottawa information is probably mistaken. I will know more in perhaps three hours."

He returned to the dining room. He sipped a second and a third morning coffee while Jean and Pierre had their usual huge breakfasts. His obvious impatience hurried both of them into indigestion.

By noon the 1940 Cadillac was parked in front of the Wingate Inn Hotel.

Lafitte arrived at the head of the alley that led to the police station at 12:10. Jean pushed away from the alley wall where he'd been waiting for a few minutes.

"Lafitte?"

Lafitte faced him and waited.

"You made a call to Montreal?"

"Yes."

"We are at the café beside the hotel."

"Give me five minutes," Lafitte said.

Lafitte entered the police station. The night man, Parsons, yawned and looked up at the wall clock. It was his way of telling Lafitte that he was late again.

Lafitte ignored him and Parsons left. As soon as the door closed behind him, Lafitte reached the town operator and asked that any calls for him be shifted to the coffee shop.

"Where are they?"

"I will have to look around town," Lafitte said.

"Do it now," Henri Leveque said.

Lafitte looked down at his fresh cup of coffee and his breakfast, a hot pastry with butter melting on it. "Now?"

"Now," Henri said.

Lafitte returned after fifteen minutes. There was a touch of anger in the way he ignored the three men at the table and bought a cup of coffee before he approached the table. Seated, his eyes swept the surface of the cloth, and he found his empty pastry saucer in front of Jean.

"The two trucks are parked in a lot north of town," he said.

"And the Americans?"

"One is with the trucks. The old one with the bruises on his face."

"And the others?" Leveque said.

"They are probably at the hotel," Lafitte said.

Henri dropped his crumpled napkin on the table and pushed back his chair. "We will contact you later."

They left Constable Lafitte to finish his coffee and stare at his empty pastry plate.

At the Wingate Inn Hotel, Henri registered for two rooms, one for himself and a double for the men with him. The clerk, an old man with sour breath, seemed the helpful kind.

"Americans? Yes, five of them registered yesterday."

"I met a group in Gilway," Henri said. "I think those Americans said they were coming here."

The clerk flipped back a page in the register. "A Mr. Ross? A Mr. Whit?"

Henri shook his head. "I don't recall their names." He looked at the room keys in his hand. "Perhaps they are not the same men. Are they still registered today?"

"Yes, sir. They have Rooms Two-fourteen, Two-fifteen, and Two-sixteen."

Jean and Pierre entered the lobby. They carried the luggage from the Cadillac.

"I will stop by and see if they are the ones," Henri said.

The clerk touched the pigeonholes where the keys were stored. "They are not in their rooms now," he said. "They had breakfast and went out."

"It doesn't matter," Henri said. He passed the keys to Jean. To the clerk he said, "You have a nice town here."

The clerk looked down at the final entry in the hotel register. "But not as nice as Montreal," he said.

CHAPTER TWENTY FOUR

arry Churchman left the rooming house around ten that morning. He felt rested. He'd had extra hours of sleep after the early-morning train-yard crew left and took the Gipsons with them.

It was a gray morning. The rain from the night before pooled here and there. The cobblestone streets were slick and treacherous. The wind was from the west, each gust like a double handful of moisture. It would rain again by night.

He had breakfast and returned to the rooming house. His bag was packed. He took a few minutes to stuff the Gipsons' belongings in their bags.

Downstairs, at the office, he paid what was owed and thanked the old couple who owned the rooming house. He carried the three bags outside and waited on the curb for half an hour before a cruising taxi passed.

The taxi dropped him at the train-station entrance below the Nova Scotian Hotel. He waited in a line and found that the next local train that passed through Wingate Station left Halifax about five that afternoon. He bought three coach tickets and checked the luggage in the baggage room.

It was going to be a long wait. And he worried about the Gipsons. Damn them. He'd trade the both of them for one railroad man who didn't have rocks in his head.

❧   ❧   ❧

The unloading of the *Emerald* continued through the late afternoon. At 1630, the starboard-watch section was relieved and given leave until 0700 the next morning. The port section took over and worked the cargo until 1800 hours.

At that point twelve of the boxcars had been filled to the weight limits, locked, and sealed. The Canadian Navy cadets were dragging, still game, but arm and back weary. And they were losing the light. Dark rain clouds were blowing in from the west.

MacTaggart boarded the *Emerald* and talked with the cargo officer. They decided to strike the work party for the day. The last of the cargo could be finished with an early start the next morning.

MacTaggart returned to the pier. The working party was dismissed and gave a weak cheer before the officer in charge called them to attention and marched them away. Within minutes the watch was posted.

Leg weary himself, MacTaggart found his bag in the end day coach. It looked like he'd have it to himself for the night. The bank officials, as soon as the unloading was under way, had been taken to town and put up at the Carleton Hotel.

He was on the pier, bag in hand, and trying to decide where the closest shower or bath was, when he heard his name called. The shout was from the direction of the *Emerald*. He headed that way and recognized young Sub-Lieutenant Carr at the head of the gangplank.

"Mr. MacTaggart."

"Mr. Carr."

"Does a wash and supper on us interest you?"

"It's got a sweet sound."

Mr. Carr caught his elbow as he stepped from the gangplank to the deck of the ship. "Do you ever get leave like an ordinary man?"

MacTaggart grinned. "In two or three days," he said.

At half-past seven, washed and shaved and with a hot meal in him, MacTaggart returned to the day coach and settled in for the night.

Richard Betts made his second trip to the area of the train depot in Wingate Station late that afternoon. On the first visit, the one the day before, he hadn't been sure. That had been Sunday, and the large brick building on the other side of the tracks had been locked tight as a bank. This time, on Monday, he had his look inside. The high metal doors weren't completely open, but the crack allowed him a brief sight down the length of it.

It was a roundhouse.

And that was another problem.

Richard couldn't see that much through the opening, so he walked around the building. It was mainly brick, but there was a deep stone foundation. And it had been built when there wasn't a shortage of steel. Thick steel beams formed the framework and the hooded ceiling that capped the building. The weakness, if there were one, would be in the huge metal doors. There was no way you could brace them so they could withstand an explosive charge.

That decision made, Betts walked back along the track to the depot. He sat on an outside bench and smoked cigarettes and considered the options. What kind of charge; how many sticks; exploded by fuse or black box?

The last telegram from Harry Churchman hadn't been exact about the time when he and the Gipsons would arrive. Until they stepped off a westbound train the crew was taking turns on two-hour watches at the station.

The tarp was spread in the back of one of the Bulldogs. To one side of it were the five Thompsons, cleaned and with the drums attached. The shotguns, in a line, took up the rest of the tarp.

Gunny lifted the bottom of the canvas where it almost touched the ground and covered the weapons.

"Good job," Captain Whitman said.

"We got to test-fire them," Gunny said.

"Where?"

"The woods somewhere," Gunny said.

Johnny shook his head. "Too risky."

Tom Renssler dropped the cover on the case of grenades. He walked over and stood between them. "They in working order as far as you can tell?"

"They got all the parts," Gunny said. "That ain't the same as being sure you'll get some rounds out of them when the time comes."

"Dry fire?" Johnny said.

"I wouldn't want to depend on it meaning anything."

Johnny looked at Tom. "What do you think?"

"You test-fire five Thompsons around here, and we'll have the whole Mounted Police coming at us on the run."

"You heard him." Johnny spread his hands. "It can't be helped, Gunny."

"This is some fucking Army." Gunny walked away.

The captain and the major left for the hotel. Gunny returned to the Bulldog where the tarp was. Vic Franks followed him and stood at his elbow.

"There ain't no way I'm going to risk my ass with a weapon that ain't been fired."

"I'm with you, Gunny."

Gunny patted the shapes under the tarp.

"When, Gunny?"

"Later. When Harry and the Gipsons get here. I taught Harry well. What I know, he knows."

"Screwed-up mess," Vic said.

"It's the only mess we've got. And it beats sitting all day on a front porch."

It was dark in the hotel room. Room 214 was on the front side of the hotel, and it overlooked the main street.

Tom reached in and found the light switch. He flipped it upward. Nothing happened. Behind him, Johnny Whitman said, "What the hell...?"

The smell reached both of them at the same time. It was a flower sweetness like perfume. "Must be some mistake." Tom stepped away and pulled the door to him so that he could check the room number on it.

Henri Leveque stirred in the chair in front of the window. The roll shade was pulled all the way down to the window ledge. "It is the correct room," he said. "You have visitors."

Next to him and to his left, Jean heard his cue and reached under the lampshade and gave the button switch a twist and stepped away.

Johnny pushed past Tom. "Who the hell are you?"

"Names do not matter," Henri said. "There is, however, another concern. There is a matter of money owed to us."

"For what?" Johnny looked over his shoulder at Tom. There was a question on his face.

"The arms," Henri said. He lifted a hand and pointed at the open door behind them. "Since this is a private business, I would prefer that it not be carried out in public."

Tom pushed the door. It closed with a slap.

Henri smiled. "See how much better that is?"

"I don't see any difference at all," Johnny said.

"I think Gunny had some business with him," Tom said. "The way I heard it from him you broke whatever agreement there was."

"I broke no agreement," Henri said. His head turned slowly until he was staring at Jean. "Are these two of the group?"

"No," Jean said.

Henri nodded, as if to himself. "I broke no agreement. My … associates may have gone beyond the limits I placed on them. I could argue that it was in your interest as well as mine."

"Dogshit," Johnny said. "Tom, what did Gunny say we still owe these birds?"

"A thousand, I think."

"It was eleven hundred." Henri's face was composed and even.

"Cheap at that price," Johnny reached into his hip pocket and brought out a wad of bills. He counted off eleven of the hundreds and replaced the rest of the wad in the pocket and buttoned it. While he moved across the room, he fanned the bills and did a final count. "That ought to do it."

Henri took the bills and folded them. He put them in his shirt pocket without counting them.

"Don't let us keep you from anywhere you're supposed to be." Johnny dipped his head at Tom. "That is all we owe them, right?"

"I believe our business is not yet done."

"That's your opinion," Johnny said, "and you're welcome to it out in the hallway or down in the lobby." As he spoke he leaned forward. His right hand reached for the lapel of Henri's jacket. "Here in my room …"

Jean moved away from the lamp table. "You are not to touch him."

"Is that right?" He didn't appear to pay any attention to Jean. His right hand touched the lapel and brushed at it. "You leaving on your own or …?"

"I told you …" Jean began.

Johnny turned. The back of his right hand, only partly closed, struck the little man across the face. The full weight of Johnny's body wasn't behind it. But there was enough force to flatten Jean,

Even stunned, Jean curled forward. He was on all fours, shaking his head to clear it, when Johnny put out a shoe and planted it on top of Jean's right hand.

"Stay there. You move and I'll kick your brains out." He stared at Jean long enough to be certain the little man believed him. He turned to Henri. "Are you leaving?"

"Hospitality seems to be a custom of the past." Henri moved his hands slowly forward and gripped the arms of the chair. He pulled himself to his feet. "But no matter about that. I will turn the other cheek. I will still give you some advice if you will be kind enough to listen to it."

"Do your talking on the way to the door." Johnny watched Henri walk past him. Beyond Henri's shoulder he dipped his head at Tom, who gave the doorknob a twist and jerked it open.

"The 1928s. You know the ones I mean?"

"I know." Johnny lifted the shoe from Jean's hand. "You too, buster. Out."

Jean used the arm of the chair to pull himself to his feet. His bottom lip was beginning to puff.

"They're stolen." Henri stopped at the doorway.

"I figured as much," Johnny said. "Unless you made them yourself."

"Two Canadian Army soldiers were killed during that theft."

"You know a lot about it." Johnny gave Jean a push that headed him toward the open door. "Thanks for the information."

"You might wish to think that it is information." Henri turned to his side to allow Jean to pass him and step into the hall. "I prefer to think I have given a warning."

"This business is done." Johnny crossed the room and pushed past Tom. "And since our business is done, I don't want to find you walking on my heels."

Henri caught the door and drew it toward him as he stepped into the hallway. "We will talk again at the proper time." He pulled the door closed.

In the room, Johnny slammed his open palm against the door. "The son of a bitch. What does he want?"

"I think he'll tell us when he wants us to know."

"And his warning, that threat …?"

"The Thompsons are hot," Tom said.

"It's got no teeth. He'd get burned himself."

Tom crossed the room and sat down on the edge of his bed. "So what do we do?"

"Nothing. We wait him out."

Lafitte, about to start his early rounds, arrived at the train station a few minutes before seven. The evening local was unloading. Lafitte crossed the platform and passed through the waiting room and out the front entrance. He didn't look back at Richard Betts or the three men who stepped down from the train and joined him.

He found Henri Leveque in the dining room at the Wingate Inn. One of his men, Pierre, sat on his left side. Jean had not wanted to come down from his room because of the puffed lip.

Lafitte stood across the table from Henri until he saw the nod at the empty chair. The waiter brought him a cup of coffee.

"I have been at the train station."

Henri smiled. He buttered a narrow crust of French bread. "It is a nice train station."

"One of the Americans has been sitting there on the platform for more than two hours."

"Is that true?"

"I assumed that the man was at the train station for some reason."

Henri popped the crust of bread into his mouth and chewed slowly while he nodded.

"The local train pulled in only minutes ago." Lafitte added a long pour of cream to his coffee and stirred it thoroughly while he let the other man wait. "The one who was waiting greeted three men from the train."

"Three new men?"

"They are men I have not seen before."

Henri swallowed and wet his mouth with a sip of wine. "Where are these men now?"

"A moment, please." Lafitte left the table and walked to the doorway that led from the dining room into the lobby. One brief look into the lobby and he returned to the table. "They are at the desk checking in."

Henri lifted his napkin from his lap. He dabbed at his mouth and placed the napkin next to his plate. He pushed his chair from the table and stood. Pierre made a movement as if to join him. Henri stopped him with a bare shake of his head. He reached the doorway and looked across the lobby.

Three men were receiving their room keys at the desk. One man was big and wide in the shoulders. Another was short and childlike. The last one was tall and very thin.

Yes, they were new men.

Henri watched the big man with broad shoulders direct the other two to the staircase. When they went out of sight Henri returned to his table. He draped the napkin across his legs carefully before he moved his chair closer to the table.

He closed his eyes. Now the five had become eight. Was there no end to the kind of multiplying these Americans were capable of? Were they rabbits that some wizard pulled from a hat? Would these eight become ten? Twelve?

He opened his eyes. Lafitte had drained his coffee cup and stared down into it.

"Do you know where this train originated?"

"It comes from Halifax," Lafitte said.

Henri nodded. The nod and the assured look on his face meant that he understood everything. In fact, he understood nothing.

Jean came to the door bare-chested, wearing only his trousers and his socks. His lower lip had a hump to it, an angry bubble.

"Is there gas in the car?"

"Yes."

"Enough for a drive to Halifax and back?"

"More than enough," Jean said.

Henri gave him a scrap of paper with a name, an address, and a phone number written on it. "You are expected."

He saw the reluctance in Jean. It was there in the way he stood in front of the mirror and buttoned his shirt. His eyes were on the swollen lip.

"It is important," he said.

"Pierre could go," Jean said.

"He is stupid, and you know it."

Vanity or no vanity, it was settled.

CHAPTER TWENTY FIVE

During the daylight hours, since his walk around town with the captain the day before, Gunny scouted the town for a barn or an old building where he could store the two Bulldogs. It wasn't easy. He and the captain had agreed that it had to be a structure set apart, isolated.

Oh, he supposed the back lot was okay if they had to settle for it. It was open ground, and there was a horse trough and a faucet at one end. There were shade trees, too. Still, it was cool at night, and he worried about his lungs during the night watches that fell to him. And that damned constable, whatever his name was—the one he'd asked about fishing in the area— was sniffing the air. It looked like he'd put the back lot on his rounds. Not that he came close, but he was always passing at a distance.

It was better to pay the highway robbery. The captain and the major agreed with him. It was a leaky and drafty old building that had housed a seed-and-feed store. The owner, a man named Bassett, wanted thirty dollars for one week's rent. You could see the sun through the roof in the day and the stars at night. It had been empty so long the rats had picked it clean and moved on.

It was almost dark by the time Gunny settled the matter with Mr. Bassett. He paid the rent and got the key and the loan of a kerosene lamp for a couple of days. Until, he told Bassett, he could buy one.

Not that he would. Another day and the business would be over. Two days at the most.

Richard Betts found them in the back lot. Gunny waved him into the truck. "Harry get here all right?"

"Minutes ago," Betts said.

Vic led the way in his Bulldog. Gunny followed.

"Where's he now?"

"At the hotel. Said he wanted to clean up and have supper."

They reached Bassett's building. Vic pulled up to the locked door. Gunny parked on the street and got out and unlocked the door. He spread the doors and let Vic drive in.

Gunny returned to his truck. "You stay with Vic."

Betts pushed the sliding door and got out. Vic came out and stood on the driver's side of Gunny. "I thought you wanted to talk it out with Harry."

"Harry's busy. I got to find me a firing range."

Vic frowned. "What'll I tell the captain and the major?"

"Any lie you want to. Or tell them the truth."

Gunny took the highway north. He'd gone about twenty miles before he found a dirt road that sliced away to the east. He took that road and followed it for five miles or so. Brush grew close in. It scraped the sides of the Bulldog. It wasn't, Gunny decided, a road that got much use.

He braked where the dirt path ended. There was a fanned-out clearing. The headlights swept across the stone foundations of what had at one time been a house. Black timbers and what had been the roof were strewn about the yard.

Probably a fire. It hadn't been recent. Time and weather had washed the smoke smell away.

Gunny got out of the truck and let his eyes become used to the darkness. Then he did a slow 360° turn. He didn't find any light in any quarter.

That meant, if he was lucky, that he was also out of earshot of anybody. He returned to the Bulldog and worked it around until it was pointed toward the dirt road again.

The tailgate was now pointed toward the remains of the house. He pulled the tarp aside and picked up the first of the Thompsons. There was a thick stump of a tree to the left of the burnt house. Probably destroyed by the fire. That would do.

He fired a short burst. Then he picked up the second Thompson. Another short burst. That way, in less than five minutes, he satisfied himself that the Thompsons were in operating order.

The stump was in splinters.

He didn't collect the brass. Screw it. It was too dark. He didn't feel like crawling about on his hands and knees.

He drove back to town. Vic had gone to supper. He and Betts swabbed out the barrels. Then he took the ammo drums and reloaded them to capacity.

No reason to spend time on a full cleaning. Not when the next day was probably the day they got used. That once, and never again. No pitting by then.

Screw the hard work. He felt tired for the first time since New York City. His lungs were sore. He wasn't coughing, and there hadn't been any blood in days. Not that he expected a miracle. It was only a matter of time. All he could hope was that it wouldn't happen before the job was over and they were back across the border.

He didn't want to die in some strange country.

Lafitte had two pieces of information for the important man from Montreal.

The first came to him during his rounds. That was after he left the hotel where he'd told the Mr. Big about the arrival of the three new men.

As he approached the back lot his mind was on other matters. He was composing a speech about ingratitude, and his text was taken from the way the man from Montreal had not said thank you even one time. He was so engrossed in his composition that he was halfway across the lot before he realized the trucks were missing.

It took him almost an hour to find them again. At that, he would have missed Bassett's store if he hadn't seen the light inside. A leak of light. He could be thankful that he hadn't searched for it during the day.

Of course, he had to be certain. At the same time, he had to be careful. That combination took him down a dark alley between Bassett's and the old stable building. He remembered that there was a window there.

Yes, the trucks were inside. Both of them. And then he realized that something strange and frightening was going on in his town. The old American and one of the younger men had their backs to him, leaning into one of the trucks. Then the old American turned and he was holding a tommy gun in his hands.

Lafitte had never seen a tommy gun in his life. Only in the movies. Had not that American gangster, Mr. James Cagney, killed several men with such a weapon in his last motion picture? And then died very sadly on the church steps?

Had it not been for the Mr. Big Shot from Montreal, Lafitte would have gone straight to the police station. He would have called the Canadian Mounted Police and told them that there were dangerous men in his town and that they had formidable weapons and that he was worried about their intentions.

He hadn't finished his rounds. He returned to the station. He needed time to think. He was at his desk, trying his best to concentrate, when the old farmer came in.

His name was Masterson. Lafitte usually only saw him on weekends, when he came in town to do his shopping or to attend church.

Masterson held out a handful of brass casings. "It sounded like a war," he said.

Lafitte had him start at the beginning. Masterson had been walking in the woods. One of his heifers was missing. That was when he heard the shooting. It had the noise of many guns firing at once. He'd been afraid and he'd waited. It hadn't lasted long. And not much later he heard a car drive away. He'd waited another five minutes and then he'd gone to the place where he'd heard the shooting.

It had been at the Hemphill place, the one that had burned down in 1936. A tree had been shot to pieces and the shell casings had been all over the ground.

Lafitte put on his best wise face. It was the face that authority gave him. Under it, he felt himself trembling. What if the timing had been different? An hour and forty minutes by the clock, and Masterson would have been reciting his tale to the night officer, Parsons.

"You will have to investigate this," Masterson said. "The sound of the firings has scared my hens. I doubt that I will find even one small egg in the morning."

The wise nod. It was what he'd seen a judge do once. "It is my thought," he said, "that this shooting at night is part of some war games. The Army is testing night blindness among its troops."

"Do you think so?" Masterson did not seem convinced.

"Usually the Army does not announce these war games. I will telephone the Army tonight and ask which unit was involved. And first thing tomorrow I will send a telegram to that unit and inform them that there *is* a chance that they have damaged your egg production for the month."

"For two or three months," Masterson said.

"You know more about chickens than I do," Lafitte said. "I have heard, through official channels, that the Army makes payments when they have done damage to farm crops."

"I have heard that also."

The fool and his chickens. It took Lafitte some minutes to rid himself of Masterson. Since he had taken the trouble to come all the way into town, he wanted to remain at the police station while Lafitte made the call to the Army. Lafitte assured him the call had to be private.

The door closed behind Masterson. Lafitte sat at his desk and looked at the handful of shell casings, and he thought of the tommy guns he'd seen at Bassett's old feed store.

Duncan MacTaggart awoke in the last coach of the formed-up train. It was completely dark. There wasn't even a light on behind the Exit sign.

He'd slept sitting straight up. Now he fumbled in the empty seat next to him until he found his coat, and he was careful as he unfolded it.

His watch was in the right-hand pocket. He found the catch and opened the cover. He struck a match on the sole of his shoe. It was a minute or two after two.

And then he heard what had awakened him. It was a *swish-swish* sound. It was his first night ashore in eight days or so, and the first night he hadn't slept deep in the innards of a ship. Down there, deep in the ship, it seemed that you were behind many inches of insulation.

After that, on land, it appeared that every sound was magnified.

Before the match reached his fingertips, he found the catch on the coach window blind. He raised the blind while he blew out the match and dropped it. The window faced the docked

Emerald. The blackout was in effect. He could see the shape of the cruiser, and then, closer in, the gusting rain that struck the coach window.

He got to his feet and struggled into his raincoat. He stumbled down the aisle and found the rear door of the coach. The heavy sheets of rain hit him as soon as he stepped on the train platform. It came at him like it poured out of a fire hose. He felt his trousers pasted against his legs and he knew that his shoes, dry for the first time in days, would be soaked in seconds.

No help for it. He took a deep breath and stepped down to the pier. He turned to his right as soon as his feet touched. When he'd checked the watch two hours before, at midnight, there had been only a light mist, and he'd reviewed four Canadian Navy guards lined up the length of the train. Now he couldn't find even one.

MacTaggart trotted the distance of the train, stopping at each boxcar to check the lock and the seal. All were intact. Nothing out of order unless you counted the guards.

Disregarding the rain, he backed away from the boxcars until his back was getting close to the *Emerald* at dockside. He cupped his hands around his mouth and yelled as loud as he could. "Guards, damn your souls, where the bloody hell are you?"

It didn't take a second shout. They came at a run from the other side of the train, the side near the pier shed. They ducked under the coupling that connected the boxcars and trotted to their assigned positions.

They'd been as dry as MacTaggart seconds before and now they were drenched.

MacTaggart gave them a moment to assume, without being told, a position of attention. "It too wet for you, laddies?"

It was a bellow. They didn't answer.

"Perhaps we could ask some sailors off the *Emerald* to take the watch for you. Everybody knows that seagoing sailors aren't afraid of water. They won't melt."

Even in the downpour, against that noise, he realized that he'd drawn an audience. He heard laughter and looked over his shoulder. The gangplank watch, a couple of ratings and an officer, leaned on the rail and gawked at him.

"Two more hours before you're relieved. You babies think you can stand the watch? If not, I'll find the watch hut and see that you're relieved. What'll it be?"

That special voice, that tone, it brought back his days as a recruit. That had been 1914, and the sergeant had his way of making you feel about as high as a dog's belly.

Since he'd started it, he decided he might as well take it the whole distance, as Sergeant Welles would have. He straightened his back and marched toward the guard nearest him. Five long paces brought him face to face with the young sailor. It wasn't exactly face to face. MacTaggart towered over him by some six inches.

"Now, son..."

"Sir... sir..." The boy's face was screwed up. He looked like he was about to cry. "Nobody said it was important."

"Important?" He bellowed until his lungs hurt. He wanted the other guards to hear him. "You have any idea what is loaded in those boxcars?"

"No, sir."

"It's a secret. You're not supposed to know. But it could make the difference between winning this war or losing it."

"We didn't know, sir."

"Now you do." MacTaggart backed away until he could look at the other guards as well. "Remain at your posts until you're relieved."

He marched away. Not toward the dry train coach. Toward the land where the pier ended. As soon as he was out of sight, he dropped all the military crap, the walk and the rigid back.

After a prowl and a blunder here and there, he found the guard hut. A rating sat there behind a desk, half asleep over a cup of cooling tea. MacTaggart marched inside and slammed the door shut behind him.

"You in charge of the guards at the train at Pier Twenty-three?"

"Yes, sir." The rating staggered to his feet and stood at a relaxed version of attention.

"It's raining out there."

The rating blinked at him.

"I know you don't furnish them umbrellas."

"Sir?"

"But perhaps you have some foul-weather gear."

The rating turned and looked at the metal cabinet behind him. MacTaggart brushed past him and opened the door. There were a number of rubberized slickers on pegs in the closet. MacTaggart grabbed several, counting them, until he had four. He walked to the rating and dumped them in his arms.

"And it's still raining, and it might rain all night."

The rating carried the armful of foul-weather gear to the door and opened it. He watched the gusting wind walk up his shoes and his pants legs.

MacTaggart returned to the closet and got one more slicker. He held it for the rating while he worked his arms into it, shifting the bundle as he did.

The rating was over the shock now. "I've got one question, sir." The *sir* seemed almost an afterthought.

"Say it."

"Who the hell are you?"

MacTaggart didn't answer him. He pushed past him and walked into the downpour. He didn't look back, but after a few seconds he heard the rating trotting after him.

Jean reached Halifax around ten that evening. He could have made better time if he'd tried, but there didn't seem to be much reason to rush. The man he wanted to talk to would not be at his place of business until some time between ten and eleven. It was misting rain the last half hour or so before he reached the town, and that same light rain covered the city.

Jean drove around the old part of Halifax for half an hour, and then he found a small dirty-spoon café that was still open. He'd ordered coffee before he remembered that he hadn't eaten his supper. Nothing on the greasy menu interested him, but he settled for a bowl of chicken stew. It was better than no supper at all. Halfway through the stew he decided that his choice had been a mistake. He finished his coffee and hoped that the acid of it would cut the pool of grease the stew had put in his stomach.

An old woman with twisted, arthritic hands took his money at the cash register. Her hands fumbled with the change and counted it onto the mat beside the register.

"Do you have a phone?"

"For a local call?"

Jean nodded. The woman had finished making his change. Now she drew a dime toward her and pointed at the wall phone behind her.

He gave the operator the number. The phone rang a couple of times before a woman with a deep voice answered. Jean asked to speak to Mr. Boulanger. The man who came to the phone sounded groggy, perhaps a little drunk, but he seemed to sober up when Jean said the right words to him.

"I need some information."

"I have been asking around," Boulanger said.

"I do not like phones," Jean said.

Boulanger gave him directions. Jean left the café and found that the rain fell heavier now. He drove through the almost-dark streets. He didn't know Halifax, and Boulanger must have assumed that he did. He lost his way several times, a wrong turn or a missed street, and it was going on midnight before he reached the right house.

It looked like a veritable mansion. It was set far back from the road. There was a high stone fence around it and an iron gate, where a man in a dark raincoat stopped his car.

Jean gave his name. The man checked it against a wet list he carried in his raincoat. The man nodded and switched off his flashlight and waved the Cadillac through the gate. Jean drove the length of a curving road and parked next to a row of official military cars.

His arrival was almost like a signal. As soon as he stepped from the Cadillac, the sky opened up. He ran through a cloudburst to the mansion door.

A tall black man answered his knock at the door. One step inside and Jean knew exactly what kind of house it was. It was all there in the smells. The perfume and powder scents.

"Mr. Boulanger expects me."

The black said, "This way, sir," and led him down a wide polished hallway. They raised the paper window passed what must have been at one time the living room. Jean had his passing look through the doorway. A number of women in thin gowns were spotted about the room, talking to perhaps a dozen men. Most of the men were in uniform. Officers with gold braid.

"This way," the black said again and led him past the living-room doorway. He stopped at a closed door and knocked and entered without waiting for an answer.

The room Jean entered had probably been the library at one time.

The black gave something like a stiff bow and backed away and drew the door closed with him. A heavy, fleshy man who looked like he might have some African blood in him got up from behind a huge desk and offered Jean his hand. The palm was soft, and there was a feeling like hand cream from it.

"You can call me Max," Boulanger said.

"Jean."

Max poured him a large shot of dark rum in a Waterford crystal glass. He didn't ask if Jean wanted a drink or if he wanted any special kind of drink.

"It must be important," Max said. He had his own drink at the desk. He lifted the glass and drained the last of it and added another two inches of rum.

"It is."

Jean sipped his rum. He looked around the room. Some of the shelves were empty now. The books that remained hadn't been touched in some months. Dust coated the tops and etched the spines as well.

"Has anything special happened in town in the last few days?"

"That covers many things."

"Tell me what you know," Jean said.

"H.M.S. *Emerald* docked this morning."

Jean shook his head. He had another sip of the rum. It burned his throat.

"Two men from a train crew were found dead in an alley in the red-light district."

Another shake of his head. Then he said, "Dead of what?"

"I have not heard for certain. It may have been an overdose of some kind of drug. Perhaps too much of a knockout potion."

A bartender who made a mistake? It did not seem to be what Jean had come for. "Do you know if any cargo of value has arrived in the last week?"

Max's head began its slow shake and then stopped. "I heard something. It meant nothing to me at the time." He placed his glass on the desk and rose to his feet. "I have to ask a question."

Jean finished his drink. He was pouring himself another when Max returned. Max got his glass from the desk and held it out so that Jean could pour for him.

"I am not sure this is what you want."

"Tell me what it is," Jean said.

"A man who works at the Ocean Terminals was here earlier this evening. He has formed an attachment for one of the girls. He is a foolish man."

"It happens that way at times," Jean said.

"The girls tell me all they learn from the customers. One never knows when this information might be useful."

"Yes." This fool was taking his own time.

"This evening this man told Lisa that they were unloading H.M.S. *Emerald*. He said there were cases and cases, enough to fill several boxcars."

"What was in the cargo?"

"He did not know. At least, he did not tell Lisa."

"Where is this man now?"

"The man from the docks?"

Jean nodded.

"At his home, I suppose."

"Is there any way to reach him?"

"The girl may know," Max said. "As I said, he is a regular."

"I need answers to these questions. What is the cargo? Where is it headed? What time will this train leave Halifax?"

"He may not know all these answers."

"I will settle for his best guesses," Jean said.

"It may be all he has," Max said. He left the library once more. He was gone for about ten minutes. When he returned he smiled and nodded. "The man's still a fool."

"A human condition." Jean had heard Mr. Leveque say that a number of times.

"Lisa called him and said she has some free time this evening and wants to spend it with him. He said he would be here in about an hour."

Jean walked to the desk and turned the clock and looked at its face.

"Are you short of time?"

"I have all night," Jean said.

"Do you want to talk to this man? I think I could arrange it."

Jean took his time. He thought about it the way he believed Mr. Leveque would think. He weighed the value of talking first-hand with the man, against revealing to him his interest. No, it was better to stay in the shadows. "Let the girl find out what she can. If she is a good whore, he will not remember he said anything to her by tomorrow."

Max dipped his head. He understood. "It is a slow evening for the girls downstairs. You have about two hours to waste. How would you like to spend them?"

It was an offer.

Jean was in bed with a tall black girl from Trinidad when the soft knock came on the door about two hours later.

The bedroom where the girl, Lisa, waited for him was a froth of lace and little-girl frills. The curtains, the canopy over the bed, and the bedcover itself. And on one of the oversized pillows was the head of a huge brown Teddy bear.

Lisa wore a long white cotton robe that reached the tops of her feet. It was not what she wore, Jean thought, when she entertained her men. This was for the mornings after, when it didn't matter how she looked, when it didn't matter that she looked her age. Her skin was like a child's, that soft, and her hair was in long curls. Blonde and thick like a Christmas doll.

He guessed that she was in her mid-twenties. In the right light, without makeup, she could probably pass for fifteen.

Jean crossed the room and sat on the low bench that went with the dressing table. It had a white satin cover, and the itch began right away.

Max had followed him as far as the door. He was sweating thick oil, the drinking he'd been doing while Jean had been with the girl from Trinidad. "Tell him what he wants to know," he said, "and then forget what you have told him."

"Yes, Max." It was a little girl's voice, almost Shirley Temple's, but not quite. What ruined it was a slightly off inflection.

Max said to Jean, "Stop on your way out," and closed the door and went away. Lisa watched him and then walked around the bed. She sat on the side of the bed near Jean. Her feet were bare. They were long and thin with the nails cut almost to the quick.

It is a child's face, Jean thought. That is her whore's edge. Old men make love to a child or a mock-child.

"Tell me what you heard about the train."

"William said they spent the whole day unloading cases from the British ship and then loading those cases on a train."

"How many boxcars?"

"He wasn't sure. He thought it might be ten or a dozen."

Jean reached behind him and scratched at his behind. "Did he know what the cargo was?"

A shake of her head. "But he heard some of the cases were heavy and some weren't."

"And the train is still there? At the dock?"

A nod. "The unloading was not finished by dark."

"Where is the train headed?"

"He thinks it goes to Montreal and perhaps on to the west."

It was a stupid question, anyway. It couldn't go east without ending up in the ocean. Of course it went west. And it did not matter whether it was intended for Quebec or Montreal. Either way, it had to pass through Wingate Station.

"Did he know when the train is to leave Halifax?"

"It was a big secret," Lisa said. "But William likes secrets. The mystery train interested him. He said he did some checking. He saw a guard-duty list. The list goes only as far as 1900 hours tomorrow night."

Seven in the evening. He stood and scratched again. The satin had him itching all over now. "And with all this interest, this checking around, he heard nothing about what the shipment is?"

"He heard one story but he said he did not believe it."

"What story was that?"

"That the cargo was the British Crown jewels."

"Why didn't he believe it?"

"There were too many cases," Lisa said. "It would not take that many cases to pack the Crown jewels."

He nodded as if he accepted that explanation.

Of course the cases contained the Crown jewels. Perhaps they also contained the Royal silver and the Royal china and God knows what else the King and the Queen wanted to protect from the air raids and the invasion that was expected.

The way the war was going, it made sense.

It was time to go. It was after two in the morning, and there was still the drive, in hard rain, back to Wingate Station. He had taken a couple of steps toward the door when he stopped and returned to her. His hand went deep in his pocket. He had some expense money that Mr. Leveque had given him. It was a wad of twenties. He took off the top two twenties and handed them to her.

"Thank you," she said.

"As a favor, you will forget the questions and the answers."

"It means nothing to me," she said.

The temptation was strong. It came on him while he stood over her. While she looked down at the twenties he put out both his hands and gripped the neck of the cotton robe where it met across her chest. He pulled the robe open.

Lisa didn't protest. She was limp and pliable.

CHAPTER TWENTY SIX

Henri Leveque awoke. The window shade was down, and he had no way of knowing what time it was. It was, he thought, either very late at night or very early in the morning.

Then he realized why he'd awakened. There was a loud knocking at the door. He got out of bed and walked barefooted across the room. It was probably Jean back from Halifax, and if he had decided to awaken Leveque, then it was likely that his information could not wait. His man, Jean, had been trained to respect his night hours of rest.

He unlocked the door and swung it inward a few inches. Lafitte stood in the doorway. His raincoat was soaked and water ran off him and pooled on the hallway floor.

"I started to come by last night."

"Isn't it night now?" Henri said.

Lafitte shook his head. "It's raining," he said.

"In the hallway?" Not very bright, he thought. He saw the puzzled look on Lafitte's face, and he backed away and opened the door wide and motioned Lafitte inside. He found the light switch and turned on the overhead globe. Then he sat on the edge of the bed. "What time is it?"

"I am not certain."

Henri found his pocket watch on the table beside the bed. It was a minute or two after seven. "I suppose you have come for some reason."

"The Americans have moved into a building a couple of blocks from the back lot where they've been."

It was hard to fight back the anger. He'd been in a deep sleep and this idiot had awakened him to give him information that could have waited until later in the day.

"And you woke me to tell me this?"

Lafitte flinched. The man's voice had a crack like a whip in it.

"There is more."

"Yes?"

Lafitte was slow. Henri could see the big gears move and then the small gears begin to grind. It was like the skin was peeled away and he could see it all.

"The old American, the one with bruises on his face from the fight..."

"I know that one." He was the man that Henri had made the arms deal with.

"About dark, last night, that man test-fired weapons in the woods north of town." Lafitte dug into his raincoat pocket and brought out a handful of shell casings.

Henri scooped the casings from his hand. He selected one shell from the dozen or so and studied it. "Do you know what kind of weapons he used?"

"They were tommy guns," Lafitte said.

"This is important to know." Henri put a hand on Lafitte's damp shoulder and turned him toward the door. "You have been helpful." He reached for the doorknob. "I will remember this when the time comes."

Lafitte mumbled something.

"I'm sorry?"

"I said I was happy to be of service," Lafitte said.

Henri had heard enough of the mumbled remark to know that it was insolent. Not that it mattered one way or the other. He had what he wanted. Now he was certain the Americans had some plan that concerned Canada. The truth was now revealing itself. Before that, before the firing of the weapons, there was always the chance the Americans intended the Thompsons for use in the States. Now, with Lafitte's new information, he believed he knew better.

He saw Lafitte out. Lafitte stood in the hall and yawned and blinked and said that he was returning to his room for a few hours of sleep before he took over the day watch at the police station.

"I will contact you there," Henri said.

He closed the door and switched off the overhead light. He bypassed the bed and raised the paper window shade. It was dark and gray, and a light rain pattered against the panes. He sat on the edge of his bed. It was a comfortable bed, full of goose feathers and light as the air. A welcome change after the lumpy bed in Gilway.

But he knew that he would not sleep anymore. Too much was happening.

He sighed and got his shaving case from the dresser top.

Half an hour later, shaved and bathed and dressed, he knocked at the room Jean shared with Pierre. Pierre answered the door. After a look over his shoulder into the dark room, Pierre stepped into the hallway and pulled the door closed behind him.

"Jean's back?"

"He arrived only two or three hours ago," Pierre said.

"He will have to catch up on his sleep later. Wake him now."

"Yes, Mr. Leveque."

"I will be in my room. We will talk first and have breakfast later."

He walked back down the hall without looking back.

The hotel dining room opened at seven. Johnny Whitman reached the lobby a few minutes after the doors were opened. He stopped at the desk. The clerk saw the five-dollar bill that was folded and covered by Johnny's hand. "The Frenchman, is he still registered?"

"Mr. Leveque?"

"That's the one." He moved his hand, and the clerk covered the bill and slid it toward himself.

"He is still registered."

"Did he say how long he'd be staying?"

"Perhaps until the weekend."

Johnny nodded and walked into the dining room. He'd finished his eggs and toast and was on his third cup of coffee when Tom entered.

Tom pulled his chair in close to the table. "The French guy is still here."

"How much?"

"Huh?"

"How much did you give the desk clerk?"

"Two dollars." Tom looked puzzled.

"That damned clerk is getting rich. He's licking his lips right now and waiting for the Frenchie to come down and pass him a few more dollars and ask if we're still in the hotel."

"What does he want?"

"What does everybody want?" Johnny said.

The waiter brought the breakfast menu. Tom ordered orange juice and coffee.

"What *does* everybody want?" Tom asked after the waiter moved away.

"Something for nothing. Cream off the top of the jar. Milk from the cow you don't own. Pork chops off somebody else's pig."

"All right," Tom said, "but what, exactly, does this one want?"

"I've got a feeling we'll find out today."

"When?" The waiter brought the juice. Tom had a sip. It had a strong metallic taste, as if the can had been opened the day before and it had been stored in the can overnight. He drank it anyway.

Johnny shrugged. He held out his empty cup when the waiter brought Tom's cup and the coffeepot. "For it to matter, it's got to be today. He waits until tomorrow, and he'll have his answer without having to ask the question."

When they passed through the lobby a few minutes later the desk clerk smiled and nodded at them. The nod was so low it was almost a bow.

The rain had stopped. It was still gray and damp. Johnny and Tom walked through the back lot, dodging puddles of water, and took a left down a narrow street.

"It ought to be here," Johnny said.

"The next block."

Down the street, on the right, Richard Betts stepped to the edge of the road and flipped a cigarette in a high arc. "Been waiting for you a time," he said when they were closer.

He led them into the building that had housed the seed-and-feed store. Gunny Townsend and Vic Franks were seated on the tailgate of one of the Bulldogs. Harry Churchman stood to one side. He held one of the Thompsons, the muzzle carefully pointed toward the back wall.

"You're up early," Johnny said.

"We found that the café down the street opens at six," Gunny said.

"Gunny thinks this soft life's getting to him." Harry carried the Thompson to the rear of the other Bulldog and placed it on the tarp.

Johnny nodded down at the tarp. "What do you think?"

"Gunny's satisfied," Harry said, "and that's good with me."

Tom counted heads. "We waiting for the Gipsons?"

Harry shook his head. "They wanted to sleep in and I wanted some peace from them."

Richard Betts laughed. "The way I hear it Harry wants to adopt them for good and forever."

"Somebody's got to support me in my old age."

"If you live that long," Johnny said.

"If they live that long." Harry worked a handkerchief from his hip pocket and wiped his hands carefully. "I've got some tales I could tell about those two in Halifax."

"Save them for some long winter evening," Johnny said. "I think we've got important matters to talk about."

"It's today," Harry said.

"When?" This was from Richard Betts.

"We'll get to that." Harry folded the handkerchief and stuffed it in his pocket. "The news you won't like is that the estimate of the take just went down. Nobody is going to be a multimillionaire."

"What went wrong?" Gunny said.

"Somebody got nosy at the pier. The Gipsons did one hotbox and had to back away."

"Shit." Richard Betts did a little kick that spread a small cloud of dust. "I knew we couldn't depend on those Gipsons to do any more than pick their noses."

"It's not small pickings," Harry said. "That one boxcar holds two hundred cases of gold, and each case weighs something on the other side of a hundred pounds."

"What's it worth?" Betts said.

"It might be anywhere between ten and twelve million. That depends on exact weight on each case."

Gunny said, "It ain't what we planned on."

"Maybe." Harry looked at Johnny and then at Tom. "But I had some time to think about it and I ain't going to whine about a million or a million and a half."

"Still…" Gunny began.

"Don't be a dummy. Anything it takes a dozen boxcars to cart here, it'll take a dozen boxcars to take across the border." Harry lifted a hand and pointed it at Vic Franks. "What'll these trucks haul?"

"Two hundred of those crates," Vic said.

"Say we got to cross open country?"

"Less," Vic said.

"Any trouble with a hundred cases?"

"A snap."

Harry nodded. He was done. He turned and looked at Johnny.

Johnny grunted. "No matter how we look at it, it's spilt stinking milk. The Gipsons didn't do all they were supposed to. No way we can change that. Any bitching to be done, let's do it now and get it over with."

The truth was it hadn't gone down too well with Johnny either. He'd had his own hard time swallowing that one boxcar.

And he thought about Lila. Wouldn't that anger her? A girl who never had more than a hundred dollars at a time, and she was going to scream and cry that she'd been robbed.

If he could find her after they crossed the border. He'd left her in New York City with the rest of his cash. She was supposed to stay there and find a job if she had to. The rest of it was waiting. If she did that.

Of course, if it came off he wouldn't have any trouble finding her. He'd have trouble losing her.

"It's locked in," Tom said. "A fact is a fact. Either we accept it and do the job or we back off and forget it."

"Those fucking Gipsons," Gunny said.

It was the statement that took all the steam from it. Agreement from everybody, and the anger went away. What could you expect of those Gipsons anyway?

"We came this far," Harry said.

"I'm still in," Vic said. Richard Betts dipped his head in agreement. Gunny said, "All right, what's a million or two more?"

"When?" Vic said.

Johnny dropped his head.

"That's the big problem," Harry said. "We don't know for sure. Today. That's all we know."

"More guessing?" Gunny pursed his mouth and spat. "This whole operation is put together like a Tinkertoy."

"Could be we could find out something at the train station. The train carrying the gold will have a clear track. What we have to find out is whether there's been any schedule change for trains leaving Halifax. Maybe it won't be exact, but it can give us a time slot."

Harry tilted his head toward Vic. "You take the first watch at the station."

"Two hours?" Vic headed for the door.

"Richard is next up," Harry said.

Vic reached the door and swung it open. The gray-haired man from Montreal stood there. He was flanked on each side by one of his men.

Vic turned around. "Captain."

"Go on to the station," Harry said.

Henri stepped through the open doorway. "He will have a long wait."

"What's it to you?" Johnny said.

"Nothing. I could not, however, help hearing the last part of your conversation. These old buildings have more holes than solid places."

Johnny waved Vic back into the building. Gunny backed slowly toward the tailgate of the Bulldog and put a hand behind him until he touched the stock of one of the Thompsons. Henri watched him and there was a flicker of recognition. He gave Gunny a thin smile. Then he turned toward Johnny.

"I think it is time we discuss a merger. I know a few facts and you know other ones. It could be that we could do business."

"I don't think so," Johnny said.

"I know when the train leaves Halifax."

"When?"

Henri shook his head. "Do you mind if we close the door? I think you will remember how I feel about keeping my business private."

"Close it, Vic." He waited while Vic allowed the three men inside and then latched the door. "Say what you've got to say."

"Cards on the table," Henri said. "I think that is how Americans talk in cowboy films. Isn't that right?"

Johnny stared at him and didn't answer.

"Very well. I will show my cards. I know that it is a matter of the British Crown jewels."

Behind Henri, Vic took one step forward. His mouth was open, as if he intended to deny it.

Johnny moved first. "I guess you've got us there, Frenchie," he said.

Tom turned slowly and looked at the other men grouped behind him. He dropped his left eyelid in a wink.

"And I think I can assume that you have some plan to stop the train here at Wingate Station?"

"Another good guess," Johnny said. "This Frenchie guesses real good."

"And there are other valuables involved besides the Crown jewels?"

"Might be," Johnny said.

"I will make a deal," Henri said. "I will give my help and my protection, and for that I will take the Crown jewels. You and your men can share the other valuables."

"No deal."

"Then a division of the Crown jewels?"

Johnny looked at Tom. Tom nodded. "You've got a deal."

"Then I suggest we do the rest of our talking at the hotel," Henri said. "It is more comfortable there."

"You lead the way."

Tom stepped in front of Johnny. "When does the train leave Halifax?"

"At seven tonight."

Use the sons of bitches. Dumbasses.

Johnny and Tom walked toward the hotel with the Montreal man, Henri. Behind them, left under the command of Harry and Gunny, the Frenchman's two men were being worked into the unit.

Half of the Crown jewels still equals nothing.

"I trust there are no hard feelings about our troubles to this point?" Henri stopped in the center of the back lot.

"Of course not," Johnny said.

Henri looked at Tom.

"No hard feelings," Tom said.

"That's good." Henri placed a hand on each man's shoulder and they began to walk again. "You have led me a merry chase since Montreal."

"Well, that's done now."

The Crown jewels. Jesus Christ, how dumb can you get?

MacTaggart was up at six. His shoes were still damp and his raincoat soaked in patches. It didn't really matter, he found when he stepped outside. The rain was lighter, hardly a mist now.

The watch stood in a plumb line the length of the train. Much better, he mumbled as he passed them.

Away from the pier and the train, he followed his nose. He found an open mess and had his breakfast with a table of casuals, seaman waiting for their new ships. A couple, he found, were going to H.M.S. *Emerald.*

A few minutes before seven he was back at the train. He watched the last stragglers from the starboard watch return from the overnight leave. Several of them remembered him from the voyage and waved and called to him before they climbed the gangplank to the *Emerald.*

He sat in the open doorway of an empty boxcar and waited. At 7:50 he heard the sound of marching boots, and the new work detail appeared around the end of the train and headed toward him.

At 8:00 exactly the *Emerald* piped the port watch to handle cargo. The unloading and loading began again. It didn't take much time. The last boxcar was loaded by 1040 hours.

MacTaggart locked these last boxcars and waited until the guard was posted once more.

The sun was out. It was going to be a beautiful day. He found Sub-Lieutenant Carr in the wardroom of the *Emerald.* Carr drew him a cup of tea and brought it to the table.

"I assume you've changed your mind, Mac."

MacTaggart had a scalding taste of tea and gave Carr a puzzled look.

"Take a few hours of leave with me."

"In that wicked city?"

"It's not wicked, Mac," Carr said, "unless you know where to look."

"And you do?" He looked at Carr. Hardly more than a boy yet. He could have been MacTaggart's son or his nephew. Carr blushed and looked away. "It's a fine offer. The truth is that I need a pen, some paper, and an envelope."

"That's easy." Carr left the wardroom. He returned a few minutes later and placed the writing materials on the table. He added a fountain pen. "I've just filled it."

"Thank you." MacTaggart turned a sheet toward him and wrote *2 July 1940* at the top of it.

"A girl, Mac?"

"At my age?" He smiled at the boy. "No, a lady." It stopped the pen in his hand. It was odd, thinking of Peggy and speaking of her as a lady. Still, the distance they'd gone together, and he was changed. Perhaps it was time that it happened. He wasn't a young-blood anymore.

Carr finished his tea standing. "I've got a few matters that need my attention. I'll check back in a time and see if you're done with it. You are, and I'll use my influence with the mail officer to see it's put on the next ship heading home."

Dear Peggy:

I think this is the 20th letter I've written you. The other 19 were written in my head to pass the time, and when I see you again I'll tell you about them. I am in Canada. What I can see of it is beautiful.

I have not seen any Indians yet. I will be disappointed if I've come this far and don't see any.

Sub-Lieutenant Carr, after thirty minutes, tapped on the bulkhead next to the doorway. He wore his leave uniform and carried a raincoat over his arm. "Done, Mac?"

"As good as." MacTaggart added a line or two to complete a thought and then he signed it. He folded the sheets and placed them in the envelope. A few moments to address it, and he carried it to Carr. He didn't seal it.

"I suppose the mail officer will want to read it through and censor it."

"You give away any military secrets?"

"Not a one."

Carr wet the flap and sealed the envelope. "Didn't I tell you? I'm the mail officer. It'll go with the crew's mail on the next ship. You've got my word on it."

"That's good with me."

They climbed the ladder to the main deck. Carr led the way toward the gangplank.

"You sure about the tour of town, Mac?"

"Perhaps on the way back." He waved a hand toward the train. "The job's not done yet."

They shook hands at the head of the gangplank.

"It was good sailing with you, Mac."

"Good luck, son."

He left the *Emerald* and settled in his day-coach seat for a long afternoon of waiting.

CHAPTER TWENTY SEVEN

The door closed behind the captain and the major and the French guy. Harry dropped the latch in place and walked back into the center of the old building. His eyes were on the ground. He stopped and bent over and picked up a piece of wood about the length of a ruler. It had probably been a part of the trim in another section of the seed-and-feed store.

He squatted and used the edge of the piece of wood to smooth and clear a space about two feet square. Then he used the broken end to draw a map. "Here's how it looks to me," he said.

The others formed a circle around him and stared down at the map.

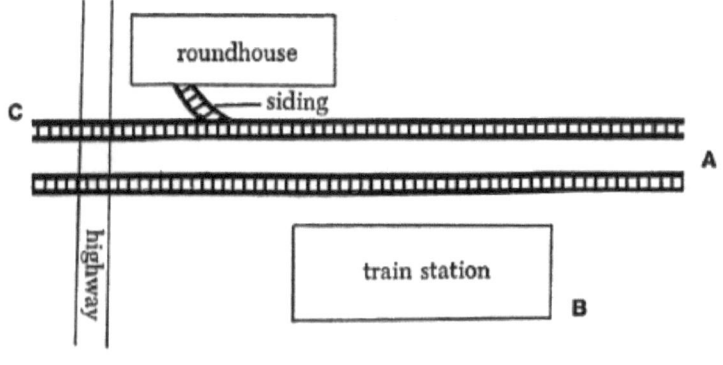

"Gunny."

Gunny stepped over the drawing and squatted next to Harry. There was a wheeze to his breathing, and Harry gave him a long stare. "You all right?"

"Fine."

"You sure?"

"Too much night air. I think it's a cold."

Harry used the stick as a pointer. "Location A."

"I see it." Gunny took a deep breath and held it. He could hear the flutter, the rattle, but he hoped that Harry didn't.

"Vic."

Vic Franks edged to the left side of the map and looked down at it.

"Location C."

"Got it."

Harry looked up at the other men. The two new men stood shoulder to shoulder. The short hairy one with the fat lip that was beginning to scab had the look of a man with a sour stomach. "You," he said.

The man's lip darted out and licked at the scab. "My name is Jean."

"You're with Gunny." He nodded at the other man, the tall one with the bald head. "That one?"

"Pierre," Jean said.

"Pierre's with Vic." Harry moved the stick pointer and touched Location A. "Here, Gunny, west of the train depot. A spot half a mile or three-quarters of a mile away from the train station. Have a look at the terrain. Pick a place to blow the tracks. That way we cut off the town from the west, from Quebec and Montreal."

"All right, Harry."

Harry pointed a finger at Vic. "Same with you. Half a mile or three-quarters from the depot. We blow the tracks there and we seal the town from the east, from Halifax."

Vic nodded. "Whatever you say."

"Betts?"

"Here."

"I want charges made up. Sticks enough to blow both sets of tracks at both locations."

"Fuses?"

"Whatever you think," Harry said.

"Twenty seconds?"

Harry turned to Gunny. "What do you think?"

"That ought to do it." Gunny put his hands on his knees and straightened up. He stood over Harry. "One thing bothers me. Two men to the east and two to the west. That thins down the firepower."

Harry shook his head. "That's not the way it'll be. You and Vic pick the spots and you make sure the charges are planted. But you won't be there when the tracks blow. You'll be with the main force." He pointed a hand at Jean. "He'll blow Location A. His friend blows Location C."

"The timing?" Gunny said.

"We'll set that later." Harry stood and raked a shoe through the dirt map until he wiped it away. "Right now what I want is for you to scout the locations at A and C. It's going to be dark the next time you're there. Find yourself markers. A tree, a building, something like that."

Gunny stepped into the middle of the map. He touched Jean on the shoulder on the way past. "That all for today, Harry?"

"Weapons check at five. Full meeting at six."

Richard Betts followed Vic and Gunny and the Frenchman's two men to the door. He saw them out and closed and latched the door after them. He returned and looked down at the scuff that had been the map. "You never did say what Location B was."

"The train depot. That belongs to the Gipsons if they ever wake up."

"They'll screw it up," Betts said.

"If they do, it breaks their string with me. And that string is about wore through."

Richard Betts leaned against the tailgate of one of the Bulldogs and reached inside. He pulled a case of dynamite toward him. The lid was nailed on tight. He looked around for something to use as a pry bar. "What about those three? The Frenchie and his men?"

"What about them?"

"We got to split with them?"

Harry grinned. "Not from my share," he said.

"There is no reason to walk." Jean led the way across the back lot. Behind them, Vic and Pierre split away and headed east. Vic was at a fast walk, almost a trot.

Gunny watched them go. Then he had to push himself to keep up with the smaller man, Jean. He was sweating. He could feel the fever coming, just under the skin, about to break to the surface.

"You're in a big hurry," he said.

Jean yawned. "I've had almost no sleep. I was in Halifax last night."

"How's it there?"

"The girls are like silk."

"Harry says it's wartime over there."

"Harry? The one who gave the orders?"

Gunny nodded. His breath was short.

"Is he as tough as he seems?"

"Nobody knows that but Harry."

They reached Wingate Station's main street. The black 1940 Cadillac was parked on the near side of the hotel. Jean cut across the street and stopped beside the driver's door. He unlocked that side, got in and reached across to open the passenger side for Gunny.

"I did not understand what you said."

"That nobody knows but Harry?" Gunny got in and pulled the door shut. "It means that people who could probably tell us how tough Harry is just aren't around anymore."

"That kind of man?"

Gunny nodded.

"You said west?"

Gunny jerked a finger over his shoulder. "That way."

Jean drove the Cadillac a block to the east and then got it turned around. As they headed west Gunny did the figuring in his head. He decided when they were about level with the train depot, and then he leaned forward and took a reading on the mileage gauge. They were parallel with the tracks, north of them. They passed a couple of intersections where streets cut south, toward the tracks. At the third street, approaching it, Gunny looked at the mileage gauge and said, "Take the next left."

He remembered the first look they'd had at the town from the rise high to the west. The way the tracks were, the delta, the fanning out before the tracks reached the edge of Wingate Station from the east. Then the tight bottleneck from there to the train station and beyond until the tracks reached the western limit of town and the land opened up again.

The Cadillac crossed the tracks. Jean gave him a questioning look. Gunny said, "Park here."

It was a good guess. Where they were now the bottleneck ended. To the east, back toward the depot, houses and other buildings lined the track, built at what must have been some pre-scribed distance. Behind them, to the west, it was as if a strong wind had cleared the borders of the tracks.

Gunny, with Jean a step behind him, followed the track bed to the west. Fifty yards and then another hundred. A crew had been out in the last week or two clearing the brush on both sides of the track. It was hard to find a location marker.

"About here," Gunny said. He lifted an arm and pointed to the north. In the middle of a field, about half a mile away, there was a weathered barn. "Level with that."

"You will be with me?"

"To set the charge." Gunny stepped over one set of tracks and stood in the space between that set and the other tracks. He checked the bed. There was a gravel surface, and the earth beneath it was packed hard. "We'll need a pick or a shovel."

Even at the brisk pace Vic set, it took him and the other man, Pierre, some minutes to reach a point about half a mile to the east of the train station.

Pierre took the dirty felt hat from his head and wiped the sweatband with a wadded handkerchief. "You have not had a lot to say to me."

Vic used the toe of his shoe to test the track bed. "I didn't come here for the conversation."

"That is not what I meant."

"You talking about that night in Montreal?"

"You have bad feelings about that night?" Pierre used the hat to fan himself. Sweat cooled on his bald head.

"I've got a bruise or two."

"But now we work together."

"That's what the bossmen say. Forget Montreal."

Vic let it go at that. To hell with these clowns, anyway. Nobody asked them to sit in on the game. And now they wanted everybody to like them.

Vic selected his spot. He marked it in his mind by a thick stand of trees on the north side of the track bed.

❧ ❧ ❧

Henri Leveque lowered himself into the easy chair that had been placed with its back to the window. It was, after all, his own room. It did not matter that it might appear impolite to the Americans. They did not seem to understand courtesy. It was just as doubtful that they would understand rudeness.

The man they called the major took a seat on the edge of the bed, hunched over, hands on his knees. It was not a comfortable position.

The captain, the one with the shoulders as wide as a doorway and the neck like a bull, did not sit down. He took a stance in the center of the room. He had the attitude of a man on a drill field.

"Now that we're here," the captain said with a curl of his upper lip, "maybe you'll tell us what the meeting's about."

It amused Henri. What kind of Army was that? The captain acted as if he were in command, and the major sat there and said very little.

"I realize I pushed my way into your operation at a late point in the planning."

"That's the Lord's truth."

Henri kept his head at an angle so that he could watch both men. He saw the major lift his head and stare at the captain. There was a brief but firm shake of the major's head before he looked down at the carpet once more.

"For this reason, I have to assume that all the plans have been formulated and that you have already decided upon your escape route."

"You're doing well at this assuming," the captain said.

"I would like to know your plans."

"In time." The captain took a step toward the major. Beneath the carpet, the floorboards creaked under his weight.

"Our plans are being worked out now," the major said.

"Isn't this late for such …?"

"The plan was made. Now it is being changed. The addition of three new men has given us some latitude we didn't have before."

"When will I know the details?"

"Later this afternoon," the major said. "We'll have a final briefing at six."

"I believe I can wait that long."

"Nice of you," the captain said.

"I have another matter that will interest you," Henri said.

"Tell us about it." The captain grinned at the major.

"Constable Lafitte is with me."

Henri saw the surprised look that flashed between the two Americans. It was a stroke, a good and solid touch.

"What watch does he have?" the captain asked.

"The afternoon and early-evening one."

The major nodded. "We were worried about him."

"But not the late-night and early-morning man?"

"My regrets," Henri said to the captain.

"The core of the plan is that we cut off the town for a period of time."

"I guessed as much."

"We'll need to talk to the constable," the captain said.

"I'll bring him to the six o'clock meeting."

"I think that's it for now." The major stood. He turned and smoothed the part of the bed where he'd been seated. He walked past the captain. The captain turned to follow him.

"One other matter." Henri grabbed the arms of the easy chair and stood.

"Yeah?" The captain whirled around. He didn't bother to hide the irritation on his face.

"The escape route."

"You go your way and we'll go ours," the captain said.

"Then you will be crossing the border into the States?"

"That's our business," the captain said.

"Come, gentlemen. The loss of the British Crown jewels and other national treasures will set off a search the likes of which we have not seen in North America since … perhaps, the murder of President Lincoln."

"Get to the point." The captain looked bored.

"With such a search expected, it might be better if I furnish you my protection."

"I don't think so." The captain looked over his shoulder at the major. "Canada's your playpen, not ours."

"What he means is that it might be wiser if we dodge the search in a country that we know." The major caught the door-knob and hesitated. "It's not that we don't appreciate your offer. We do. But it might be better if we're going about our business in the States while they're looking for us in Canada."

"That's fact." The captain grinned. "And since you've been good enough to make your offer, we'll make ours. Come south with us and we'll protect you."

"The offer has its merits," Henri said.

"Let us know."

The major swung the door open. The captain stepped into the hall. The major followed and pulled the door closed behind him.

Henri locked the door and returned to the easy chair. He slumped into it and closed his eyes.

The numbers were not equal. That bothered him. Eight of the Americans and only three in his group. Four if he counted Lafitte. Those odds, the two to one, meant trouble. It had been a reluctant bargain. The Americans had not wanted his help, and they had refused his aid with the escape route.

He thought like a man who only kept his bargains when it was to his advantage. Were the captain and the major the same kind of men? Was there any advantage for the Americans that would force them to keep the bargain? He did not think there was. His only value was that he added three more men, and that would be useful in the taking of the train. Once the job was over, there would be no more need of him or his men. That would be a dangerous time.

And, yet, there was a way. The men from the States had two trucks. He, himself, did not even have one truck. Would it appear odd if he sent for a truck and for two men to drive it? He did not think so. It was his right and he could argue that. Let them believe he was bringing in reinforcements to protect himself. It would, if nothing else, inform them that he was not a complete fool.

Henri opened his eyes and sat forward. The time, however, was short. There was a number in Quebec that he could call. Quebec was too far away from Wingate Station for a truck and men to arrive from there in the time there was. No, the men and the truck would have to be recruited and sent from some town nearby.

He left his room and headed down the hallway toward the staircase. Halfway there, he passed an open doorway and heard voices raised in argument. They were American accents, and he hesitated as he reached the doorway.

A tall, lanky young man with dark hair was in the entrance way, about to leave the room. Past him, in the center of the room, there was another young man. This one was short and had close-cropped hair.

The tall American saw Henri and stepped away and slammed the door.

Odd. The whole hotel was filled with Americans. On his way down the staircase he remembered those two Americans. They were two of the three recent arrivals.

In the lobby he placed his call to Quebec.

CHAPTER TWENTY EIGHT

Clark put his back to the door. "Who was that?"

"Where?"

"In the hall."

"How the hell would I know?" Randy sat on the end of the bed and pulled his shoes, with the socks balled up and stuffed in them, from under the bed. He used his hands to dust the soles of his feet. That done, he pulled on his socks.

Clark stared at the socks. As far as he knew, Randy hadn't changed socks in a week. The socks were stiff and crusty. "You coming down for dinner?"

"Breakfast," Randy said.

"Are you coming?"

That was what the argument was about. Randy didn't want to leave his bed. He wanted to stay there all afternoon. Clark, the night before, had promised Harry Churchman that he would have Randy up and around by noon or not much later.

"I'm awake, ain't I?"

Clark decided that that was as close to a yes as he was going to get. He dropped the room key on the bed next to Randy and went downstairs to the dining room.

The waiter said that they were serving lunch but he could still order breakfast if he wanted to. Clark ordered ham and eggs and coffee, and he'd just received his plate when Randy walked across the dining room and slumped into the chair across the table from him.

"You order for me?"

"I didn't know what you wanted."

Randy looked at Clark's breakfast. "The same for me," he said to the waiter. He unfolded the morning paper he'd bought in the lobby and placed it on the table.

It was the Wingate *Morning Star*. It was a thin paper, only ten or twelve pages, and Randy flipped through it rapidly. He found a sports page and pulled that section out before he pushed the rest of the paper toward Clark.

Clark wasn't interested in the news. The front page was mostly about the war in Europe. Still, there wasn't much to do after he'd finished his breakfast. He drew the paper toward him and read the front page. The main article was about the French fleet. The British were saying that the French had broken an agreement about what was supposed to happen to the French ships that were left after their surrender to the Germans. It didn't make any sense to Clark. He couldn't see any reason to fuss over some ships. He turned to page 2.

One item down the left side caught his eyes. It was headed DEATHS INVESTIGATED. It was the same all over the world. They were always investigating deaths, even down in North Carolina. He started to move away from the item. Then he saw the dateline. *Halifax, N.S., 1 July.*

His eyes skipped down the short article, and when he saw the names, he returned to the first of the item and read straight through it. The shock was in his stomach and he could feel sweat begin to break out between his shoulders.

The bodies of two young workmen were found today in an alley in the waterfront section of Halifax. Robert Mass, 28, and Andrew Phillips, 19, were discovered in the late afternoon by a Royal Canadian Navy patrol....

After Clark finished the article he lowered the paper and stared at Randy. He was stuffing his mouth with ham and eggs, and the egg yellow spotted the corners of his mouth.

Clark creased the page so that the article was set apart. He put some money on the table to cover the cost of both breakfasts before he pushed back his chair and stood.

Randy's head jerked up from his plate. "Where you going?"

"To the lobby." He edged around the table and placed the folded paper beside Randy's plate. He touched the article about the deaths and said, "Read this."

"What's it about?"

"Just read it." He left the dining room and found a chair in a corner of the lobby. He sat down and put his head back and closed his eyes. He felt like crying, but he couldn't. The anger and the pain choked him, and he tried to bring up an image of Andy's face. What came was shadowy, an outline without features. And then that outline was replaced by one that he could see clearly. It was a face that he'd only seen once, the time Andy had shown him the snapshot. Susan. The sister that Andy thought plain.

He opened his eyes and looked across the lobby. It destroyed the image, and when he closed his eyes once more there was only darkness.

"So what?"

Clark opened his eyes. Randy stood over him. He'd brought the paper with him. He dropped it into Clark's lap and backed away.

"It didn't have to happen."

"It was a mistake. Harry must have got the wrong stuff. Knockout drops didn't kill me the time I had them that place in New Orleans."

"Harry told you one eyedropper for each man. How many did...?"

Randy turned away. Clark pushed up from the chair and caught his arm. He jerked him around. The slyness was on Randy's face. It was a look Clark knew too damned well.

"How many...?"

And he knew. He knew without listening to what Randy said, either his denial or his confession.

"It wasn't like they were family," Randy said.

"When did that ever make a difference to you?" He might have added some words about how Mama had died in the charity ward while Randy was on the chain gang, and how the worry she had about him had helped to kill her. He didn't. He realized that his voice was too loud. He could see that the desk clerk was staring at him. He swallowed the rest of what he wanted to say and pulled his brother toward the door that led outside.

He released Randy's arm when they were on the sidewalk. Harry had given them directions to the building where the trucks were stored. He took a few seconds to get his bearings before he headed in that direction.

Randy followed. He wore his hangdog look. "I swear I didn't know it was going to hurt them."

"You insisted you had to do it. You remember?" Clark looked back at him. "You put in the whole bottle?"

Randy dipped his head and looked away.

That tore it. It ripped it all the way open.

A heavy weight fell from Clark. He was free. He could breathe again. It was fresh air, breath that hadn't been sucked out of his lungs by Randy.

"I swear..."

Clark looked at Randy's I-am-sad act. He looked away. Lord, he thought, who is this stranger walking beside me who thinks he is my brother?

"We'll walk through it," Harry Churchman said.

He led the Gipsons down the street and across the back lot, toward the main street where the hotel was. It was a fair and bright day. The high-noon sun was drying the rain from the night before.

"You'll be issued handguns," Harry said.

"The two men you sent us drinking with in Halifax," Clark said.

Harry stopped. He looked puzzled. "What about them?"

"They're dead," Clark said. "It was in the papers."

"Is that right?" Harry swung around and began walking again.

Clark followed. "You interested in how it happened?"

Randy, his head down, lagged a couple of steps behind.

"Not especially." Harry didn't look at him. "Dead is dead, and there's nothing you can do about that but pray."

Randy recovered. He saw that Harry wasn't going to join in an attack on him. In his eagerness he stuttered. "You're … talking … to the … right man … Harry. Clark knows how to pray."

Harry ignored Randy. He lifted a hand and patted Clark on the shoulder. "Look, that's tough, but there's nothing we can do about it now. It's done."

They approached the train station.

"Exactly at eight," Harry said, "you two enter the train depot and take seats. You act like you're waiting for a train or waiting for somebody who's arriving on a train."

Him too, Clark thought. Lord, he is as bad as all the others.

They walked around the station and climbed the steps to the platform. Harry leaned against a window and stared into the waiting room. "You handle a telegraph key?"

"Like a beginner," Randy said. "There's no way I could fool anybody with my hand."

"But you read it?"

"Some."

Harry turned to Clark. "You?"

"About the same as him."

Harry put his back to the waiting room. "Then we don't try to fool anybody. Nothing tricky. Soon as the action starts we close the train station down, telegraph and all."

"It'll look suspicious."

"That's right," Randy said.

"We'll have to live with it." Harry crossed the platform and started down the steps. Randy followed. Clark trailed them, several paces behind.

It was two in the afternoon.

The trees along the back lot threw long patches of shade here and there. Harry watched a young boy water a mule at the dark metal trough. The mule lowered his head until it was an inch or so from the water. It snorted to clear the green slime away. Then it began to drink.

"It's a nice little town," Harry said.

Constable Lafitte stood with his back to the sun. His face was in shadow, but Harry could read it like the headlines of a newspaper.

"It can be pleasant in the spring and summer."

"How long have you lived here?" The boy grabbed the head harness on the mule and tried to pull him away. The mule snorted into the water again and wouldn't move away.

"Five years this fall," Lafitte said.

"You married? Own property here?"

"Neither."

"Then you wouldn't mind leaving town if you had to?"

"If Mister Leveque wished it, I would."

"He say anything to you?" The mule had shown he couldn't be forced. Now he backed away on his own. The boy led him down the street.

"He said that I was to do what you said."

"It's the same thing," Harry said.

"Is it?"

"Take my word for it."

"If I must." Lafitte nodded. "What am I to do?"

Harry dropped his voice to just above a whisper. "All hell is going to break out at the train station a bit after nine tonight. I don't want any trouble with the police. That means you. It also means the night man if he comes charging up and wants to mix in this business."

"I can handle Parsons."

"You got a jail cell over there?"

"Two," Lafitte said.

"Might be Parsons could end up in one of them."

"It is possible."

"Besides that, the main problem could be the phones." They talked for a few more minutes. At the end of it Lafitte returned to his office, and Harry went over and stared down at the horse trough.

The coolness, the green feathery slime, made him think of summer days in Texas when he was a boy.

It was a long, long time ago.

At five that same afternoon Duncan MacTaggart sat on the cool fold-down steps of the last day coach, the one next to the caboose. After the slow, leisurely early afternoon there was a sudden increase of activity around the train.

Mr. Craig and the other specialists from the Bank of England were deposited by a staff car at the far end of the pier a few minutes after five. MacTaggart watched them march the length of the train. When they reached him he moved to the side of the step to make room for them to pass.

Craig let the others board the train before him. He peered at MacTaggart. "You look tired."

"You look rested."

"It was a pleasant visit." Craig started past him.

"See any Indians?"

Craig stumbled and caught the rail to steady himself. "Not a one."

MacTaggart nodded. It was a thoughtful nod. Only after Craig went inside did he grin to himself. Maybe there were no Indians left in Canada.

At half-five he heard the smart quick-step march and pushed himself from his seat on the coach stairs to watch the Canadian Army unit round the far end of the train and head straight for him. It was dress parade, the heavy boots in time and the hands swinging in the best British drill.

He did his estimate. About sixty men and two officers. The ranking officer was a captain with a wide red mustache and a limp. About fifty, MacTaggart thought, and that probably meant the limp went back to World War I. The young lieutenant with him had the straight back and the airs of a man just out of military college. In his twenties and full of piss and vinegar and wanting his men to make an impressive show of it.

The young lieutenant called his men to a halt one coach away from the spot where MacTaggart stood. The boots hit the pier like thunder and there was an echo in the stillness that followed.

The captain left the lieutenant with his men and marched toward MacTaggart. He tried his best to conceal the limp. It was his left leg, up high near the hip joint.

"You'd be Mr. MacTaggart?"

"I would."

"Captain McGuire." He lifted a hand and gave a casual touch to his cap, a gesture that was almost a salute.

"An Irishman in Canada?"

"Why not? Did you think all Irishmen preferred the peat bogs?"

"But you're Canadian?"

"Three generations," Captain McGuire said.

MacTaggart looked down the ranks of men. The row was straight as a line drawn with a ruler. "Your troops eaten yet?"

"Not since lunch."

"Maybe you'd better see to that," MacTaggart said.

Captain McGuire turned. It was a slow, awkward movement that favored his bad hip. "Lieutenant."

The young officer arrived at a fast walk.

"Mr. MacTaggart, Mr. Foster."

The young lieutenant put out his hand. MacTaggart took it and gave the boy a grin.

"He believes we ought to see the men have a meal."

"Do we have time?"

"An hour or so," MacTaggart said.

"Send them off with Sergeant Jones," McGuire said.

While Foster handled that detail, Captain McGuire paced in front of MacTaggart. When he stopped he grinned and said, "And our own supper?"

MacTaggart waved a hand at the docked cruiser. "I have connections on the *Emerald*."

"Would you be a man who believes in a drink before supper?"

"A taste of Irish?"

"Man, are you serious?" Captain McGuire stared at him. "On the *Emerald*?"

"In my kit," MacTaggart said.

Craig and the bankers had taken seats in the middle coach. The last coach was empty except for the three of them. MacTaggart passed the bottle. Lieutenant Foster, careful of his reputation, had only a token sip. The captain drank next, a full-throat quiver of a taste. MacTaggart matched him drop to drop.

Captain McGuire stared out the window at the *Emerald*. His red hair and mustache were streaked with gray, and his eyes were a dark blue. "I was ordered to report to a Mr. MacTaggart, but I was not told what we were supposed to be guarding."

MacTaggart held the bottle to the light. It was the last of the bottles, and there was only a quarter of it left. He tipped the bottle and had about half a sip. He ran that around his tongue before he swallowed. "Valuables," he said.

"Valuables?" Captain McGuire took the bottle and allowed himself a polite sip that matched the one his host had taken. The young lieutenant shook his head at the offered bottle. McGuire inserted the cork and tapped it lightly with the palm of his hand. "I hope you are not one of those closemouthed Scots," he said.

"Later." MacTaggart took the bottle and placed it in his bag. "I think it's time we did our begging at the *Emerald*." He stood.

"How's the food aboard ship?" Lieutenant Foster wanted to know.

"Better since we reached port," MacTaggart said.

Leading the way, going up the *Emerald's* gangplank, he turned and looked back at the train. The four-man watch was still in place. There had been no lapses since the night before.

CHAPTER TWENTY NINE

The weapons' check at the run-down building they'd rented began a few minutes after five. Harry and Gunny handled the check-out and the assignment.

Handguns for the Gipsons. These were the target pistols Harry had stolen in New York. They'd been used in the bank robbery in Renssler, and they'd been packed over the border in Gunny's heavy suitcase.

Harry passed them, butt first, to Randy and Clark. "Pack them in a gym bag or a big paper sack. Too much bulk to stuff them under your shirts."

"I'd rather have a Thompson." Randy tilted his head toward the trap on the tailgate of one of the Mack Bulldogs. "One of them."

Gunny looked away. It wasn't worth discussing. He left it to Harry.

"I don't think so. The ticket clerk probably won't be armed. How're you going to explain walking in with a Thompson under your arm?"

"A shotgun then."

"Same answer," Harry said. He put his back to Randy. Henri Leveque was next. "How about you?"

Leveque shook his head. There were two Thompsons in the boot of the Cadillac and the .44 revolver for himself. "We came prepared."

"You, Gunny?"

"The pump gun."

That left Thompsons for Captain Whitman, Major Renssler, Richard Betts, Vic Franks, and the last one for Harry.

Gunny passed around the spare drums for the Thompsons. The whole matter hadn't taken more than fifteen minutes.

Harry sent the Gipsons and Henri Leveque's men, Jean and Pierre, away to an early supper. Their part in the operation was already established. After eating, the Gipsons would remain at the hotel until time to leave for the train station. Henri's men, when they'd completed their meal, would return and wait at the barn until eight o'clock, the set hour for their departure for Positions A and C.

"It might be a good sign. We're running early. Any objections to going on to the briefing?" Johnny looked around and nodded to himself. "I guess there isn't. All right, the main strike..."

"How large a part of the train are we speaking about?" Henri Leveque asked.

"One boxcar."

"The correct one?"

Johnny passed that answer to Harry Churchman. "Unless there was a mistake in Halifax," Harry said.

"I would hate to involve myself in an illegal activity and discover that it was not worth it."

"It'll be worth it," Tom said.

"The Crown jewels?"

"If we've crippled the right boxcar."

"And if you haven't?"

"Other valuables," Tom said.

"What other valuables?"

"Goddammit." Johnny pushed past Harry and faced Leveque. "If we don't get this operation organized, it's not going to matter what's in the boxcar. Your percentage of nothing is nothing, and that's the Lord's truth."

Henri absorbed the burst of anger. He let it blunt itself on him. Then he gave Johnny a humorless smile and backed away. "First things first? I believe that is an American expression as well?"

"Does that mean I can get on with it?"

Henri dropped his chin on his chest and didn't answer.

The briefing meeting broke up at six-thirty.

Gunny remained with the trucks and the weapons. He'd have his supper after the Frenchman's two men returned. Not that he would eat much. A light meal before a fight, that was the soldier's maxim. It was a truth that went back to his time riding along the Mexican border and his tours in the trenches in France during the Big One. Stomach wounds and gut shots, the advice went, healed better if you didn't have a mess of undigested food in you.

Soft scrambled eggs, some dry toast, and a cup of hot tea. That kind of supper. Nothing heavy. Only what would be digested fast and leave you empty.

At the hotel Henri Leveque stopped in the lobby. The Americans, led by the captain, brushed past him and headed into the dining room without inviting him to join them. Henri followed them as far as the dining room entrance. Satisfied that they were seated and about to order, he backed away and returned to the desk.

"Has anyone asked for me?"

"Two men," the desk clerk said.

"Where are ...?"

"They rented a room." The clerk turned the hotel registry toward him. "They are in Room Four-ten."

❧ ❧ ❧

"Where's the Frenchie?" Harry lowered his menu and looked around the dining room."

"A gentleman like him?" Johnny said. "He's in his room pouring on some more perfume before supper."

"You never get enough of that," Harry said.

Tom placed the menu on his plate. "You think this is going to work?"

"This partnership?"

"Yes."

"It was going to work before these clowns forced their way into it. Now it's going to work with them or in spite of them." Johnny shrugged. "To hell with him. God, I'm starved."

"Gunny says to eat light," Harry said.

"That old soldier's tale?"

"Might be. But you know what?"

"What?"

"I look around this patchwork army and I don't see anybody but Gunny who's been in a war."

"With lungs like cheesecloth, he's worried about his stomach?" Johnny waved a hand at a passing waiter. "Ready to order here."

Harry Churchman ordered a small steak, rare, and toast and hot tea.

The others ordered full dinners.

The two men in Room 410 looked like lumberjacks. They wore cord trousers, flannel shirts, and heavy boots. They smelled of old, dry sweat and rum.

Henri introduced himself and had his careful look at them. They were cousins, but they could have been twin brothers. Both had square, blocky bodies, weathered faces, and close-cropped black hair that might have been cut using a bowl as a pattern.

They were the Bouchards, Pete and Charlie.

"You brought the truck?"

"There was no truck to bring."

"Didn't the people in Quebec ...?"

Pete was the older of the Bouchards. He did the talking. "I told them we had no truck. I said if we needed one we could steal it here in Wingate Station."

It made a certain kind of sense. And there was no way that Leveque could argue with them. If he argued that they had not done what he ordered, there was still no truck. Arguments did not furnish a truck.

"Do you have weapons?"

They didn't. He gave that some thought. Finally he left the hotel with them through a side entrance and escorted them to the police station. There he turned them over to Lafitte, who was just returning from his first rounds of the evening.

Lafitte would tell them where there was a truck they could steal and where they could hide it until it was needed. And he would keep the Bouchards with him until the action at the train yard began.

Henri entered the hotel dining room as the Americans were leaving and heading back to the seed-and-feed building.

It was a pleasant supper.

Sub-Lieutenant Carr had not returned from leave, but the other officers remembered MacTaggart, and an invitation to dine aboard the *Emerald* was extended to him and his guests.

By six-thirty they'd eaten and toasted the King's health.

A few minutes later they were back on the dock. Lieutenant Foster saw to the boarding of his troops. MacTaggart and Captain

McGuire relieved the four-man watch and remained on the pier until the engineer, the fireman, and the brakeman arrived.

At 7:00, exactly, the train pulled away from the dock. H.M.S. *Emerald* disappeared behind them.

There was a clear track all the way to Montreal.

The last local train that left Halifax departed about twenty minutes after five. It arrived at Wingate Station two hours later. The final coach in that train carried troops. At each major stop along the route, two armed soldiers were dropped off. These guards took up positions in the waiting rooms of the depots.

Five passengers disembarked from the civilian coach and crossed the platform at Wingate Station. Two soldiers, a private and a corporal, swung down from the military coach and walked along the track bed to the station. The corporal was Robert Lester from Medicine Hat. The private was William Carpenter, and he was from Calgary. The corporal wore a web belt and a canvas holster with a Webley in it. The private carried a Springfield '03.

Corporal Lester and Private Carpenter entered the waiting room and had their careful look around the station. The room was empty except for the ticket clerk and an old man who'd arrived on the same train. The old man was waiting for a suitcase that he'd checked at Halifax. The two soldiers watched the old man until the suitcase arrived and was passed to him through the baggage window. About that time the train pulled away from the station.

The old man shouldered his suitcase and left by the door that faced the main part of town. When the door closed behind him, Corporal Lester took a seat on the bench that faced the platform and the tracks.

Private Carpenter stood behind him. "We staying here the whole night?"

"Don't you ever listen?"

"I was listening."

"A train's passing through here and it ought to arrive around twenty-one hundred hours. That's the one we're supposed to guard. About forty-five minutes later, the regular train from Montreal comes through. We get on that and we're back in Halifax by twenty-four hundred hours."

"If there's no trouble," Private Carpenter said.

"Who's expecting trouble?"

"You're not?"

Corporal Lester smiled. "This is a holiday trip."

Satisfied, Private Carpenter left the waiting room and took up a position on the platform. When he got tired of standing he found a baggage cart and sat down. But that wasn't regulation, and now and then he looked over his shoulder into the waiting room. Lester didn't seem to mind.

When Carpenter was comfortable and about to nap, a clock in the distance struck eight.

At 8:00 exactly, Gunny carried the twin bundles of dynamite with the rattail fuses attached out to the 1940 Cadillac. He got in the front seat next to Jean. Vic followed him and entered the back seat and sat next to Pierre. He carried identical twin bundles.

"No smoking," Gunny said over the seat back.

"I'm not even breathing."

Jean drove. Vic directed him to a spot to the east of town. Vic and Pierre got out, Vic carrying the explosives and Pierre carrying a pickax.

Jean turned the Cadillac around and headed back through town. Without being told, he took the proper turnoff, the one they'd scouted that afternoon. He parked in the same place, and they got out.

It was dark now. It took Gunny a few seconds to decide if he'd reached the location they'd chosen. He wasn't sure. He couldn't see the barn he'd selected as a marker. So he said to hell with it and that fifty feet one way or the other wouldn't matter.

He handed the explosives to Jean and took the pickax. He stepped into the space between the sets of tracks. He worked fast and hard. He dug a hole between the ties on the inside rails of each track system.

When he was certain the bundles would fit, he backed away and leaned on the pickax. The exertion had placed a cough just at the back of his throat. He fought to hold it there. A few seconds, and he knew he had it under control. He dropped the pickax and took the twin bundles from Jean.

He went through it once, showing Jean how the bundles were to be placed and how the fuses were to be laid out.

"Got it?"

"I have."

Gunny took the twin bundles from the holes under the tracks and handed them to Jean. "The next train passes by here is the right one."

"I understand."

"Soon as the train passes you plant the dynamite and wait. You're going to hear all hell break out around the train station. That's your signal to light the fuse. You got matches?"

"A whole box."

Gunny left him. He set out toward the center of town at a fast walk. It would be at least an hour before the train arrived. It might be longer than that.

He wanted a rest before the long night began.

Vic wasn't about to bend his back when there was another mule in the yard. Pierre, with the felt hat pulled down tight, dug the twin trenches beneath the rails. Vic kept him at it until he was sure the bundles of explosives would fit with some give.

When he was satisfied, Vic went through the drill, the placing of the charges, three times.

With some people you just couldn't be too careful.

The Gipsons were late leaving the hotel lobby. That was Randy's fault. He got his back up and said that he didn't see any reason to rush over to the depot and then have to sit there in the waiting room for more than an hour.

They'd checked out of the hotel earlier. Their bags were stored at Bassett's seed-and-feed store. Randy kept his battered gym bag with him. In it he'd packed the two target pistols and a spare box of shells.

It was half-eight when they left the lobby. Randy carried the bag. It was a short walk to the train station. The night was clear and warm. Clark entered the waiting room first. He took a seat on the bench that faced the entrance on the town side of the depot. Randy followed him, and his eyes flicked a time or two at the soldier who sat on the bench facing his brother. Clark didn't look at him. He was staring at the soldier. Randy backed his way toward the ticket window. He turned and leaned on the counter until the ticket clerk noticed him.

"When's the next train to Montreal?"

"You just missed it."

"Maybe there's another one," Randy said.

"I can't be sure."

"Huh?" Randy looked over his shoulder and grinned at Clark. There was an expression on Clark's face that Randy couldn't read. "Run that by me again."

"A special troop train's passing through. I won't know if the scheduled express…"

"When will you know?"

"When they tell me," the clerk said. "You want tickets?"

"For a train that might not show up?" Randy laughed at him. "We'll wait."

He was still laughing when he sat on the bench next to Clark. "How do you like that nonsense?" He placed the gym bag on the floor between his feet. When he looked up again that same odd look was on Clark's face.

The soldier on the facing bench uncrossed his legs. His boots had a glossy spit shine. His trousers had a crease like a knife edge. Randy's study of the soldier stopped at his waist.

The corporal tugged at his gun belt. The holstered Webley pistol shifted on his hip until it was balanced, braced on the front edge of the bench.

CHAPTER THIRTY

O f the three day coaches between the freight cars and the caboose the most forward one had been taken over by the Canadian Railway Express representative and the Bank of England specialists led by Mr. Craig. The Railway Express man was a Mr. Bruce Telford, a pudgy man in his late fifties who wore heavy convex glasses that were about a double thickness of window glass.

Mr. Telford wasn't with the train because Railway Express had insured the shipment. No one, not even the Canadian government, would insure a cargo as valuable as this train transported. However, the freight charges would amount to almost a third of a million dollars, and Railway Express had assigned their top troubleshooter to the project.

As a part of his watchdog role, a telephone had been installed in Telford's coach. This instrument placed him in the middle of any communication between the brakeman in the caboose and the engineer in the locomotive.

The soldiers under the command of Captain McGuire were assigned seats in the final two day coaches. There was no dining car. At breakfast time, some distance down the line, a mess car would be taken on.

Duncan MacTaggart selected a seat in the last coach, next to the caboose. After the troops were settled in, Captain McGuire made his halting way down the aisle and tapped the empty seat next to MacTaggart. "You mind company?"

"Glad of it." He watched McGuire pivot toward the seat. He kept his hand on his left hip, supporting it, and he didn't relax completely until his behind hit the cushions. He sighed, and when he leaned back MacTaggart could see that the perspiration from the strain was oil-slick on his forehead.

"It looks easy from here in," Captain McGuire said.

"I'd like to drink to that." MacTaggart toed the bag that held the last of the Irish. "But I think I'd better save the drop that's left for the real celebration."

"I'll have it with you."

"I thought you might." MacTaggart looked the length of the coach. The soldiers were straight up, at the ready, their rifles braced against their legs. "You've a good outfit."

"You noticed that, too?" McGuire smiled. "Good, but green as gooseberries."

"Hard to tell that from here."

"We've done our best, young Foster and me, in the time we've had to work with them. Two months aren't a God's plenty."

"You've done the job."

McGuire shook his head. "It's a beginning. The rest will be done in England." He saw MacTaggart's questioning look. "That's right. They're shipping for England as soon as this detail's completed."

"The boy ..."

"Young Foster?"

"Seems a fine type."

"The best," McGuire said. "I knew his father in the other war, our war."

"France?"

"A year of it."

"I was there myself. And it was our war. I figure one war to a man's lifetime."

"It works out that way." McGuire patted his left hip. "I won't be going with them. I'm with training."

That explained it for MacTaggart. He had his doubts about the captain. The hip was more than enough to keep him out of the war. It wasn't, it appeared, enough to keep him from a position in training command.

Lieutenant Foster pushed open the door that connected the final coach with the one forward of it. He stopped in the aisle, and his eyes swept the seats until he located Captain McGuire. A jerk of his head, and he worked his way to the back of the coach. On the way he stopped here and there to pass a word or two with his men. He reached McGuire and leaned on the headrest of the seat. "They're settled in, Captain."

"Stay alert. Have Sergeant Jones pass that on."

"Yes, sir." Lieutenant Foster smiled and turned away.

McGuire watched him go. "It's hard on the boy. I attended his wedding a month ago."

"Hard on a lot of people."

"Some more than others. The lad's been like a son to me. His father, Robert, died in the trench right next to me. A sniper. We thought the morning mist covered us."

"That drink we take," MacTaggart said. "We'll drink some luck to him in England."

"I'll look forward to that drink even more now."

That said, McGuire settled back against the headrest and closed his eyes. MacTaggart watched him attempt to work his left leg, the hip, into a comfortable position. His teeth gritted with the strain. After a minute or so, either he got it right or he accepted the discomfort.

Gunny Townsend arrived at the old seed-and-feed building. He stood outside for a couple of minutes to get his breath after the fast walk. His shirt was soaked, and he could feel the toothache warning of the chill that was under the surface, about to break through.

When he was steady he went in and got the pump shotgun from the back of one of the Bulldogs. He shucked the shells and loaded it from a fresh box. The rest of that box and one other box he divided and stored away in his pockets. He didn't think he would need that many shells, but it was always better to have more than you needed.

He propped the pump gun against the wall to one side and sat down. He closed his eyes and waited. He drew all his strength from deep inside him to fight the chills.

"Gunny?"

He opened his eyes. He wasn't sure how long he'd been resting. The nightmare fever dreams had just started. He blinked and looked around the room. Nothing much had changed. He decided only minutes had passed since he'd closed his eyes.

Major Renssler leaned over him. "Is it done?"

"The west approach to town is."

"Good."

He heard his own voice. It sounded thin and reedy. "I did as much as I could," he said. "Everything but light the fuse and hold his hand while it blew."

"It'll work out." The major backed away.

Gunny's eyelids fluttered. He closed them tight.

Before the fever dreams began again he heard Vic arrive. Vic said, "... clown will probably blow himself up along with the track."

A bull's roar of laughter from Harry. "What's wrong with that?"

"Nothing," Captain Whitman said. "Good luck to the dumb burrhead."

Randy jerked his eyes away from the holstered Webley. The corporal was staring at him.

"Americans, aren't you?"

"Us?"

"I heard you talking to the ticket clerk. You know, I was in Detroit last summer."

"Is that right?" Randy swung his head toward Clark. "I've never been there."

"I saw a baseball game. It was a pretty slow affair."

"You've got to grow up with it," Randy said.

"The whole Sunday afternoon, two games, and ..."

"A doubleheader," Randy said.

"...nothing happens."

"You don't go there expecting..."

Randy let it trail off. The telegraph key began its chatter. He heard the first part of the message. The telegrapher's hand wasn't that practiced. He was slow as a beginner.

EXPECTED ... TIME ... ARRIVAL ... TWENTY ... ONE ... HUNDRED ... HOURS ... PLUS ... TEN.

"But the man who throws the ball," the corporal said.

"The pitcher."

"He takes his own good time with it."

Randy lost the rest of the message. That damned soldier. Had to be talking. He looked to the side and saw that Clark had left the bench and was stretching as he paced back and forth in front of the ticket window.

He relaxed. Clark could read a key as well as he could. The corporal leaned forward, caught up in the conversation. So Randy settled into it with him. He told the Canadian about the lazy man's game. How you went to a game and sat in the sun and got a tan, and you had a couple of bottles of pop and some hotdogs, and even if you had to take a trip to the bathroom, there wasn't much chance you'd miss anything important.

The key stopped. Clark returned to the bench and sat and crossed his legs. Randy looked over his shoulder at him. Clark shrugged. Whatever had followed hadn't been important.

About seventy miles out of Halifax, Billy Jeffers, the brakeman, closed his lunch pail. He had a final swallow of the ink-thick coffee. Still chewing the last of his cheese and tomato sandwich, he mounted the steps to the perch. From this seat—a kind of tower that projected above the caboose—he looked down the full length of the train ahead of him.

It had been ten minutes since he left the perch. During the time he took for his meal something had changed. Ahead, where there had only been darkness before, now there was a shower of sparks.

Hotbox, he thought. Before he left the perch he counted the cars. Three day coaches ahead. Then four boxes beyond that. The seventh box in front of the caboose, that was where the hotbox was.

He pressed the buzzer that connected the phone to the engineer's station forward. When he heard two clicks, he remembered that there was also a phone in the Railway Express station three coaches forward.

He began his report.

The first sign MacTaggart had that all was not well was the gradual slowing of the train. It wasn't for a brief period, what might be an adjustment to the terrain. No, this was an all-out slowdown.

He got to his feet and stepped over McGuire's legs. The captain didn't move. His breathing was a blubber of a snore.

He rushed through the middle coach and into the forward one. Telford, the Express representative, was on the phone. MacTaggart circled Telford and got a nod and a wiggle of a finger from him.

"And it will mean how much additional time?" Telford blinked behind the thick glasses. "Twenty minutes? No more than that?"

Telford placed a hand over the mouthpiece of the phone. "We've a problem with one of the boxcars." Before MacTaggart could speak, Telford shook his head at him and lifted his hand from the mouthpiece. "And that would be Wingate Station? The first available siding?"

Behind Telford, Craig and the bank experts leaned forward, listening.

"Very well, if that's the best we can hope for." Telford broke the connection and placed the phone on the hook. He turned back to MacTaggart. "We have to slow the train down to just this side of a crawl."

"Why?"

"We've got a hotbox acting up."

"What's that?"

"The axle's seizing up."

"And what does that mean?" MacTaggart asked.

"We'll have to cut that boxcar out of the train the first chance we get. That's at Wingate Station."

"No one cuts a boxcar from this train without my say."

"Mister, you'd better speak fast," Telford said. "If we don't remove that car we could have hell's own fire. It's sparking right now. You can smell the smoke from the caboose. Some more heat, and that boxcar could burn."

"That's possible?"

"It's happened," Telford said. "I've agreed to slowing the train. When we reach Wingate Station we'll shunt the car with the hot-box on a siding for repairs."

"How long with that take?"

"It will depend on how long it takes the crew at Wingate Station to form up." Telford removed his glasses and rubbed his eyes. "Perhaps you know what is in the fourth car forward of this one?"

"It's not the paper," MacTaggart said.

"You'd better make plans."

"Can we hold the train at Wingate Station while the boxcar is repaired?"

"I don't think it's practical," Telford said. "As it is, we've tied up the track all the way west to Montreal. This shipment is certainly important, but so's the rest of the war."

"That's the decision?"

"That's it."

MacTaggart went looking for Lieutenant Foster. He found him in the middle coach writing a letter to his new wife by the beam of a flashlight.

"I need you," MacTaggart said. He led the young officer into the car where Captain McGuire was sleeping.

The telegraph began its brittle tapping all of a sudden. The corporal, by then, was on his feet showing how a certain ballplayer had swung and missed a third strike. He swept the air with his clenched fists and an imaginary bat. Randy said, "Do that again," and he pretended that all his attention was on the corporal's stance. It wasn't. He was reading the telegrapher's hand. A different man. Faster and with an exact spacing and a sure rhythm. It was too professional, and Randy missed about as much as he got.

He pushed the gym bag under the bench when the ticket clerk–telegrapher acknowledged the message. He stood next to the corporal and said, "You've got to get your hips into it," and he took an exaggerated swing. "Like this."

Behind the ticket counter the clerk left the table where the key was and pulled the phone toward him. He gave the operator a number.

"Like this?" The corporal put his hips into the swing at the imaginary baseball.

"You've got it."

"Brian," the ticket clerk said, "how soon can you get a crew together?"

"He's got it, hasn't he?" Randy said to Clark.

"The sooner the better." The clerk tapped a pencil on the counter. "The special's got a hotbox, and they'll be shunting off one car here in Wingate."

"He's my clean-up man," Clark said.

"On the siding in front of the roundhouse. How long?"

Randy backed away and sat on the bench next to Clark.

"The estimate is twenty-one-thirty hours."

Randy reached under the bench and pulled the gym bag forward.

"See you then." The ticket clerk placed the receiver on the hook and cleared his throat. The corporal looked over his shoulder and discarded the batting stance. "Over here," the clerk said to the corporal.

Randy watched the back of the corporal as he leaned across the counter to listen to the ticket clerk.

"I said it would work. I told them."

Clark looked away. Pride and the fall that came after it. In time, all in good time.

"How big a guard detail?" Captain McGuire leaned forward and stifled a yawn.

"What can you spare?" MacTaggart asked.

"Fifty men if we have to."

Lieutenant Foster stared past McGuire. "What happens with this detail after the boxcar's repaired?"

"There'll be a relief engine sent from Halifax. Perhaps from a town closer if there's one available. The relief engine will pick up the boxcar when it's ready to roll again. The detail will remain with the car until it catches up or it reaches its destination." MacTaggart closed his eyes and tried to remember the schedule. "That would be at Montreal. Of course, the stop at Montreal won't be that lengthy. Only long enough to shunt off three boxcars."

"So there's a chance that the relief engine won't catch up with the main train?"

"That's true."

"Eight men and a sergeant," Lieutenant Foster said.

"Twenty," McGuire countered.

"No." Foster dipped his head toward MacTaggart. "Can you promise another car or two won't go bad between here and Montreal?"

"I'm afraid I can't."

"Twenty men on the detail would stretch us thin. Say these disasters come in threes. Twenty men with this car, twenty with the next detail some miles down the track. Where would we find the men for the third detail?"

"I'm not sure I agree with the premise of the threes." Captain McGuire grabbed the headrest of the seat in front of him and pulled himself to his feet. He kept most of his weight on his good leg until the stiffness left the crippled one. "But I do agree that we should be cautious with our manpower. That's a point well taken." McGuire's left hand rubbed at the hip joint. "Mac, what's the value of the cargo in the one boxcar?"

MacTaggart looked over his shoulder. "Somewhere between three and four million pounds Sterling."

McGuire let out a low whistle. "Then it can't be a sergeant. It has to be an officer."

"We have more sergeants than officers," Foster said.

"The detail will consist of an officer, a sergeant, and eight men."

Foster smiled. "What I meant is that we only have two officers."

McGuire returned the smile. "We have Mister MacTaggart with us. He was an officer in the last war."

"Hardly." MacTaggart let a rumble of laughter go. "My highest rating was that of lance-corporal."

"In that war lance-corporal outranked most wet-eared lieutenants."

Young Foster blushed at the teasing. "I'll pick my men."

"The next detail's mine," the captain said.

"The third one's mine." MacTaggart patted McGuire on the shoulder as he passed him. He headed up the aisle toward the Railway Express coach. Maybe it had not occurred to Telford that, when the crippled boxcar was repaired, they would need a coach to transport Foster and his squad to Montreal and perhaps beyond that city to Ottawa.

Gunny opened his eyes. A heavy cloud of cigarette smoke floated above him.

Harry Churchman pushed away from the tailgate of the Bulldog where he'd been sitting and squatted next to him. "You look done in."

"I'm out of shape," Gunny said. "I'm too old to be running around dark streets." He took a deep breath and didn't hear a rasp. The rest had helped him. "How's the time?"

"Nine o'clock on the button."

"No sign of the train?"

"No need to worry," Harry said. "We'll hear it."

"It set?"

"Everybody's here but the Frenchie."

Gunny got to his feet. His legs felt weak, but he covered the trembling by leaning against the wall until he was stronger. "What's the drill, Harry?"

"With this group, who can tell?"

Harry turned and nodded in the direction of the captain and the major. They sat cross-legged in the center of the building. They were drawing lines and circles in the dirt floor.

"Last-minute changes?" Gunny asked.

"More like last-minute decisions." Harry tapped Gunny on the arm. "Let's see what stew they're cooking up now."

Captain Whitman looked up from the dirt drawings. "You don't have a mortar with you, do you?"

"Not with me," Harry said. "It's back at the hotel."

"Too bad. I'd like to put a few rounds on the track at both ends of the boxcar before we make our push."

"Grenades," Harry said.

"How do we get close enough?" Johnny pointed at the drawing in front of him. The lines and circles represented the siding, the roundhouse, and the road that ran past it toward the south.

Harry put his toe on the road line and pushed it south. "A pass in the trucks."

"How?"

"Easy. We roll them off the tailgate as we go by."

A moment of hesitation before Johnny said, "It might work."

It was 9:05. The Frenchie still hadn't arrived.

CHAPTER THIRTY ONE

enri Leveque slapped the dashboard of the stolen Ford with an open palm. "Stop here," he said. He could see the faint, leaked light from the seed-and-feed building. It was straight ahead, half a block away on the right.

It was 9:10.

The Ford had wooden sides and a plank bottom. It was used to transport crates of chickens, and the cab smelled of their droppings. Back in the load space, feathers were caught, almost imbedded in the planking. There was crude lettering on both cab doors: WILLIS POULTRY COMPANY.

Lafitte had fingered the truck for them. It had been parked for the last week on a side street. The owner, Phil Willis, was in Montreal having a goiter removed from his throat. He had left the key with Lafitte before he took the train. He was not expected back from Montreal for at least another week.

Pete Bouchard cut the engine. He switched off the headlights.

Henri Leveque had no illusions about the intelligence of the Bouchard cousins. A leader could not always choose the tools he used. "Once more," he said, and he could feel the restless shifting. "The important matter is that you don't lose us. Stay close enough that you can follow but not within the distance that they will know you are there."

"We understand that," Pete Bouchard said.

Henri hoped they did. He got out of the cab of the Ford and closed the door carefully so there would be no audible slam. He leaned on the window of the cab. "It will not be long. You will know that it is time to prepare when you hear the train arrive."

"You can depend on us," Charlie Bouchard said.

"I do."

Henri Leveque walked away. The Bouchard cousins watched him until he stepped from the sidewalk and turned right and went out of sight.

Neither man knew exactly what Leveque expected of them. It was easier to pretend that they did.

"Well," Harry said as he stepped away from the door, "I guess we can start the dance now. Everybody we invited is here."

Leveque watched Harry walk away. Then he turned and latched the door that led to the street. "I assume that I did not miss much. I decided upon a nap and overslept."

"You didn't miss much," Harry said. "We decided on how we'd divide the Crown jewels. You weren't here so we figured you didn't want a share."

"Americans have such a fine sense of humor."

"Is that right?" Harry whirled around and grinned at him.

"It is in all their films," Leveque said.

"We don't make those films in Texas."

Pierre Picard, from his position in the brush below the track bed to the east of town, saw the train first. The probe of the headlight on the engine could be seen several miles away. It was a pinpoint at first, even before he could hear it, and then the train was closer, and the noise was deafening, and the light flooded the tracks and the track bed on both sides as far as the recently cut brush.

When the train was closer, seconds before it passed him, he saw the cascade of sparks. Those and the plumes of smoke came from under a boxcar about two-thirds of the way back toward the end of the train.

When that boxcar passed Pierre, he could smell the burning, the hot iron and steel and the scent of wood overheating and about to burst into flame.

The caboose clacked by. Pierre climbed to the track bed. The smells were stronger, more acrid there, and he saw wisps of smoke from the undergrowth where the sparks had landed. He stood in the middle of the tracks and waited until he was certain there would be no fire. Then he took the twin bundles from under his arm. He placed them as the American, Vic, had shown him, one bundle in each trench beneath the rails. He duck walked between the tracks as he spread the pig-tailed fuses.

He was ready. He sat on the rail and waited. It was a warm night, and he took off his battered felt hat and fanned himself.

After a couple of minutes the scent of the burning had blown away.

Randy heard the train first. A few seconds later Clark caught the low sound. His head jerked around, and he saw Randy's dip of his head and slow wink.

It was thirty seconds later before the corporal heard the train approaching the station. He rushed from the bench to the door that led to the platform. "You can wire that it's arrived," the corporal said over his shoulder to the ticket clerk.

The telegraph key started up as the corporal rushed outside.

Randy shifted down the bench until he was closer to Clark.

"We didn't plan on him," Clark said.

"He seems friendly enough."

"He's armed."

"So are we," Randy said. He touched the gym bag with the side of a shoe.

It was a short message. Information had been passed down the line that the special train had reached Wingate Station.

Johnny pushed open the double doors and said, "Let's go shake the peach tree." Vic was behind the wheel of the Mack Bulldog on the left. Johnny passed two of the Thompsons through the driver's side. Before he entered the passenger side he circled the tailgate and received four grenades from Gunny.

Vic kicked over the engine and started backing into the street. Gunny yelled, "Hey, there, Vic." Vic braked and waited for Gunny to place his shotgun in the back and step in with both hands clutching grenades.

Richard Betts placed two prepared charges of dynamite on the seat of the other Bulldog and stepped in and rammed the sliding door closed. Tom dropped four grenades on the seat next to the explosives and braced a Thompson against his knee before he closed the passenger door.

"All right," Gunny shouted.

The first Bulldog backed through the building doorway. When it reached the street Vic turned it and pulled forward far enough to clear the driveway. He edged to the curb and braked.

Henri Leveque stood to one side. He'd watched the first truck leave the building. Now he stared at the second one. Harry passed him and dumped four grenades in his hands. Harry pointed at the second Bulldog. "You can ride with me." He followed Henri and caught his elbow and boosted him over the tailgate. Harry stepped around the side of the truck.

"Move it," he said to Richard Betts.

Betts backed out. Harry watched him clear the doorway. He stood in the center of the barnlike room and looked around for his final check. It was clear except for the suitcases. The men had checked out of the hotel after supper and moved their gear to the meeting place.

Satisfied, Harry lowered the wick on the lamp and blew across the globe to extinguish the light. He replaced the lamp on the nail on the beam, and, leaving the building, he closed the doors and attached the padlock. He climbed into the second truck beside Henri.

Vic put the lead Bulldog into gear and pulled away from the curb. The headlights swept across a battered Ford truck with wooden sides and a wide bed that was parked across the street.

Vic slowed when the truck was beyond the back lot. He wanted to be sure Richard was behind him. He caught the streak of the headlights in the road as he began the right turn that took them toward the main street where the Wingate Inn Hotel was. A left on the main street and he drove past the hotel. At the corner beyond the hotel he took a right. The train station was dead ahead, a block away on the right.

"Pull over here," Johnny said.

Vic pumped the brakes and edged to the curb. He cut the engine and switched off the lights. Straight ahead, a few feet this side of the railroad tracks, there was a flashing light and a barrier that had lowered into place.

The barrier was a good touch, Johnny thought. He didn't want to cross the tracks yet anyway.

"We're going to look silly," Vic said, "if they don't drop that freight car off for us."

Even as Vic spoke, the train began to back up, passing the crossing. The caboose went by, then three lighted coaches and the first of the boxcars rolled by. The fourth boxcar that passed the crossing threw out a shower of sparks.

"Tell me," Johnny said, "if those sparklers don't look golden to you?"

There was a shaking sound, a noise like thunder, as the train was braked. There was a short wait, and then the train moved forward again. The caboose, the three coaches, and the first three freight cars had been uncoupled. The last boxcar now was the damaged one. Smoke and sparks poured from under it, even though it was hardly moving at more than five miles an hour.

"We're lucky or good." Vic hunched forward and planted his elbows on the bottom curve of the steering wheel. "They're switching our bank to the siding."

"You know something about trains?"

"Only what I learned stealing in the Detroit yards."

The yard crew from Wingate Station hadn't arrived yet. Crewmen from the train accomplished the uncoupling and the switching.

While the engine nudged the crippled boxcar onto the siding, MacTaggart and McGuire swung down from the last coach. They were on the south side of the tracks. They stood aside as Lieutenant Foster, a young sergeant, and eight men dropped from the same doorway and formed up.

"Good luck, lad," MacTaggart said as the detail marched by.

Captain McGuire called out, "Stay alert, men, and I'll see you at breakfast."

The detail marched toward the road. When they reached the point where the tracks and the road met, they took an oblique turn and angled for the center of the separated boxcar.

"They'll be fine," MacTaggart said.

"I wanted to stay with them."

"You can't baby the boy all his life."

"You bastard." McGuire grinned at him. "Of course, you're right."

At a distance the switch was thrown again and the engine and the remaining boxcars were on the main track once more. There was a rattling as the train backed toward the three boxcars of paper wealth, the three day coaches, and the caboose. The brake-man hung on the last boxcar, a lighted lantern in one hand.

"We'd better board," MacTaggart said.

He stepped up and inside. He stopped and watched as Captain McGuire took his last long look at the detail. When McGuire was done and turned, MacTaggart offered him a hand and swung him aboard.

There was a jolt as the cars met. MacTaggart and McGuire found their seat. After a long pause the train began to move forward.

McGuire leaned across Duncan to get his clear view of the siding. Lieutenant Foster and his men were spaced the length of the single boxcar.

Foster lifted a hand, and then the coach passed the siding, and the depot and the town were behind them.

The stolen Ford truck was parked on the main street, the grill and part of the hood showing beyond the corner of the side street that led to the railroad crossing.

Pete Bouchard had been about to make a right into that street when he saw the two trucks parked and dark in a line. At the last moment he corrected the wheel and continued on the main street. He crossed the intersection and braked against the curb. "Have a look," he said.

Charlie dropped from the cab and trotted to the corner.

Pete pulled away, half a block, and did a U-turn. Returning, he cut across the lanes and parked the Ford level with his cousin. Before he switched off the headlights he saw Charlie shake his head. Not yet. He killed the engine and settled down for a wait.

The train passed Location A. Jean waded through the heavy brush and reached the track bed. He carried the twin bundles of explosives in front of him, clutched in both hands.

He planted the charges the way the old man, Gunny, had shown him. He stretched the fuse toward him, and then he stood, one shoe on the end of it, while he stared in the direction of town.

At the railroad crossing the flashing light went off. The barrier swung upward, wobbled for a few moments, and then pointed straight for the sky.

Vic shifted gears and looked past his right shoulder at Captain Whitman. "Now?"

"Not yet." Johnny wanted to allow the train time to put some distance between it and the town.

Straight ahead, off to the right, the front of the roundhouse was lighted. Several large lights lit the closed high doors.

"Two or three minutes more," Johnny said.

In the back of the second Mack Bulldog, Henri Leveque sweated with the wait. He'd heard the train pull away. That seemed hours ago. The grenades that Harry had given him were slick in his hands, like they'd been oiled.

"Is there some reason we don't move?"

The coal of a cigarette wagged in Harry's mouth as he talked. "The same screw-up. With this setup why expect anything else? We got here early." He took a final puff from the cigarette and mashed it into the floorboards at his feet.

"Something has gone wrong. I know it."

"Don't be a cunt," Harry said. He didn't say that he'd be happy when the truck moved, too. The scent the Frenchie wore was making him sick. The nervous sweating of the man made it even worse.

Charlie Bouchard circled the Ford and climbed in the passenger side. "We will hear it start up," he said.

On the seat between them were the two pistols that Lafitte had offered them. Both were rusted and scratched, weapons that the constable had taken away from drunks on Saturday nights. "I can't swear they'll fire," he'd said.

In some ways that information had not frightened the Bouchard cousins. Not as much as it should have. Neither of the men had ever fired a gun at anyone in their lives.

Three minutes passed and then two more.

Randy had done the figuring in his head. All hell would be breaking out any minute now.

He said, "I got to bleed my lizard." He caught the gym bag at his feet by the cloth handles and stood.

Corporal Lester watched him, but it was not with any special interest. After he'd returned from the platform outside, after the train left, he appeared tired. Most of his attention was centered on the ticket clerk behind the wire cage. There'd been a call from the foreman of the yard crew. They'd had trouble with the truck, and they were coming in soon in their own cars.

Randy faced Clark. "Got to bleed yours?"

"Not yet."

Randy carried the gym bag into the bathroom. Both rest rooms were to the left of the ticket window, toward the door that led to the town.

The door closed behind Randy. Corporal Lester smiled at Clark. "Is that an American expression? I've never heard it before."

"Down home and country," Clark said.

"I'll have to remember it and use it on my mates," the corporal said.

In the bathroom Randy unzipped the gym bag and took out both target pistols. He emptied the spare box of shells into his right-front pocket.

Nerves were getting to him. He went into one of the stalls and pissed long and hard.

Nothing like a good piss to take the strain away.

Lieutenant Foster had chosen the youngest of the noncoms, Sergeant Winston. That done, he'd left the selection of the eight men to him. It was the way the chain of command was supposed to work.

After the train left the station, Foster drew Sergeant Winston aside for a talk. They decided that four men would form the guard detail and the other four would take a break on the other side of the boxcar. It would be one hour on and one hour off. There was no way to know how long the detail would last. It might go on all night.

Sergeant Winston set the first watch. He sent four soldiers to the other side of the boxcar for their rest time. Winston wanted the first watch, but Foster decided that he would take it.

Winston joined the second watch on the far side of the car.

Lieutenant Foster stood at the edge of the road, his back to it, and stared at the boxcar. He hadn't told anyone what was inside. He could keep a secret with the best of them. But in his mind he was thinking about the letter he would write Mary Ann before he shipped out of Halifax. Wouldn't she be surprised when he told her that he had been left in charge of a cargo worth between three and four million pounds?

He was framing the words when the strong beam of the truck headlights washed the length of the boxcar and lighted him.

He turned to face the truck. He raised a hand the way a traffic cop did. The command to stop was on the tip of his tongue. But whoever was driving the truck pressed down on the gas, and the truck took a leap and sped level with him and beyond.

He turned to look after that truck. It was then the headlights from the second truck placed their strong beam on him. He felt like a bug pinned to a board. It was a feeling he had only for a short time. He whirled to his left to face the second truck. It was then he realized that something had been thrown or had fallen from the back of the first truck. One of the objects…a rock…a stone…had landed at his feet. He looked down but the glare had blinded him. He couldn't see what it was. Other objects were hurled from the back of the second truck.

He opened his mouth. He began to shout, "Stop in the name…"

The first grenade exploded almost exactly under Lieutenant Foster's feet. It split him from crotch to neck like a freshly slaughtered beef.

"Now," Johnny had shouted.

Vic jumped the truck across the tracks and headed for the siding where the boxcar was parked. Johnny eased the sliding door on his side open. He grabbed two grenades from the seat next to him and pulled the pins. He held the levers down until the truck was abreast of the boxcar.

A young man in an officer's uniform held up a hand as if to stop them.

"Floor it," Johnny said.

The second the headlights left the young officer, Johnny tossed the two grenades through the open doorway. In the back of the same truck Gunny tossed two grenades past the tailgate and then pulled the pins on two more and tossed them under-handed toward the boxcar.

The second Bulldog, with Richard Betts at the wheel, had its hood on the bumper of the truck ahead. After he was rid of the second pair of grenades, Gunny rolled away and pressed against the right side of his truck so that he could not be seen in the headlights. He covered his face with his hands.

In the cab of the second Bulldog Tom Renssler pulled the pins on a pair of grenades and held the levers down. At the last moment, level with the boxcar, he released the levers. The blast of air poured on him through the open door. And for some reason he hesitated. He wasn't sure that he could throw the grenades.

It was then he heard Richard Betts yelling at him. "Throw the goddam…"

He did. It was that or blow up.

The truck roared past the siding. Richard Betts was still shouting at him. He didn't hear the most of it. "…What the fuck did you think…?"

The first grenade went off and he didn't have to listen to the rest of what Betts said.

Harry Churchman threw one grenade and then a second one. He rolled to his side and stared at Henri Leveque. "You going to toss them?"

Henri didn't move. His hands were clenched white over the slippery grenades.

Harry gave him a shove and then fell down next to him. "Worthless as pigshit," Harry said.

"I couldn't."

"Pigshit."

The Ford turned the corner and headed for the railroad crossing. Pete Bouchard was following the two trucks the way Mr. Leveque had told him to. When he crossed the tracks he was about a hundred yards behind the second truck.

The Ford was almost level with the near end of the boxcar when the first grenade exploded. Charlie Bouchard said, "Great God, what is …?"

Pete grabbed the wheel with both hands and swung it hard left. The headlights told him there wasn't much space in that direction. The side of another building was there. But he moved into the other lane. A hard right and he was straight and level.

Sergeant Winston had his back to the wall on the other side of the boxcar. He heard the trucks approaching and got to his feet. A young soldier, Private Pitts, looked up at him.

"What is it, Sergeant?"

"I'll see." He turned back to the four men. "Rest easy. It's probably nothing."

The closest way was the gap between the back of the boxcar and the roundhouse entrance. He reached the end of the boxcar when the first headlights passed. He stopped and said to himself, What the hell?, and reached for his holster flap.

He was still fumbling with the holster flap when the second truck passed. At that instant the first of the grenades went off. He wasn't hit by any of the flying metal, but the concussion pushed him back. He used his left hand to grab at something on the boxcar. He righted himself.

He heard screaming then. It was close, but it sounded far away. The blast had almost deafened him. Other grenades exploded, and he pressed against the end of the boxcar. The bulk of it shielded him.

His Webley was in his hand. He didn't remember when he'd drawn it.

A third truck was passing. It was cutting across the road into the other lane when Sergeant Winston braced his service revolver against the side of the boxcar. He pulled the trigger as fast as he could. He emptied it into the cab of the Ford truck.

Window glass shattered. The Ford seemed to hesitate, slowing, and then it curved hard left and rammed into the side of the brick building on the other side of the road. The hood buckled and flipped upward.

The screams pushed at him. He was shaking while he broke the pistol and dumped the spent shells and began to reload.

"Form here, form here," he shouted over his shoulder. "Damn your hides, form up."

His four men, the ones who'd been on break and had been shielded by the boxcar, pressed close to him. He could see their pale, sweaty faces.

"Lock and load."

He heard the bolts snick and the rounds ram into the chambers. "Prone position," he shouted.

When they were belly flat he put one knee on the rail and waited.

To his left, he heard someone scream, "Oh, God, somebody help me."

Sergeant Winston didn't move. The boxcar, the safety of that, was his first concern. Only when he was certain that it was secure would he have time to take care of the wounded.

CHAPTER THIRTY TWO

The *crump, crump, crump* in the distance brought Pierre Picard to his feet. He clapped the battered hat on his head and the clammy inside liner started an involuntary shiver down his spine. He waited until it passed, and, after he located the tip of the fuse, he brought the penny box of matches from his hip pocket. He squatted over the pigtail and selected a match. But he hesitated. He wasn't sure that the explosions were the ones that constituted the signal.

Barely moments later he heard small-arms fire. One or the other, it didn't matter which was the real message. He tried to strike the first match. It broke and he tossed it away. Nerves, just nerves. The second match caught and flared. He touched the flame to the fuse and it hissed at him.

He jumped over the rails and ran as hard as he could along the track bed toward town. He'd gone about a hundred yards when the blast came. It rocked the ground under him. He staggered and landed on all fours. A dust cloud swirled toward him and a hail of small stones showered down. Dust reached him and clogged his nostrils.

Time passed. Only seconds, but it seemed longer. He got to his feet and walked the distance to the spot where he'd planted the explosives. The dust was thick, so dense that he didn't believe it would ever settle. He found the place and stopped a few feet away.

The inside rail on each set of tracks curled upward and outward. The wood ties had been blown to splinters on both sides of the trench where the bundles had been placed. A deep crater had been scooped away beneath the tracks.

He'd done his part. It was a curious satisfaction. Mr. Leveque would be pleased. He turned and ran through the dust clouds at a fast trot. He'd gone perhaps two hundred yards toward town when he heard the massive explosion in the west. He had no way of knowing that this detonation marked the blowing up of tracks at the west end of town. Pride soured in him. He thought he'd blown the tracks early.

The same confusion bothered Jean. He hadn't known what kind of signal to expect. The grenades exploding, the small-arms fire that followed, didn't sound like the "all hell breaking loose" that Gunny had warned him to listen for.

Another thirty seconds passed while he squatted over the fuse. Then he heard the heavy explosion to the east. It was the signal, he knew, and he congratulated himself for not letting panic push him into making a mistake. Mr. Leveque did not appreciate mistakes.

He struck the match on the side of his shoe and touched the flame to the fuse. He sprinted down the track toward the parked Cadillac. When the twin bundles of dynamite blew the rails apart he stopped and looked back. He did not, however, return to the location to check. He assumed that the American who had made up the explosives knew his business. Otherwise, why had he been given the job?

The grenades appeared to have exploded directly outside the waiting room. Corporal Robert Lester leaped to his feet. He said,

"God Jesus damn," and his right hand went to the flap that covered the Webley in his holster.

He took a long stride toward the door to the railside platform. Behind him, Randy pushed open the bathroom door with his shoulder. He carried a long-barreled target pistol in each hand. "You," Randy said to the corporal, "you stand still."

Clark circled Corporal Lester, careful not to walk between him and the pistols Randy held. He tugged the Webley from the canvas holster and stepped away. A few strides and he reached the ticket window. He ducked through the baggage-claim opening.

The clerk was there. His first instinct had been to run for the window and look outside. Now he whirled around and said, "Soldier, you'd better ..." The rest of it died in his throat when he saw the Webley pointed at him. His eyes flickered toward the table where the telegraph key was. Clark took two steps to his right. He stood between the clerk and the telegraph unit.

"No messages tonight," Clark said.

Using one hand, Clark stripped the wires from the telegraph. He pulled and twisted at the key until it broke away in his hand. He tossed it in the corner of the room.

"Tell me what this is about," Corporal Lester demanded. His face was flushed, and he could barely force the words past his teeth because of the anger.

"This is the seventh-inning stretch," Randy said. He wagged the pistol in his right hand until the corporal got the idea and lifted both hands high above his head. "See how much real baseball you're learning?"

Randy laughed. He cut his eyes toward Clark to see if he'd properly appreciated his wit. It was then that the door to the platform jerked outward and Private William Carpenter took a step through the doorway and froze in surprise at what he saw.

⚜ ⚜ ⚜

Private Carpenter had been sneaking a smoke, seated on the baggage cart and looking over his shoulder now and then to see if the corporal was watching him. Not that he expected a lecture out of Lester. Lester was a good guy. Still, some of the squad thought he was too much a stickler for what he thought didn't look military. Smoking on duty was high on his blacklist.

He crimped the cigarette and field-stripped it, and he was scattering the tobacco when he saw the line of trucks cross the tracks and head south. The first two trucks were close together, and the other was about a hundred yards behind them.

The blast of the grenades stunned him and so unnerved him that, when he reached for the Springfield '03, he knocked it clattering to the platform. He grabbed it and worked the bolt and put a round in the chamber. His first urge was to run for the siding. He reached the edge of the platform before he realized he could not go anywhere without receiving orders from Corporal Lester. No matter what was happening at the siding, if Corporal Lester came looking for him and didn't find him, you could bet that Carpenter would lose a few strips of hide.

He returned. He jumped the baggage cart and grabbed the knob on the door that led into the waiting room. He swung the door open and took one stride through the doorway. What he saw in the waiting room shocked him. Corporal Lester was over to his right, his hands raised above his head, just like in a film, and a short little man with cropped hair held two guns on him.

Carpenter's rifle was at his right hip. His finger was outside the trigger guard. When he skidded to a stop, his finger slipped past the guard and touched the trigger. He didn't realize he'd fired until the rifle kicked at him. The recoil almost twisted the Springfield from his hand. As luck had it, the rifle happened to be pointed in the general direction of the little man with the two guns. Randy gave a frightened yell that was almost a scream and fell or dived behind a bench.

Private Carpenter thrust the Springfield in front of him and grabbed the bolt and started to put another round in the chamber. A shot deafened him, and glass in the door behind him shattered and rained down on the platform. He looked to his left. A tall man behind the ticket counter was leveling a huge revolver at him, ready to fire again. Private Carpenter's knees buckled under him; that weakness probably saved his life. The second shot splintered wood on the door frame behind him. From all fours he twisted around and made a dive for the platform outside.

He landed on the platform, directly on the shards of glass. He felt the glass rip at his hands and his forearms but he still held the Springfield. He was struggling to get to his feet when a heavy weight fell across his back. He dropped the rifle and shook the weight from his back. He twisted around and hit the man with a clenched fist. The man groaned, and he realized that he'd struck Corporal Lester. "God damn you," Lester wheezed at him, and then both of them rolled to the left, away from the open doorway and the light.

A shot was fired inside. It tore into the platform. Another shot sounded. Corporal Lester said, "Oh, shit," and he pointed at the Springfield '03. It was in the wedge of light just outside the doorway.

Private Carpenter realized that Lester's holster was empty. He patted himself. All he wore that could be considered a weapon was the bayonet in the sheath at his hip.

"Got to get that rifle," Lester said.

"How?"

"How the hell do I know?"

They crouched on the platform, in the darkness below the windows. They were breathing hard, like big dogs in hot weather.

"Randy? Randy? You all right?"

"Yeah." Randy lifted his head above the top of the bench back and peered out the doorway.

Clark looked down at the ticket clerk. He was on his backside, where Clark had pushed him when the soldier walked in and pulled the trigger and shot at Randy. "What now?"

"They said for us to hold the depot." Randy poked a pistol over the back of the bench and fired two rounds into the platform. "I guess we've got it."

The coach windows shook in their frames with the first blast. MacTaggart said, "What the bloody hell?" and stepped over Captain McGuire.

McGuire sat up and rubbed his eyes. "Huh?"

"I don't know."

"Earthquake?"

"I doubt it." MacTaggart listened. After twenty seconds he started up the coach aisle. "I'd better check this with Telford." He'd taken only a few strides when the second large blast rocked the rails.

He met Telford in the middle coach. He'd come looking for MacTaggart. As if on cue, both men said, "Did you hear…?" and then they looked at the awakening soldiers. Telford took MacTaggart's arm and they hurried into the lead coach where the Railway Express operation was set up.

"What do you think those were?"

Telford closed his eyes. It was as if he were picturing what had happened behind them. "Somebody blew the tracks."

MacTaggart nodded.

"That boxcar is reason enough."

Telford reached across the seat and grabbed the emergency cord. He yanked at it twice. Only seconds later the train came to a full stop. About the same time the phone buzzed. Telford lifted the receiver. "Hold it a minute," he said into the phone.

He turned to MacTaggart. "Put a party together. All the men that can be spared."

"Good as done."

Telford put the phone to his mouth. "Engineer, I want this train backed up toward Wingate Station. I want it done at all safe speed. Rear brakeman, I think the track's been blown away. I want you to get us as close to Wingate as you can without derailing us."

Telford looked at MacTaggart. His eyes were small and pink behind the thick glasses. He covered the phone mouthpiece with a hand. "You armed, Mr. MacTaggart?"

"An Army .45."

Still holding the phone to his ear, Telford reached into the luggage compartment above his seat. He pulled down a sawed-off double-barreled shotgun. He passed it to MacTaggart. Another reach of his arm and he drew out a heavy belt with about two dozen shells inserted in the loops. "My eyes aren't as good as they used to be. Consider this a loan."

MacTaggart slung the shell belt across his chest.

Telford moved his hand away from the mouthpiece. "Move as soon as the rear brakeman signals you," he said.

MacTaggart reached his seat. Captain McGuire stood in the aisle. A jerk, and the train began to back slowly down the track. MacTaggart reached out a hand and braced himself against a seat back.

"Pick me a dozen men," he said.

"Thirteen is the proper number," McGuire said.

"Pardon?"

"I'm going with you."

"Who's going to handle security on …?"

Captain McGuire leaned past him and yelled the length of the coach. "Sergeant Jones."

"You certain about this?"

"Sergeant Jones," McGuire yelled again.

Sergeant Jones, a huge man in his early forties, waddled down the aisle toward them at a trot. "Yes, sir."

Captain McGuire lowered his voice so that only MacTaggart could hear him. "That boy back there is my godson. More than that, he is under my command." As if that hadn't been enough, he added, "All those men are my responsibility."

MacTaggart moved around him. He lifted his bag from under the seat. He drew out the Army .45 automatic. "Pick your men." He jammed the automatic into his waistband.

Captain McGuire caught Sergeant Jones by the arm and turned him. "I need a dozen of the best men you have," he said.

"Captain?"

McGuire turned to face him. "Yes?"

"As soon as you're done with Sergeant Jones I'll need him."

"Huh?"

"If you and I are going flower-picking we'd better let Mr. Telford know who's left in charge."

"By the book," McGuire said.

"It's the only way."

McGuire limped away, leaning toward the huge sergeant and in lively discussion. There wasn't any way to know that he was worried sick about the boy, Foster. MacTaggart knew. He was worried as well. The boy was a damned fine lad.

After the first run by the boxcar, Captain Whitman nudged Vic in the ribs and waved him to the right, off the road. Vic parked the truck in the dusty field behind the roundhouse.

The second truck followed their lead and parked level with them. Johnny rammed the sliding door to the rear and jumped out. The headlights from both trucks illuminated the field with its sparse grass and, about seventy-five yards away, a low mound of stacked steel pipe.

Vic switched off the headlights and circled the cab to join Johnny. "On foot?"

Johnny pulled the slide back and let it travel forward: the Thompson was charged. "We can't risk the trucks."

The flat *pop* of a handgun sounded on the other side of the roundhouse. Johnny said, "What the...?" He ran the length of the truck and stopped at the edge of the field, where it touched upon the road. He arrived in time to see the Ford truck careen across the road and stab its nose into the brick wall of the building there. The hood buckled from the impact, and water spewed from the smashed radiator.

Harry trotted from the darkness behind Johnny and stopped at Johnny's shoulder. "What was that?"

"I'd guess a mistake." Johnny watched as the others gathered in a loose half-circle behind him. "That's the danger of driving down the wrong road at the wrong time."

"One piece of information we got from that mistake," Harry said.

"What's that?"

"Some of those dogfaces are still alive."

Johnny gave him a sour grin. "You notice all the good news."

Two shots sounded. The gunfire was from a distance, and the echoes were soft and flat.

Next to Gunny, Henri Leveque flinched and backed away. Gunny said, "The ones you hear ain't the ones you worry about."

"Locate those for me, Harry."

"I'd say the train depot, Captain."

Vic spat into the dust. "Another screw-up for the Gipsons."

"Gunny."

Gunny stepped forward. He carried the pump shotgun over his shoulder like he was on a bird hunt. "Yeah?"

"While we mop this up, you loop over and check on what's going on at the depot."

"Fine with me, Captain."

"You want help?"

"Don't need it." He turned and walked away, past the trucks and into the darkness. He circled the mound of pipe and went out of sight.

"Betts?"

"Yo."

"You made some charges?"

"That's right." Betts held up a bundle of six sticks taped together, the blasting cap and the fuse already attached.

"How far can you lob that?"

"Fifty yards more or less, if the wind's right."

"That ought to do it." Johnny waved a hand at the round-house wall on the left side of the road as he faced in the direction of the tracks. "That'll give you cover until you're close enough. Harry, you back him."

"Good as done."

"The rest of us …" Johnny broke off and stared at Henri. "You got a weapon?"

"It's in my car."

"Jesus." Johnny held out a hand toward Richard Betts. Betts passed him the Thompson he carried under one arm. Johnny said, "Don't lose this one," and tossed the Thompson to Leveque. "You know how to fire that?"

"Of course."

Johnny laughed. "I didn't think it hurt to ask."

Harry and Richard Betts trotted away and reached the rear corner of the roundhouse. They stopped there and looked back.

"The rest of us do a little Sunday stroll down the street."

Johnny stepped into the road. Tom followed him. "How you like soldiering, Tom?"

Vic crossed behind them and took a position in the center. Henri Leveque charged the Thompson and took his place on the far side of Vic.

"You didn't answer me, Tom." Johnny began his slow walk down the road.

"It's a new experience, Johnny."

When they were level with the rear wall of the roundhouse Harry Churchman nodded at Johnny. His Thompson at the ready, his back to the roundhouse side wall, he kept pace with the four men in the road.

Richard Betts was one step behind him.

Corporal Lester said, "Let me have your bayonet."

Private Carpenter reached behind him and drew the bayonet from its canvas sheath. He passed it to the corporal. Lester held it by the heavy handle, and then he switched it and gripped the blade end.

Carpenter stared at him. Was he going to try some kind of knife throwing?

"Hold it like this."

"Yeah?"

"Over there. The last window. You get there and I'll give you the signal. You reach up and smash one of the panes."

"What...?"

"Do what I say."

Private Carpenter crawled the length of the platform. When he was below the last window he sat up straight and looked at the lights.

"Now," Corporal Lester hissed.

Private Carpenter swung his arm upward and slammed the heavy bayonet handle against one of the bottom windowpanes. It shattered. Two shots fired inside the waiting room smashed into another part of the window. Glass showered down on Carpenter.

Corporal Lester lunged as soon as Carpenter smashed the pane. He made his dive across the lighted area in front of the open doorway. He grabbed the Springfield and rolled away into the safety of the darkness on the other side of the doorway.

A bullet scarred the platform behind him.

He clutched the Springfield to his chest. That was better. He didn't feel naked anymore. He thought back through it. Carpenter had fired one round. The Springfield '03 clip held five. That left four rounds.

He worked the bolt and put a round in the chamber. He lowered the rifle and placed it on the platform. "Throw me your ammo pouch," he said to Carpenter.

Private Carpenter unclipped his belt. He duck walked from beneath the lighted window. He drew back his arm and tossed the belt. For an instant he was stretched out, extended, and he was lit by the spill of light from the window beyond him.

The belt flew past the open doorway and landed in front of Lester. He grabbed it and drew it toward him.

That same moment, to Lester's right, at the track level, a shotgun boomed. One blast and then a second one. Both patterns of shot struck Private Carpenter and tore him almost in half before it bounced him against the station front.

Corporal Lester grabbed the Springfield in one hand and the ammo belt in the other. He took a headlong dive off the platform. He landed in a patch of cinders. He was so afraid, he didn't feel the rasping that tore the skin from his hands and arms.

Gunny lowered the shotgun. He selected two shells from his pocket and fed them into the slot. He remained crouched in the darkness at the track level, below the platform.

"Randy?" He had to shout again. "Randy?"

"Yeah?"

"How many are there?"

"Two." The voices of Randy and Clark overlapped.

"Stay put."

"Gunny. Hey, Gunny…"

"Shut up."

They did. One man left. If the man made his move, Gunny would be ready for him. A wing shot. Otherwise it was a standoff, and he would have to find a way to flush him.

At the first rumble of the battle at the train station Constable Lafitte lifted the phone receiver from the hook and waited until the town operator came on the line.

"Who is this?"

"Irene."

"This is Constable Lafitte. For the next hour there will be an Army exercise at the train yard. If anyone calls and asks, you tell them that. And don't put any calls through to this number. I'll be at the train station. You got that?"

Irene said she did.

Lafitte broke the connection. He opened the lower desk drawer on the left and took out a shot-loaded blackjack. He crossed to the door and locked it, and then he switched off the lights.

The only instruction they'd given him was that he was not to allow the night man, Parsons, to interfere. And that was all that he was going to do.

He knew Parsons's schedule. He took a nap in the early evening before he left for work. But by now he'd be awake. And if he heard the explosions, he'd come running across town. Though he kept his handgun with him, he would stop by the office for one of the Winchesters. That was the way Lafitte figured he'd act.

He was right. After ten minutes he heard the running footsteps. The door was tried and found locked. A key scraped against the lock front.

Lafitte stood with his back against the wall beside the door. When Parsons entered and turned to reach for the light switch, his heavy breathing covered the sound of Lafitte's movement. Lafitte took two steps and swung the blackjack. He struck Parsons behind the left ear. Without a sound Parsons fell face down on the floor.

Lafitte dragged him across the office and into Cell Number One. He dumped him onto one of the bunks. As an afterthought Lafitte unbuckled his gunbelt and relieved him of his revolver. On the way back into the office he locked the cell.

There. His part of the job was done.

CHAPTER THIRTY THREE

Jean drove Mr. Leveque's black 1940 Cadillac in a wide circle that avoided the center of Wingate Station. He kept to the back streets and he found the old seed-and-feed building with hardly any trouble at all. He parked in the driveway. The headlights, before he switched them off, lit the huge shiny padlock on the double doors. So they were all gone? He had expected that.

He remained behind the wheel of the Cadillac for a time. He had a decision to make, and he wished that Mr. Leveque were there to help him with it. He was expected at the train siding. But, even at a distance, he could hear the gunfire. The battle was far from over yet, he thought. Therefore he would need a weapon. He knew there was a Thompson in the boot of the car. In fact, since Mr. Leveque hadn't taken his with him, there were two. The question was whether he could cross the town while carrying a Thompson. He did not think so. He could, of course, drive to the area of the depot. That way, no one would see the Thompson. There was risk in driving. The Cadillac was Mr. Leveque's pride and his prized possession. Any damage to it from stray gunfire, and the Devil would receive his pay before the morning.

No, the pearl-handled .32 would have to do for him. Once he reached the train yard he could find another weapon if he needed it. Later, when the boss wanted his car, he could return for it.

He stored the keys in the space between the sun visor and the roof. Just in case something happened to him. Pierre or Mr. Leveque would know where to look.

He hurried along the dark street and crossed the back lot. As he approached the brightly lighted main street he slowed to a casual walk. He wasn't prepared for what he saw when he turned a corner. The central block of the town swarmed with people. He estimated two or three hundred people, more than he'd seen there during the daylight hours. Men, women, and even little children clustered in groups.

All faces turned toward the train station. No one paid any attention to Jean. He started across the street toward the hotel. He'd reached the far curb when he heard shouting behind him. He turned and looked.

Constable Lafitte stalked from the alley that led to the police station. He looked angry. He pushed people aside. The questions people shouted at him didn't stop him.

"Lafitte, what is …?"

"Is it the war?"

"Are we under attack from the Germans?"

In the middle of the street the constable raised his hands high over his head. He planted his feet firmly in the wide-legged stance that meant business. The shouting ended.

"I have told you. There is a night exercise being carried out by the Canadian Army. It will not last long, but until the operation is finished anyone found on the streets will be arrested." His voice increased to a bellow. "Get off the streets."

There was a mumbling, a low rumble. A path cleared for him. Head down, Lafitte angled for the sidewalk in front of the hotel. Jean watched him and drifted over a few feet so their paths would cross.

"I'll go with you," Jean said in a low voice.

Lafitte didn't raise his head. "I told you to get off the streets."

"Lafitte."

The constable looked at him. "You?"

"I'll walk with you."

"If you like." They walked side by side toward the corner of the street that led to the train station. A few steps before the corner Lafitte turned on the crowd again.

"Get off the streets."

No one moved. It was quiet at the train yard. That silence was broken by the two booms of a shotgun. "Now. I said now."

One man moved and then a woman. A little boy began to cry. The crowd melted away. A stream of people filed into the hotel, others entered the café next door.

Jean had a last look before they turned the corner. The street was almost empty.

Four abreast they reached the Ford that had smashed into the building opposite the side wall of the roundhouse. Johnny broke step and waved his free hand at the cab. Tom crossed behind Vic and the Frenchman. The door window had been shattered by gunfire. Tom leaned in and had his look. Two men, neither one stirring, were huddled against the far door.

He returned to the line and took his place between Vic and Johnny Whitman.

"Know them?"

"I don't think so. I didn't get a good look." What Tom Renssler didn't say was that he didn't want a good look.

To their left Harry Churchman and Richard Betts crabbed their way along the wall. Twenty feet from the front corner of the roundhouse, where it joined the siding, Harry stopped. He motioned to Richard and then to Johnny. Betts moved up closer. He unwrapped the fuse and reached in his pocket for a match.

"Twenty rounds cover fire," Johnny said. "When I cut it loose."

Johnny moved forward. A few paces and he could see the boxcar, the two-thirds of it that was nearest the railway-crossing end of the siding. He jammed the butt of the Thompson against his shoulder and dropped to one knee. He didn't see anyone, but that didn't matter. He squeezed off a short burst and then another one. Down the line the others did the same. Harry Churchman lunged forward and reached the corner of the roundhouse. He poked the Thompson past the corner and triggered a long blind burst.

Betts struck a match and touched the fuse end. It was a ten-second fuse and he let about half of it burn away before he tapped Harry on the back and yelled, "Now." Harry ducked and backed away. Betts stepped around Harry and sidearmed the bundle of sticks toward the boxcar. It slammed against the near end of the boxcar and bounced a few feet away.

"Down," Betts yelled.

The explosion almost blew the boxcar from the tracks. It rocked away and then settled into place again.

Sergeant Winston was on one knee. That knee rested on a section of the rail that was between the freight car and the high double doors that led into the roundhouse. He heard voices, someone coming down the road toward them, and he lifted the Webley revolver and pointed it toward the road.

"Ready now," he said to his four remaining men. "Before you fire, be sure of a target."

It should have worked that way. It didn't. His first glimpse of the men coming down the road, and he thought, they are ducks on the water, and he shouted, "Fire."

His yell was lost in the harsh thunder of automatic weapons. The angle was bad for the men in the road. The hail of .45 caliber slugs tore into the side of the boxcar. The fire was not even close to Winston and his men. It should have helped him, but it didn't. His men were frightened, and the ones that fired didn't pick their targets. Winston turned to try to settle them down and he watched as one soldier screamed and jumped to his feet. The other three followed the first. It was then that the package of explosives went off a few feet away from them. The blast was fire and shock waves, and it threw the four soldiers through the air. If they screamed anymore, he didn't hear them. He was stunned, a stone man on his belly.

He thought, I can still get one or two of them, and he forced his eyes open. He pushed his right hand forward, and that was the moment he realized he wasn't holding the Webley anymore. In fact, he saw that he didn't have hands either.

Both hands were jagged bone stubs and he got to his feet using his elbows, and ran toward the line of men in the road. He didn't get far. A huge man stepped away from the side of the building, and there was a Thompson at his shoulder. Sergeant Winston saw the flame spout from the barrel, and the slugs stitched him from his neck to his groin. He did a skip and a jump and fell forward on the stubs of his hands. He didn't feel the shock. He was already dead.

It took a few minutes to clear the bodies from the track bed below the freight-car doorway. Johnny directed it and made a final check to be certain the trucks could back up flush against the boxcar. Satisfied, he used the butt of his tommy gun to break the seal and the lock.

"Richard. Vic. Bring a truck here."

A burst of fire from the other side of the freight car brought him to a crouch, the Thompson at the ready. He relaxed when he recognized it was automatic fire, and that meant Harry Churchman was mopping up.

A few seconds later Harry stepped around a crater and spat dry cotton on the rails. "There wasn't much left of him," he explained.

"Who?"

"Some poor dog-assed soldier."

"That all of them?"

"I've seen neater slaughterhouses." Harry tried to spit again, but his mouth was dry. "You see the poor bastard who made the run at me?"

Johnny checked him. "You knew we weren't making mud pies." He handed Harry his weapon and grabbed the freight-car door. A hard pull, and it rolled open. "Let's see what all this was for. It'll make you feel better."

Harry moved aside as the first Bulldog, driven by Vic, pulled past the boxcar entranceway and then backed across the track bed. When it was almost flush, Harry said, "That's it."

Johnny stepped onto the tailgate and jumped from there into the freight car. Harry stood in the space between the truck and the boxcar until Johnny returned. He was straining, grunting under the weight of one crate. He lowered it to the tailgate. "It's heavy enough," Johnny said.

Working together they unstrapped the case and lifted the cover. Harry struck a match and held it close. The four ingots of gold glowed in the weak light.

Tom pushed in past Harry. "Is it ...?"

Johnny laughed. "And you said we couldn't do it."

Tom put both hands into one compartment and lifted an ingot. "It must be twenty-five pounds if it's an ounce."

"What do you want me to do, Captain?" Harry asked.

Johnny pointed toward the railway crossing. "I think you'd better cover the road from town."

Harry leaned the major's Thompson against the side of the truck and walked away. Johnny grinned at Tom and swung to the ground. Vic passed him and pulled himself up into the boxcar.

The Frenchie stood at the edge of the road, head down and the borrowed Thompson under his arm. Johnny reached him and took the weapon from him.

"Give them a hand with the loading."

"Is it the correct car?"

"It's the right one."

"The Crown jewels?"

"Oh, shit," Johnny said, "we missed those."

"You promised me the Crown jewels."

"Sue me."

Henri looked at his empty hands and at the Thompson Johnny had just taken from him. "Nobody makes a fool of me."

"Nobody had to. The Crown jewels? Jesus Christ."

"What is in the boxcar?"

"Gold. Tons of it."

"And we still split?"

"The same split," Johnny said.

"Then I will help with the loading."

"Wait a minute." Johnny pointed one of the Thompsons in the general direction of the wrecked truck across the road. "You knew those men, didn't you?"

"I needed a truck to haul my share away."

"Bad luck for them."

"Yes, it was bad."

Leveque walked toward the rear of the truck. Johnny turned the Thompson and pointed the barrel of it at him. It would be damned easy. Screw him and his share. He lowered the Thompson. There would be plenty of time later to deal with the Frenchman. Right now, without the man's helpers, he would need every strong or weak back he could muster.

Harry had taken his post at the crossing. Johnny set his watch at the back side of the roundhouse. From there he could cover any approach from the south.

Corporal Lester knew he was in a bad spot.

At a distance the Springfield '03 had the advantage over a shotgun. But, close range as he was now, he didn't think he had a chance.

The man on the dark track knew what he was doing. He didn't waste rounds, and he was patient.

There just wasn't any percentage. Not the way he saw it. He was outgunned by the shotgun, and there were two crazy Americans in the depot. You couldn't predict what they might do.

He buckled the belt with the ammo pouches on it around his waist and gripped the Springfield. He dropped to his stomach and began crawling away from the train station. He told himself, when he was a good distance from the depot, he would find a sniper position and see how much damage he could do.

A hundred yards from the platform he convinced himself that it would be better if he went looking for some help. One man could not do much.

Some hundred and fifty yards away from the station he knew he was safe. He scrambled to his feet and trotted down the side of the tracks toward the west. There wasn't any special reason to head west. He had run out of reasons for anything he did. Now he was running in panic and confusion.

The train backed slowly. It seemed to move at little better than a snail's pace. Impatient, worried, MacTaggart stomped the aisle between the seated soldiers. Captain McGuire watched him. He'd selected his men, and now he rested his left leg and felt the time slip by.

There were two kinds of time. Slow time on the train and fast time in the town back there where young Foster might be fighting for his life. The more McGuire thought about the difference in times, the less sense it made. Bugger it.

"You say something?" MacTaggart stared down at him.

"Nothing of any importance."

Standing over him it occurred to MacTaggart that he ought to ask the captain if his leg was up to the strain of the forced march and the battle that was back there in the town. A look at the set and determined face, and he decided that the question would have to be answered in Wingate Station. Now wasn't the proper time.

A jerk of the train almost threw him off balance. He sensed that it was a gradual slowing before the full stop came.

McGuire struggled to his feet. "My squad, load up."

MacTaggart shouldered the sawed-off shotgun.

Telford, the Railway Express man, pushed past him. MacTaggart followed him and stood aside as Telford swung the heavy metal door open. Telford jumped. MacTaggart landed a couple of feet behind him. The train shuddered and shook and became still. Steady, balanced, he returned to the doorway and gave McGuire a hand down.

Telford waited for him about thirty yards beyond the caboose. The lights of Wingate Station were bright in the distance.

"They blew it all right," Telford said.

MacTaggart joined him and looked down at the crater in the track bed. He edged around the crater and gripped one of the twisted rails. "What are your plans?"

"I don't have much choice," Telford said. "They're expecting me in Montreal."

MacTaggart gave the rail a push. "You'd not be in any danger from another train if you waited here."

"I can't. But you've help coming from Halifax."

"Two hours away," MacTaggart said.

Telfold spread his hands in a gesture of helplessness and said, "You have to handle it."

Telford returned to the coach and stood there with one hand on the door rail. Captain McGuire formed his men in twos and marched them away from the train. After they passed the caboose Telford swung aboard the coach. The rear brakeman moved the lantern in a rippling upward and downward movement. The train began to pull away.

McGuire reached MacTaggart. He waved his squad around the crater and the twisted rails. "Well, Mac?"

"Let's see how the nightlife is in Wingate Station."

"I hear the ladies are lovely."

"That's a warming thought."

They joined the men and the march toward the town.

Lafitte got up and dusted his hands against his trouser legs. Jean was still on the sidewalk, his hands pressed over his ears. "I think it's done." He reached out a hand and pulled Jean erect.

The big man they called Harry loomed in the dim light on the far side of the crossing. He cradled a Thompson in his arms.

Lafitte spread his arms wide and walked into the center of the road. Jean kept pace with him. His hands were high above his head.

"We're coming over," Lafitte shouted.

The Thompson shifted from the cradle and the barrel swung toward them. "Who is it?"

"Lafitte and one of Leveque's men."

"Jean."

Harry relaxed. The weapon eased into the crook of his arm. "It's about time the working party arrived."

The two men crossed the tracks. A dark shape edged from the shadows to the east. It was Pierre Picard. "I am here as well," he said.

"What took you so long?" Harry grinned at him. "We had to start without you."

"You were killing everyone in sight."

"That's done. Now the real work's started." He waved them down the road to the boxcar and the truck.

Gunny stepped into the cinders and stopped and listened. The man was not there, and there was no sound of him, no breathing and no noise of his movements. The soldier had been there minutes before. Now he was gone.

He took a giant step from the ground up to the platform. He squatted and kept his head down. "Randy. Clark. I'm coming in."

"Walk in."

The waiting room was lighted bright as day. Randy was behind a bench. Gunny passed him and saw he was sweating. He smelled the stink of fear on him.

Clark was at the ticket window, behind the wire cage.

"The telegraph out?"

"It's wrecked."

"The soldier outside's disappeared on us."

Randy said, "That's good news." He gripped the back of the bench and stood. He rubbed his thigh muscles.

Gunny couldn't resist it. "Keep a good watch. He might come back."

He chuckled to himself at the fright that fixed itself to Randy once more. He walked from the waiting room and across the platform. Some fucking soldier that Randy would have made. In the old days on the Mex border, he couldn't have cleaned horse stalls.

Harry met him at the crossing.

"A man with a rifle's over there somewhere," Gunny said.

"One man? With any sense he's running."

"Could be." It was what he believed as well. "I'll relieve you, Harry."

"It's yours."

Harry leaned his Thompson against the side of the Bulldog and hoisted himself into the boxcar. The sooner they got the gold loaded, the sooner they could make the run for the border.

MacTaggart heard it first. He put out a hand and touched Captain McGuire on the arm. Macguire raised his arm, and the file of soldiers behind him halted. In the quiet that followed they could hear the running man.

Corporal Robert Lester was within fifty feet of MacTaggart and the squad before he raised his head to gulp for air. He saw the tall man with the shotgun, and he skidded to a stop and dropped his rifle at his feet.

"I give up."

MacTaggart lowered the shotgun. "He's one of ours," he said.

CHAPTER THIRTY FOUR

Captain McGuire put a man on point fifty yards ahead of the detail. He was a young man with dark skin and bowed legs and a nose so large it almost filled his face. "He's part Indian," the captain said as the soldier headed down the track at an effortless lope.

"What?"

"Cree, I think."

MacTaggart squinted into the darkness ahead. His first Indian, and he'd hardly got a look at him. When this was over, when he had the time...

Macguire dropped his hand, and the squad moved out.

But the march slowed. After the point man reached his forward position he eased into a bare trot. It wasn't long before MacTaggart felt the bottled-up rage and impatience. He caught the arm of Corporal Lester and pulled him forward until he was abreast of the captain. "They blew the tracks at both ends of town, didn't they?"

"I heard explosions to the east and the west."

MacTaggart moved next to the captain. "They think they've cut both approaches. They won't be expecting us."

McGuire wasn't sure. "If I ran this operation I'd blow the rails *and* guard the approaches."

"We don't know how many men they have." MacTaggart tugged the shell belt away from his neck. It was beginning to chafe. "Unless they've got a whole company, they're running against the clock. How long can they control a whole town?"

The information they'd received from Corporal Lester, after he'd calmed himself, had made them aware that the boxcar hadn't held up against the attack. The silence from the town, the fact that there was no continuing arms fire, confirmed this fear. "They've got to unload the boxcar. They've got to get on the road. It might mean they've pulled back to a line near the siding."

"Fewer guards and more workers, you mean?"

"That's it."

"Will you take the responsibility if we run into a buzz saw?"

"I know my responsibility," MacTaggart said. "Perhaps you don't know yours."

"Damn you, Mac."

"Sorry."

"You're right." Captain McGuire gave Corporal Lester a push. "Let me know when we're a hundred yards from the train station." A deep breath and McGuire lunged forward. He set a grinding pace.

MacTaggart matched him step for step. He felt the jolting in his stomach. Lord, he wasn't in shape, he wasn't the lad he'd been twenty years before.

He thought his lungs would burst. He looked past his shoulder and saw the distilled agony on Captain McGuire's face. It wasn't pretty to watch. There, we're even, he thought, pain tears running down the lines on his cheeks.

He had his doubts then. He was afraid that his anger had pushed the captain beyond what he knew he was able to do. It could have been that the pace he'd set early had been to reserve himself for the fight that might come. And for all his regrets he knew that there was no way to change it. The captain would not stop unless the leg fell off.

Another fifty yards at the same pace and MacTaggart told himself it was foolish to worry about Captain McGuire. The captain might survive it. He was not so sure about himself.

He was running half blind. He slammed into someone, and he might have fallen if the hand hadn't clutched his arm and steadied him. He stared at the man for a long time before he realized that it was the soldier they'd met on the tracks, the corporal.

"It's there," the corporal said.

"What? What's where?"

"The train station," Corporal Lester said.

They sprawled on a grassy field to the right of the track bed. "Two minutes," the captain said. And then he sat down next to Corporal Lester and MacTaggart.

"You think the telegrapher is still alive?"

"He was when I took my dive onto the station platform."

McGuire turned away. "Private Black."

The point man, the soldier who was part Indian, walked over a couple of soldiers and stood in front of the captain. He was breathing evenly. "Yes, sir."

"Pick one man. Take the corporal here with you." He nodded toward Lester. "I want you to take the station and hold it."

"If I can," Private Black said.

"You're in charge, Black." McGuire faced the corporal. "Is that agreeable with you?"

"If you say so, sir." Lester couldn't hide his relief. He'd decided he didn't like command.

"Is there a signal or a time?"

"Twenty minutes or the first firing you hear...whichever comes first."

They compared watches. It was exactly 10:00.

A minute later, Private Black, the other soldier he'd picked from the detail, and Corporal Lester crossed the tracks and melted into the darkness of a row of buildings that lined the north side of the track.

"And the rest of us?" The two-minute rest was over. MacTaggart staggered to his feet and swayed from side to side.

"Our objective is the boxcar." Captain McGuire stood, putting most of his weight on his right leg. He teetered for a long second before he got his balance. MacTaggart put out a hand and withdrew it when he saw that McGuire was steady.

MacTaggart looked down the track. That way led past the train station. "Which way?"

"From the south. This side of the tracks." The captain led them across the field to the east. The field ended. Dark buildings loomed in front of them. Beyond those buildings, if they had their bearings, was the brick shell of the roundhouse.

It was backbreaking work. The bullion cases weighed every bit of a hundred pounds and probably more. After handling thirty of the crates, Vic said, "Shit, it's hot in here." He moved to the side of the boxcar and leaned against the doorway and took a few deep breaths. One of the Frenchman's men, the one called Pierre, jumped from the tailgate to the boxcar and worked that end. Richard Betts took a case Pierre passed him. He paused in front of Vic.

"How's it going?"

"I'm going to drop a hernia any minute."

"There'll be gold dust on it," Richard said.

"Now you've made me feel better." Vic backed into the boxcar once more. He and Pierre took turns passing the crates through the doorway. Betts and the little man, Jean, alternated meeting them and stacking the bullion in the truck.

After they passed the fifty mark Harry Churchman pulled himself into the truck. "What's the count?"

"A fourth of it is loaded." Betts took a shuddering breath and wiped a hand across his forehead.

"Too slow," Harry said.

"You try it a few minutes."

"I might." Harry reached for the next case. The breath whoofed out of him. "Jesus, it's pure stone."

Richard Betts caught the side of the truck and swung down. A cool breeze blew down the road and chilled him. He felt sweat slick the length of him. He shivered and clenched his hands into fists to control it.

Richard heard voices. He stepped away from the truck and saw the major and the constable, Lafitte, leaning against the hood of the Bulldog. They were talking in low whispers.

Why the fuck not? Wasn't this a democratic army. "Major?"

Tom lifted his head and looked around.

"Vic and one of the Frenchies need a break."

"Thanks, Richard."

The major and Lafitte passed him and climbed the tailgate of the truck. Betts laughed to himself. Now that was a democratic army for you. You got to order a major around, and he thanked you for it.

When they were relieved, Vic and the little man, Jean, joined him for a smoke. They were tired, and the smoke stung their lungs. The smell of death blew at them from all sides.

Maybe you were supposed to get used to that smell. Betts wasn't sure that he ever would.

"Richard." Harry stuck his head past the side of the truck. "We're going toward the hundred cases. You'd better bring the other truck over here."

Betts flipped his cigarette into the middle of the road and walked away. Captain Johnny met him at the rear corner of the roundhouse. "How does it look?"

"First truck's almost loaded."

"How's the time?"

"Harry's worried."

Someone moved on the other side of the captain. It was Henri Leveque.

"Give them a hand with the loading," Johnny said.

"The smell ... the smell there ..."

"Not up to it?"

"I will do anything else," Leveque said.

"Weak stomachs." Johnny saw that the Frenchman was unarmed. He passed his Thompson to him. "You take my watch, and I'll break a sweat."

He got into the truck with Betts. Vic started the engine and pulled it in a wide circle and headed down the road to the siding. He parked the Bulldog a few feet beyond the one that was being loaded. He left room for it to pull away from the siding.

The headlights lit the crossing. Gunny turned with the shotgun over his shoulder. He blinked into the lights. Betts switched the headlights off and leaned against the steering wheel and waited.

After five minutes Vic got into the loaded Bulldog and drove it away from the boxcar. He gave the horn a playful toot before he went out of sight behind the roundhouse. Betts answered with his horn. Then he backed the truck down the slot the first time and braked when Harry yelled at him.

"Get your wind yet?" Harry met him when he stepped from the cab. Johnny circled the front of the truck and stopped next to Harry.

"You lose yours?" Betts asked.

"Every bit of it," Harry said.

"My turn then." He was passing Harry when he heard Harry lower his voice and ask, "When do we deal with the Frenchman?"

"When we don't need him anymore."

"I don't need him now," Harry said.

Betts nodded to himself. That was only right and proper. Screw them for mixing in another man's business. His arm muscles screamed at him as he pulled himself through the boxcar entrance.

He took a couple of steps into the boxcar until he located the major. Tom was seated on a low stack of the bullion crates. His head was down and his breath was ragged.

"Take a break, Major."

Tom staggered to his feet and wobbled to the doorway. Richard Betts watched him grab the side of the truck, hang there, and drop out of sight.

After that it was all work. He geared himself to go all out. The frenzy he created passed to the other men. He wasn't aware of time and he didn't see faces, and as he worked he felt like his brain had turned itself off. This crate and that crate and the one after that.

He didn't hear his name when Vic called him. Vic had to step into the boxcar and jerk a crate away from him. "Harry says you got to drive, so you'd better take a rest."

"Huh?"

"Take a rest until we're ready to move out."

He understood at last. He said, "How about you, Vic?" but the words didn't come out straight. They came out garbled, and he had to repeat it so that Vic could understand.

"In a few minutes," Vic said.

Richard sat in the boxcar entrance, off to the side, for a couple of minutes. His strength was slow returning to him. Finally, still unsteady, he lowered himself to the ground and staggered to the cab of the Bulldog. The sliding door on the driver's side fought him. He finally made it work by kicking it. He fell inside and caught the steering wheel to right himself. He leaned back and covered his face with his hands. God, he was tired, and his arms didn't seem to belong to him anymore.

The last thought that came to him before he blanked his mind, before he emptied it, was that those goddam Gipsons hadn't broke a sweat yet.

It was a dead town, the part-Cree soldier, Private Black, thought. There were lights on, the town glowed with them, but there were no people on the streets and no cars moved on the roads.

Ghostly.

At 10:05 Black left his rifle with the other private, Cooper, and crawled the final twenty yards to the train station. He thought of himself as the other spirit that was in him, the one that was an animal, and this time the spirit was a snake. He crawled and flowed. The ground was his natural element.

When he stopped thinking of himself as a snake he was on the station platform. No one had noticed him and he peered over a window ledge and into the waiting room. One bench had been moved to the doorway that led to the platform. It had been tipped on its side to form a barrier. The other bench had been placed flush against the other doorway, the one that led to the town.

A man sat on the floor with his back to the bench that blocked the town entrance. He was smoking a cigarette and staring down at his hands. There were two long-barreled pistols on the floor next to his right leg.

This man had close-cropped hair, and he was short, a runt.

Another man leaned on the ticket counter. He held a service revolver, a Webley, in a lax hand.

Private Black did not see the ticket clerk. He backed across the platform and slid over the side of it and reached the ground. He did not crawl this time. There was no reason to. The two men inside were not watchful.

He returned a minute later with Cooper and with the corporal who was not of his outfit. He stopped them at the side of the platform.

"A man over there," the corporal said.

A large man stood at the crossing a distance away. He had a shotgun or a rifle over his shoulder.

"I saw him," Black said. He had not. The snake did not see everything. He did not, however, want to admit it to a stranger.

"That loaded?" He touched the Springfield '03 the corporal carried.

"Yes."

Black saw it in his head, the way it was going to be. "Wait here," he said to the corporal. He touched Cooper on the back and led him down a narrow alley that ran beside the train depot. They reached the other side, and Black positioned Cooper so that he could watch the doorway on the town side of the station.

The corporal did not hear Black when he returned. The surprise showed on his face when he turned and realized that Black was there.

"In a few minutes Captain McGuire will start the attack over there." A vague nod in the direction of the roundhouse. "I will be at that window." Black pointed at the window above them. "Or at the doorway. One or the other. When I fire into the waiting room I expect the man over there, the one watching the road, to run in this direction."

"Yes."

"I want you to kill him."

"All right."

"Can you do it?"

"Yes."

Private Black reached up and placed his rifle on the platform. One step to the side, and he eased upward and was belly flat on the platform flooring. He hadn't made a sound, and he seemed to blend into the shadows.

Corporal Lester lifted the Springfield and settled the weight of it on the edge of the wood. He lined up on the man at the crossing. It was at least a hundred yards. He took a deep breath and let it out slowly. A jerked trigger, and he would miss the man.

An ache started in his shoulders. He tried to relax.

He had never fired at anything but a target. A man was not a series of circles on a piece of paper. A man could shoot back. It was not a thought that helped him relax.

❧ ❧ ❧

Captain Whitman pushed away from the side of the truck and stretched. Harry Churchman watched him. "See how the loading is going."

Harry stuck his head into the space between the truck and the boxcar and asked his question. He walked back to the captain. "About twenty cases to go."

"I think it's time I had my talk with the Frenchman."

"Want me along?"

Johnny shook his head. "Three of his men in there. Might be they'll be disturbed."

"I'll calm them." Harry lifted his Thompson and watched the captain head for the rear of the roundhouse.

"I'll take over," Johnny said.

"Is the loading finished?"

"Almost." Johnny took the Thompson from Leveque. "Quiet here?"

"I thought I heard something a few minutes ago."

"Where?"

"Where the pipes are stacked," Leveque said.

"You check it?"

"No, it is quiet now."

"Probably nothing." Johnny lifted the Thompson to his shoulder. He pointed it in the general direction of the mound of pipe. "Where exactly was it?"

Henri Leveque stepped in front of him and lifted his arm to point.

Johnny touched the trigger and fired a short burst that blew off the top of the Frenchman's head.

Bone fragments and blood and brain tissue mushroomed in a pink spray above Leveque as he pitched forward and fell on what was left of his face.

Now the animal in Private Black, his other spirit, was the great black bear, sometimes six feet high when he stood on his hind legs, and weighing as much as five hundred pounds. A fabled hunter, the black bear did not know what fear was when he was angry. There was nothing in the north woods that was a match for him.

The rifle he held was an extension of his claws.

A wind that blew across the platform ruffled the heavy fur on his back.

A black bear knew of time only what his body told him. He did not understand the ticking of a watch. But the rattle of gun-fire on the other side of the tracks brought the itch of a growl to the back of his throat.

Private Black, the man-bear, reared to his full height and blocked the doorway. His claws reached inside the waiting room and ripped and tore at the little man who sat with his back to the other doorway.

Two rounds were fired through the open doorway. The first one splintered wood from the bench to the left of Randy's head. The second shot should have hit him low in the chest or the stomach. It didn't. Randy turned to his right and reached for one of the target pistols. The second round struck him low in the back.

Randy clutched his side and opened his mouth.

At the ticket counter Clark braced the Webley and fired twice at the soldier in the entrance. He didn't know if he hit the soldier but the man disappeared.

Randy's mouth moved without sound. The scream that he thought was there didn't come out. Instead there was a choked cry. "Clark, help me."

Clark looked down at the ticket clerk. He was facedown on the floor.

"Clark, you going to help me?"

Clark ducked through the baggage window and, bending over, ran to his brother. He fell to his knees over Randy. He was turning Randy on his stomach when he heard a rifle fire outside the building. It didn't strike him or anywhere in the waiting room. Intended for someone else, he thought, and he placed the Webley on the floor next to him and reached for his brother once more.

Behind him, at the ticket window, the clerk knew that he had his best chance and that another one might not come. He didn't take the time to step through the baggage window. The fear was so great in him that he ran for the counter and took a headfirst dive through the opening in the cage. He almost cleared the counter. A trailing foot caught the side of the cage and turned him. Instead of landing on his hands and knees his left shoulder took the impact. He heard the tearing as the shoulder separated. He got to his feet. His left arm dangled useless. He pulled the arm across his chest and jumped over the overturned bench. When he reached the platform he stopped. He might have jumped from the platform and down to the tracks if he hadn't heard Corporal Lester yell at him. "Over here."

He ran in the direction of the voice. Out of the light and into the darkness, he didn't see Private Black, who crouched there. He tripped over Black's feet. Corporal Lester had to back away to avoid the flying form as it hurtled toward him.

Part of the plan hadn't worked.

Corporal Lester had had the huge man at the railroad crossing in his sights. He had aimed for the widest part of him, his body trunk. He'd sighted in and relaxed and then sighted in again.

The sound of gunfire from the other side of the roundhouse had startled him. He'd been between sighting in and relaxing, and he'd had to move his finger away from the trigger to keep from sending a round into the sky.

He had taken a deep breath, had let it out slowly, and had been lining up on the big man again when the Indian, above him and to his left, had stood in the lighted doorway and had fired twice. His shots had been answered from inside and the Indian had swung away and dropped in the shadows.

Corporal Lester had forgotten all his basic training, his time on the rifle range. His finger had jerked at the trigger. The Springfield had moved, and the round had gone high and wide of the man's left side.

Lester had cursed. He had fumbled with the bolt and rammed another shell into the chamber. He'd sighted in, but the huge man was not at the crossing anymore.

CHAPTER THIRTY FIVE

It happened so fast that Duncan MacTaggart wasn't certain what he was seeing or hearing.

The progress along the back streets was smooth enough. Captain McGuire had the lead. MacTaggart was on his heels, and the other ten men dogtrotted in single file behind him. Urgency pushed them. They didn't use a scout, even though it was unknown land. All the talking, the questioning of Corporal Lester hadn't furnished a single fact about the alleys, the back lots, or the buildings on the south side of the tracks. What Lester knew of Wingate Station he'd seen from the platform of the train station.

And, sure enough, they got trapped in open land. It was a flat dirt field that was a potential killing ground. First they reached a stack of pipe that was about nine feet long and perhaps four feet high. It was a natural barrier that ran at a right angle to the rear wall of the roundhouse. About eighty yards away, straight ahead, was the road.

Captain McGuire stopped behind the mound of pipe. It was good cover for a couple of breaths. He allowed his men a blow. He counted to thirty in his head, and when he didn't see anyone in the field in front of him he decided it was clear, and he led his squad around the left end of the stacked pipe.

Most of his men cleared the pipe. The last man in the file was level with it when they heard the truck. Bright headlights stretched down the road. As the driver cut the steering wheel hard right, the twin beams swept toward the twelve startled men.

McGuire went down fast. Behind him, without a signal, the rest of the squad landed on knees and elbows. The headlights never quite reached them. The driver braked the truck, and the lights faded immediately.

MacTaggart kept his head raised. He saw the man's shape detach itself from the far corner of the roundhouse. The man had gray hair that was almost luminous in the dim light.

The driver stepped down from the truck's cab and walked past the gray-haired man and out of sight down the road. A young soldier beside MacTaggart hadn't seen the guard at his post. He shifted, and there was the scrape of a belt buckle against a stone. MacTaggart clamped a hand on the man's arm. "Be still."

The guard took a couple of steps toward the center of the field. He stopped as if to turn an ear toward that section of the field where the squad was. MacTaggart had the sawed-off shotgun in front of him. He placed his finger on the double triggers. Ahead of him, the gray-haired man, after about thirty seconds, lowered his weapon and backed away. He reached the corner of the building and melted into the shadows there.

It was 10:05. Still fifteen minutes before the attack was to begin.

Next to MacTaggart the soldier who'd made the noise had been holding his breath since then. Now he released it and it came out like a thin whistle.

Jesus God, MacTaggart thought, but the whistle ended and the guard hadn't moved. He hadn't heard it.

A soundless shift in front of him, an inching backward, and Captain McGuire was shoulder to shoulder with him. His lips were only an inch away from MacTaggart's ear.

"No way to take him without sound."

"No."

"Got ourselves trapped."

"Yes."

"The best cover's behind us ... the pipes."

"I'll pass the word," MacTaggart said.

"We'll have to wait for Black to begin it at the station."

"I don't like it."

"Make another plan."

MacTaggart couldn't. He leaned toward the soldier on his left and passed the message. "If the shooting starts, take cover behind the pipes."

Ten minutes passed. Five minutes to go.

It was then the strange thing happened.

Another man joined the watch. They talked, though the words weren't audible to MacTaggart, and the man with the gray hair passed the weapon to the other man. He backed away and took a couple of steps toward the section of the field where the squad was hidden. He spun and lifted a hand. At that moment the other man pointed the weapon and touched the trigger. The gray hair exploded and turned into pink dusting powder.

Shocked that it had happened so fast, MacTaggart raised the shotgun and lined it on the man with the Thompson. Until he heard the Thompson fire he hadn't known they were dealing with automatic weapons. It changed the game, and he made his decision to try to take out the man with the Thompson. That weapon could not be matched by rifles and pistols.

Before he placed the shotgun's butt against his shoulder, there was a yell at the far side of the building. The man with the Thompson backed away from the man he'd just killed.

The butt settled on MacTaggart's shoulder as the man reached the corner of the roundhouse. MacTaggart realized he had missed his chance. He pulled the double triggers, and the pellets smashed into the bricks and threw out a dust storm. The man he'd aimed for, however, was beyond the wall, and he didn't think he'd hit him.

"Bloody hell," MacTaggart said. He broke the shotgun and peeled out the casings with his thumbnails. Next to him Captain McGuire staggered to his feet and ran for the mound of pipes. He made it to the cover, and the eight men who followed him were safe as well.

Two other soldiers, slower to react, started their run late. A hail of .45 caliber slugs cut them down in mid-stride.

MacTaggart remained flat on the dirt, below the Thompson's fire. He thumbed a pair of shells from the belt across his chest and inserted them. He closed the breech and swung the shotgun toward the corner of the building.

The deafening clatter stopped. The barrel of the Thompson was pulled away. The drum is empty, MacTaggart thought, and he considered his options. He could retreat to the stacked pipe. But off to his right was the parked truck. It would spread the line of fire. It would almost give them a cross fire. If he could reach the truck. He scrambled to his feet and took off at a low run. He kept waiting for the renewed blast of the Thompson. He braced himself for it. It didn't come. He reached the front of the truck. He left his feet and rolled and clawed through the dust until he was under it.

The blasting began seconds after he was behind the front-right tire. A second automatic weapon had been added to the first, and the heavy hail of fire rattled and screeched off the hollow pipes.

It was a questionable distance for the sawed-off shotgun. It was probably beyond its killing range. Cutting and stinging only, he thought. Still, facing a shotgun would make you wet your pants, and the men behind the pipe needed time to steady themselves and get ready to squeeze away a few rounds of their own. MacTaggart could buy them that time.

No other way. The Lord be with me. He had a quick thought about Peggy waiting for him in London. What was he doing here when he could be there? Being foolish, that's what. And then he placed two spare shells on the ground in front of him.

He settled the shotgun at his shoulder. He pulled both triggers.

❧ ❧ ❧

At the first sound of the gunfire the major was in the doorway of the boxcar. He'd carried a case of the bullion from one of the far corners, and now he held it out to the little man, Jean. "God's mercy," the little man said. He lowered his hands and backed away. Tom clutched the case so it wouldn't fall between the box-car and the tailgate of the Bulldog.

"What was that?" Jean asked.

"Trouble." Tom carried the crate into the truck and stacked it in place. When he returned to the tailgate Jean was at the side of the truck, about to swing down to the ground.

Harry met him there. "Go on with the loading. We'll handle this." He looked past the little man. "Major?"

"Here." Tom pushed past Jean and dropped to the ground. He took a deep shuddering breath and followed Harry. "What's going on?"

Harry stepped close to him and lowered his voice. "That Frenchie just..."

Harry's jaw fell. From the left, the direction of the depot, there was rifle fire and then pistols.

"What the hell?"

Another rifle fired. This time it was closer. They watched as Gunny ran toward them. He fell to his knees, and Harry thought he was hit until he saw Gunny begin a roll and a crawl away from the tracks.

Tom reached for the Thompson he'd left propped against the side of the truck. Just then there was the harsh boom of a shotgun at the rear of the roundhouse.

Harry yelled, "See to Gunny." He sprinted down the side of the road toward the post the captain had set up. He found Johnny there, rubbing brick dust from his eyes.

"How many?"

"I don't know." Johnny edged forward and stuck the barrel of the Thompson past the corner of the building. He fired a sustained burst that burned air over the field behind the roundhouse. He backed to the cover of the wall and looked down at the Thompson. "Shit, the drum's empty."

Running footsteps approached them from behind. Richard Betts might have run past them if Harry hadn't put out an arm. He pressed Betts against the wall and jerked away the Thompson he carried. He passed it to the captain and handed the one with the empty drum to Betts. "Put a full drum on that one."

"Together?" Johnny said.

"I don't see why not." Harry charged his Thompson and stood next to the captain. "You say when."

"Now."

They stepped away from the covering wall, firing as they moved. The short bursts from the two weapons swept the field from left to right. Each man fired about twenty-five rounds. When they ducked behind the corner, Harry thought he was blind and deaf. He leaned against the wall and waited for the sensation to pass.

Richard Betts returned with three spare drums. He squatted over Johnny's Thompson and replaced the empty one. He tossed the drum aside.

"That truck out there," Harry said. "I don't like six million dollars in no-man's-land."

"A lot of work for nothing," Johnny agreed.

Harry tapped Richard Betts on the chest. "We cover you, you think you could reach the truck?"

"Might be."

"We'll keep the heads down for you."

Betts hefted the Thompson and edged forward.

"You say when." Harry watched him.

"When." Richard Betts stepped past Harry and bent low. The first five yards, and he decided it was going to be no trouble at all.

Another long stride. Behind him Harry was about to move away from the wall when the blast of the shotgun checked him. He pressed so hard against the wall that the bricks cut into his back.

The flare of the shotgun at the front of the Bulldog was the last thing Richard Betts saw. Something as wide as green chain lumber slammed against him and threw him high into the air. For the whole time he was in the high curving leap he was still alive. His mind registered the flare, and he thought it was an explosion under one of the green stumps. He knew that what tore his chin and throat apart was a green root, and his mind told him he had made a mistake with the time count on the fuse.

The leap ended.

Blood pooled under Randy.

The entry wound was below his ribs on the left side. The exit hole was slightly lower.

"I can't move my legs," Randy said.

"You will." Clark took off his shirt and pressed it over the two wounds. The blood continued to pour. It soaked through the shirt in seconds and covered Clark's hands. "It's the shock. You'll get the feeling back when the shock's over."

"Bubba, I'm freezing."

That nickname. What Randy called him when they were children and Randy was just beginning to talk. He hadn't used that name in years, not since he'd started doing all those crazy things.

"I'm scared, Bubba."

"You hold on. Soon as I can I'll get the captain over here. He'll know what to do. And if he doesn't, Gunny will. He's been in a war."

He smelled it then. Randy's bowels had loosened.

"You still cold, Randy?"

He shoved one of his bloody hands under Randy. He moved it to the chest area. He was searching for a heartbeat.

There wasn't one.

Private Black crawled the last few feet across the platform and dropped over the side with hardly a sound. He stared over the planks at the crossing. He didn't see the man who'd been stationed there.

"You get him?"

"This is the ticket clerk," Corporal Lester said. He nodded at the man who sat clutching his left shoulder.

"That is not what I asked."

Lester looked away. "He moved. There was gunfire and he …"

"So you didn't?"

Corporal Lester didn't answer.

There was the chatter of automatic fire to the south. A shotgun boomed its deeper voice.

Private Black looked at the corporal with contempt. This man had no other spirit. He was a dog without teeth and with no courage.

"There is one man left inside. We see what he decides to do."

Watchful, he became the owl.

Captain Whitman grabbed his left forearm and clenched his teeth. "Shit."

"You hit?" Harry caught Johnny's wrist and turned the arm.

"Stung." Johnny rubbed it. The skin wasn't broken. Some pellets, almost spent, had found him when he began his move to cover Richard Betts. Lucky, he'd been lucky. "It's all right. You locate the shotgun?"

"At the truck."

"I wish I knew how many..."

"It might be one farmer for all we know."

"One dirt digger?" Johnny considered that possibility. He jerked a thumb in the direction of the train depot. "That wasn't a farmer. It sounded like an '03."

"I hear Canada picked up some of our surplus."

"That could mean Army."

"Question is: How big an army?"

"Beyond me." Johnny heard scraping sounds and looked behind him. Gunny Townsend, pale and shaky, lumbered toward them. "Yeah, Gunny?"

"Major says we better get out of here. It's falling in on us from all sides."

"The second truck loaded?"

"Just about."

From the direction of the truck a blast of the shotgun. It did no damage. The slugs rattled against the wall and down the street past them.

"How about the other truck? We just leave it?"

"He's telling us something," Harry said to Captain Whitman. "That shotgun says we don't go in his direction. I say we cut our losses."

"Down from twelve million to six?"

"We've already lost two shareholders. We might lose a few more."

It made sense. Johnny pressed against the wall and backed away. He made a flat loop around Gunny. "Cover us here until we're ready to leave."

Gunny let Harry pass him. He brought the shotgun high, at the ready.

MacTaggart stared at the lump, the form of the man he'd just killed. He'd been the first man MacTaggart had killed since the Big War. And that poor fool had been an accident. He'd been putting down cover, and the man had run right into the full pattern of it.

Still no sound from beyond the stacked pipe. Perhaps that was the sensible choice. From that angle there were no targets. From his own position, from beneath the truck, he couldn't see elbows or knees either.

A handful of rock rattled against the hood and the windshield of the truck above him. It came from the direction of the stacked pipe. He shifted about and looked past the tire. As he watched, three soldiers broke the top line of the pipe and moved along it. Their heads and shoulders were like a row of mechanical ducks in a shooting gallery. The soldiers reached a point almost level with the truck and waited there.

MacTaggart knew what they wanted from him. He turned his upper body and drew the shotgun toward him. He set the butt in the hollow of his shoulder and lined up on the corner of the roundhouse. He fired one barrel. A quick look behind him and he saw the three soldiers vault the pipe and run toward him. He faced the building again and fired the second barrel.

Clark knew there should have been some tears in him. There just weren't. His mother, if she'd been alive, would have cried for a solid year. It would have been a year of weeping and wearing black and only eating enough to keep her alive so that she could carry out the mourning.

But his mother had never been Randy's keeper. His mother had birthed him, and there must have been pain in that, and she had worried about him those long nights when Randy had been on the chain gang. All that was true. But she had never seen the true meanness in him, the Devil's hand on him, the way he fought the Lord's good in him and twisted it like a dirty joke.

Maybe he could cry in five years or ten years. When he could forgive, if the Lord would show him the way. If the Lord cared about either of the Gipsons anymore.

Blood coated his hands, thick as red mud.

Sick to almost vomiting, he looked around the waiting room. The door marked GENTLEMEN was there. He duck walked in that direction. He twisted the knob and lunged inside. The overhead light was on. The gym bag Randy had carried was in the center of the floor, empty except for a shell box.

Clark washed his hands and then his face. He looked at himself in the mirror above the washbasins. There was blood smeared on his undershirt.

He stared at his eyes. He did not look like a man whose brother had just died.

He dried on a damp roller towel. One step took him toward the waiting room. He stopped then and looked behind him. A breeze was blowing in on him through an open window above one of the toilets.

A string with a metal bead on it hung from the overhead light. He yanked the cord, and the bathroom was dark. He crossed to the window and stepped up on the toilet seat.

An alley was below him. A short drop. He looked in both directions. He didn't see anyone. He pulled himself up until he sat on the ledge. A jump might make too much noise. He grabbed the ledge and lowered himself until his toes touched the ground.

He heard firing from his left, the direction of the railroad siding. Not that way. He headed toward town. He reached the corner of the station building and stopped. He drew back. A soldier stood in his path, rifle up, watching that entrance to the waiting room.

Clark watched. The soldier didn't move. He was there for the night, it seemed, and Clark backed away. He whirled and started down the alley toward the tracks. He'd gone only a few feet when he heard the man coming toward him. "Cooper? You hear me, Cooper?"

Clark dropped to his hands and knees. The man was only yards away. Clark pressed against the wall. He lowered his head and saw the narrow opening above the foundation of the depot that led into the crawl space. He pushed upward and his head was inside. His shoulders scraped and he twisted his body to free them. He clawed and scratched, and his legs went in and out of the way only seconds before the soldier passed the opening.

Private Black said, "You see anybody?"

"Not a soul."

"You keeping a good watch?"

"I got no reason not to," Private Cooper said.

Black nodded. "You hear me, you come running."

"I'll do it."

Clark crossed his arms under him to keep his head above the dust. He was boxed and he knew it.

Maybe it was what Harry had said. That the whole operation was planned like a picnic for idiot children.

In the distance, muffled by the closed space, the gunfire was heavier. It went on and on, and it was like it was never going to end. Not in this lifetime. Not ever.

CHAPTER THIRTY SIX

Gunny Townsend didn't have to check his pump gun. It was packed to the slot. He'd reloaded after he fired those two rounds at the train station. That was a part of soldiering the way he knew it. No mistakes and no excuses. You took care of what was yours, and you let the Devil do his best with the rest of the world.

He held a hand in front of him, palm down, and watched the barest tremble and shake to it. Being shot at could do that to you, but he knew he could settle it down. He'd get it back to normal in no time. But, Lord, it was embarrassing to have that major leaning over him and asking him if he was all right. Him, a man who had fought in the Big One and had killed his share and had even killed some spies in that Mex border war.

It soured him some to have that major acting like he was some raw recruit.

He pressed against the wall when the shotgun by the truck burned more powder. He heard the shot whap against the rear wall of the roundhouse. No way of knowing who that idiot was there by the truck. Or how many of them there really were.

Not that it mattered a bit. Let them come one at a time or all in a bunch.

The cutter he carried could clear a trench five yards wide and five men deep.

Just walk your ass into it.

❧ ❧ ❧

Even with all the activity around him, the firing and the running and the shouting, Vic remained in the cab of the Bulldog that was backed up to the freight car. His head back, his eyes closed, he was trying to get some rest. He'd quit the loading a time after Betts did, and he'd gone out, expecting to join him in the cab. Betts hadn't been there. Vic was too weary to wonder where he'd gone. He got into the cab and pulled the sliding door closed. To hell with everybody, unless they were two times as tired as he was.

The truck shook, it shifted under the weight as men worked in the bed of it. He felt each crate of bullion as it was dropped or stacked back there. It didn't bother him any more than the gunfire did, as long as it remained at a distance. As long as nobody dropped a gold bar on him.

He didn't sleep. His mind was full of bits and pieces of dreams. It was the way he'd felt when he was twelve and had the flu that winter in Detroit. Dreams that grew out of fire. He was in his office. The Franks Trucking Company. There was one gold bar on his desk, just to hold the paperwork down. And when he went outside, the Mack trucks were lined up, a dozen of them, the hoods raised. He walked the length of the yard, stopping to listen to each engine for a minute. The song, the sound of the perfect tuning.

And at his trucking company nobody made fun of anybody. A man who gave a dollar's work for a dollar's pay was just as good as anybody else. That was the first rule at the Franks Trucking Company. And rule number two was ...

"Time to move out," the captain said.

Vic grabbed the steering wheel. This sliding door on the passenger side rasped open. Johnny was there and Harry Churchman stood behind him.

"That way?" Vic pointed past them toward the rear of the roundhouse. "South?"

"Not directly," the captain said. "North first and we work our way to the border."

"How do we stand?"

"We lost a couple. We're left and so's the major and Gunny."

"Betts?"

"He walked into one. So did the head Frenchie."

"That leaves the three that don't belong to us," Vic said.

Johnny backed away from the door. "Harry, you get the major."

Harry shifted the Thompson on his shoulder. "What about those three?"

"Like Vic said, they don't belong to us. Do what you think best."

"That's easy," Harry said.

Harry walked away. Captain Whitman stepped into the truck. He left the door on his side open. He could look down the road and see Gunny.

"You got any love for the Gipsons, Vic?"

"I wouldn't walk across the street to piss on either one of them."

"That's what I thought. Of course, there's been shooting at the train station. It might be the Gipsons aren't with us anymore."

Tom put a hand on the roof of the cab and leaned in. He was sweating and his breath was ragged. "The loading's done."

"Get in," Johnny said.

"Harry said he was going to deal with those three men. What did he mean …?"

Someone shouted at the back of the truck. It was a plea, almost a scream. It was split down the middle by a long chatter of a Thompson.

"Get in," Johnny said.

"What the …?"

Johnny grabbed his arm and pulled him into the truck cab. He reached across Tom and dragged the sliding door closed.

Vic started the engine. He eased the truck away from the siding. He swung the wheel to the left. The railroad crossing was straight ahead.

"Wait for Gunny."

Vic braked.

"No lights," Johnny said.

Harry was belly down in the back of the truck. He cupped his hands around his mouth and yelled, "Let's go, Gunny. I'll cover."

Gunny pushed away from the wall.

"Gunny."

Gunny started for the truck at a shambling, bearlike trot.

After the three soldiers reached the other truck they spread themselves on the ground around MacTaggart.

"Where's the captain?"

"Gone by now," one of the soldiers answered. "He said to tell you he was circling back to close off the road where it crosses the tracks."

"That puts the cork in the bottle," MacTaggart said. "You lads fire those rifles you've got there?"

"Yes, sir," one soldier said.

"I want the three of you to crawl to the back of this truck. Once you're there, I want you ready to move into the road and fire down the road when I tell you. Got that?"

A whisper of yes-sirs, and the soldiers moved away. Minutes passed. There were almost no sounds at all. A long burst of automatic fire broke that silence. It was at a distance, on the other side of the roundhouse. MacTaggart wasn't sure what the firing meant. It might mean that Captain McGuire had reached the other side and had stumbled into something.

"Get ready to move," he called.

He heard a truck engine start. From the sound he thought it was moving away, going in the other direction. He hadn't decided what to do when he heard someone yell down the road. It sounded like "Guns" or something like that.

"Now, lads." MacTaggart got his feet under him and ran away from the cover of the truck. With any luck he could reach that corner of the building, the one he'd been chipping away at all night. Even as he ran he saw the three soldiers leave the cover of the truck and step into the road. MacTaggart lunged the last few steps and rammed into the brick wall. He looked back and saw that the soldiers were kneeling in the road, firing together, putting round after round down the road as fast as they could work the bolts on their rifles.

Gunny Townsend saw the Bulldog pull away from the freight car. The driver got it straight in the road and braked. Harry was yelling at him from the back of the truck. It was time to move out. Gunny raised the shotgun to port arms and began his run toward the Bulldog. His breath came hard; he thought he was choking, and his heart beat against his chest like it was trying to break its way through.

He heard firing. His head down, he thought it was the cover fire from Harry. Another half-step and he heard his lungs tearing apart. He staggered, and the blood roared upward from his lungs. The dark flow choked him. It filled his mouth and gushed down his chest like vomit.

That close. He'd been that close before the lungs failed him the way he'd known they would.

He tossed the shotgun aside. He tried to right himself. Only fifty yards. He could still make the tailgate. Harry would help him.

A staggering step, another one.

He couldn't breathe. Now blood was flowing from his nose. He tried to clear his throat. The cough drowned in the back of his mouth.

He lifted a hand toward the truck and fell face down in the road.

There were three wounds in his back. One round had hit the lower corner of his left lung and ruptured it.

Harry thought Gunny was going to make it. That was before he heard the rifle fire behind Gunny. Some rounds lashed against the truck. Harry gutted it up and brought the Thompson to his shoulder. When he looked down the barrel he knew he couldn't fire. Gunny, wide as he was, blocked any sight of the riflemen in the road.

He wanted to yell, Get down, Gunny. It shaped his mouth. The "get" was on the front edge of his tongue. It was on his bottom lip when he saw Gunny stagger and almost fall. There was still some bull reserve of strength in the old man. He straightened himself, and his head lifted. His mouth made a scream that didn't have a sound. What came out, Harry saw, was a pulsing rush of dark blood.

Just before he fell, Gunny lifted his right arm and reached for the tailgate. His arm wasn't that long. It was fifty yards short. The hand changed into a claw and Gunny fell into the road.

Harry touched the trigger on the Thompson. A short burst streaked down the road above Gunny. It was only five or six rounds. Harry lowered the Thompson. The drum was empty.

A tall lean man in a dark raincoat stepped into the road. He had a shock of gray hair and he carried himself at his full height, straight up. He swung a blocky weapon at his right hip. A sawed-off, Harry thought, and he realized this was the man who'd checked them from the Bulldog parked in the field.

The man ran toward the rear of the truck. It was the easy, long-legged lope of a man trying to catch a bus.

Harry slapped the side of the truck with his open hand. "Drive it, Vic." Hardly breaking his stride, the gray-haired man leaned down to scoop up Gunny's pump gun. A few more strides, and the tall man dropped to one knee. He placed the sawed-off on the road next to his left knee. He put the pump gun to his shoulder as the Bulldog jumped forward and began to pull away.

Harry doubled over and rolled away from the tailgate. His shoulder struck a stack of the gold crates. He couldn't move any deeper into the truck. He brought up his hands and elbows and covered his face and neck.

One round. Low, Harry thought, and he was pleased until he realized the man was firing at the tires.

Better the tires than me.

Another round from the pump gun. Harry reached for the side of the truck as the left rear tire blew and the Bulldog wobbled and swerved hard to the right.

The hip, the whole leg, throbbed like a toothache now.

Starting from the hip joint, it had raced down the back of his leg. It throbbed in the calf. "Damn the fucking leg," Captain McGuire hissed through his teeth as he ran along the track bed. Even as he cursed, he dropped his left hand and grabbed the hip. He pressed as hard as he could.

He knew he'd reached the train station when Private Black, his rifle pointed at the depot front, side walked away from the platform to meet him.

"Careful, sir. There's still one in there."

McGuire dug his fingers deeper into the flesh around the hip. He stopped with all his weight on his right leg. "We'll deal with him later." He waved the five men in his detail past him, toward the railway crossing.

"I'm going with you, Captain." Black didn't wait for agreement from him. "You," he shouted at Corporal Lester, "you watch that door."

McGuire limped along in front of him. He'd gone about another ten yards when he stopped and bent almost double. The left hip had locked on him. Private Black ran forward and caught McGuire's left arm.

"Help me, son."

Black leaned toward him. McGuire swung an arm over the private's shoulder and straightened when Black did. The leg dangled between them as they hobbled toward the crossing. Just ahead of them the five soldiers had stopped just short of the crossing and were waiting for him.

Rifle fire searched the road to their right. The chatter of an automatic weapon began and died abruptly. In the silence that followed, before the shotgun boomed twice, Captain McGuire heard the racing truck engine.

"Firing positions." He removed his arm from Black's shoulder. He fumbled with the flap that covered the Webley revolver at his hip.

The truck, headlights dark, careened down the road toward them. Some force pushed the truck to the right and the driver fought to steady it in the center of the road. The front tires bumped across the first set of rails, and it was directly in the center of the crossing when Captain McGuire sighted in with the Webley and shouted, "Fire."

Harry's hand pounded against the side of the truck. "That's it," Johnny said. "Gunny's aboard."

Vic gunned the engine. The Bulldog took an easy leap forward.

"You think you can find the border crossing south?" Johnny faced Tom.

"If we can ..."

Two booms from a shotgun. At the second one the truck shivered. It appeared to jump into the air, and it began to pull to the right. Vic said, "That's a tire," and he fought the drag and turned the Bulldog into the center of the road. The rail crossing was straight ahead. The steering wheel jittered in Vic's hands when the front tires rode over the first set of tracks.

The left side of the truck cab exploded. Round after round smashed into it. Vic clawed at the steering wheel as he fell against Johnny. Vic had been hit several times, but the bullet that killed him entered his left ear and angled upward. It blew away the left side of his skull.

Johnny pushed him away with an elbow and reached for the steering wheel as the truck resumed its curl to the right. Johnny was swinging it hard left again when a blow struck him in the side. Another hit him in the armpit, directly under his raised arm. He couldn't hold the wheel. The truck had finished its crossing of the tracks. It headed for the sidewalk and the building to the right. The front tires climbed the curb. That bump swung the truck to the left again. The driver's side of the cab scraped a telephone pole. The right side, in front of Tom, plowed a deep groove in the brick wall of the building. Metal screamed and tore away. The Bulldog slammed to a full stop. The impact threw Tom headfirst against the windshield.

"Tom?" Johnny couldn't speak above a whisper. "Tom, I'm hit. You've got to ..."

He lifted his head. Turning to his right was the effort it took to move a thousand pounds.

Tom didn't answer. His head had smashed into the windshield. The blow had flattened the top of his skull and glued it to the glass. Blood trickled from his ears.

The darkness began to blow across Johnny Whitman. It was thick and heavy and it smelled of coal dust. He closed his eyes and thought, *if I have to go back down into the mine I will, but...*

Captain McGuire lowered the Webley to his side. He reached across his body and lifted the holster flap with his left hand. He shoved the revolver deep in the holster as Private Black said, "Captain...there."

McGuire looked up and saw a man who'd just jumped from the tailgate of the truck. He carried a Thompson in one hand. A big man, an agile man. He didn't hesitate. He ran directly for the tracks. For an instant it seemed that he might turn the Thompson on McGuire and his detail. He didn't. He threw the weapon away and took a sharp turn to his left. He jumped from the road to the track bed and sprinted toward the darkness.

A young soldier was still on one knee in front of Captain McGuire. Bracing himself against the pain McGuire limped forward. He grabbed the young soldier's rifle and swung it to his shoulder. He sighted down it and took in a breath and let out half of it. He squeezed the trigger and felt the recoil slam the butt against him.

Like an echo to his round a shotgun boomed from the road to the captain's right.

It was better in the flop hotels in New York.

It was better mugging drunks when you needed a few dollars.

Damn Mr. Arkman for playing cards with cowboys.

But he was going to make it. Harry Churchman was nobody's fool. He didn't play with people who used shaved cards.

The dark shadows were right ahead of him. He was going to make it, and twenty years from now he could tell people about this Canadian adventure he took once against his better judgment.

Fools. All fools.

And then a mountain fell on him.

Two forces appeared to strike the running man at the same time. He was pushed forward and, at the same time, he was slammed hard to his left. He seemed to trip. He tumbled away into the darkness.

"Here, son." McGuire lowered the rifle and passed it to the kneeling soldier. From behind him, Private Black moved forward and offered him a shoulder.

As Captain McGuire hobbled toward the stalled truck he looked over his right shoulder and saw Duncan MacTaggart crossing the tracks.

Except for the dirty raincoat he looked like a Scots gentleman out on a morning shoot.

Private George Cooper thought that all the action had passed him by. The whole night he'd done nothing but stare at the entrance to the waiting room.

When he heard the firing close by he thought, it ain't over yet, and he forgot his post and ran toward the road. He reached the sidewalk in time to watch the truck hurtle from the road onto the far sidewalk and ram against the brick wall.

With his back to the depot, intent on firing at anyone who tried to leave the truck, he did not see the tall angular man with dark hair. The man ducked low around the back corner of the depot. A fleeting look at Private Cooper's back and the man headed in the opposite direction, to the west.

The sound of his footfalls was covered by the boots of the soldiers who trotted past Private Cooper and lined up beside the truck.

The first soldier to reach the Bulldog jerked the sliding door on the driver's side. It slid open. He grabbed the arm of the man behind the wheel and pulled him into the light. One look at the head wound and the soldier released him and let him tumble into the road at his feet. He backed away and gagged.

The man in the center of the cab was huddled forward, as if he'd tried to lower himself to the floorboards for protection. A second soldier replaced the one who'd walked away. He leaned across the seat and grabbed the man under the arms and dragged him from the cab. When the soldier lowered him to the road, there was a hisslike breath from him, and his lips moved. The soldier bent down and turned an ear toward his lips.

Captain McGuire dropped his hand from Private Black's shoulder. He stood over the young soldier. "What did he say?"

The soldier turned his face toward the captain. "He said something about a mine."

"A gold mine?" MacTaggart lowered the shotgun and tapped the butt on the sidewalk. "That's presuming." He walked around a couple of soldiers who were staring into the truck cab. A look at the third man, the one on the far right, told him that he was past help. "Leave him," he said. "He's not going anywhere."

He backed away from the truck and squatted over the man with the bull neck and the wide shoulders. The man's eyes were open and they flickered at MacTaggart.

"Who are you?"

The man closed his eyes. Breath hissed out of him. Before MacTaggart could repeat the question the man died.

❖   ❖   ❖

The Frenchman's black 1940 Cadillac was parked in the driveway of the old seed-and-feed building. Clark Gipson leaned on the dusty hood for a couple of minutes while he got his breath back to normal.

He staggered to the double doors and tried them. A heavy padlock rattled in the hasp.

He yanked at the lock. He could feel the screws give in the rotten wood. Some, but not enough. He released the padlock and returned to the Cadillac. He felt around in the back seat. Nothing to pry with. He found nothing he needed in the front seat either, but when he gave the sun visor a shove, the car keys fell at his feet.

He unlocked the trunk. The jack handle he found there was the right tool. One heave at the lock and the hasp pulled away from the splintered wood.

The kerosene lamp hung from a nail on a rafter. He lit it and adjusted the wick. He carried the lamp to the side of the building where the bags and suitcases were stored. He located his bag and unstrapped it. One quick dig through it and he realized he didn't have a clean undershirt or a shirt. He tossed his bag aside and moved on to the next one. A look at the size of the shirt and he knew it was Harry's suitcase. There was no way he could wear one of them.

The third suitcase was imitation leather. He opened it and stared down at the contents. Banded bundles and bundles of money. Ones and fives and tens. He remembered the bag. The last time he'd seen it Captain Whitman was carrying it. It was, he realized, what was left of the money they'd taken from the bank in Renssler, New York.

Clark closed the suitcase and buckled the straps. He placed it beside the lamp.

With the next suitcase he was in luck. He recognized a green shirt that he'd seen Vic wearing a few days before. The undershirts were a couple of sizes too large, but they were clean. He peeled away the bloody one he wore and pulled on one of Vic's. He added the green shirt and made a few tucks in the side so it didn't bag.

After a last look around the building he carried Captain Whitman's suitcase and the lamp to the doorway. Nothing else he needed. He snuffed out the lamp and placed it on the floor. He went out and closed the double doors.

The Cadillac engine kicked over the first time. It purred. As he backed down the driveway he had a look at the fuel gauge. There was a quarter tank of gas.

He drove north.

MacTaggart stood in the road beside the boxcar and waited for Captain McGuire. He'd retrieved the sawed-off shotgun that belonged to Telford, and he held it in the crook of his arm and watched the flicker of the flashlight on the far side of the freight car.

It wagged, it swept, it hesitated, and then it switched off. MacTaggart listened to the *thump-thump* of the butt of the rifle that McGuire used as a crutch.

The captain stopped at the edge of the road. He placed the rifle in front of him and clasped the barrel with both hands. He stared down at the road.

"Who were these people?"

MacTaggart shivered at the rage in the other man's voice. The pain, too. He felt the same pain in his chest that he knew McGuire was suffering. It tightened across his chest until he could hardly breathe. And then, MacTaggart realized that Captain McGuire was crying. It was not a woman's crying. The rage, the grief, and the pain mixed and churned in the captain. It poured out of him in coughs and sputters and gasps.

MacTaggart walked away without looking back. A man had the right to some privacy when he cried for his dead.

AFTERWARD

By midmorning the next day the damaged rails on the east and west approaches to Wingate Station had been replaced and the track bed restored.

The original freight car, scarred by grenade fragments and explosives and .45-caliber fire, still had the hotbox problem that had placed it on the siding. MacTaggart requested a baggage car as a replacement. It arrived in time to test the rails east of town. While MacTaggart had a bath and a nap in a room at the Wingate Inn Hotel, an Army working party transferred the two hundred bullion cases from the two Mack Bulldogs. In the late afternoon MacTaggart climbed aboard the baggage car. Two armed guards from Railway Express joined him. The sliding doors were locked from the inside, and MacTaggart kept the key. After an hour's wait the next scheduled train heading west took the baggage car as far as Montreal, where it was shunted to an express bound for Ottawa.

It was a long trip, a nightmare journey, with one man sleeping while the other two had the duty. Eight hours on and four hours off was the way it worked out. MacTaggart took his rest breaks, but he didn't sleep. He allowed himself to relax only after the baggage car reached Ottawa and the gold was hauled away to the vaults at the Bank of Canada on Wellington Street.

The Canadian government's official version of the events at Wingate Station was in the papers and on the radio the next day. A fire and related explosions had created one of Canada's worst rail disasters. A train transporting troops, ammunition, and aviation fuel was rammed by a truck at a Wingate Station crossing. The newspaper account celebrated the exploits of members of a Canadian Army unit aboard the train. One officer and twelve enlisted men died while fighting fires and attempting to unload a boxcar of ammunition and explosives that overheated as flames raced the length of the train. Seven American tourists died in the same disaster. They'd joined with their northern neighbors in the heroic struggle that contained the fires and kept the whole town from being razed.

Through other channels, however, the American State Department was informed of the real nature of the deaths of the seven Americans. The State Department had no explanation for the excursion across the border, and it was argued that it was obviously an isolated outlaw action that should not spoil the good relationship that existed between the two countries.

Six Canadian civilians perished at Wingate Station as well. Two died in the truck that rammed the passing train and initiated the disaster. Three more were tourists from Montreal. The final civilian death was that of a respected local lawman, Constable Lafitte. The confusing story he'd told townspeople about night Army exercises was explained away as a well-meant lie that was intended to keep townspeople away from the dangers at the train yard.

MacTaggart was to pass through Wingate Station three more times. His next journey through, certain that it would be his final one, he sat at a coach window and looked for the scars of the nightmare. Most of them had disappeared. It amazed him what some rebuilding and a few hundred gallons of paint could do to disguise the horrors of only a week before.

He arrived at Halifax only to learn that his trip east was not for the purpose he believed. He was not in Halifax for transportation back to England. Instead, he was billeted at the Nova Scotian Hotel in a room fit for an admiral and told to await his orders.

On July 13 a second shipment arrived from England. Six British ships of the line, including a battleship, H.M.S. *Revenge,* and a cruiser, H.M.S. *Bonaventure,* formed the escort. Three refitted passenger liners, *Monarch of Bermuda* and *Sobieski* and *Batory,* the last two of these Free Poland ships, carried the consignment. The cargo, of which $773 million was gold bullion, had a value in excess of a billion dollars.

MacTaggart assisted with the security. It took five trains to transport the gold and securities across Canada. Departures from Halifax and the arrivals at Montreal and Ottawa were scheduled over a five-day period so that the cargo could be unloaded during the late-night or early-morning hours.

This time he passed through Wingate Station while locked in a baggage car. It was a cloudless night and all he saw of the town was a glow of lights. Darkness and then the glow and then the darkness again. It could have been a passage through hell, he thought.

He remained in Ottawa until the end of July.

When his orders came he was booked space on a local. It stopped in every town that had a depot. He was not surprised when the schedule called for a ten-minute layover at Wingate Station. It was high noon when MacTaggart left his coach and walked along the platform. He stood in the doorway and stared into the waiting room. A new coat of paint covered the walls, and the newly replaced window panes had already collected an ageless layer of dust and soot.

Across the tracks to the southeast the huge doors of the roundhouse were wide open. A crew of workers swarmed over the sides of a locomotive. If anything had happened at the siding three or four weeks before, there was no sign of it now.

His orders called for passage to England by the next available transport. Within a week he sailed from Halifax on a troopship, *Lady of the Highlands.* After a stop at Iceland to unload troops the liner reached the River Clyde without incident.

The first Sunday in September Duncan MacTaggart married Peggy Sloan in a civil ceremony in London.

❦   ❦   ❦

Turbeville, South Carolina, in 1940 wasn't a town or a village. It was a crossroads with a couple of stores, a cotton gin, and a tobacco warehouse, where the auctions were held in July and early August.

In the early fall of 1940 a young man arrived in Turbeville. He drove a black 1939 Ford sedan, and he wore a new black suit that he'd bought at J. C. Penney's. There wasn't a hotel in Turbeville. The young man took a room in the hotel in Sumter, a short drive away, and people got used to seeing him in Turbeville almost every day.

He seemed to be interested in land. Often he was seen driving slowly along the highway, or his Ford would be parked on the shoulder of the road, and he'd be standing, deep in thought, at the edge of the field.

The piece of land that appeared to interest him the most belonged to Addison Malachi Turner, "Uncle Ad" to his friends and neighbors. People thought of Addison as a bit of a wild man. He was a deeply religious person, and his friends said that it was his own business if he wanted to let his hair grow long, all the way down over his collar.

In season Uncle Ad sold the vegetables he grew on the farm from the back of his truck. He was in Sumter most mornings, six days a week. Sunday was the Lord's Day, and he didn't even allow cooking in his house on Sunday.

Nobody seemed surprised when they heard that Uncle Ad had sold the young man the ten acres of land that was across the highway and half a mile down from the Turner farmhouse. The land was cleared, and some people thought that Uncle Ad had taken advantage of young Mr. Gipson. The land was dead played out, those people said.

The fall was mild that year and the foundation and the framework were completed on the highway side of the ten-acre plot by the first of November. The building continued with a full crew on the job and with payment for labor and materials cash on the barrelhead. The structure was, onlookers said, large for a house, and there was a running debate about what the young man intended to build. One lady said it looked like a schoolhouse.

The curiosity was satisfied in early December. A brick mason worked all morning one day putting up some kind of brick framework in front of the building. It was about four feet high and five feet wide and it faced the highway. The sign and the plate-glass cover arrived two days after the brick mason finished his work. The sign had been painted in Sumter. The plate glass came all the way from Columbia.

THE CHURCH OF THE LORD JESUS CHRIST
THE REDEEMER AND THE FORGIVER
PASTOR: REV. CLARK GIPSON SUNDAYS
AT 11:00 A.M. AND 6:00 P.M.

The first service was held on the Sunday before Christmas. More than a hundred people, Methodists and Baptists, crowded into the church that morning. They sat in the newly painted pews and smelled the paint and the fresh wood, and they stared at the dark-haired young man who leaned on the unpainted pulpit. Young Mr. Gipson was perspiring even in the cold, and his face was the color of bleached flour.

Uncle Ad had arrived early and had taken the front pew. With him were his wife and his granddaughter, Edna. Edna was just back from her first semester at Winthrop College in Rock Hill. She was a plain girl with long black hair and the luminous glow of thyroid eyes.

"I am a sinner," Pastor Gipson said. "And all of you are sinners, too."

A lengthy, brittle silence followed the opening statement from Pastor Gipson. The joints in the new pews creaked as the gathering of farmers and their families became restless and shifted in their seats.

The pastor's mouth opened, it closed, and it trembled open again, like a beached fish gasping for air.

"Amen," Uncle Ad Turner shouted from the front pew. "Amen, Pastor."

Young Mr. Gipson stared down at him. His expression was a mixture of shock and confusion.

Next to Uncle Ad, dressed in a dark skirt, a white blouse, and a dark sweater, the school uniform for Winthrop College, Edna Turner smiled shyly at the new preacher.

And then the Lord God touched his tongue the way he knew He would.

From the Montreal *Star,* August 31, 1945:

POLICE GUARD RICH CARGO
VALUABLE U.K. SECURITIES LOADED ON SHIP HERE

More than 1,000 cases containing millions of pounds worth of British securities, sent to Canada in 1940 to avoid possible capture by the Germans, were packed aboard the British cruiser, *H.M.S. Leander,* in port here today under close R.C.M.P., naval and harbor police guard. The vessel is leaving shortly for England.

A British warship brought these British assets here in June, 1940. They comprised millions of pounds worth of securities that had been collected by the British Government from private owners under their finance regulations, and a lot of gold. The gold was sent to the Canadian mint and to Fort Knox in the United States for storage.

The hundreds of thousands of stock script securities were stored in the specially built vault in the Sun Life Building, 50 feet below street level. R.C.M.P. men were kept on duty guarding the securities.

At 7:30 o'clock this morning, trucks began the job of loading the cases into which had been packed the valuables. Before 11 A.M., the cases were on the waterfront.

Harbor police stopped all traffic along the waterfront where the ship was docked, near Pie IX Boulevard, and requested passes from anyone attempting to get into the marked-off area.

Newspapermen were refused permission to approach the ship as the Canadian Pacific Railway Express trucks unloaded the precious cargo on the east-end dock this morning. Naval authorities said the work being done was of a confidential nature and that they did not want "publicity" on the shipment.

ABOUT THE AUTHOR
AND THIS BOOK

The original version of this novel, entitled *MacTaggart's War*, was published in hardcover in 1979 and was Ralph Dennis' final, published work. It failed to reached the wide audience that he and his publisher had hoped for. This new edition is a substantial revision of the original manuscript. Several scenes and chapters were deleted, while others were moved to earlier or later in the narrative, to improve pacing, sharpen characters, and heighten suspense. The editing was done by Lee Goldberg, a *New York Times* bestselling author, who has acquired all of the rights to Dennis' novels, published and unpublished, from his estate.

Ralph Dennis was born in 1931 in Sumter, South Carolina, and received a masters degree from University of North Carolina, where he later taught film and television writing after serving a stint in the Navy. He is perhaps best known as the author of the twelve novels in the *Hardman* series. At the time of his death in 1988, he was working at a bookstore in Atlanta and had a file cabinet full of unpublished novels.

Brash Books will be releasing the entire *Hardman* series, his two other published novels, and his long-lost manuscripts.